I received my first pie in the face as a Stooge in a film called *Pies and Guys*. Pies had long been the Stooges' specialty and it's true that Moe threw all the pies in that film, as well as the other Stooge pie comedies. Moe always had a musclebound property man offstage stirring up the pie goop in a vat while Moe piled the stuff on pie plates; the ingredients were Moe's own special recipe.

I had never been hit by a pie before—on camera, that is!—so when we did the party scene where pies went a-flying I wasn't sure how to react when I got mine until Jules instructed me. He made me count to three and on three I was to be prepared for Moe to smack me with a pie. I remember Moe tossed the pie on schedule but when it struck me I just stood there wondering what I should do next. Finally I started eating the pie off my face. Then, looking straight into the camera, I said, "Oooh, that's delicious!"

ONCE A STOOGE,
ALWAYS A STOOGE

The forgotten Beatle, Joe. Actually from The Joey Bishop Show.

Once a Stooge, Always a Stooge

Joe Besser
with
Jeff and Greg Lenburg

KNIGHTSBRIDGE PUBLISHING COMPANY
NEW YORK

To my lovely wife Ernie,
the same woman who told me
to quit show business 54 years ago,
and who's been my wife just as long.

This paperback edition of *Once a Stooge, Always a Stooge* first published in 1990 by Knightsbridge Publishing.

Originally published by Excelsior Books in 1985 under the title *Not Just a Stooge*.

Published in the United States by
Knightsbridge Publishing Company
255 East 49th Street
New York, New York 10017

ISBN 0-877961-42-6

10 9 8 7 6 5 4 3 2 1

FIRST EDITION

Contents

Foreword *vii*

Introduction *1*

1 That Crazy Old Childhood of Mine *5*

2 Bitten by the Show Biz Bug *17*

3 Hocus! Pocus!—Joining Thurston *27*

4 Learning New Tricks *35*

5 Touring with Alex and Ole *43*

6 Ernie *53*

7 Vaudeville! Vaudeville! Vaudeville! *67*

8 Broadway, Marriage, Hollywood, London . . . and the Stooges *77*

9 Lights! Camera! No Joe! *91*

10 Playing Around with the Son's of Fun *101*

11 Teaming Up with Renny, Allen, and Cantor *109*

12 My Hollywood Dream 121

13 Uncle Miltie and the Shoe That Didn't Fit 131

14 The Movies and Lou Costello 141

15 Hey, Stinky! You're a TV Star! 155

16 The Third Stooge 167

17 Stooging Around with Moe and Larry 177

18 A Stooge Solos 195

19 No Business Like Cartoon Business 211

20 Once a Stooge, Always a Stooge 223

Filmography of Joe Besser 231

Television Appearances of Joe Besser 235

Afterword 242

Index 243

Foreword

For over fifty years, the critics have called Joe Besser an innocent pixie and a cherub. For that same fifty years, I have called him a friend.

When I read an advance copy of this book, it brought tears to my eyes . . . tears of laughter and tears of nostalgia.

The Joe Besser story, in essence, is a journey back into my own life. In Yiddish, the word "Besser" means better. In view of Joe's talent, he was very appropriately named. Joe's style of comedy was indeed Besser than all the rest!

I strongly recommend this book to you . . . I loved it as much as I love Joe.

—Milton Berle

Introduction

August 30, 1983: The Hollywood Chamber of Commerce honored the Three Stooges with a star on the world-famous Hollywood Walk of Fame.

Even though being a Stooge was only part of my life in show business, I accepted the chamber's invitation to attend the festivities with mixed emotions. Moe, Larry, Curly and Shemp were all gone. Now, twenty-six years after we had left Columbia Pictures, Hollywood was finally recognizing us for being "the greatest motion-picture comedy team of all time."

Better late than never, I guess!

The turnout for the spectacle was tremendous. An outpouring of more than two thousand loving fans crowded around the small area on the sidewalk where the star was to be unveiled. More than twenty-five camera crews from around the world and one hundred still photographers lined up behind crowd-control ropes—looking more like a firing squad—to capture the best possible angle.

A dozen guest speakers including: Gary Owens, who was the master of ceremonies; Milton Berle; Jamie Farr; Adam West; Joan Howard Maurer, Moe's daughter; Phyllis Fine Lamond, Larry Fine's daughter; Jean DeRita, the wife of Curly-Joe DeRita (who replaced me as a Stooge); and Jeff and Greg Lenburg (who helped Gary Owens organize a nationwide campaign to get us our star). We all reminisced about "the boys," and our speeches took more than one hour in the baking sun. The induction was reportedly the largest gathering—if not the longest ceremony—ever for any Walk-of-Fame proceedings. It had even outdrawn the inductions for such name stars as John Wayne, Frank Sinatra, and Barbra Streisand!

So at least our ceremony was done with style!

Throughout the entire ceremony, however, all I thought about were the memories of my life in show business for more than 64 years—memories and accomplishments that have often been overshadowed by my association with the Three Stooges. Memories that people from all walks of life still remind me of in their more than two hundred letters monthly. It's hard to believe I've done everything during my career—vaudeville, Broadway, radio, movies, and television . . . I've done everything except radar!

As the cheers went up during the introductions of each invited guest, I remembered the many cheers I had received when I played on vaudeville and Broadway stages. Cheers and applause that had started the moment I was introduced. Laughter that never stopped for every "Ooh, you crazy y-o-u!" or "Not so f-a-s-t!" catch phrase and mannerism I delivered. The cheers I received the day of the star induction matched those I had received while working with the best of Broadway: Al Jolson, Sophie Tucker, Paul Ash, Harry Richman, Carmen Miranda, Sammy Davis, Jr., Ethel Merman, and Olsen and Johnson.

More memories boggled my mind when Milton Berle got up to give his testimonial. He had used me exclusively on his radio show, *Let Yourself Go*, in the mid-1940s. At that time, he wanted me all to himself to bolster the laughs on his show and to keep me from his comic contemporaries—Jack Benny, Fred Allen and Eddie Cantor—whose shows I also had worked on regularly. I must have tricked Miltie because he kept me for five years!

Ooh, what memories!

Jamie Farr, Corporal Klinger on TV's *M*A*S*H* and an avid Stooge fan, followed Milties's speech. Before the ceremony, Jamie had recounted how he had been a fan of mine since he saw me in the first starring wartime feature, *Hey, Rookie!* with Ann Miller. *Hey, Rookie!*? That's right, I made that, too! I starred in forty features at Columbia, Universal, United Artists and Twentieth Century-Fox, besides making my own comedy short-subject series at Columbia, where I worked for fourteen years! Gads, I almost forgot!

Jamie set off another flood of memories. What names I had worked with at these studios: Abbott and Costello, Donald O'Connor, Jackie Gleason, Ida Lupino, Paulette Goddard, Bing Crosby, Debbie Reynolds, Robert Wagner, Jerry Lewis, Marilyn Monroe and others.

Gee, that didn't even include my work on television!

I've appeared in more that 250 television shows. My most famous character was "Stinky" on *The Abbott and Costello Show.* Now, three decades later, new generations of fans are watching the show in reruns and hearing me tell Lou for the first time, "Ooh, I'll give you such a pinch!" And I'll never forget my role as "Jillson," the apartment superintendent on *The Joey Bishop Show*, from 1962 to 1965.

Gosh, where did I find time to do all these things!

My thoughts remained in a turmoil until Gary Owens asked me to unveil the star with Joan Howard Maurer and Phyllis Fine Lamond. Flash bulbs popped. Cameras clicked. Fans cheered. And after the ceremony ended, the flood of memories that had haunted me all day returned. I wished I had had more time to share them with the fans who were there that day and with the thousands of other Three Stooges fans around the world.

It was then that I started thinking about writing my life story. The hardest part was to come up with an angle. But it hit me once I had reviewed everything I've done in my career. Six words stuck in my mind:

"Once a Stooge, always a Stooge!"

So I'm happy to tell you about my days with and without the Stooges. And, if you don't believe me, you crazy, just read on!!

Chapter 1

That Crazy Old Childhood of Mine

If somebody had asked me when I was a child if I ever expected to become a famous comedian, my answer would probably have been, "Maybe." I never intentionally did things to make people laugh, nor did I realize that making audiences laugh would be my calling for the rest of my life.

Those who knew me best during my childhood might disagree after they considered all the stupid things I did to myself and to my parents. They always asked, in horror, "What did Joe do now?" Sometimes I wonder how my poor parents put up with me. I, alone, probably gave them all their gray hairs! No kid got away with as much as I did, yet lived to see his next birthday! Fortunately, my parents were unusually patient with me, and they always saw past my misbehavings.

Fanny and Morris Besser brought me into this world on August 12, 1907 in St. Louis, Missouri, and without them my life would never have been as complete. They were the warmest parents any kid could have hoped for; they were also the firmest when it was necessary. Poppa had been raised in Czarist-controlled Russia; Momma in the impoverished country of Poland.

Poppa was a tall, willowy man with deep-set blue eyes, a tubular nose and a bald (wonder where *I* got it!) head. Momma was short, impish, and childlike. They were married in England, where Poppa had been employed as a baker, before they emigrated to America in 1895. Their first stop was New York.

They stayed in New York for some time—long enough to give birth to three children: two daughters, Esther and Molly, and a son, Manny, who also entered show business and was ten years older than me. Three children were enough of a burden, but our family never stopped growing. It was always enlarging by leaps and bounds. Eleven children were born—two of whom died at birth—and seven of whom were girls. My third-oldest sister, Gertrude, was born in Cincinnati, where Poppa and Momma had temporarily relocated. They finally settled permanently in St. Louis, and that's where Rose, Lilly, Henrietta, myself, and Florence entered the picture.

Poppa and Momma were proud Europeans. They knew what it was like to be poor, to struggle, and to make the most from what they had. Living in America seemed to fit their lifestyles. They worked hard for what they got in life, as did every American.

For the first five years of my life, we lived in a cozy two-story duplex apartment at 1313 Carr Street—the same house in which Al Hirschfield, St. Louis' bearded gift to the cartooning world, had been born several years before me. We rented the upstairs and downstairs apartments. The downstairs contained the living room, the dining room, and Momma's and Poppa's room.

The dining room became my room. I slept on a couch behind the dining table. (I always held onto one of the table legs; if I didn't hold onto something I couldn't fall asleep.) My sisters were camped in the upstairs apartment in three rooms with beds of their own. Manny had moved out by the time I was born. He had joined the Buffalo Bill Traveling Show and was doing quite well on his own.

How Poppa provided for us on a baker's salary, I'll never know. Living conditions were better after the turn of the century, but poor is poor. Poppa must have struggled to feed eight mouths (nine when Manny was around) and to keep a roof over our heads. I have to give Poppa credit; he never once complained. Poppa was truly a rare breed. He was forever devoted to Momma and us, and he religiously maintained his responsibilities as a husband and as a father.

Poppa also found enough energy to help move his three brothers to this country. They were Leopold, Lepold and Isadore Besser. Leopold and Lepold settled in Little Rock, Arkansas, while Isadore came to St. Louis, where he opened a tailoring store. I remember my uncles and father were always close, even though they often tried to outdo each other—often succeeding!

Leopold owned a dry goods store, while Lepold managed a hardware store. Lepold's business had more prestige than Leopold's because Lepold had found his store in a town he and his son named, "Besserville."

Yes, Besserville!

Besserville, Arkansas was a real small town all right. Leopold hung an electric sign that flashed over the entrance to town. It read: "You are now entering and *leaving* Besserville." . . . I told you the town was s-m-a-l-l!!

The rivalry among the brothers hit epic proportions when Leopold's and Lepold's sons got into the act. They opened gas stations across the street from each other on separate corners where they regularly staged "gas wars." The rivalry between my cousins kept the town buzzing with activity until business finally died down. Since then, Besserville has never been the same!

Isadore was the most successful brother. He was, perhaps, luckier than Poppa. Of course, with luck came hard work. He and his wife never had as many children as we did—just a son and a daughter—which explains why they were better off than us. Isadore also wisely invested his money into a two-block stretch of apartments. He appropriately called them "Besser Apartments." I don't know if the buildings are still standing today, but they were very prominent back then. With the added cash flow from this property, Isadore's money went further.

Even though Poppa didn't earn the kind of money Isadore did, he was clearly the happiest. I never detected any bitterness on Poppa's part. He was proud to be an American, and he realized his opportunities for success would eventually come. In the meantime, he always encouraged his brothers to succeed. Unfortunately, Poppa's luck never changed much, but neither did his atttitude toward his brothers. He always loved them and pulled for them.

What we lacked financially, we made up for in our faith. As Orthodox Jews, Poppa and Momma raised our entire family under the law of Moses. Although Poppa wasn't as religious as Momma, they took us to synagogue every Saturday, nonetheless. There was never a more perfect Jewish mother. Momma won hands down! She followed every custom to the letter. Saturdays were considered a day of fast and prayer and, as part of this weekly ritual, Momma taught us the Jewish alphabet to strengthen our religious vows.

I remember how Momma and I sat behind the kitchen table—me usually wearing a yarmulke—while she reviewed each letter of the alphabet with me, one by one. She found me to be a lost cause. However, my comic nature surfaced during our first lesson.

Reading from the Bible, Momma told me to repeat after her.

"Alah," she said.

"Alah," I said.

"Baz," she said.

"Baz," I said.

"G'muwl," she said.

"G'muwl," I said.

Before going on to the next word, Momma looked at me. I didn't have my yarmulke on. So she said, "Jessel, *una hattel*?" I didn't know what she meant, so I repeated, "Jessel, *una hattel.*"

Momma burst out laughing. Then she said, "Jessel, I said, where's your yarmulke?"

"I'm sorry, Momma," I said. "But you told me to *repeat* everything you said!"

As Jews, we were restricted to a specific diet. We were never allowed to eat pork, and Momma always adhered to this diet—except once when she made an exception for me. That happened years later after I had entered vaudeville and was playing at the American Theater in St. Louis. Whenever I was in town, I always stayed with my parents instead of renting a hotel room. By that time though, even though I had been brought up as a religious Jew, I had fallen away from one of the basic tenets: abstaining from pork. I loved to eat, and it's no wonder I got fat!

One morning as I waited to leave for the theater, I sat around in the kitchen until it was time to go. Poppa and Momma were both gone; Poppa had gone to work, and Momma was out shopping. I helped myself to a cup of coffee from the pot I had been brewing. I heard footsteps at the front door. It was Momma—I could always tell!

"Jessel," she yelled, in her typical Jewish monotone, "it's me!" ("Jessel," in case you didn't know, means "Joe" in Hebrew.) "I've got something for you, Jessel," Momma continued happily, as she walked in with groceries. "Get everything off the table."

I cleared the table in record time, for the idea of food always aroused my appetite—especially when Momma was doing the cooking.

While I was cleaning off the table, I noticed Momma had something wrapped in newspaper. She laid the bundle down and opened it. Inside was a freshly cut ham. "Jessel," Momma said sweetly, "I know you're on the road a lot, and I know you eat pork. So why shouldn't you have it here? It isn't going to hurt anybody."

She was right, it didn't. My stomach agreed! I made myself a ham and cheese sandwich, and it tasted twice as good because Momma had bought the ham. Momma was always very loving, and she always looked after my best interests—as a child and as an adult.

I still recall how Momma tucked me into bed every night when I was a child. She'd cover me with a yellow wool blanket, kiss me on the head, then read me a bedtime story. Sometimes she would sit with me and stroke my shoulder-length curly hair with her coarse hands until I fell fast asleep.

I remember these things because I always kept one eye partially open so I could watch her.

Momma was extremely close to us kids; she was protective, and she always tried doing things as a family. At night, Momma, my sisters, and I would gather in front of the hot, burning stove in the kitchen to listen to fairy tales. Momma never read them to us; Gertrude did. Momma liked listening instead. Every story was written in Hebrew, and even though she was a grown woman, Momma was really a child at heart. She never tired of hearing the fairy tales—even though she probably had heard them dozens of times!

Momma was also charitable—not that we had much to offer. I remember a black man who used to come by the house to light our gas stove when it went out because Momma was afraid she'd light it wrong and cause an explosion. We never paid the man much, but once he received more than just compensation for his services.

The man arrived in his customary tattered suit. Momma felt sorry for him and said, "You could stand a new suit. The one you're wearing is too old. You'd be better in a new one." Momma then left the man in the kitchen, went into the bedroom, and pulled out a suit from Poppa's closet. The suit was made of pure wool and was one of his most expensive garments. (We were sometimes short on money but Poppa always dressed as though he were a millionaire!)

When Momma told the man he could keep the suit, he was speechless! He couldn't believe her sudden act of charity, but he thanked her and took the suit anyway.

Now, most husbands would have gotten mad at their wives for giving away their best duds. Not Poppa. He admired Momma's kindness toward those who were down on their luck, so he kissed Momma on the cheek after she explained what had happened. "It's okay," Poppa told Momma. "I'll just buy another suit." Poppa never replaced the suit. He figured he would be justly rewarded later, in some way, for helping his fellow man.

In the spring of 1912 Momma and Poppa decided we had outgrown our home on Carr Street, and they moved us to a bigger two-story duplex apartment on Stoddard Street, where most of my childhood memories originate. I went to school here. I made my first friends here. I also got into more trouble here!

I became extremely curious at five and created so much mischief that my parents were lucky to keep up with me. I always had my hands into everything and tried everything, even trying to fly once.

We had a woodshed in back of the house where Poppa stored his tools and other personal items. One afternoon—I don't know what got into me (the devil made me do it!)—I wondered what it was like to fly. Birds could, why not me?

I climbed on top of the shed, taking an umbrella with me to break my fall. When I jumped, the umbrella went one way, and I went the other. I didn't get hurt, but I remember Gertrude watching my "flying" act and screaming, "Momma, Joey's being bad again!"

You'd think I would have learned to stop my shenanigans, but I didn't. The worst—almost fatal—episode happened early one morning when the milkman was making his delivery. He drove a horse-drawn truck that was stocked full of milk. The milk was stored in bottles and big metal canisters for larger deliveries. When the milkman took our milk inside, I went out to investigate. Actually, I did more than th-a-a-a-t!

I sat down in the driver's seat and pretended I was driving the truck. Automobiles were becoming popular around this time, and the Model T was the vehicle people were driving. Horse-drawn vehicles were slowly becoming extinct. And I almost did, too!

While I was playing in the truck, one of those new-fangled Ts drove by and suddenly backfired. The explosion frightened the hoofs off the horse—who tore off with the wagon, throwing me headfirst from my seat into one of the big metal canisters. What was worse was I couldn't move after being thrown because my head was stuck in the canister! (Fortunately, no milk was inside or else I would have suffocated.)

As the horse galloped away faster than a Kentucky Derby race horse, Momma "died." I was told that when the horse took off, she couldn't believe her eyes and fainted. The milkman couldn't believe his eyes either and dropped his delivery. Somehow I was miraculously rescued; just how I'm not sure. Momma scolded me royally. That I *do* remember! And, afterwards, I was reluctant to look at another milk can again.

My parents watched me more carefully after that hair-raising experience. I guess I couldn't blame them. They made me stick closer to home, so I wouldn't get in as much trouble. That was when I started becoming friendly with our neighbors, among whom were the Carusos. Although the name meant nothing to me then, it did later when I learned they were related to the world-famous opera singer Enrico Caruso. Even though Enrico used to come over for dinner when he visited St. Louis, I never had enough brains then to figure out who he was.

Enrico's relatives were very generous to me when they heard that my folks were poor and couldn't afford to buy me any toys. I never owned a toy until the Carusos, who lived next door in a fancy two-story house, gave me the toys their children had played with.

Mr. Caruso bought new toys for his children every week. So once they outgrew them, Mrs. Caruso would walk over to the fence that divided our properties and holler after me. "Joey, come here. I have some toys to give you." I'd skip over to the white picket fence, and she'd hand me a new toy that would keep me entertained for hours.

When our family celebrated Hannukah, I never received any toys. My sisters and I saw how other children celebrated Christmas, receiving toys from Santa Claus, but we realized that our situation was different from other children. We were happy with whatever Momma and Poppa gave us.

One time my parents celebrated Christmas after my sister Florence and I complained that they didn't put up a Christmas tree or yule-time decorations. They put Christmas stockings on the mantelpiece, and when we woke up on Christmas morning we found them filled with candy. What an unexpected treat!

Although the Carusos lavished me with toys, I never counted on ready-made ones. I often built my own toys. The kids in my neighborhood used to ride on their scooters, and it wrenched my heart that I didn't have one. But they were too expensive, and Poppa couldn't afford one. Rather than pity myself, I built my own.

With Poppa's help, I took a wooden box, hammered on a piece of board as the bottom, attached two metal pie tins to the front for lights, and separated a roller skate and nailed the wheels to the bottom of the board—one in front, one in back. That became my scooter! It even had a bell to warn pedestrians!

The scooter kept me out of trouble for a while. I wish I could say the same thing happened when another neighbor gave me my first boomerang!

Mr. Youmans, who was related to the great composer Vincent Youmans, gave me a boomerang as a present. He and his wife lived on the other side of us, and they rented both levels of another duplex apartment. Mr. Youmans used the lower level to manufacture and distribute men's caps to local clothing stores.

Mr. Youmans became my friend also, and he used to give me an occasional toy or game to keep me occupied. One Saturday afternoon after I had run out to play, he hollered at me to come over. Reaching behind his back, he produced an honest-to-goodness boomerang! He placed it in my hand and said, "It's yours, Joey. Why don't you make a test throw?"

I couldn't wait!

Although Mr. Youmans showed me how first, he probably should have given me better directions. His house was on the corner and faced the three other corner houses that made up the intersection to our street. I don't think he took this into consideration when he told me to throw the boomerang. I gave the boomerang a whirl and—whoosh!—away it soared. I watched its flight in awe until, suddenly, I noticed it started coming back to me. Mr. Youmans never told me that boomerangs always returned to the same spot from which they were thrown. He also forgot to tell me to stand away from the front of the house, because the boomerang crashed right through the front window!

I ended up working odd jobs for Mr. Youmans to pay for a new window. Afterwards I still went boomerang-throwing with the other kids on the block, but I never hit any more windows.

If I wasn't playing, I was looking after my younger sister Florence. She looked up to me because I was older. If anything ever happened to her, I would stand up for her. Heck, that's what big brothers are for!

I also taught her the difference between right and wrong. One day I'll never forget she was sitting on the steps in front of the house, and her panties were showing. Being the righteous kid that I was, I went up to her and slapped her. I said, "Don't you ever sit like that!" She never did it again, and afterward she respected me for pointing out her mistake.

By age six, two important changes occurred in my life. My parents enrolled me in school for the first time, and my life became more structured and disciplined. In the fall of 1913 I began attending DuVall Elementary School, which was only four blocks away from home, so I walked there. In the beginning, I was hungry to learn everything there was to learn about reading, writing, and arithmetic. I bore down every night to study my homework, and Momma and Poppa were extremely proud of my progress. My grades were better than average my first two years.

At DuVall I never spoke out of turn or did anything disrespectful to my classmates or teacher. I was more well-mannered at school than at home because my teacher was a strict, older woman who wore dresses with high collars and smacked you on the hand with a ruler if you caused any trouble. I was so frightened of her that I postponed my mischief until after school.

However, in 1914, my second year there, my clean record at school became tarnished. One day during lunch, a classmate blamed me for starting a fight with another boy. The accusation wasn't true. (I wouldn't become aggressive until two years later.) Nevertheless, the teacher escorted me back to the classroom and as my punishment, she tried washing my mouth out with soap. Just as she went to rub the bar in my mouth, I couldn't let her go through with it and threw my hands in front of me, knocking the soap from her grasp. I then ran away until she caught me in front of the principal's office. (What a place to wind up in!)

When I went to school a principal had the authority to issue severe punishments for students who misbehaved. The teacher explained how I had resisted having my mouth washed to the principal, so he decided to teach me a lesson. He ordered me to lie over a chair and bend over. Then he reached for a rubber hose and prepared to whip me.

Again this punishment seemed unfair—I was innocent! As the principal rocked back his arm to smack me, I ducked off his lap, and he hit his hand on the chair and writhed in pain. He was lucky he didn't break his hand, because the chair was made from pure mahogany. He came after me again, only this time I crashed through the office window and ran home.

I emerged unhurt, and the principal later forgave me after my parents had the matter investigated. The other boy was punished and got his just desserts. At least the principal had a sense of humor. Following the incident, whenever I passed the principal's office, he jokingly looked at me in horror, said, "Don't come near me!" then laughed teasingly.

Momma and Poppa never found the incident funny. They immediately checked out another school for me. In the fall of 1915, they sent me to the Glascoe Elementary School. DuVall was four blocks east of our house, while Glascoe was four blocks west. So the distance was the same. Only the school and teachers were changed.

The change turned out to be just what the doctor ordered. My new teacher was a doll. Her name was Miss Bartlett. She was young, pretty, and bubbly compared to the sourpuss who taught me at DuVall. She also took a liking to me. At seven, I was the age when every schoolboy develops a crush on his teacher. Miss Bartlett was my crush all right.

Several classmates thought I was Miss Bartlett's pet because I always hung around with her. I guess they had their reasons to believe this even though I never thought so. I just liked Miss Bartlett, and she liked me, that's all. She'd invite me to her place every Sunday and bake cakes and pastries for me. I'd stay long enough to gobble down these tasty delicacies. Then I went about my merry way.

Having Miss Bartlett as my teacher made school more enjoyable than before—that's for sure. I couldn't wait to get up in the mornings. When I woke up around around seven o'clock, Momma always had breakfast waiting for me. I dressed the same way for school every day: knee-high knickers with a belt, a polo shirt, and regular wool socks. During the winter I dressed more warmly.

Walking to school gave me my exercise every morning. The Glascoe School was nestled on top of a rolling hill that was beautifully landscaped with grass from top to bottom. I loved climbing to the top. It gave me great pleasure to know Miss Bartlett would always be in class with a kind word and a cheery smile for me.

Recess was fun, too. I got along with the other kids in my class, and we'd either play volleyball, tag, or swing on the swings to see who could go the highest and who could fall the hardest. I always fell the hardest!

At lunch time I went home, and Momma cooked lunch for me. Sometimes she packed my lunch or gave me lunch money—ten cents a day—to buy my own. Ten cents went far in 1915, for a kid anyway. I'd walk to the corner drugstore on Stoddard Street and, with my dime, I would buy a sandwich for a nickel, a drink for two cents and a package of animal crackers for three cents, which sometimes was more than my little stomach could hold.

At Glascoe I experienced my first run-in with a bully. He was jealous of my friendship with Miss Bartlett, and he thought I was an easy target because any boy with long curly hair didn't look as if he could defend himself. The boy was older than me and called me "stupid" and other names when we played during recess. Sometimes he'd follow me home, and I'd run inside crying because he never stopped picking on me.

Although my brother Manny was still working with the Buffalo Bill Traveling Show at this time, he returned home. I don't have too many memories of Manny because his annual visits home were the extent of our brotherhood. Luckily that year's visit coincided with when this kid had started harrassing me.

Because Manny was older, I naturally sought his advice on how I should deal with this bully. He said, "You're not going to let him get away with that, are you?" Nervously, I replied, "What else am I supposed to do?" Upset with my apparent cowardice, Manny said firmly, "Joey, if you don't go and hit this guy back, I'm going to give you the licking of your life!"

I didn't know what would be worse: to be bullied around every day by this kid or to have my own brother beat me up . . . I decided to beat up the kid!

The next day he followed me home and started pushing me around. But when we reached the front of my house this time, I suddenly grabbed him by his shirt collar, closed my eyes, said a prayer, and then decked him with my best punch. (Muhammad Ali would have been proud!) I kept hitting him until Manny came running outside to referee. As the kid started retreating I turned to Manny and said, "Should I stop?"

Smiling, Manny said, "Yeah, I think he's had enough."

The kid ran home and never bothered me again. Manny walked me back inside, proud that I had stood up for myself. I was never afraid again.

When weekends arrived, Poppa put me to work around the house. I'd help him clean out the stove downstairs and the heater, or we'd shovel coal for the stove and wash the windows and doors to the house. We were poor, but we were definitely proud! I also took Poppa's suits to the Chinese cleaners. The couple who owned the shop liked me. Normally they rewarded each kid with one lichee nut who came in with their parents to leave a load of laundry. They liked me so much they gave me *three*!

Poppa also entrusted me with the responsibility of picking up beer for him every week from the local tavern. The owners knew me, so they never questioned my being underage. They were good friends with Poppa, and they knew I wasn't the guzzling type! This system worked perfectly until the time somebody else was working there. When I stopped in to refill Poppa's beer canister he refused. "Sorry, son," the man said, "but I don't sell to kids!"

Well, I was flabbergasted! Nobody had ever turned me down before. What would I tell Poppa?

I returned home and found Poppa sitting in the living room reading the newspaper. I handed him the canister, empty, and said, "Poppa, here's your beer!"

Glumly, Poppa noticed the can was dry. "Jessel," he said, "there's no beer in here!"

"Poppa, anybody can drink beer if it's in the can," I said, in jest. "But try drinking beer when it's *not* in the can!" (This may have been my first actual comedy line, but I am not sure.)

Poppa laughed loudly at my joke, but it was the last time I got him beer!

Chapter 2

Bitten by the Show Biz Bug

Poppa eventually forgave me for coming home without any beer, and he and Momma soon entrusted me with other responsibilities around the house.

At the same time, they noticed I had become increasingly restless. School had held my attention because Miss Bartlett was a fun teacher, but I had other interests. One of them was going to the movies.

I enjoyed going to the movies every week, sometimes after school or on weekends. The downtown business area was loaded with theaters. My favorite theater was the Hamilton Skydome, which was one of the first open-air theaters. St. Louis was one of the first cities to pioneer these theaters. They had no roofs (thus the name "open-air"), but were simply surrounded by four walls. Customers sat on benches and watched the latest movies. During the winter there was a definite problem when it rained or snowed, and the theaters would then have to be shut down. On a normal evening in St. Louis, however, the Skydome offered the most beautiful sight in the world. As the movies flickered on the screen, the stars shone in the heavens above. You couldn't have asked for a more magical atmosphere.

For a while Momma and Poppa used to give me ten cents to cover my admission. Then I discovered another way to get in. I started sneaking in over the fence before the shows started. I admit this was wrong of me, but I didn't know any better. I knew the owners of the theater, and sometimes between shows I cleaned up the place for them. Still I should have never taken advantage of them. They finally caught me and said, "Joe, you don't have to sneak in. Come in the front way. We'll let you in for free." From then on I did. I only wished they had told me before, because it would have saved me a lot of splintered pants!

The movies I watched were silent, of course. Talkies hadn't come into existence yet. But the movies they showed in 1915 were very entertaining. The scripts were well written. The acting was good. The directing was good. Even the theater's popcorn was good!

Every program featured a newsreel, serial, comedy short, and feature. I remember seeing classic movies such as *The Red Circle*, *The Man With The Claw*, as well as Pearl White serials, and comedies starring Charlie Chaplin, Fatty Arbuckle, Harry Langdon, and Harold Lloyd. My favorites were the comedies. Something about those movies attracted me. Something about the way the comedians entertained audiences made me want to do the same.

Eventually I became obsessed with watching more movies and started missing school. (In other words, I'd play hookey and go to a midday matinee as my "daily assignment.") Although Miss Bartlett understood my dilemma, she could not approve. She'd send me home with a note to my parents, and they'd warn me never to skip school again. Momma and Poppa soon learned, however, that they would never be able to stop me from repeating the same mistake. They didn't stop me because they realized that movies meant everything to me. They refused to kill my dream.

One Saturday night I almost made them change their minds when I went to the evening show. I took the streetcar to the theater as usual. My parents weren't worried about me because I made this trip dozens of times. They only became concerned when I wandered off without telling them (a habit I never broke until later in my young life.)

On this particular Saturday night, I was so thrilled about going to the movies that I forgot to tell my parents. I took a front-row seat and gorged myself with popcorn and other refreshments as the main feature began. The theater was filled nearly to capacity, which wasn't surprising because weekend matinees were big.

I kept my eyes glued to the screen and studied every movement the actors made. However, the film and the actors didn't entirely capture my interest because gradually my eyes became heavy. I had had a rough day working at home with Poppa, and I must have been tired. In no time I fell fast asleep. By the time I woke up, it was pitch dark outside, the theater had emptied, and the theater was closed. That's when panic set in!

Why didn't someone wake me up when the show ended? How could I get out? What were my poor parents thinking?

My parents and sisters were dressed in their pajamas and searching in front of our house for me. They had started worrying about me because I had never stayed out this late before. Poppa had finally called the police, who had joined the search.

Back at the theater, I was still sleepy. My only thought was, "What time is it?" The theater didn't have a clock, but I could tell that it was late. I guessed it was about midnight. Now I was really worried!

I finally realized there was only one way out. The theater was enclosed on each side by a picket fence. I made my escape by hopping the fence nearest to me. Momma and Poppa were waiting outside the theater. They'd had a hunch they'd find me here and, fortunately, their hunch was correct. They grabbed and hugged me and were very happy that I was safe. But they didn't forget to scold me. But at least they didn't try to keep me from going to the movies again.

My interest in show business was heightened whenever I saw my brother Manny perform. He left the Buffalo Bill Traveling Show early in 1915 and became a burlesque comedian. Manny billed himself as a Jewish comedian. He wore a charcoaled beard on his face, and he told Yiddish jokes using a Jewish dialect. He usually followed three other comedians who were Dutch, Italian or "tramps"—which was the vogue at the time.

Momma and I went to see Manny perform once, and we never laughed so hard in our lives. He practically stole the show. Afterwards we visited him at the Alamack Hotel, where he stayed whenever he was in town (once he entered burlesque he stopped staying at home). I remember his picture was encased in glass in the front lobby of the hotel, along with pictures of the other comedians in the show. Seeing Manny's success made me think about my own future in show business. I was sure it was what I wanted to do. I wasn't sure about exactly how yet.

Every year Manny played the American Theater in St. Louis. I made a point to see him. He was an inspiration. Sometimes I would play hookey just to see him, but I was never malicious. I was always honest with Miss Bartlett. The week Manny arrived in town I'd walk up to her desk and say to her, "Miss Bartlett, my brother's playing in town this week. Can I go and see him? I only see him once a year." Sometimes before she'd even have a chance to answer, I'd add, "If you don't say yes, I'm going to go anyway." Miss Bartlett realized how much I idolized Manny and that I was telling the truth, so she'd excuse me every time. I'm surprised she never got into trouble with the school officials, but somehow she covered for me.

While I was deciding what area of show business I wanted to pursue, I started going to vaudeville shows after school. I went to three theaters in the area: the Columbia, the Orpheum and the Grand Opera House. The Columbia became my main hangout because they always had three shows a day. I never paid more than five cents to get in and after each show I met all the performers. They seemed to like me, and I liked them, which made me feel as though I really belonged in the same business.

My favorite act was Gus Edwards' School Days, which featured a group of entertainers in childish escapades centered in a schoolroom setting. I went to see their act three or four times a week when they played in St. Louis. They always seemed to have a lot of fun, so one day I finally became convinced I wanted to do the same. So I approached Mr. Edwards about joining the act, but he turned me down. "You're too young, kid," he said. "You lack any stage experience." Being rejected didn't discourage me; at age eight, I felt my day would come.

My desire to perform kept burning brightly. I still went to school, but on weekends Momma and Poppa let me go to the Forest Hills amusement park. I rode there on the back of a streetcar and visited the park daily during the summer to take in as many shows as possible. The park had rides, game booths, fortune tellers, a bearded lady, and other attractions. I had another motive for going there: I hoped to get a job to gain the experience Mr. Edwards said I lacked.

The owner of the park saw how I always helped out the other workers, so he hired me. With Momma and Poppa's approval, I worked in the game booths. I worked there the entire summer before returning to school. Like Manny, I had finally gotten my foot in the door.

My sister Esther recognized my interest in show business and also tried helping me. That same summer, she took me to my first opera at the Municipal Opera, which was down the street from the amusement park. The production we attended was Gilbert and Sullivan's famous Japanese opera, *Mikado*. I vividly recall how the actors' faces were painted and the Oriental costumes they wore. The dance sequences were so exquisite, I almost wanted to paint my face and join them.

After having this much fun I almost hated to go back to school. In the fall of 1916, I entered the fifth grade at Glascoe. I was a little smarter, but less enthusiastic. Miss Bartlett was still my teacher (in the old days you had the same teacher every year until you graduated). And she was my only consolation for being there. I started getting restless again; I wanted to work in show business. I spent most of my time in class daydreaming, and my grades suffered dramatically as a result. However, I bided my time and persevered.

That winter became the worst on record. We were snowed in a couple of times a week and temperatures dropped below freezing. Sometimes, though, I didn't mind the snow because, like every kid, I dreamed about playing in it.

I recall one day when the snow almost spelled my doom. I was looking out the front window watching the frost on the rooftops of every house in the neighborhood. My sisters were helping Momma in the kitchen. They were preparing a big kettle of soup. Poppa had weathered the snow storm and reported to work safely. I went back to playing with my toys, and Florence joined me. The fury of the wind made the trees thrash against the side of the house. Momma kept working in the kitchen when all of a sudden I heard a thud.

I turned around and found Molly on the floor. She laid there motionless. Momma and my sisters ran to her side, and they converged over her. They weren't sure what they should do. Nobody knew what was wrong with her. I didn't wait around to find out. In the midst of Momma screaming, "Jessel, wait!" I ran barefoot in the snow to get a doctor who was located downtown, but I almost didn't make it.

The snow was so cold that it almost froze my feet. By the time I arrived at the doctor's office, the doctor noticed my feet had turned blue. The blood had stopped circulating. Quickly he bundled my feet in towels to warm them up. Meanwhile, I explained what had happened to Molly. After my feet thawed he carried me out to his horse-drawn carriage, and we went back home to check on Molly. When we returned, however, we were too late. Molly had regained her consciousness minutes before we entered the front door; she had only fainted!

The good doctor never charged us for his time. Momma thanked him for braving the snow and offered him a bowl of soup before he returned to his office. The doctor accepted and, as he went into the kitchen, Momma cradled me and kissed me for trying to be a hero.

Despite my futile attempts to help Molly, I always seemed to balance my good deeds with bad deeds, or vice versa. Once spring rolled around and the weather warmed up, I started making trips downtown after school to go to the movies and vaudeville shows again. Sometimes I had plenty of time to tour the city after going to the theater before dusk fell. At this time of day delivery trucks were making their final rounds. The most popular delivery workers were from Anheuser Busch, which was a cornerstone of the city of St. Louis and the beer industry for many years.

The delivery men were not popular because they worked for Anheuser Busch; they were popular because of the Clydesdale horses. The horses were the company's mascots, and they pulled the delivery trucks throughout the city to drop off barrels of beer at local taverns and restaurants. Every kid in town loved to pet the horses as they waited for the driver to make his deliveries.

Late one afternoon I had a sillier notion. While the delivery man was making his delivery, I thought: "Why not jump into the back of the wagon as it's moving and try landing successfully on top of the barrels?" It sounded like fun . . . until I tried it!

As the delivery truck pulled away I timed my jump . . . but I missed. I landed on the board that held the barrels in place, but then I slipped and knocked the board loose. One by one the barrels bounced into the street, bouncing me to the ground with them! By the time the delivery man stopped the truck, I had disappeared, unhurt. He found the beer barrels, however: The suds covered the street!

Every school year went by faster and faster for me. Soon the summer of 1917 was upon me. Poppa's business had begun to flourish a little over the previous year. Part of the improvement was because of the breakout of World War I. Many businesses in the area, including Poppa's, had increases. People started panic buying because nobody was sure whether the government would start rationing as a result of the war. However, how that relates to people needing their pants and suits pressed is beyond me.

In any case, Poppa was able to buy more things when we needed them. It also meant an occasional surprise, such as my very own bicycle! I wanted to start a newspaper route, since show-business jobs were few and far between, and buying me a bike was Poppa's way of encouraging me.

Before I landed a route, I rode my bike every dayout of sheer happiness. It was the most thoughtful gift I had ever been given. It was even better than Mr. Youman's boomerang. I soon put the bike to good use when I found work as a delivery boy for Western Union. I worked after school and on weekends. More people began sending telegrams rather than using their telephones as the war escalated. I delivered these messages and received a dollar a day for my efforts. Since the job never paid much, I supplemented my income by working as a baggage boy at the Union Railroad Station, the main train depot in St. Louis. This helped me pick up a couple of extra dollars a day in tips.

Neither of my jobs nor my bicycle lasted long, however. One Friday evening during the summer, after finishing my deliveries and working in the railroad station, I got a sudden urge to travel. Working two jobs and owning a bicycle were big responsibilities for a ten-year-old. They made me more restless! That's when I thought, "Why not go to Little Rock?" My sister Esther had moved there earlier in the year after she married Harry Snyder, who owned a tailor shop there. Harry designed uniforms for the local policemen and firemen, and made custom suits for men.

At the station I decided to sell my bike and put the money toward buying train fare. I wasn't keen on selling the bike, but I was too stupid to think about going home and just asking my parents if they would help pay for my ticket. Several hours passed before I found a taker. A man stopped and said, "I'll buy your bike. How much?" Poppa had paid $20 for the bike, but I only needed $10 for a round-trip train ticket to Little Rock. So that's what I took. The man paid me, I bought the ticket, and boarded the outgoing train without calling my parents.

Yes, I forgot to tell my parents where I was going again.

I arrived in Little Rock at seven o'clock the next morning. Trains were slow in those days. Esther and Harry lived in northern Little Rock and, because I didn't have their phone number, I walked the fifteen miles from the station to their home. All on sidewalks. After an hour or so of walking, I was lost.

I stopped a man on the street for directions. "Mister, do you know where my sister lives?" I asked wearily.

"Do I know where your sister lives?" the man said, amused. He must have thought I was nuts! "Who's your sister?"

"Her name's Esther Snyder," I said. "Her husband is Harry Snyder. He runs a tailor shop."

The man looked at me in disbelief. "I don't believe it," he said, amazed. "Of course I know where she lives. Harry's shop is right down the street. Your sister lives in the apartment building next door."

Talk about luck or the powers from above!

I thanked the man and ran to my sister's apartment. Before I knocked on the door, Esther came out to greet me. "Joe, I knew it was you! I had a dream you were going to be at the door."

Of all the things to dream about!

"Do Poppa and Momma know that you're here?" she asked.

"I . . . I . . . I," I stammered.

"Well?" she insisted.

"I forgot to tell them!"

Esther immediately called and told my parents not to worry. "Joey's here. We'll keep him for a while," she said. "Everything's going to be all right." I talked to Momma next. "Jessel, why do you do this to your poor Momma and Poppa?" she said, her voice sounding disturbed. "At least let us *know* when you're leaving town!"

It didn't take long before Esther and Harry wished I had stayed in St.

Louis. They never realized what trouble I could be. Everyday I followed Harry to the shop. The tailor business was not unfamiliar to me because I had watched Poppa work in his store before. But I didn't prove to be much help to Harry. He actually found me to be more of a nuisance! I'd play with the sewing machines while he worked. I never broke any, but I did break plenty of button holders and tools just by touching them. I never intentionally meant to bring Harry any misfortune; I was just a boob at times!

Harry decided to put me to work before I got him further in debt. Before he did, however, I increased the cost of my damages tenfold. The first morning I was to report to work I spotted his car in the garage and discovered the key was still inside. Every kid has probably pretended to drive their mother's and father's car at least once or twice.

Well, I did more than pretend!

I started the ignition and, as a favor to Harry, I decided to back the car out for him before we went to work together. Instead I drove the car right through the front wall of the garage! I forgot to put the car in reverse!

Harry came running out after he heard the crash and his first words to me were, "Joe, how could you do this?" He pulled his hair and grimaced even more when he saw the damage to the car and to the garage. The car had gone halfway through the garage and most of the car needed repair work. The hole in the garage was big enough to park the Queen Mary in!

I apologized repeatedly for my stupidity and started crying. Harry put his arms around me assuringly, and once he cooled down he said, "Don't worry, Joe. It's an old garage anyway. I'll have it and the car fixed tomorrow."

The following day he and Esther didn't punish me by chaining me in my room, but they did devise another method to keep me out of trouble. They bought me a saxophone and had me practice in the back room of Harry's shop everyday. The only thing that drove them crazy was the constant sound of the saxophone, since I practiced for hours. Otherwise they were happy to have me around so long as their eardrums held out! I played the sax religiously, but, like any kid, my enthusiasm only lasted until I found something else that grabbed my attention. Harry was smart enough to notice when I lost interest in playing the saxophone and quickly put me to work. What else could he do?

Harry always pre-shrank the clothes he designed in a ringer-washer tub in back of the store. My job became wringing out each piece of clothing in water then hanging it to dry. This time, I was successful. I didn't ruin his tank or his clothes. I just got tired of working there and felt another change was necessary.

So I found work at the local movie theater as an usher. Since movies were my first love, the job seemed only natural. I ushered every customer to their seat and, once they were seated, I bought a hotdog and popcorn and watched the movies myself. The job was easy, and I saw a lot of movies. Eventually, however, I became homesick, and I returned home to Momma and Poppa before the summer ended.

Esther and Harry loved me dearly, but they must have been quite relieved that my adventurous summer in Little Rock had drawn to a close!

Chapter 3

Hocus! Pocus!—Joining Thurston

The year was 1918. In the fall, school was to begin again—only this time I didn't return. The sixth grade became my last year of school. I decided to concentrate on breaking into show business—with my parents' blessings, of course.

Momma and Poppa understood my decision. Show business had gotten into my blood, and they realized if they had forced me to go back to school I would have been miserable. Even Miss Bartlett wished me good luck. To earn a living in show business burned ever more passionately in my soul. Even at such a young age, 11, I couldn't stand being idle any longer.

My decision to make my way in the world followed my sisters leaving home. They had all moved out of the house by now, except Lilly and Florence. Lil was working full-time for the Wabash Railroad Company as an office clerk. Although she never paid room and board at home, she bought Momma and Poppa things they could use around the house—such as a beautiful brass bed and their first Victrola. Rose had married and become the wife of Nathan Gershner, a jeweler by trade. Like Esther and Harry, they also moved to Little Rock. Gertrude, Molly, and Henrietta were also leading responsible lives, holding down respectable jobs. Manny was still traveling the country working in burlesque.

Now it was my turn to branch out.

I didn't have to look far for employment. I heard about an opening for a song-plugger job with a song-publishing firm in St. Louis called Waterson, Berlin, and Snyder. They published the sheet music for popular songs of the day, which were sold locally in dime stores.

Harry Lorenz was the manager of the local office, which was located in the Columbia Theater. When I applied in person for the job, Harry hired me on the spot. My job was to supply, free of charge, sheet-music versions of the firm's songs to performers at the various vaudeville theaters. Harry hoped by having the performers sing these songs in their acts, it would encourage theatergoers to buy copies of the songs at local dimestores and drugstores. That's how the publishing firm made money.

Fortunately, my hard work created business for the firm, thereby keeping me in the good graces of Harry Lorenz. At the same time I believed that I was heading in the right direction. Seeing the success of others working in show business made me realize that hard work and determination eventually pay off...even if you're only a song plugger.

So by June of 1919, without hesitation, I left my job with Waterson, Berlin, and Snyder and went to work as a singing usher at the Missouri Theater. The theater was beginning its second year, and to celebrate their first anniversary the owners assembled a stage show featuring vaudeville acts, singers, dancers, and who else but the ushers.

We actually introduced the show by singing a song that put the greatest MGM musicals to shame. I can still recall the lyrics: "Ushers hearts won't break/But their soles will ache/As skipping down the aisles they go/So let our acquaintance be forgot/And keep your eye on this grand ol' show!"

With lyrics such as those, no wonder the show ran only three months! But, seriously, I really enjoyed working before a live audience. Nothing beat entertaining people. Afterward I was even more determined to become an entertainer. Notice I said "entertainer." I still wasn't sure about becoming a comedian.

I still lived with Momma and Poppa and gave them a cut of my weekly salary for room and board. I was out of work for two weeks before I found another job. The Fox Theaters had the largest chain of theaters in St. Louis, if not Missouri. They were owned by Spyros Skouras and his brothers, George and Charles. (By 1926, they owned a chain of thirty-seven movie theaters in St. Louis!) They placed an ad in a local newspaper advertising for a boy to pass out circulars promoting the programs for their theaters. I got the job and Spyros Skouras gave me my first assignment. He wanted me to distribute five hundred handbills to pedestrians on the boulevard in front of his office.

Simple enough.

So I did what he told me and went through the handbills fast. Every time I returned for more, Skouras was impressed. He'd say, "Boy, you got rid of those fast!" He never had a worker as efficient as me, so he handed me some more. Surprisingly, each time I returned faster and faster and each time I gave him the same excuse, "There's a lot of people out there!"

All this happened my first day on the job.

The next day I reported, and the same thing happened. I went through one pile of handbills after another. By the fourth day, Skouras figured something was up. So he started following me. I was going through these handbills fast because I wasn't telling him the truth. I often got tired of waiting for people to take the fliers from me, so I tossed whatever was left down the sewer and went back for more. That day Skouras caught me. I turned around, and he was right behind me. He grabbed me and said, "Now I know how you do it so fast!"

"Ooh, you caught me!" I said.

"I sure did," he said, his eyes livid, "and now you're not going to get in to my theaters for nothing." Because I was an employee, he had always let me in the movies for free.

Since he was taking my favorite pastime away from me, I retorted childishly. "Okay, but you wait," I said, "you'll be sorry. One of these days I'll . . . I'll . . . I'll be a big actor. I'll play one of your theaters, and you'll have to pay me a lot of money."

Skouras laughed. But twenty years later, my prediction came true.

After the Ambassador Theater was built, I returned to St. Louis in 1938 as a name comedian, and the manager booked me at this same theater, which the Skouras' owned. Benny Ross and Maxine Stone, the show's master and mistress of cermonies, just loved me. So did the audience, which included Spyros Skouras.

Impressed, he came backstage to see me in my dressing room afterwards. Of course, he didn't know that I was the same little boy who had worked for him many years before. We shook hands and he said, "Mr. Besser, you're the funniest man to ever play this theater. What a great act you have."

"That's nice," I said, reluctantly. "But I want to tell you something that you won't find so hysterical. Do you have any of those circulars you used to hand out to people?"

Skouras stared at me, confused, and said, "I don't have those anymore."

"Gee, I guess I threw them down the sewer so often that you don't have any left," I mused.

Skouras paused, turned beet red, then looked at me in disbelief.

"No, it can't be!" he said.

"Oh, yes it can!" I said. "Remember the little boy who used to hand out leaflets for you. Well, that was me. And now you're paying me back!"

Embarrassed, Skouras apologized, which wasn't necessary, and after that he couldn't do enough for me. I played his theater three times a year from then on.

Getting back to early June of 1919, I found an even better job after my stint with Skouras. The Barnes Carnival was in town searching for workers. It traveled throughout Missouri to every small town, including Hannibal and Springfield, and operated only during the summer. All the towns were so close to each other that the carnival pulled up stakes and arrived in the next town in less than an hour.

Still ambitious, I wanted to entertain and became enthralled with the idea of joining a traveling circus. I went to see the owner about a job, but the only thing he had was a vending job, which wasn't what I had in mind. He did say, however, that the job might lead into work as a performer, so I accepted.

Before the job became mine, the carnival owner discussed my employment with Momma and Poppa. Since I would be traveling, he felt it would be better if they approved. My parents never stood in my way. Whatever made me happy, made them happy. The man didn't have to say much to sell them. All he said was, "Mr. and Mrs. Besser, the carnival is only in the summertime, and it will be good experience for Joe. It's better than having him hanging around the streets." My parents couldn't have agreed more. Anything to keep me out of trouble was fine with them, so they let me go.

I was paid $5 a week, including food and housing, and I sent part of my salary to my parents every week. I never needed much money at my age. The people I worked with always took care of me. I never starved, and I never went without a bed to sleep in. Everybody in the carnival knew me, so if I needed food I'd walk over to the hot-dog stand, and the vendor would give me whatever I wanted, free of charge. Living in boarding houses was also fun. I didn't feel restless anymore; I finally felt responsible and independent. Sometimes we'd run into summer rainstorms and couldn't perform. I'd stay inside my room and put my hand out the window to feel the warmth of the summer rain.

What a life!

And I finally did get my chance to perform! I was selling peanuts and popcorn one night when one of the performers suddenly got sick in a show. So the owner asked me to fill in. He never regretted it. I played a small part in the show; it was a melodrama staged beneath the big top. The applause of the audience did my heart and soul good and fueled my desire to be a performer. After the show, although I was extremely proud of my performance, I went back to selling peanuts and popcorn and told people as they exited the tent, "I'm the same guy who was up there a minute ago!"

My favorite act on the bill was a magician. I loved magic, and the chemistry between the magician and the audience thrilled me. Being a magician seemed like a wonderful way to perform. I had had these feelings earlier because, before (and after) I joined the carnival, there was one magician who came to St. Louis every year, and I always made it a point to see him. His name was Howard Thurston.

Thurston was born in Columbus, Ohio in 1869, the second of three sons of William H. and Margaret Thurston. His father was a carriage maker and inventor who manufactured simple household aids. He had lost his business during the financial panic of 1873. As a result, Thurston and his older brother, Harry, went to work to help support the family. Thurston took on jobs as a hotel bellboy and as a newsboy, selling papers at street corners and on trains.

Thurston's love of magic began at age seven when he saw a performance given in Columbus by the magician Alexander Herrmann. The master's magic completely intrigued young Thurston and made a permanent impression on him. So he set out to learn the art of legerdemain (in other words, the tricks of a magician) and later gave his first formal magic show as a student at Mount Hermon School. His show's success further spurred his interest.

By 1905, after years of traveling and playing in side shows, dime museums, tents, halls, and minor theaters, Thurston became world famous. He became internationally known and worked in Australia, China, and India, as well as in the United States. Thurston was still enthralling audiences when I first saw him.

In December of 1919, three months after the carnival had disbanded, Thurston played an engagement at the American Theater in St. Louis, and I didn't miss him. It was the fifth year in a row that I had seen him, and every time I had gone backstage to ask if he'd let me join his act. Each time Thurston gave me the same emphatic answer: "When you get a little older I'll take you."

Well, how much older did I have to be? I was already twelve. This year Thurston finally gave in . . . but only a little. He agreed to use me as a plant in the audience during his disappearing clock trick. He said to me after I made my customary plea to him backstage, "I'll tell you what. I'll let you work in the audience for me." I came to the theater wearing a plaid jacket and sat in the third row. Thurston stood near the steps to the stage and made one watch after another disappear. Each watch got progressively larger until the last one was an alarm clock. Completely amazed, the audience cheered wildly with Thurston's every move. When it came time to make the alarm clock vanish, that's when I became involved.

Thurston had planted an identical clock in my coat pocket and had an electric bell nailed under my seat. After he made the real clock disappear, he'd craftily ask the audience, "I wonder where the clock went?" At that precise moment the bell rang under my seat and everybody around me stared at me. I acted innocent until I realized the clock was near me. Then I'd scream, "Gee, it sounds like it's close to m-e-e-e-e!"

The audience would laugh and Thurston would then come down from the stage, reach into my pocket and—voila!—he'd produce the missing clock to everyone's astonishment. I always reacted as though I was stunned, in a comical way, of course, "Oh, no," I'd scream, "it was m-e-e-e!!"

This brief taste of working with Thurston made me want more. So the night Thurston closed his show I executed my plan. I went down to the train yard after his final bow. The train yard was directly in back of the theater, and it was also where the baggage cars were parked. Freight workers loaded props and other accessories from Thurston's act into the freight cars. When they weren't looking, I jumped into one of the cars they had left open, and hid behind a cage. I didn't know what was inside the cage nor did I care as seconds later, they locked the door to the car. I was safe for the moment. As usual, my parents didn't know where I was.

The train pulled out from St. Louis, heading for Detroit, and I fell asleep like a little cherub on top of the cage. In the middle of the night I awoke when I heard heavy breathing and growling coming from the cage. When I peeked under the cover that was draped over the cage I discovered who the occupant was: a lion! Believe me, caged or not, I was scared! How I braved this crisis during the night I will never know.

Somehow I survived until the next morning when the train came to a screeching halt. We had arrived in Detroit. Now you can imagine what my poor parents must have been thinking by this time. Here it was the next day, and they still didn't know where I was. What a terrible thing I had done to them. I kept worrying about them, but I also had other worries. One was being discovered by the freight workers, who never liked stowaways.

Minutes after the train stopped, the workers started unloading the cars. When they got to mine, George White, Thurston's head assistant, who supervised the unloading, couldn't believe his eyes. He just moaned, "Oh, no!" then reluctantly escorted me to the car where Mr. Russell, Thurston's manager, was staying. George bravely announced, "Mr. Russell, I've got a surprise for you!" He pulled me from behind him, and an angry Russell smacked his head and moaned. George explained how they had found me asleep on the lion's cage but didn't know what they should do with me.

All Russell kept repeating to himself was, "The kid's from St. Louis. What are we going to do with him?" He decided to keep me until Thurston saw me the next day at the theater. Russell took me to see him, announcing, "Thurston, look who's here!"

Thurston's face immediately went pale. He couldn't believe it. The same boy who had begged him to be part of the St. Louis show had now followed him to Detroit! Quietly impressed, he told Russell, "You know, Russell, any boy who wants to be with me this bad, we've got to keep him. Get in touch with his folks."

I jumped high in the air and hugged Thurston in appreciation. He started my salary at $12 a week and planned to use me the next day.

Meanwhile, Thurston wired my folks to tell them I was all right. At first, the news that I had run away bothered Momma and Poppa, but they knew me better by now. Even when I did something crazy, it was usually for a good reason.

And what better reason to stow away than to work with Thurston and see my dream of performing finally come true.

Chapter 4

Learning New Tricks

For a boy who was almost thirteen, the city of Detroit represented a whole new start.

The downtown section buzzed with excitement: Skyscrapers towered high into the sky; movie and vaudeville houses cluttered the main boulevard; people were helpful and courteous. My enthusiasm for this great city got me so sidetracked that I almost missed my first performance with Thurston altogether.

Thurston asked me to report to the theater on Wednesday (we usually performed two matinees a week, on Wednesdays and Saturdays). I reported to him at nine o'clock in the morning. He told me that I would be working as his assistant in the noontime matinee and said I was free to go anywhere I wanted as long as I reported back to the theater in time. So I went sightseeing. I walked downtown and boarded a double-decker bus that took me on an excursion tour through the city. I climbed to the second deck for the best view, all for ten cents!

Unfortunately, I became so enthralled by the sights that I lost track of time, and the bus went off course. Worse, I didn't know where to tell the driver to let me off. My mind suddenly went blank. What was the address of the theater? What was the theater's name? I couldn't remember. And now Thurston would probably fire me for being late!

I frantically informed the driver about my plight. "I'm supposed to be at the theater where Thurston the magician is performing," I quavered. "If you know where he's playing, would you please take me there?" The driver calmed me down, telling me he knew exactly which theater Thurston was playing at. He personally dropped me off at the backstage entrance.

I immediately dashed up the stairs through the backstage door and hurried to my dressing room. Performers from Thurston's show were already creating a flurry of activity as they were getting ready to go on. The show started in five minutes! As I reached the dressing room, there he stood, with glaring eyes and stern face. It was Thurston, my mentor. And was he mad!

"Joey," he said to me firmly, "remember this for the rest of your life in show business. Never be late again. Always be to the theater a half-hour before you go on."

I felt terrible, but that's because he was right. I should have been more responsible. Surprisingly, Thurston never reprimanded me; that was his first and final warning. Since that time I have *never* been late to any engagement. In fact, I have always been early.

During my first performance, Thurston had me assist him with his rabbit-in-the-hat trick. The trick was simple—so simple that I ruined it! I earned my first laugh on the professional stage by pulling the rabbit from Thurston's coat pocket too soon. He always used two rabbits in this trick, but gave the audience the illusion that he used only one. He'd put the first rabbit in the hat and make it disappear. Then I was supposed to take the hat from him before he showed the audience that the rabbit had disappeared to his coat pocket (where the second rabbit was all the time). But I beat him to the punch, and the audience just howled!

At first Thurston got angry, since that was the second blunder I had made in one day. But once he saw how the audience reacted, with gales of laughter, he whispered to me above the cheers, "Keep on making mistakes. We could stand a little laughter every once in a while."

Despite my tardiness and my "comic" mistake, the show was a huge success, and the audience applauded wildly after the curtain closed. Afterwards they called on Thurston to take a bow, as well as everybody else from the cast. Thurston's popularity never surprised me. His magic act had a cult following that was second only to Houdini's. And no wonder. His show was always a spectacle! He used one hundred and fifty people and a myriad of tricks and props during the course of his act. It took fifty-two boxcars to transport his stock company from one town to the next.

Thurston used me more and more as comic relief. I spoiled other tricks by tripping over my feet while fetching props for him, and the audience laughed louder every time. Sometimes Thurston wasn't aware of everything I did behind his back, however. Many times I let the audience in on my joke by giving them a silly look or by winking at them. Slowly I began developing into a comedian, but I never went overboard. Nobody upstaged Thurston; he was the star!

Thurston's magic captivated audiences of all ages. I can still remember his many great illusions. In one, he levitated a woman in midair and pulled a hoop over her to show that she wasn't suspended by any wires. He even made an elephant disappear! The elephant was placed on a steel platform and was raised up in the air by pulleys with a curtain draped over it. Thurston then fired a gun, the curtain fell to the ground, and only the platform remained suspended. No elephant.

Another trick Thurston performed was a colorful stage number that used all the women in his act. They dressed up in Chinese costumes and, in an Oriental setting, assisted Thurston as he made water squirt from any object, including portions of their bodies. He waved his hand and water gushed from their fingers, ears, eyebrows, the backs of their heads—just by touching them. He also made water spout from the Chinese folding fans each girl carried. The audience, of course, was awestruck by Thurston's wizardry. They had never seen anything like it before. This was one act I *couldn't* ruin!

Thurston was a perfectionist with his craft. That's why he was so successful. During every performance, his wife sat in the box and critiqued the show. If anybody did anything wrong, she reported the problems to Thurston and after every show they held a meeting to discuss them with us. With his wife's keen eyes to aid him, Thurston could never fail. She always found room for improvement.

I measured Thurston's success by the number of engagements we played yearly. We played every city across the country at least once! We only got time off in June when Thurston returned to his home in Whitestone Landing, a suburb of Long Island, New York. He made his headquarters in an old church he had converted into a home and workshop. I was fortunate to be able to stay with Thurston every summer rent free. He had an extra room and since it was too much trouble to return to St. Louis every year and then rejoin the act before we went back on the road, my parents, who I wrote to often, agreed to this set-up. I was having too much fun to come home!

My time with Thurston wasn't always devoted to leisure, however. I painted props and fixed other gadgets that he used in the act. This experience taught me how to use my hands creatively. I continued on this same work schedule for three years until I was fifteen.

Then, in June of 1923, I decided to leave Thurston and pursue another act or another line of work. Although I wasn't looking to become a comedian yet, I did enjoy making people laugh. I was torn between being a magician and a comedian, and felt I needed to do some exploring first.

Thurston was sorry to see me go. He had always treated me like a son.

When I left he said, "If there's anything I can do for you, you let me know. My door is always open."

Packing my belongings, I moved to a boarding house on 45th Street in midtown New York City and went job hunting immediately. The pains of unemployment lasted several weeks, but, fortunately, I had saved enough money from working with Thurston to hold me over until another job came up. I went to one job audition after another, but nothing happened. I soon realized I wasn't the only struggling artist in New York; there were thousands of them—all in unemployment lines. Although he later became a household name, I used to run into one gentleman who was then in the same dilemma. He rehearsed his act in the building where I lived, and his name was Cab Calloway—the "King of Hi De Ho" himself. Cab's individual style of singing contained a joy and festive spirit that moved one into instant gaiety.

Cab's producer, Hazel Green, lived in an apartment that was on the main floor of the building I lived in—right below mine. She helped Cab rehearse daily. I have always enjoyed meeting show people, so one day I dropped in to Hazel's apartment to hear Cab sing. Hazel let me in, but was suspicious of me. She explained why later. Hazel didn't have enough money to buy the rights to first-rate songs for Cab to use in his act, so he sang many hit songs without acquiring permission. As Hazel told me after she realized I was just an admirer, "You be a good boy and don't tell anybody the numbers we're using." Of course, I didn't. Why would I? Cab had talent that hadn't been properly discovered yet, and I wanted him to succeed.

Hazel could sense my sincerity, so she invited me down for coffee or dinner all the time. If Cab was there, he would end the evening by entertaining us with his singing. As show people do, we always pulled for each other. I remember telling Cab, after he finished singing another one of his songs, "You're going places, Cab. Keep singing. You wait and see. Things will start happening for you."

Hazel loved hearing my words of encouragement. But I knew Cab would become a nationally famous singer without my praise. And he did. Several years later he joined Duke Ellington's band and toured the country before he recorded his most famous song, "Minnie the Moocher." The song headed all the national recording charts and from then on Cab was in. Years later, he never forgot me either. Whenever we ran into each other we always reminisced about our days on 45th Street.

A job at last! Another magician, Madame Herrmann (who had taken over the act of her late husband, Herrmann the Great), hired me as her new assistant. I figured working with her would expose me in front of the right people. Maybe I could use the job as another springboard.

Neither happened. Instead, joining Herrmann became the worst decision of my life. She was always mean and criticized my work; she didn't like my clowning. Every day she complained about something, and every day I wished I had stayed with Thurston. My association with her lasted a couple of weeks before I quit and asked for help.

Our last performance was at the Coliseum Theater in New York. On the bill with us was a black minstrel group called the Dixie Four. Backstage I explained my dilemma to them, and they offered to help. They said, "Joe, when you finish here, quit. Don't take that from her. We'll watch out for you, and help you get a job."

Sure enough, they did. A week later they were playing at the Royal Theater and an aerialist named Queenie Dunedin was in the show. She needed a helper. The Dixie Four immediately recommended me. "We've got somebody for you. We'll bring him by tonight."

That evening they took me to the theater to meet Queenie face to face. She was a young, petite girl, in her twenties; a brunette with a pixie face and a shapely figure. Too shapely for being a wire walker! She and I hit it off right away, so the next day I was in the act.

Queenie was an expert at walking and riding a bicycle across the wire, and my job was to bring her props to her, but I always stirred up laughs from the audience first. I'd stumble and fall while taking her bicycle, and every time the audience erupted with laughter. Like Thurston, Queenie loved my bits of comedy and told me to keep them in. Gradually I regained my confidence, which Madame Herrmann had practically destroyed.

Queenie kept me in her act for two years and, during that time, we became close friends. By the winter of 1925 I was nineteen and like most boys who reach that magic age, I became interested in girls. I became interested in Queenie, which proved to be fatal. I fell for her in no time flat, even though her feelings about a serious relationship with me weren't mutual. She liked me as a friend, but that was the extent of our relationship in her eyes. When I found out she had been seeing another man who I didn't like, I started to interfere. She didn't like my meddling into her personal affairs, but I didn't listen.

The delicate situation reached a boiling point when we were playing an engagement at a theater in Richmond, Virginia. Queenie started arguing with me, telling me to back off. Looking back, I should have minded my own business. It's never smart to become too concerned about another person's life unless they ask you for your help first. Since then, I have always lived my life by the following motto: "Close one eye and see your friends. Then close both eyes and keep your friends." If only I had thought that way then, but I was too young to understand.

The argument with Queenie abruptly ended when she asked me to leave the act. I stubbornly refused, so she called on the stagehands to throw me out. They tossed me out the backdoor with my baggage, then slammed the door behind me. What a hollow feeling this gave me. I had never been fired before. It took hours of soul searching and growing up before I realized I was to blame.

I didn't see Queenie again until many years later when I was a comedian headlining in a theater in Cleveland, and she came backstage to see me. We talked, and she forgave me for trying to get close to her in the past. I felt sorry for her because the man she had been seeing had used her, and afterwards her life was never the same. Unfortunately, you can't change the past, so we both learned from our mistakes. But after our visit, I never saw her again.

I returned to New York by boat—reluctantly I might add. I was afraid of traveling on water because I always got seasick and this trip was no exception. I was sick from the minute we set sail until we docked again.

After I arrived home, my future seemed even more clouded. Then I found another job as a busboy at the St. Regis Restaurant, a quaint eatery in downtown New York next door to the Palace Theater. Being a busboy provided me with a steady income, but it never fully paid for my room and board and other expenses. So before and after work, I shoveled snow for people and picked up a couple of extra dollars a week that way until my financial picture improved.

I remember starving for a month before that happened. Every performer has gone through the same financial hardship, so I wasn't any different. I am proud to say, however, that I never asked my parents to help me. I managed to pay off my debts and remain confident that things would turn around.

I have to give credit to two people who helped me get through this crisis emotionally. They became my new neighbors at the boarding house: Frank and Helen O'Connor. They lived two doors down from me. Frank was a reporter for *The Daily Mirror*, and Helen was a nurse. Frank was also an alcoholic, but his drinking never seemed to interfere with his work.

Whenever I went by to visit, Frank always had a drink in his hand. He'd invite me in and offer me a drink, but since I never drank I turned him down. Sometimes he and Helen would have me over for dinner, and I would discuss my plight as an out-of-work performer with them. They knew I worked as a busboy and that the restaurant's owner didn't pay me much, so Frank helped me. He didn't have to, but he did. He got me a job at the *Mirror* bundling newspapers. I picked up ten dollars a week doing that. Frank also paid me to pick up food when he had his weekly poker game. The players he invited would place their orders, and I would pick them up. At the end of the evening, Frank would pay me a couple of dollars more for helping. These little jobs helped put me back on my feet financially, and with friends like Frank and Helen I no longer worried.

I admit that working at the St. Regis became frustrating at times. What made matters worse was that the performers who played at the Palace ate at the restaurant after every performance, then hung around there until their next show. Sometimes seeing them inspired me; but there were other times when I wanted to beat my fist into the silverware tray. The front window to the St. Regis didn't help my mental state either. It faced the Palace. Talk about a daily reminder! I wanted to perform badly, and I used to think to myself as I glanced out the window, "You wait. One day you're going to play that theater."

Somebody finally heard me because I did play the Palace—not then but later. I also found stage work for the first time since returning to New York. In April of 1926 my brother Manny was in town for a six-week engagement at the Alhambra Theater. His wife with whom he'd been working, had left the act and he was working with another Jewish comedian—Irving Irwin. They billed themselves as "Besser and Irwin."

Manny came to visit me, and you can bet I was happy to see him! I needed advice once more. With his current success on the stage, he seemed like the best person to help me. I explained my desire to work on the stage, and Manny said, "Joe, you should come by the theater. Maybe you'll find work there. Besides, there's an act you'll just love. They're called Alexandria and Olsen. They're a real scream."

What did I have to lose?

So I took Manny up on his offer and caught his act one night. He was funnier now than the first time I saw him! The audience laughed so much that afterward Manny and his partner took several bows. They were a great success, but they were not without any competition. The Alexandria and Olsen act was also a scream. The audience laughed louder and longer than they had for Manny—that's how funny they were. The act consisted of Ole Olsen (the brother of John Olsen—who *also* called himself Ole and later became part of the comedy team of Olsen and Johnson) who was the slender comic straight man and Eddie Alexandria (Alex for short) who played the fat, dumb comic.

Watching these two buffoons rekindled my desire to become a comedian. I felt best suited for their style of comedy. After the show Manny introduced me to Ole, and during our visit I was real blunt with him. I said, "Ole, I'd love to be in your act. Please take me with you. I can do some funny things. I want to be on stage. I'll do anything to be with you."

Ole gave me a noncommital, "I'll see what I can do, Joe. I'll see what I can do."

His answer didn't satisfy me. I never left him alone.

Ole and Alex played ten theaters in New York during the next six weeks, and I went to *every* one of them every night. Manny was on the same bill each time, so he thought I was coming to see *him* perform. I never told him otherwise. I kept hounding Ole about joining his act until he finally gave in. He told Alex, "Let's take Joe with us. Give him a couple of bits to do. Maybe he'll work out."

That's all I wanted—a chance—and I don't think they ever regretted their decision.

Chapter 5

Touring with Alex and Ole

My first booking with Alexandria and Olsen was in Connecticut in 1926. They started me at $35 a week, including room and board, and became my official tutors in the comedy world.

In our first year together we played a gamut of theaters from Connecticut to California. Vaudeville was a big-money business in the mid-1920s, and it became a perfect training ground for a clown like myself. I couldn't have asked for a better place in which to develop.

My task was made easier because vaudeville folk were a close-knit group. The loyalty and love they had for each other ran deep. If you needed help, nobody was hesitant to offer you a helping hand. Everybody helped each other.

Vaudeville had been a form of entertainment since the eighteenth century, when jugglers and other acts first performed before the townspeople (this was the first "variety show," which we later called "vaudeville"). The humor was cruder than in the 1920s, and the acts were not as diversified. After the turn of the century, however, the shows were clean and fun, lasted two hours, and were packed with eight to ten entertainment acts: comedians, jugglers, acrobats, magicians, singers, midgets, and others.

The stages on which vaudevillians performed had come a long way, too. They no longer performed on platforms in town squares but in thousand-seat theaters from the Palace on Broadway to the Orpheum Theater in Los Angeles. As a result, theater owners never complained because they did such bustling business.

By the time I entered vaudeville, theaters were jammed to the rafters every day—whether it was a matinee or evening show—with people coming from all over to be entertained. Admission was ten cents for children and twenty-five cents for adults. At those prices, no wonder you couldn't keep the people away!

Playing the vaudeville circuits also became a great way to see the country—at its best and its worst—and get paid at the same time. The vaudeville circuits guaranteed you a minimum of a week's work, meaning three or four shows a day, and I never had a week when I didn't work! Entertainers were always put into hotels or boarding houses that had cold rooms in the winter and hot ones in the summer. Not every city had such luxurious accomodations, however. In some towns the theater dressing rooms were in terrible shape, and the food and rooms were lousy. But seeing the good and the bad helped educate me on all walks of life. And that was something I couldn't learn in the classroom.

I'll never forget how Momma and Poppa gave me the chance to perform regularly. If they had been different parents, I probably would have wound up being a plumber or an electrician!

I always felt indebted to them for putting up with me all those years. So I sent them ten dollars a week from my salary to help take care of their needs. I'm sure, in their minds, the money was immaterial. Half the time they didn't spend it; instead they bought presents with it for my sisters. They rarely treated themselves. But, at least, through this weekly contribution they were constantly reminded of how much I loved them.

In 1927, my second year with Alexandria and Olsen, I had the most exciting event of my career. My name was added to their billing! This was the first time I had received a billing at any theater, so I knew they appreciated my work.

What a change working with Alexandria and Olsen was for me. No more magic. No more playing assistants to anybody. No more bussing tables at restaurants. No more bundling newspapers or shoveling snow (pretty dramatic, isn't it?). Instead I was making people laugh regularly.

People laughed all right, and that's because there was something in our act for everybody. Everything we did was simple and nonsensical, which prompted Alexandria and Olsen to call our show, "What's It All About?" At first the title was misleading. But audiences found it appropriate once they'd seen us perform. I remember one noted critic who wrote, "Alexandria and Olsen have been in vaudeville for a good many seasons, and yet they continue to delight and attract large audiences with their slapstick and hokum. It is hard to recount the fast-moving and utterly ridiculous antics of Alexandria and Olsen so that some idea of their comedy can be obtained. There is no semblance of plot or outline—simply a lot of fun!"

That critic couldn't have come closer to the truth—not that I'm biased or anything!

I still recall how our act began, just as though it happened yesterday.

There were actually four of us in the act: Alex, Ole, Sammy (a midget), and myself. We always opened with a round of jokes. Ole and Sammy would remain on stage, while Alex and I went up into the theater boxes and heckled them. The audiences loved our silly patter and enjoyed this part of the show the most. Ole and Sammy performed a mind-reading routine, and our job was to interrupt Sammy before the audience found out Sammy didn't know how to read minds—he was just faking.

The jokes we used might be considered primitive today, but when we told them they always left the audience in stitches. Some were simple jokes.

For instance, I'd scream to Ole, "Hey, Ole, it's all over the house!"

Playing it straight, Ole would yell back, "What's that, Joe?"

"The roof!"

After the audience stopped laughing, Sammy went back to reading minds before we interrupted him again. This time I would be holding a fishing pole with an apple on the hook as bait. Ole would spot me, and before I said anything, he'd say, "Hey, Joe, what are you doing?"

"I'm fishing," I'd say.

"Then what are you doing with an apple?" Ole would ask. "Don't you know you have to have worms?"

I'd stare at him stupidly, then say, "Well that's what the apple is for . . . the worms are in the apple, silly!!!"

There would be another slight pause so Sammy could resume with his mind reading. But then Alex would let another joke fly. He'd say, "Hey, Joe, what's good for a bald head?"

"That's simple," I'd say. "Plenty of hair!"

With each joke Sammy pretended he was getting more flabbergasted. Alex and I never quit, we were just warming up! We kept pumping jokes until the audience became exhausted from laughing. Next I tried an animal joke on Ole. "Hey, Ole!" I'd scream. "How do you keep a dog from going mad in September?"

At his wit's end by now, Ole would say, "I give up, Joe. How do you keep a dog from going mad in September?"

"Kill him in August!"

Sammy never did get around to reading anybody's mind.

In show business you'll find some performers are superstitious. Alex was in that category. I remember he owned a black cat that he brought with him to every theater. The cat's name was Puss, as in "Puss n' Boots," because she was black with white fur on her feet, which gave them the shape of boots.

Alex loved Puss so much, he later worked her into our act as the *fifth* member. Puss was definitely the first trained vaudeville cat. Alex trained her to play the xylophone: she'd walk across the keys and create musical sounds that delighted everybody. She always received standing ovations and bouquets of flowers from the audience. Then, one night her career was cut down in the prime of her life.

That night was when Sophie Tucker was on the bill with us. Puss disappeared. Alex was frantic! He looked everywhere for her. She was a show business oddity. Losing her was like losing the first talking frog! Unfortunately, Alex never found her, so he went on that night without her.

I couldn't resist making light of the situation, however, when it came time for our heckler interlude. My ad lib caught Alex completely by surprise. We had just finished telling one of our routine jokes when I blurted out, "Hey, Alex, I know where your cat went!"

Startled, Alex fumbled around. "Where Joe?" he said. "Where?"

"Sophie Tuck-her!" I quipped.

The audience burst into laughter, and they laughed even harder after Alex explained to them that his cat actually was missing. The ad lib became the highlight of the evening. Even Alex laughed, in spite of how much he missed his cherished cat.

Sometimes other famous comedians and performers from the show worked with Alex and me in the boxes. I remember Ken Murray and his wife Charlotte once did when they were in a show with us. Ken went on to become a big star on stage, screen, and television. He also stockpiled the largest collection of home movies ever taken of known and unknown Hollywood celebrities. He probably has one of me doing an Esther Williams pose around the pool when I wasn't looking!...Ooh, he was such a sneak!

When Ken and I worked together, I wore a straw hat every night. Ken's job was to whack me on the head with a rolled-up newspaper after I finished each joke. Simple enough, right? That's all he had to do. Then I'd yell, "Ooh, you crazy, you, s-t-o-p!!"

Ken's job was so simple, he became irritated. I'll admit almost anyone could have done what he did and for smaller wages. Ken finally came to me and said, "Joe, come on. You've got me sitting in the box. At least give me one joke." I did, and he was happy for the rest of our engagement together.

Following our heckling routine, Alex and I would then return to the stage and participate in a comical musical number with Ole and Sammy. Alex played the xylophone, I played the ukelele, Ole blew into a wine jug, and Sammy sang. We reprised many popular show tunes and other melodies, such as "Ain't She Sweet." After we completed our last number the audience usually gave us a rousing ovation. Many times we had to come back out on stage for an encore performance. That kind of applause made us perform even harder the next time.

Afterwards Ole would step back on stage and conduct what they call an afterpiece. It consisted of stand-up material with Ole as a master of ceremonies and other performers from the show coming out for a final bow, interrupting Ole with *schtick* in the process.

One time Al Jolson, who was on the bill, walked on stage in front of Ole carrying a step ladder and interrupted Ole in the middle of a story he was telling the audience. Irritated, Ole would say, "Al Jolson, what are you doing with that step ladder?"

Al would chuckle a bit, then say, "I've got to get *up* in the morning!"

Al would then walk off stage and another performer would appear. Perhaps Ed Wynn. Ed would also interrupt Ole, only he'd come out holding a pot of coffee. Ole, always perceptive, would say, "Ed Wynn, where are you headed?"

"Why I'm going to the courthouse," Ed would say solemnly. "I'm getting a divorce from my wife, you know."

"Too bad, Ed. Too bad," Ole would sympathize. Baffled, though, he would then inquire, "Then what are you doing with the coffee pot?"

"I've got the *grounds* in there!" Ed would quip.

Ed would exit and Sophie Tucker would then follow. And she would come out carrying a long board. Ole would stop in the middle of his story again, and he'd say, "Sophie Tucker, what's with the board?"

Sophie would wisecrack, "Can't you tell, honey? I'm looking for a room . . . I've got my *board*!!"

Playing with Alexandria and Olsen also gave me many opportunities to work with other name people. Besides Al Jolson and Sophie Tucker, I also worked with the one and only, Sammy Davis, Jr., when he was five years old! The only difference between the Sammy of then and now was that he didn't wear as much jewelry in those days! Sammy was a featured dancer in his father's and mother's act. He was an adorable kid, and we played on the same bill together at least twice a year.

Sammy's parents always gave me a big bear hug when we worked together. They knew how crazy I was about Sammy—and I still am. Sammy used to sit on my lap before every performance, and we'd talk shop. He'd talk dancing; I'd talk comedy. Sometimes we'd also take long walks backstage before he went on, which settled Sammy down from being so hyper. On stage, however, Sammy demonstrated that he had the poise of a veteran. Nobody doubted he would be successful.

As Alex, Ole, Sammy (the midget), and I traveled, our act became increasingly popular. Some theater owners demanded repeat engagements or would hold us over for another week to meet the demands of ticket buyers.

At the beginning of our third year together, I hit a minor snag in my relationship with Alex and Ole. They were still paying me $35 a week. By all rights, I deserved more because every employer's responsibility is to increase an employee's wages. At first Ole and Alex balked at the idea of a salary hike. When they refused to change their minds, I quit.

They called me back to work, with a raise to $40 a week, after they discovered that theater owners wouldn't book them unless I worked with them. Several owners told them, "No Besser, no bookings!" They were happy to have me back, and so were the owners!

By the spring of 1928, however, I felt it was time to move on and explore other challenges in my career. Ole and Alex had given me the opportunity to develop into a respectable comedian. Now I needed to prove my ability—alone. In March of that year, Ole and Alex reluctantly gave me my release. It wasn't long before I made a new connection.

Just a week later, the manager for Loew's Theater on Delancy Street in Brooklyn heard I was available and signed me up for two weeks. His theater was located in a neighborhood that had a strong Jewish flavor—right down to an appetizing bagel store. I felt right at home.

I basically maintained the same kind of material I had performed with Alex and Ole, except the show's master of ceremonies served as my straightman. He happened to be the best. His name was Richy Craig, Jr., and many considered him to be the Bob Hope of his time. There was a singer who went under the billing of Ethel Zimmerman in the show with us. She later changed her name to Ethel Merman.

The theater manager couldn't have been more pleased. We knocked the audiences dead for four straight weeks and created so much excitement he held us over for two additional weeks! I wasn't completely satisfied with my work, though. I was still working on my character. It took a while before everything fell into place. Since I always came across as childlike, I decided to create a character everyone could identify with. The character I decided on was an overaged Lord Fauntleroy who always thought the world was crashing down on him. His only defense became his exasperated mannerisms and catch phrases like, "Ooh, you crazy y-o-u!" and "Aw, shut uuupp!"

Everything clicked with Richy. At first it was an adjustment working with him as my straight man. My attitude changed when he told me the laughter our act was receiving wasn't for him, but for me. I never realized people were laughing at *me*. I had thought they were laughing at Richy. The compliment was a big boost to my confidence—although Richy deserved credit for helping me get those laughs. After that I felt like nothing could stand in my way.

During our engagement, I'm proud to say, Richy and I became good friends. We stuck close to each other and roomed in the same hotel—buddies to the end. During our final week together, in April of 1928, we hoped to work together regularly. One night that week our dream looked as though it would come true. Rich barged into my dressing room with some exciting news. "Joe, several scouts from Paramount Publix are going to be in the audience tonight," he said. "They're looking for new acts to play their circuit, mostly comedians!"

I could have fainted! Paramount Publix happened to be one of the largest vaudeville circuits in the country. If you landed a contract with them, you were guaranteed work for 52 weeks a year in big-budget stage shows.

Richy rehearsed his lines extra hard before the show. While he was enthusiastic about this opportunity, truthfully speaking, I was scared. The idea of performing before several bigwigs from a major theater was new to me. Richy was excited and sure they were going to sign him to a contract. I wasn't as sure myself.

We went on that night and did our normal *schtick*. My hands sweated abnormally during our routines—I was that nervous! You couldn't tell by the laughs we received, however. The audience went bananas.

After our performance I collapsed in our dressing room, while Richy couldn't wait to hear from the scouts. He was positive they would come back to see us. He was so positive that he went out and bought a bottle of champagne on ice. As we wiped our makeup off, there was a knock at the door. Richy opened the door, smiled, and reached to shake hands. It was *them*! Richy thought for sure they had come to offer a contract to him. I was, too, until, they bypassed Richy and offered a contract to me instead! Richy couldn't believe it. He thought they had made a mistake!

Paramount signed me to a one-year contract, and Richy breathed a sigh of relief when I offered to take him with me. He went on the road with me and wrote material for my act. He didn't work exclusively for me, however. If somebody wanted him to perform at another theater, I let him go and had another emcee fill in. I tried to convince Paramount to sign

Richy up as my straight man, but they demurred. So Richy *wrote* material for me instead. He knew how to instigate comedy—on stage and off. He kept me laughing, even when we were miles apart.

I remember one time we had been working together in the same town, but after the show closed we went our separate ways. I went to California; Richy returned to New York. Richy left me at the train station at midnight. I got on my train, and he got on his.

At two-thirty in the morning, there was a knock on the door to my state room. It was the porter.

"Mister, Joe," he said, "I hate to wake you, but there is an urgent telegram here for you."

I tipped the porter and closed the door to read the telegram. It was from Richy. It said:

You're a fine pal. Why don't you write?

Signed,
Richy Craig, Jr.

I had just left him!

Richy definitely was a master of one-liners. I remember another time when we went golfing together. I had never golfed in my entire life! I borrowed Richy's clubs and lost six balls, slicing them all over the green. Then I left to play an engagement in the next town. Later, I received another telegram from Richy: "You can come home now. We found the balls."

Richy was far ahead of his time in terms of humor. After we first met we decided to exchange autographed photos. I gave Richy an early shot of me on stage in my vaudeville costume, and he gave me the only picture he had of himself. It was framed with a pretty border and engraved at the bottom of the frame was "Richy Craig, Jr., 25 Years Ago."—The frame was empty!

Richy was clever on stage, as well. He slayed audiences with a rapid fire delivery of jokes. Later, as part of his act, he also danced. Richy would take an ordinary phonograph record, lay it on stage, then tap dance on the record without breaking it! That's how light on his feet he was!

As the finish to his act, Richy would come out and take a bow and make an announcement. "Folks, I've got to take a picture of you and send it to my Mom and Dad to show them what a wonderful audience you've been." He then produced a camera with a flash and snapped a picture.

My years with Richy and the Paramount Publix circuit were very happy ones. I was able to establish myself and broaden my style of comedy (even though I later added improvements), and I was also able to shape and define my character. And the money they paid me was a big improvement from the salary Alexandria and Olsen paid me. I now earned $150 a week!

During my first three months with Paramount, I played at least twelve Publix theaters across the country by early June of 1928. I worked the Olympia in New Haven, the Metropolitan in Boston, the Loew's Palace in Washington, D.C., the Metropolitan in Los Angeles, the Granada in San Francisco, the Uptown in Chicago, the Rivera in Omaha, and so many others that I don't have room to mention them all.

I was always booked with other major acts and performers at these theaters. I worked with giants of the business like Ruth Etting, who sang her hit "What Can I Say, Dear, After I'm Sorry?"; Clara Bow, the noted film actress; the famous bandleader, Paul Ash; Ginger Rogers, who wore her hair in a "sheik" bob and talked baby talk; and Ethel Merman, when she was *really* Ethel Merman—and those are just a few.

Just like Ole's afterpiece, Publix's people liked to feature these performers in my act. I remember using Ethel Merman and Clara Bow on separate occasions, but with very different results. Singing, not comedy, had become Ethel's true talent. The night she worked with me, Paul Ash, "The King of Jazz," was the master of ceremonies. Ethel had one problem: She couldn't deliver the straight line. Everytime when she was supposed to set up the punchline for me during rehearsal, she started laughing uncontrollably. Paul finally interceded. "Joe, you can't have her laughing all the time," he said. "It's going to ruin your act." He was right, so I gave Ethel the big hook.

Clara Bow was a vast improvement. She and I worked in another show, and she definitely knew how to milk a joke for laughs. Theaters used to stage vaudeville shows before the main feature, and Paramount often booked the star of the movie in our show to promote their work.

Clara Bow was the star of a movie that was playing in a theater I was appearing in. The front office asked me to put her into my act, so I came up with a clever bit that she helped pull off magnificently. The skit had me running on stage, tumbling to the ground, and picking myself up. Just then Clara would appear in the wings wearing a bathrobe, clapping her hands in a cleaning motion. She had supposedly thrown me out of her room! The bit got laughs everytime, and Clara became a great addition to the show.

After that particular engagement closed, my greatest challenge lay ahead of me.

Chapter 6

Ernie

In mid-June of 1928 Paramount Publix announced that I would be starring in their first musical revue entitled, *Main Street to Broadway.* The show opened at the Paramount Theater in New York the last week in June.

As I recall, the production was labeled "the most ambitious project ever" from producer Frank Cambria, who became an absentee backer. Although he got the show going in the beginning, he didn't return until the show closed five months later to collect the profits! The show had dancing, singing, ballads, acrobatics, more dancing, more singing, more ballads, more acrobatics, and a short pudgy guy doing comedy—me! Yes, my belt size had increased, as had my stomach. My weight was up from 140 pounds to 165 pounds. Nobody believed in health spas then—including me!

The show was first-rate all the way. Frank cast a talent-rich selection of prominent entertainers in the show with me that included Almira Sessions, the hottest new singer recruited from vaudeville; Arthur Campbell, a singing juvenile; Ruth Witmer, another singer who was billed as "The Dixie Nightingale"; Burday and Norway, who performed an acrobatic waltz; Calm and Gale, another eccentric dance team; and Barnett and Clark, a boy-and-girl tap-dancing duet.

I told you there was a lot of singing and dancing! The show was made up of three segments presented before the main feature at every Paramount Publix theater. The movie was different in each city, as was the master of ceremonies. We played in Buffalo, Cleveland, Boston, Chicago, Baltimore, Detroit, St. Louis, Philadelphia, and every other major city and small town. Each time a different bandleader emceed the show. Paul Ash handled the chores at the Oriental Theater in Chicago, while Teddy Joyce did the Loew's Penn Theater in Pittsburgh, and Wesley Eddy did the Loew's Palace in Cleveland.

No matter who our emcee was, the show's results were always the same: sold-out performances and rave reviews. One Pittsburgh critic acclaimed:

"The audience encored heavily for *Main Street to Broadway*, a crazy gathering of odds and ends of talent. Most of it so crazy, it's funny; most of it is so funny, it's good. It was cheered all the way."

The critics were unbelievably kind to me. I hate to brag, but they never gave me a bad review—not once. I recall one critic wrote: "Joe Besser indulges in a lot of eccentric comedy that quite often hits the spot. He is about the brightest member on the stage show." These reviews always surprised me; the same went for how the audiences loved me. In Dallas, Texas, the bandleader Ray Teal forced me back on stage for a brace of bows because the audience wouldn't let him continue with the show after I performed my act. Audiences like those made performing a real pleasure.

Such favorable responses on the part of audiences and critics soon impressed the brass at Paramount's New York office. Enough so that, after *Main Street to Broadway* closed in November of 1928, they signed me to a thirty-five week extension. I was to headline additional vaudeville shows with an increase in pay. My salary was increased to $175 a week! I couldn't have been happier.

The busy schedule I worked gave me little time to socialize, however. I guess there's always some drawback to becoming successful, especially in show business. Paramount gave me one day off a week—every Monday—and I normally relaxed on that day. I spent mornings of the other days preparing for and working on my shows. I was twenty-two and ready and waiting for the right girl to come along. Despite my recent success, my life seemed empty. I badly wanted to share my good fortune with somebody, and being patient until the right girl came along was hard.

Paramount next assigned me to open a new show just before Thanksgiving with Paul Ash at the Chicago Theater in Chicago. We were booked there for one week, then moved to the Paramount Theater in Brooklyn for eight weeks—a record for a single vaudeville engagement! I enjoyed working with Paul. He was personable, quiet and reserved. And what a bandleader! He always asked for me in order to bolster his show, even though he didn't actually need me to elicit a great audience response.

I'll never forget how much business Paul brought to the theaters of Chicago. Mounted police were needed to control crowds outside the theater; the customers were wrapped around the entire block! Several theater owners had to band together when the theaters in the area could no longer accommodate the crowds. They ended up building the Oriental Theater exclusively for him.

We worked long and hard hours in Chicago, and I remember the night our show closed I couldn't wait to go home. This was at two o'clock in the *afternoon*! Three shows a day had begun to wear on me. I needed rest—lots of rest. I took out my frustration on the doorman, saying, "I'm tired of working all these shows. Sometimes this is too much."

A smartly dressed woman heard my complaint, and she walked up to me and said, "If you don't like the business, why don't you get out?" She then walked away with a troupe of dancers following her. They were the Allan K. Foster Girls. They had just arrived in town to prepare for their own show, which started the day after ours closed.

I thought this woman had showed a lot of nerve, and her comment really annoyed me. I angrily said to the doorman, "Who's that fresh dame?" He said, "Why, she's the captain of the Foster girls."

That's all I wanted to know. I never forgot a name or face, but in her case I was willing to make an exception!

That night I went to my hotel room, more exhausted than ever. I was tired from my head to my toes. I didn't even take my clothes off before going to sleep. However, in my dreams, that woman's comment still irritated me. All night I swore if I met up with her again I'd give her a piece of my mind.

I got that opportunity when Paramount put me in another musical revue, *Carnival Cocktail*, which opened in Buffalo in late December of 1928. My contract with Paramount had been extended for another year! The show featured Frances Willis, a trick dancer; Ethel Dallon, a dynamic singer; Moore and Pal, a popular acrobatic team; Julia Dawn, a singing organist; and Charles Marsh, who was our master of ceremonies. To my surprise, Paramount gave me top billing in the show—a first for me. Because I had been so successful in *Main Street to Broadway* the executives at Paramount thought I deserved it.

Oh, yes, I almost forgot. There was another act starring in our show: a stunning array of dancers known as the Allan K. Foster Girls. Not that it mattered, of course.

Charlie Niggemeyer, who later became a good friend of mine, produced *Carnival Cocktail*. The woman who had rudely insulted me in Chicago was also in the show. And she didn't want to be there. Charlie told me she said to him, "You're not going to put me in a show with him," meaning me. "I'm going to have trouble with this guy."

Actually it was the reverse. She caused trouble first. I still didn't know her name, nor did I care to, until . . . .

One night following a hectic late show, I was lying in bed listening to music on my radio. The radio was portable and had pushbuttons. I took it everywhere. It was my constant companion. Unlike modern radios, mine was so primitive that it didn't have a built-in aerial. You had to attach a wire to the radio that was placed outside the window to improve the reception. I followed this procedure in the hotel, and the reception greatly improved.

Music always lulled me to sleep, and that night was no different. My eyes got so heavy, I fought to keep them open. Finally I gave in, and I was out—fast asleep, in a deep sleep. Suddenly I heard a loud crash. As I turned, I saw my radio flying out the window! I pinched myself to see if I was dreaming . . . ouch!! I wasn't! The radio had suddenly launched itself into outer space!

By the time I reached the window, it was too late. The radio had plummeted to the pavement below. At first I was pretty broken up about it (so was the radio!). Then I got mad! Who was responsible for destroying my radio? Well, the culprit had left behind the evidence: The aerial wire to the radio had been severely shredded, as though someone had tried pulling it from the room below.

I called the manager of the front desk and angrily complained. "I want the person responsible for stealing my radio," I said. "It just flew out the window!" The manager, in a calm monotone, said, "Mac, I've heard everything. But I've never heard about a radio that flew! We'll check into it anyway." Then he hung up.

The manager checked into the matter, but by the next morning he had come up with nothing. That's when I stumbled onto who the culprit was. Her name was Erna Kay Kretschmer, dancer. "Ernie," for short. She worked for the Allan K. Foster Girls. She was the girl who had bawled me out in Chicago. The girl who bawled me out?! Wait a minute! It couldn't be! It was.

Ernie found out my room was above hers, and she brought up the remains of the radio to me. Nothing was left but splinters of wood and broken tubes, but she thought I might be able to use the parts. "I'm sorry about the radio," she said. "I feel like a heel!"

"You look like one," I said.

Touche'! Now we were even.

Ernie explained that the radio flew out the window when she accidentally pulled on the wire trying to pull down the shade to her window.

The story was so funny, because it was true, that I couldn't help but laugh.

To show that I didn't harbor any hard feelings, I invited Ernie to have an ice cream soda with me down the street at a place called "The Ice Cream Store" (pretty clever name, huh?). They served a soda there that was named after me. No, not a "Soda Jerk," it was called "The Joe Besser Ice Cream Cocktail." I ordered two, and we dug in. I saw a different Ernie, unlike the one who picked on me before. She was short and thin, with slender legs, a heart-shaped face, brown eyes, and brown hair. She was older than me, by seven years, and her background was as interesting as mine.

As we sipped our sodas, Ernie told me her parents, Herman and Anna Kretschmer, had emigrated to this country from Europe. Ernie was born on March 17, 1900, in New York City after Herman moved Anna to America because he realized it was a land of opportunity. However, after Herman found an apartment for Anna and little Ernie to live in, he returned to Europe where he worked as the head guard at the Kaiser's Palace. He had been granted a temporary leave, but his position was like that of any serviceman's—he was committed to serving his country first. So Ernie was raised fatherless, but Herman always provided for her and Anna by sending money to help out.

Ernie was blessed with a natural-born ability for dancing, and she started when she was five. An organ grinder and his monkey used to perform outside her apartment. The monkey danced, then held out a tin cup for donations from the passersby who crowded around to watch them perform. One day Ernie got into the act and started dancing for the organ grinder, too. She made more money than the monkey, so when the organ grinder came by later he had Ernie dance instead!

Ernie first worked professionally on the stage when she turned fourteen. Then if you were fourteen you could acquire working papers. So Ernie did, and she worked in a number of shows. Her first was as a hootchy-kootchy dancer in an all-men's burlesque show. Originally, Ernie's mother didn't approve of her daughter's show-business aspirations; she changed her mind once she saw how successful Ernie became.

Ernie next joined a dancing group of four girls called, "Mary Astor's Dancing Dolls." Then producer Joe Wood signed her to work in his school act, which was similar to Gus Edwards'. Impressed with her work, Wood cast Ernie in his long-running stage show, *Mimic World*, in which members of the cast impersonated famous performers of the time. Seymour Felix directed and starred in the show.

In 1925 Ernie joined the Foster Girls when her friend, Dolly Nutter, who later married Charlie Niggemeyer, got her the job. Ernie had had several sweethearts along the way, among them, Charlie Chase, a famous motion-picture comedian and a critic for *The Daily Mirror.* At least that's the story she gave me, unless there were more!

We had sipped our sodas dry by the time Ernie finished telling me about herself, and I walked her back to the hotel. For the most part, I was interested in her, but I was also afraid. I was already seeing another girl in the show, also a Foster girl, so I had that girl's feelings to consider. For this reason, I didn't pursue Ernie until she pursued me, which happened that week.

Allan K. Foster was strict with his girls. He set down one guideline for employment: There was to be no dating men from the same show. The girl who was seeing me had already broken this commandment, and the rules didn't stop Ernie either! Luckily Foster never found out.

Ernie came to my dressing room that day, shoved the other girl aside, and said, "You'll be seeing *me* from now on!" Now that's what I like—a girl with brute force! So I became hers, and she became mine—or however that goes.

We dated secretly until *Carnival Cocktail* closed, after a year-long engagement, in December of 1929. None of the other girls ever squealed on Ernie because, after all, she was the captain! We went out during the day or before we performed our matinee and evening shows. Sometimes we spent time strolling through the local parks, going to parties with other performers from the show, or catching a late showing at a movie theater after we finished our last performance.

In every town we either found something to do or somebody invited us for dinner. Sometimes these people just invited me, but it must have been love, because I'd always say, "I'm sorry, but I can't come by myself." I couldn't leave Ernie. I never went anywhere without her.

After the show closed, Ernie and I returned to New York so she could introduce me to her mother. When Ernie told Anna what I did for a living, Anna screamed, "Not another entertainer!"

I could tell that Anna liked me right away. So could Ernie.

We were going to get along just fine!

You laugh and I'll harm you. At age five, with curls yet!

My parents Morris and Fanny Besser.

My brother Manny's success as a stage comedian inspired me to enter show business. At Manny's right, his partner Irving Irwin.

Magician Howard Thurston gave me my first break. Circa 1923.

See, I did have hair! From my days with Alexandria and Olsen.

No, this is not me! It's my wife Ernie as a dancer in the mid-1920s.

The greatest day of my life: The day I married Ernie. 1932.

On stage with Jimmy Little, 1940.

Backstage with Olsen and Johnson. From *Son's of Fun,* 1941.

Hey, Rookie! elevated me to a movie comedian in 1943. With Ann Miller and Larry Parks.

With my biggest fan and best friend, Lou Costello. He never "harmed me."

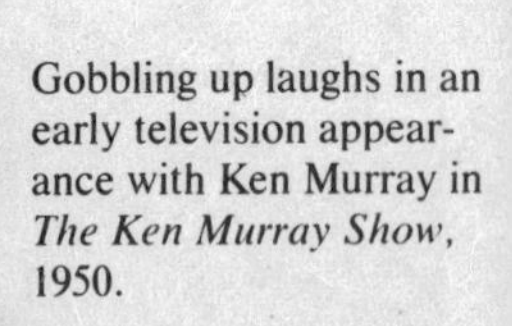

Gobbling up laughs in an early television appearance with Ken Murray in *The Ken Murray Show*, 1950.

My character "Stinky" from *The Abbott and Costello Show* first evolved in a TV sketch on *The Alan Young Show* in 1951.

A familiar scene from *The Abbott and Costello Show*.

Jack Benny loved using me on his own television show—seven times! From my most memorable episode with Tennessee Ernie Ford on *The Jack Benny Show*.

You'd do this kinda stuff too if a major studio signed you to star in a series of two-reel comedies. From *Fraidy Cat* (1955) with Jim Hawthorne.

Chapter 7

Vaudeville! Vaudeville! Vaudeville!

In February of 1930 I was separated from Ernie for the first time when she and the Foster Girls were sent on a six-month tour through Europe and Germany to entertain audiences at the London Palladium and the German Winter Garden. Those months became the loneliest of my life.

Ernie and the girls embarked by boat from the New York harbor on a cold wintery day. An early-morning haze covered the sky, and my pal Richy Craig and I waved goodbye to Ernie as the ship steamed away into the morning mist.

I continued working in vaudeville shows in New York around this time, but it wasn't as much fun without Ernie. My life seemed empty because I couldn't see her every night. Richy finally helped me curb my loneliness by helping me write love letters to Ernie overseas, so I wouldn't be so depressed. I often had difficulty expressing myself on paper, so Richy said, "Don't worry, Joe. Whatever you write, I'll type for you."

Indeed he did.

Richy typed the most hilarious lover letters you've ever read in your life! He refined what I wrote with his comic touches, and they undoubtedly kept Ernie's heart throbbing for days. Ernie never knew that Richy helped me co-write these letters—and she still doesn't know. Oops! . . . She does n-o-w!!

When letters were not enough to show my love, I started sending Ernie bottles of expensive perfume. She loved receiving them until she learned she had to pay duty on them. What a *schmoe* I was! (That's idiot in Yiddish!) I never knew she could buy the same perfume in England, where it was manufactured! The bottles I bought her were originally shipped to America from England! Ernie finally wrote me and said: "It's cheaper for me to buy the perfume here, you dumb cluck!"

Ernie always worried about Anna while she was gone, so I checked on her periodically. At that time she lived in a modest two-story brownstone on Thirty-first Avenue in Astoria, Queens, which was just north of downtown New York. My visits brought us closer together, and Anna soon learned to trust me more. She also helped me gain weight!

Everytime I went over, Anna wouldn't let me leave without giving me something to eat. She served me platters of food and pitchers of drink. She must have thought she was feeding a moose, not a man! After one week of eating there I started looking more like a sumo wrestler. That wasn't an earthquake theatergoers felt in the theaters; that was me walking on stage!

I became more concerned about my diet when Anna invited me to move in with her and Ernie, permanently. They had a spare bedroom, and she thought it was silly for Ernie and I to be apart. Living there would definitely help me save on rent, and I would be able to take care of Anna by being there. I was sure Ernie would approve. So I lived there until Ernie and I got married. I accepted Anna's generous offer under one condition, "Please, Anna, not so much food!"

The brightest day of my life came in June of 1930: Ernie returned!

We made up for lost time and spent every evening together going to the movies, eating out at restaurants, and sitting up with Anna. Anna enjoyed having us around, and every night she would make bite-sized sandwiches for us to snack on while she worked on a jigsaw puzzle in the living room. Every night she worked on a different one. She was just crazy about puzzles!

When Anna came close to completing the puzzles, she'd go to bed and leave out the last four or five pieces until the next morning. Then she would put them in and announce to us, "I finished it! I finished it!" She actually left the pieces for us to put in, but we never touched them, leaving her with the final glory the next day.

Ernie and I were never apart until my contract with Paramount Publix expired in late June, and I received a lucrative offer from the RKO Keith Theater circuit. They promised to increase my salary to $200 a week and said they wanted to send me on tour to promote my act, which was more than Paramount was doing for me.

At first I was hesitant about accepting their offer because Ernie and I had already been separated for six months, and the tour RKO had in mind was going to last for two months, covering parts of the West and Midwest. But Ernie insisted I take it. "Joe, don't pass it up," she said. "Go ahead, darling. I'll be all right."

Before I left on tour, I finished writing a new act with a writer named Lester Lee. It was called, *Wild Cat Dugan*. It was based on the misadventures of a member of the Northwest Mounted police with me as, you-know-who!

The act needed four other people; three characters and a straight man. I held auditions before the tour began. I broke in the new straight man first: Sam Critcherson (who changed his name to Dick Dana after he left my act). Of all the candidates I interviewed, Sam was the best. A magnetism instantly flowed between us when we played out the skit. I hired Sam right away without looking at any more candidates. We were never billed as a team. Later, when it was just the two of us, the billing read, "Joe Besser with Sam Critcherson." (Which was the case with all my straight men.)

Then I hired three other people to round out the act: Harry Lang, Dorothy Ellsworth, and Dorothy Wallace. Sam and Harry played the villainous heavies in the act; Sam was Bill, a gambler, and Harry was a French bartender named Pierre. The two Dorothys were cast in the roles of Daisy and Chici, both singing heroines. RKO billed us as "Joe Besser and Company," and we became an instant hit.

Our first stop was San Francisco, California. The sky was a smogless blue. The ocean was crystal clear. The Golden Gate Bridge was as breathtaking up close as it had been on picture postcards. You could even see the prisoners on Alcatraz on a clear day!

We opened at the RKO Golden Gate Theater the last week of July. The other acts on the bill included singer Frank Devoe; comedian Hap Hazard; and an acrobatic family, Wyse and Company, that featured Ross Wyse, Sr. and his son, Ross, Jr. With acts like these we offered a balanced and entertaining revue that was enjoyed by audiences and critics.

To my surprise critics called my act the highlight of the show. I remember one critic who said, "The laugh hit of the entire comedy opera was Joe Besser, who, with a company of four, unfurled a comedy characterization with some breezy lines that totaled about 15 minutes of continual hee-haws."

The constant hee-haws were the result of *Wild Cat Dugan*, which was a parody of old-fashioned melodramas in which my assignment was to capture Bill for murder. In the skit I meet him in a northwestern barroom before arresting him. He put up a great deal of resistance and tried scaring me with his meanness:

Bill: "Who are you?"

Joe: "Who wants to know?"

Bill: (gruffly) "I want to know."

Joe: (imitating him) "Oh, yeah? Well, who are you?"

Bill: "Who wants to know?"

Joe: (playfully) "That's my question, you answer first!"

When his menacing words failed to scare me, Bill tries to prove which one of us is a man:

Bill: "Say, in case you don't know it, I'm a pretty tough guy."

Joe: (calling his bluff) "Oh, yeah? Well, I'm pretty tough t-o-o! With the switch of this hand (pointing to my right) last week I killed fourteen people!"

Bill: (laughing at its scrawniness) "With that hand?"

Joe: "Yes, with this hand!"

Bill: (getting tough again) "Well, then, what would you do if you had a fist like this?" (He sticks his fist under my nose.)

Joe: (examining it) "I'd wash it!"

Such nonsense continued until I successfully hauled Bill off to jail just before the curtain closed. I'd always end the act with a laugh by sticking out an inflated hand from underneath the curtain. Sweeping the hand across the stage, I would then scream to the audience's delight: "Ooh, you crazy yooouuus!"

The tour became a whopping success,and the executives at RKO couldn't have been more pleased. In each city, we played before standing-room only audiences! The tour ended in, of all places, St. Louis. That gave me a chance to visit Momma and Poppa and to tell them about Ernie and our plans for the future. I could tell they were happy for me, but Momma's first question was no surprise.

"When are you getting married?" she asked. "After all, you've been going together for two years."

"Yes, Momma, we have," I said. "But there's something you should know. Ernie's not Jewish."

Momma smiled and said, "What does that have to do with me? As long as you love her and you will be happy with her, then I will love her and be happy, too!"

Poppa nodded his approval; he was never one to make speeches.

Momma and Poppa really approved when they met Ernie for the first time. That happened when we were sent on tour with another vaudeville show for the RKO circuit, which made its debut at the RKO Palace Theater in Cleveland before moving to the East Coast.

When the show moved to St. Louis, Momma and Poppa were overwhelmed after they caught their first glimpse of Ernie; they couldn't believe how charming she was. Momma instantly fell in love with her and treated her as though she was already part of the family. She'd lovingly say to Ernie, "Come, *kindle*," which means child in Yiddish, "sit on my lap." She would then rock Ernie for hours on her lap, and they'd laugh and have a great time.

In Cleveland the show became another can't-miss production. It featured Charlie King, Jane Withers, and the Harmonica Rascals. My luck for working in one hit show after another remained unblemished, even though the show did have its share of problems.

The same week the show opened, the city of Cleveland was the site of a national businessmen's convention. So every hotel was booked solid. Not a single vacancy. In other words, "Sorry, Charlie!" Well, the manager who handled hotel reservations for us at RKO's office in New York didn't plan ahead. When the entire cast arrived for our show in Cleveland we discovered that he had only made room reservations for Charlie King and me, but forgot to get rooms for the others in the show, including the Foster girls.

A scandal was fortunately avoided when Ernie came up with a solution: The girls could sleep in my room. But where? I only had one bed, and there were fifteen girls in the dancing troupe! Being the gentleman that I am, I let them in. They slept on the floor, in the bathroom, in the closet, in the medicine chest, under my bed, or wherever they could find space. The funny thing is, the manager of the hotel never questioned the sight of fifteen girls coming in and out of my room. Maybe in Cleveland this wasn't so unusual!

The hours Ernie and I put in for rehearsing and performing in the show were often grueling. Sam and I rehearsed the *Wild Cat Dugan* sketch with the other members of the act and performed it three times daily. After a while I used to go to bed thinking I was a Royal Mountie.

Between shows, several members of the cast and I used to relieve our tensions by playing a game of hearts. Playing cards became our way of socializing backstage, too. Only we didn't play for the high stakes some performers did; we played for pure enjoyment.

Charlie King was also one of the participants. He never won a game, but he became a sure loser fast. Everytime he needed a queen of spades to win, he came up short. Night after night Charlie's luck never changed, and he'd say disgustedly, "Why can't I get the queen of spades just once!"

Finally Charlie couldn't take losing anymore, and he decided to get even. During a supper show when I was in the middle of my act, Charlie stormed out on stage carrying nine decks of cards. He glared at me, playfully, then at the audience, and then threw the cards at me! Each deck was loaded with nothing but queens of spades! I broke down laughing—Charlie had won this match. He got the biggest laughs that night, even though when we played hearts on the following day, he continued right where he'd left off—he lost again!

The show finished touring at the end of 1930, and by January of 1931 I was mostly working on the East Coast and in the Midwest, which enabled me to stay closer to Ernie. In the meantime, I also changed my act. *Wild Cat Dugan* had had its run, so Lester Lee wrote a new act for me called, *Spanish Omelet*. The act contained one comedy blackout after another, in typical vaudeville fashion, and featured my best bits from my days with Alexandria and Olsen as well as several new routines Lester and I developed.

I retained a stock company for this act, too. Harry Lang remained from *Dugan* and two new girls were added: Adele Wolf and Ann Ellsworth (who was later replaced by Alice Cavin). I never enjoyed doing this act as much as *Dugan* because the material was old, and I wanted something fresher. But with the managers of the RKO Keith Theaters demanding my performances, I didn't have time to construct an entirely new act. So I settled for this one until I could come up with something better.

One routine Lester and I created always launched audiences into a laughing tirade. It was called "The Paint Bucket Routine." Sam would be standing on stage telling jokes to the audience when I would rush out from the wings to interrupt him. He would spot me wearing two overcoats and carrying a paint can and brush and say, "Hey, Joe, where are you going?"

"Ooh, you're such a dumb," I'd say. "I'm going to paint my house."

Sam would scratch his head dumbfoundedly and say, "Paint your house? Then what's the idea of wearing the two coats?"

"Don't you see what it says on the paint can?" I'd say. "It says for best results put on *two* coats!"

This bit became the audience's favorite in every town we performed in. I guess the audiences loved me because I always played to *them*. A simple routine like painting a house was something they were faced with in real life; only they never misread the directions like I did!

I also got great pleasure from mixing with the audience. I was one of the first comedians to go down into the audience and let them in on the jokes. I'd run down to the front row, sit next to a kid with his popcorn, munch on his popcorn, then I'd look up at Sam and say,? "Okay, now *you* try being funny?"

Performing in vaudeville had as many highs as it did lows for me, however. Not every audience was as appreciative. Some theaters were located in rundown neighborhoods where the theatergoers worked hard for their money, and they expected more from your performance as a result.

One such theater was the Jefferson Theater on Fourteenth Street in Brooklyn. It was on the same street as two other vaudeville houses—the Fox Theater and the Strand Theater—which I also played. Even though the Jefferson was perfectly suited for on-stage entertainment, the audiences were not perfectly suited for the entertainers who played there!

The theatergoers were basically a hostile and rowdy bunch. If they liked you, they let you know. If they disliked you, they let you know that, too! The audiences were usually unemployed people from various ethnic groups as well as mobster types. I remember Webb and Hayes; Don Loper, a famous dancer; Rooney and Bent; and Joe Laurie, the acts I followed, were also terrified when we played before this crowd. For fifteen cents the audience was more critical than the critics! They often made obscene remarks during our acts and could certainly be unkind.

When my turn came, I was equally petrified. For some reason, though, the audiences never got hostile or disrespectful toward me. My entire week there I became the crowd's favorite. Even the mobsters loved me. I'll never forget how one of them came to my aid the night I became hoarse in the middle of my act. I didn't feel up to par before going on, but I went on anyway, even though I could barely talk above a whisper.

When the audience noticed I was having trouble talking, one Italian member in the front row showed empathy. He pointed at his throat to acknowledge that he knew something was wrong with mine. I looked at him, pleading for help. "I'm hoarse," I said. The man got up from his seat and left. I watched him leave the theater in such a hurry that I was afraid I had offended him. I could see it now—a black limousine would pull up behind the theater, and the same man would emerge packing a violin case...and you know what they pack in those violin cases!

So after the show I frantically returned to my dressing room. Minutes later, there was a knock at the door. I froze. I slowly opened the door, cracking it, and expected the worst. It was him—the man who had left the theater! Only he wasn't carrying a violin case; instead he was carrying a care package.

"Hey, Joe," he mumbled in a Godfatherlike accent."We like ya, and we want ya to get well. So ya take this, and yer sore throat will go away."

He handed me rock-and-rye whiskey (rock candy). It's supposedly the best cure for colds and sore throats. "Don't take too much of this," he added.

"Just a little bit because it has a rotten taste." Believe it or not, I trusted the guy. He didn't seem like he came to bump me off. The following day his remedy worked. My throat was normal,and my voice returned to its familiar whiney sound.

A couple of nights later this same man returned to watch my act. This time when I noticed him in the audience, I stopped the show and told the audience what a kind act he had done for me. They gave him a standing ovation, and you could tell that he was elated by my acknowledging his good deed. He never forgot me, and every time I returned to play the Jefferson he always appeared at the door to my dressing room with more rock candy!

In time, the audiences at the Jefferson Theater proved to be tame compared to the ones I performed before in college towns. In New Haven, Connecticut, the hometown of Yale University, students from the university would come to watch me perform at the RKO Polei Palace.Theydidn't come to be entertained, however; they'd come to the matinees to memorize each performers' lines. Then they'd return for the evening show and say the performers' lines before they did.

While the other acts before me went on, I noticed how these students interrupted them, and I prepared myself for the same. The part of my act they learned was from the paint bucket routine. They tried catching me off guard during the punchline of "Don't you see what it says on the paint can? It says for best results put on two coats!" So when I got to this line, they all screamed at once: "For best results put on two coats!"

Now most performers would have become annoyed. I didn't. I laid down on the stage and laughed my head off. I was being on the level, too. I never knew how funny their interrupting me would be. What cracked me up was that they'd go to all that trouble just to interrupt me! I finally picked myself up from the stage and told the audience: "That's the funniest thing I've ever had happen to me. You guys are geniuses!"

They gave me a big hand for being such a good sport and, as a result, word got around to the other students at the college: "Don't bother Joe Besser. Don't interrupt him. He's on to us!"

The college students in other towns were just as demonstrative. In Notre Dame, Indiana, the students from the University of Notre Dame were a prime example. The manager of the theater where I played told me, "Don't pay attention to them, Mr. Besser, because they'll try ruining your act."

That didn't bother me. I knew how to handle them after my experience with the students from Yale. When they tried to interrupt me during the same punchline, I said it before they did, then afterwards I proudly turned to them and said childishly, "See, I beat ya!"

I continued to play in vaudeville theaters for another year, before the opportunity of a lifetime arrived: working on Broadway.

Chapter 8

Broadway, Marriage, Hollywood, London . . . and the Stooges

In August 1932, I was booked at the Palace Theater in Chicago with singer Harry Richman. Ernie and the Foster girls were in the same show.

One night J.J. Shubert was in the audience. J.J. and his brother Lee were theatrical producers. They went into partnership with their brother Samuel and formed the Shubert Theater Corporation, which controlled theaters in practically every major city in the country. Their domain included theaters in Philadelphia, Baltimore, Buffalo, and Cincinnati, and leading Broadway theaters such as the Hippodrome and Winter Garden.

After my performance, a note came back to me in my dressing room from my straightman, Sam Critcherson. It said: "Joe, J.J. Shubert is in the audience. He wants to see you. Sam."

Until then, I had never heard of J.J. Shubert. I thought it was a joke, so I asked Ernie if she knew him. She told me she had worked for Shubert before in a stage production with Al Jolson called *Great Temptations* and that he was legit.

Since I've always been skeptical about people I've never met, I sought a second opinion by asking Harry Richman. "Harry, there's a man out there who wants to see me," I said. "His name is J.J. Shubert. Is he a phony?"

Harry laughed uncontrollably and almost fell off his chair. "Joe, he's for real, all right," he said, still catching breath. "But I've never heard of him waiting to see anybody right after their act. He usually has them come to his office in New York."

Well, Harry convinced me. So I had Ernie introduce me. In so doing, when J.J. got one look at Ernie he gasped, "What are you doing here?"

"You wanted to see my boyfriend," Ernie said with a laugh.

J.J. couldn't believe what a coincidence this was and right away he felt comfortable. "Joe, what brought me here is I'm producing a new Broadway revue called *The Passing Show of 1932*. I want you in it, and I'll pay you $500 a week for starters."

Immediately my eyes beamed the size of silver dollars. "Five hundred dollars!" I screamed. I had never made that kind of money in my entire life!

I didn't even think the deal over. I consulted with my agent Bill Miller, and the next day I signed a contract. It wasn't every day somebody came knocking at my door with an offer to work on Broadway. This was my chance. It would also be my first time!

The Passing Show of 1932 was going to be another one of those star-studded extravaganzas featuring name vaudeville acts such as Lester Allen, Florence Moore, Jack Osterman, Ara Gerald, Jack McCauley, Joan Carter-Waddell, Jerry Norris, Gertrude Neisen, Peggy Hoover, Ernest Sharpe, Eddie Shubert, Dot Rotay, Kendall Capps, George Marshall, Dorothy MacDonald, and forty luscious dancing beauties! I performed my popular *Wild Cat Dugan* for the show. The show also contained thirty musical comedy segments and ten hit songs.

The top headliner of the show was Ted Healy and his Racketeers, with Healy serving as the master of ceremonies. Ted was the highest paid vaudevillian at the time; he earned approximately $8,500 a week! His "racketeers" were three other noted comedy troupers, only they earned considerably less than Ted: $100 a week (slightly higher for a Broadway show). They weren't paid nearly enough for the physical abuse they took from Healy in the act, however. Their names were Moe Howard, Larry Fine, and Shemp Howard. They had been Ted's "stooges" since the mid-1920s.

I had always wanted to work with these fellows, but never had the chance until now. They had quite a reputation in the business for creating "surefire laughs," as a result of their knockabout brand of humor, which, in my opinion, was crazier than the Marx Brothers, to whom they were often compared in their vaudeville days. I actually looked forward to seeing them up close myself to see what all the fuss was about.

The first day of rehearsal I met Ted and the boys, and we became good friends. Believe me, having them around was a laugh a minute. Rehearsals were never as much fun. I was in the middle of setting up my act for rehearsals when suddenly I felt a tap on my shoulder. I turned around and saw Ted and—in the distance—three unusual haircuts—one shaped like a bowl, one like a head of snakes, and another like that from a barbershop quartet.

"Joe Besser, I presume," Ted said.

"That's right," I remarked.

"I'm Ted Healy of stage, screen, and rain gutters," he cracked, leading into the introductions. "These are my three traveling comedy rogues—Moe Howard, Larry Fine, and Shemp Howard."

"Hi ya!" they rang out in unison.

"We have a bone to pick with you," Ted continued, his Irish brogue cracking through as he spoke.

"What's that," I said.

"We want to know why we've never worked with you before," Ted mused.

We all laughed, and right away I could tell Ted and the boys liked to have fun.

In the days ahead, as we bore through one rehearsal after another, I got to know Ted and the boys more personally. In show business you constantly hear rumors, and sometimes it's difficult to separate the fact from fiction. In the case of Ted Healy, I found that the rumors I heard were true.

Much like his on-stage persona, Ted Healy was a real character offstage. Noted for his sharp wit, he made as many headlines for his offstage antics as he did his rapid patter and broad, slapstick style. Actually, Ted never wanted to get into show business, so maybe that had something to do with how he handled his stardom. Originally, he had aspired to be a high-powered businessman. But for a man once known as Charles Earnest Lee Nash, his name by birth, his childhood dream got derailed when he suffered an incurable case of the "show business bug." Once he got it, he was hooked . . . permanently.

Ted initially got his start as a comedian by doing impersonations of show-business greats such as Ed Wynn, Eddie Cantor, and Al Jolson, in a blackface act he originated. Using this as a springboard, the act soon catapulted Ted's career to new heights. Before World War I, he set the world of show business on its ear. Within a short amount of time he became known as "the greatest straight man" in show business, a Broadway star, and a household name. After watching him work, I would have to agree. He was definitely comic artistry in motion. He always used a theater audience to his advantage, making them part of his act. On stage he either settled himself behind a piano in the orchestra pit or seated himself at the lip of the stage. Saying in so many words, "Most comics come out here breaking their necks to make you laugh, but not me! Not me! To hell with you!"

Without fail, the audience burst into laughter, and seconds later he had them virtually eating out of the palm of his hand.

Another thing Ted should also receive credit for is creating the concept of "stooges." In the act as it stood in vaudeville, Ted was the head boss of the team, and he dished out all the orders to Moe, Larry, and Shemp, while Moe was the boss of Larry and Shemp in their own group, yet still answering to Ted. Ted helped originate some of the many Stoogelike mannerisms and routines that have since become legendary. For example, the now-famous "triple slap" whereby Ted slaps all three stooges in unison, giving off the sound of a machine gun, or the "football huddle," a time devoted to brainstorming amongst the stooges. If it hadn't been for Ted there may have never been a Three Stooges comedy team as we know them today.

Ted's only downfall was how he handled his fame; he definitely reacted to it differently than most performers. You could undoubtedly classify him as a rabble-rouser. He developed a real love for the bottle, and sometimes in interfered with his work. He would reel in late for work, and sometimes it would affect his ability to perform. He was as much a ladies man as he was alcoholic, too. As I remember it, he was a constant flirt with the showgirls in this revue and others, but most of the girls were on to him. You could say his reputation preceded him. These two factors, as I later learned, led to the split between him, Moe, Larry, and Shemp—even prompting Shemp to leave on his own earlier in their working relationship. In Shemp's eyes, Ted looked like a hypocrite. He often professed to Shemp, Larry, and Moe that he expected to set examples for them, yet he could hardly set a proper example with his own life the way it was.

On the other hand, Moe, who sported the sugar-bowl haircut, was as much a businessman as Ted and was the most serious of the bunch. It seems fitting that he took over control of the trio many years later. I mean, let's face it, you have to have brains to succeed in any business and Moe had brains all right. One of five brothers—their real last name was Horwitz—Moe hailed from Bensonhurst, New York, a small suburb of New York City. Of his brothers, only two never entered show business: Jack and Irving. Moe's other brothers were Shemp (Samuel) and Curly (Jerome), which, to my amazement, some fans don't initially realize. Moe was actually christened Moses Horwitz (he later adopted the name Harry). He adopted the name Moe after he cut his hair in the shape of a bowl (the result of constant heckling from classmates jealous of his shoulder-length curls).

As Moe once explained to me, he had always wanted to be in show business from a young age. He tried many stints along the way in pursuit of a full-fledged career as an entertainer. His earlier accomplishments included a blackface with Shemp that fizzled, showboat dramatizations, and even singing jobs in a saloon where he was paired up with Shemp . . . all to gain more experience in front of an audience.

How Moe went to work for Ted is a fascinating story in itself. It turns out that he and Ted were childhood friends. Ted had always remained in touch with Moe through the years and during his own rise to fame. One day he called and asked Moe to come to work for him as a "stooge" in his act. Ted was playing the Prospect Theatre in Brooklyn, only miles away from where Moe lived. The fellows who had been working with Ted walked out one night in the middle of the act when Ted made a vulgar gesture on stage. The spur-of-the moment gag got laughs but enraged Ted's coworkers to the point that they sought work elsewhere. Stoogeless, Ted worked himself out of a jam before the next show by calling Moe, who gladly came to the rescue. From that night on, Moe never stopped stooging.

Finally getting a chance to work with Moe, I noticed that he clearly looked after Larry's and Shemp's best interests; he was their boss on stage and off. He never let them socialize with any of the girls from the show because they were married men, as was Moe. If he did catch them, he grabbed them by the hair and pulled them away.

Larry was the one who got his frizzled hair yanked the most. He was the most sociable stooge, and he always liked to entertain everybody when there was a break in the rehearsals. He'd either do soft shoe or tell funny stories, which is exactly the way he was when I later became a Stooge myself. Everybody from the show got along with Larry.

Like Ted and Moe, he was another naturally gifted showman. Philadelphia born, he changed his name, Louis Feinberg, to Larry Fine for marquee purposes.

Larry came to demonstrate his talent and show-business potential as a consequence of a freak accident. His father, a local jeweler, left a bottle of acid (which is used to test metals for gold) unattended. Young Larry waddled up to his father's work table and went for the bottle. In trying to quickly move it out of the way, Larry's father accidentally spilled acid on Larry's left arm. After a successful skin-graft operation, doctors advised that Larry needed to strengthen his arm; the instrument they most recommended was the violin.

As a result, Larry's first love soon became the violin, and through daily practice this wooden instrument also brought renewed strength to his arm. In time the violin also converted him from an amateur violinist into a semiprofessional one. The violin helped launch Larry toward a successful show-business career. He also soloed for many years before linking up with the Haney Sisters—Mabel and Loretta—a popular singing duet. Larry got more out of the act than repeated bookings; he also landed himself a wife in Mabel.

The violin became an issue when he joined Ted Healy's act as a stooge. In 1925, Larry was playing the Rainbow Gardens in Chicago. Moe, Shemp, and Ted Healy were in town, also playing out an engagement at a local theater. At the time Shemp had already informed Ted that he wanted out of the act, thus creating the need for a replacement. After seeing Larry perform one evening, Moe quickly suggested that Larry's appearance—frowsy strawberry blond hair, tubular nose—plus Larry's comic repartee would make him a good replacement for Shemp as a Stooge. Healy liked the idea and at the conclusion of the show the boys went backstage to meet Larry. In making his offer, Ted supposedly told Larry, "I'll pay you $100 a week to be my stooge; that's $90 a week and an extra $10 a week if you'll throw that fiddle away."

It seems strange that Larry would become a Stooge by way of Shemp's leaving only because Shemp would return to the act after his other stints failed and work with the boys again in numerous Broadway shows, *A Night in Venice*, *A Night in Spain*, and, of course, *The Passing Show of 1932*, which we all starred in together.

Shemp was as down to earth as Larry. You could talk to him about a variety of subjects. He always started a conversation—whether you were interested or not. He definitely enjoyed people, and I think he thrived on making them laugh. I know he made me laugh, not once or twice, but often. Shemp was always jovial, the life of the party. He had the appearance of a court jester, with his hair parted down the middle over his ears and a face that only a King could appreciate! Since he was such a good-humored man who loved to laugh, I hung around him the most.

Shemp had become a Stooge the same night Moe went to work for Ted Healy at the spur of the moment. Only Moe and Ted had no idea that Shemp was going to be there. Ted and Moe were in the middle of their act, which was totally improvised, when, all of a sudden, Moe heard this unmistakable, almost obnoxious howl. Turning to Ted, he said, "There's no mistaking that laugh, Ted. It's Shemp's."

Right away Moe and Ted called Shemp up from the audience and, after indoctrinating him into the act with a few slaps and other *schtick*, Shemp was a Stooge to stay.

It's funny now, but I never thought our paths would cross again as they did many years later when I replaced Shemp as the "third stooge" and became a member of the Three Stooges. It just goes to show you that life is full of many surprises.

We started rehearsing for *The Passing Show of 1932* four weeks before it opened in Detroit on Sunday, September 4, 1932 (the show was to be test run in other cities before opening on Broadway). We then moved to a theater in Cincinnati where the show folded after three weeks . . . without Healy and without the Racketeers. The show was doomed from the start after the Shuberts had a run-in with Healy. Ted possessed a sharp wit, and he knew how to keep audiences riveted to their seats with laughter while introducing each act. Therefore, he was a tough man to replace . . . as the Shuberts soon found out.

Slowly Ted's relationship with J.J. deteriorated. One day it reached the boiling point when Ted had an argument with J.J. over his billing in the show and his salary. J.J. was the stingiest producer, even though his productions never showed it. I understand he tried to renege on paying Ted his customary salary of $8,500 a week as well as giving him top billing. When Ted realized that Shubert wasn't going to budge on either front, he found a loophole in his contract and left the show, taking the Stooges with him.

Only Shemp refused to go on with Ted. He put up a battle. Healy had two vices that disturbed Shemp terribly; he drank and his behavior was often erratic. Moe repeatedly tried to convince Shemp into staying, but he was unsuccessful. "I'm tired of Ted's shenanigans," Shemp said.

Moe was saddened to see Shemp go, because he truly loved working with his brother. Ted wasn't the kind of person to forgive and forget. So if Shemp left, he was out of the act. And Shemp did leave. Now short a stooge again, Ted found another replacement: Moe's kid brother, Jerome, whom they nicknamed Curly after he agreed to shave his head.

Curly seemed like a natural candidate, because he always hung around the theater during rehearsals and watched Ted, Moe, Larry, and Shemp rehearse. He'd fetch sandwiches and Cokes for us when we broke for lunch. He was very reserved, compared to Moe and Shemp. So what he later exhibited on stage was a complete surprise. Curly became the most popular third stooge when he, Moe, and Larry signed with Columbia Pictures as "The Three Stooges." And, as they say, the rest is history!

So on opening night, with Healy's spot vacated, J.J. inserted Lester Allen in Ted's place as the master of ceremonies. Unfortunately, in insisting on carrying through on their production schedule, the Shuberts made the grave mistake of not adjusting the comedy material to Allen's style. Therefore, he never won any bouquets from the audience that night at the theater, and it was obvious he just couldn't carry the show. Critics rapped him and the length of the show, which lasted three hours. Normally two and a quarter hours is the limit. A deletion of forty-five minutes would have definitely helped the show.

Although the Shuberts ignored the critics' comments about the length of the show, they recognized that Allen had to go. The following week, after the production shifted to Cincinnati, J.J. had no choice but to drop Lester and substitute Jack Osterman in his place. Jack was a slight improvement, as his timing was impeccable. He was effective in drawing laughs from the audience when he chatted with them at infrequent intervals, and he practically stole the show with his wise-cracking and a song he sang called, "I Want to Go Home."

I understand, however, that the Shuberts quietly wished that Healy would return. They were biding time until Ted cooled off. I recall one columnist reported, "It is possible Healy will relent and join the show later in Chicago. But two weeks of public apathy toward the production proves the need of him or another of equal talent."

Well, the show never made it to Chicago, and Healy never changed his mind. Instead, the most critical time in which the show had to succeed had passed. It failed at the box office in Detroit and lost money in Cincinnati before it was finally cancelled. The Shuberts only kept the show running this long because, according to labor laws for the Actor's Equity Union, a show must run at least two weeks and actors must be guaranteed at least that much time in work.

Besides lacking a name emcee, *The Passing Show of 1932* was also killed by the bad press it received. The press unfairly attacked the nudity of the dancers in this revue. In each city, even New York, the segments featuring the girls were deemed "objectionable" because of their skimpy costumes. As one critic wrote, "Mr. Shubert believes that the public wants to see the girls practically naked—and lots of them. Therefore, he is offering an assortment of beauties scarcely clad at all, notably one titan-topped lass whose costume would not make a fair-sized handkerchief."

Worse, another critic noted, "Mr. Shubert believes the public wants its comedy played in bedrooms . . . he believes that people with enough money to pay $3.30 per seat have no delicacy, no taste, no decency in their minds."

With all those elements against us it's no wonder *The Passing Show of 1932* flopped. It was, of course, disappointing because it was my first Broadway show. But that's show biz!

In late September of 1932 I returned to vaudeville where I continued to have great success. I headlined theaters in various cities across the country and Ernie remained busy working with the Foster girls, so we managed to see each other from time to time.

I didn't return to New York until early November to play at the Proctor Newark Theater in Newark, New Jersey. Two other acts were on the bill with me: The Radio Rogues, who performed impersonations of famous people, and a former great movie comedian who was trying to make a comeback. I had always watched his movies as a kid but never dreamed I would ever work with him on the same stage. Eleven years earlier, he was wrongfully blacklisted after being accused of raping and murdering actress Virginia Rappe in a hotel room in San Francisco. His roly-poly presence had made millions laugh up until then. Now he was recreating those same antics on vaudeville stages across the country. His name was Fatty Arbuckle.

Fatty traveled with his second wife, the former Addie MacPhail, who also worked in the act. They performed a comedy skit similar to those Fatty had done in his silent comedies for Keystone. Sam Critcherson was still my straight man and together we marveled over Fatty's ability to overcome adversity. He never seemed embittered toward the San Francisco judge who had ruined his life. Nor did he begrudge the producers in Hollywood who told him he was through.

Fatty never knew what it meant to quit. I could tell he was a fighter. He worked himself back into filmmaking with his own short-subject series for Vitaphone. Fatty loved talking about comedy with me between shows, and his eyes gleamed with enthusiasm as he spoke. That gleam showed me he still had the desire to entertain.

Fatty and I became such good friends during our two-week engagement together that before it ended he wanted to cast me in a new comedy series he was planning to star in for Vitaphone. The series didn't have a title yet, but I was going to play his kid brother. We were even going to dress identically. Fatty thought since our physiques and mannerisms were similar, this would be a good gimmick. He had the deal all worked out with Vitaphone. Before we parted company in Newark, he promised to contact me once the studio gave him the go-ahead.

The last time I heard Fatty's name was almost one year later. On June 28, 1933, Fatty died. Unfortunately, he never saw the series through, and his death left a definite void in the entertainment world.

In the second week of November, 1932, I was playing an engagement at the Loew's State Theater in New York when a strange feeling overcame me: I decided to marry Ernie!

That week I proposed to Ernie. "Let's get married. I want to take care of you for the rest of my life," I said. "Also, to take another burden off your mind, I'll take care of your mother."

Ernie jumped into my arms—she had waited for four years!— and sealed our engagement with a kiss. We were married in a private ceremony by a justice of the peace on November 18, 1932 (not November 19 as reported in some publications) in Woodbridge, New Jersey. Lou Randall, who was my business attorney, and his wife stood up for us. Afterward, they drove us to their home for a wedding dinner, which also became our honeymoon!

The next day I was booked into a theater in Baltimore, so Ernie and I hopped a train that night, leaving from Woodbridge. We rolled into Baltimore late that evening. The next day, another scandal almost developed when several performers from the show were surprised to find a woman in my dressing room. They thought there was some hanky-panky going on between us until Ernie announced that we were married . . . ooh, did she have to tell?

I guess you might say Ernie's honeymoon with me lasted for four years. She decided there was room for only one entertainer in the family and quit the Foster girls after we were married, with no regrets, and traveled extensively with me for four years. The Shuberts signed me for one more Broadway show, *The Greenwich Village Follies*. Then I worked in three long-running vaudeville shows for producer Harry Rogers: *Spices of 1934*, *Spices of 1935*, and *Spices of 1936*, all with Count Berni Vici and fifteen symphonists. Each show received better reviews than *The Passing Show of 1932*. Like Shubert's production, they featured many alluring dancing girls, only this time the critics never complained about a lack of taste.

When Ernie didn't travel with me, she stayed behind with Anna in Astoria. We wanted to have children, but it seemed impossible to plan for them until my work schedule lessened. Unfortunately, we waited too long as Ernie's age was against her. She was in her late thirties by the time we could have children, and doctors warned her that she would be risking her life if she tried. Today the medical risks are much less for older women having babies. I guess we could have adopted children, but we felt it wouldn't be the same as bringing our own baby into the world.

In the fall of 1937 I starred in another lavish musical revue entitled, *You're in the Army*. Producer Harry Rogers offered me the lead and wrote a scene in the show especially for me in which I played an exasperated Army recruit. The story revolved around my being drafted into the service and the comic trials and tribulations that followed the first day I reported to boot camp.

When the show opened in New York, critics raved about the routine. (I later rewrote it, adding new material, and incorporated it into my vaudeville act.)

You're in the Army ran almost a year, and it was so successful that it helped bring about my first movie role. For the first time the thousands who laughed at my antics on stage would be given a chance to laugh at my antics on the screen.

The deal that brought about my film debut occurred in late September of 1937 after *You're in the Army* premiered. The show had shifted to the West Coast, and we were playing at the Orpheum Theater in Los Angeles. During our engagement I learned that several studios had been scouting me (I had received movie offers from Educational, Warner Brothers and Republic previously, but turned them down). I had never given making movies that much thought because I was content working on stage. That feeling changed one night when Jules White, the head of the short subject department at Columbia Pictures, dropped by to watch my act. His scouting me didn't make me nervous, since I had been scouted before, and I had plenty of confidence in myself.

Well, needless to say, my performance that night sent theatergoers home reeling with laughter. Afterward Jules visited me in my dressing room to discuss my future in motion pictures. His hair was slicked back, and his pencil-thin mustache bristled as he puffed intently on a cigar. I didn't know much about the man, other than that he had directed comedies at MGM before hooking up with Columbia in 1933. He wasted no time before delivering his *spiel*.

"Joe, I enjoyed you very much," he said. "But I don't think you're ready to star in pictures."

Jules' comment threw me. Why would he come back to tell me this? A producer only wants to *kibitz* with you when they're *interested*. I didn't know what he wanted to prove, so I scoffed at his remark. "Well, if I'm not ready," I said. "I'm not ready. I'm not going to lose any sleep over it."

Jules took one more puff on his cigar, thanked me, then left.

Surprisingly enough, I received an offer the following week from Columbia, but not from Jules. In early October, after I returned to New York to play a date at the Strand Theater, another man from Columbia looked me up. His name was Jack Cohn, and he was the brother of Harry Cohn, the West Coast chief at Columbia. Jack headed Columbia's production offices in New York, and he apparently wasn't aware that Jules had made a report on me the week before. Nor did he care.

He phoned me the day after seeing my performance and offered me a job in a musical-comedy short that Ben K. Blake was producing and directing entitled, *Cuckoorancho* (it was originally to be called *Rancho Bango*). It was filmed entirely in New York, and I was paid $1,000 for one week's work. Ben worked the filming schedule around my play dates for *You're in the Army*, and we finished filming in four days. In the movie I played a wanderer who is mistaken for an American millionaire by an impoverished hacienda owner.

Cuckoorancho was released six months later on March 25, 1938, but the positive reviews my performance received didn't turn my career around overnight. Jack Cohn was satisfied with the fine critical reaction the film received, but he never discussed the possibility of using me in any other movies afterward. However, I cast aside my desire to star in more movies as my career started picking up momentum in another direction: the stage.

Sam Critcherson remained my straight man until *You're in the Army* shut its doors in December of 1937. He left my act when he contracted emphysema, which prevented him from traveling extensively. His services were truly missed, as he had become an integral part of my act. However, I was able to find a replacement for him before I hit the road again in the spring of 1938 by the name of Lee Royce. Lee was a baritone singer whose rendition of "Ol' Man River" was as smooth as his ability to deliver straight lines. We played the RKO and Orpheum circuits together for six months, and the combination of his singing with my comedy style became a highly touted box-office draw.

By May of 1938 Lee and I became such a major force on the vaudeville circuit that more producers started noticing us. Among the offers my agent Bill Miller fielded was one to play the London Palladium for two weeks. At first I was thrilled about the chance to visit a foreign country and make my international debut. However, I was also scared; I still hated boats! Bill and Ernie finally convinced me to go, and Lee and I were set to open at the Palladium the first week in June.

We steamed to our destination on the S.S. Paris. I'll never forget right after we passed the Statue of Liberty, just as I had feared, I lost my lunch! I was sick for four days, and when we arrived in London the producers had to postpone our opening until I recovered.

I was still pretty wobbly after we got off the boat. We tried walking from the pier to our hotel, but my legs kept giving out on me. Then they suddenly cramped up; I was suffering from a severe case of sea legs. Bill and Lee broke my fall and sat me down on a bench to rest...Where was Dr.

Watson when I needed him?

Well, Dr. Watson was probably on another call , but an Englishman who noticed my faltering ran over to help me. After I told him my legs were giving me trouble he sat down next to me and massaged my legs until the feeling came back in them. If this was what English hospitality was like, I never wanted to leave!

Once my strength returned, Ernie and I spent our second week seeing the Paris-sites (as we used to say in our show). We stayed at a hotel in Trafalgar Square, which was on a main strip in downtown London. From there we visited such popular tourist attractions as Piccadilly Square, the London Tower, and Scotland Yard. We also went shopping in a Jewish neighborhood. We bought Poppa a new shawl and Momma several fairytale books written in Yiddish.

Meanwhile, the Palladium attracted record crowds during our two weeks there. In fact, so many people were turned away that the theater owner held us over for three more weeks! The program we were featured in was definitely a show-stopper; Harry Richman and Cicily Courtnidge were among the headliners. Lee and I also were a hit with the British, despite my problems on opening night with the censors. That's when I made the first stage blooper of my career!

In the beginning of my act, Lee came out on stage first and then I followed him dressed like a cowboy, swinging a rope in the air and screaming like an Indian: "Woo, woo, woo! Woo, woo, woo!" After jumping through the center of the rope and falling down, I announced, "I'm a cooow-boooy!!" Well, unfortunately, the audience never heard me say the word "boy" in cowboy because I had one hand partially cupped over my mouth from my "woo-woo-wooing." All they heard me say was, "I'm a cow . . . " and they started laughing hysterically. I didn't understand why they laughed at this line until we were finished. Backstage, the stage manager came up to me and said, "Joe, you can't say cowboy anymore."

"Why?" I asked, feeling disturbed.

"Because, even though I heard you say cowboy," he said, "the audience only heard you say cow, which, in England, means a whore!"

I turned pale. I had never used any dirty humor in my act. The next night, I changed the line to: "I'm a Texas Ranger!"

Besides my act, I was also featured in other bits during the show, one of which was with Harry Richman. After my act Richman went on stage to lead his orchestra in another round of his songs. But I interrupted him. I came running out on stage like an autograph hound with an autograph pad in my hand. I said to him, gleaming, "Would you mind autographing this book for me?"

"Why, certainly," Richman would say enthusiastically, signing his name on the pad as I stood and watched.

After he finished I'd look at his signature and frantically say, "You're Harry Richman!?"

"Why, yes!" he'd say, impressed.

"You mean the Harry Richman who sang 'The Birth of the Blues'?" I'd continue.

"Why, yes!" he'd say again.

"And . . . and . . . and 'Walking My Baby Back Home'?" I'd ask.

"Why, yes, yes, yes. That's me!" he'd boast.

"Oh, boy, are you lousy!"

I'd then tear up Richman's autograph and run off stage.

By providing these kind of laughs, I was also booked at the Trocadero Club. The owners of the Trocadero wanted to extend my engagement, too. I would have accepted, but my plans to stay longer were suddenly aborted when Ernie received word that Anna was ill.

We immediately returned to New York by boat. However, when we arrived home, we found out that Ernie's mother wasn't sick at all—she was just lonely. She faked an illness and hoped we would return home after we received her telegram . . . Well, it worked!

I didn't get angry, though. Ernie and I would have left sooner or later anyway, and being on the road for long periods of time was always grueling. So, for me, it was good to be back home.

Chapter 9

Lights! Cameras! No Joe!

In January of 1939, Hollywood again beckoned for my services after another studio executive had viewed my performance in *Cuckoorancho*.

I was performing at the Orpheum Theater in Los Angeles with Lee Royce when Cliff Work, the then-head of production at Universal Pictures, called on me. He and director Christy Cabane had seen my act one night. Cliff and I were old friends. He used to manage the RKO Golden Gate Theater where I had played hundreds of times. It was good seeing him after all those years, but his visit was more than a social call.

Cliff wanted me to make a screen test for a new movie tentatively called, *Hot Steel*, that he and Christy were casting and which Christy was going to direct.

"Cliff, you've got to be kidding," I said, after he gave me the news.

"No, I'm not, Joe. I'm serious," Cliff said. "Christy and I think we might be able to give you a part in the film provided we can convince the executive board at Universal with a screen test."

It didn't seem fair to film the test without Lee, but Cliff opposed including him. "We don't want your straight man, Joe," he said. "We want *you*! You'll rehearse with Larry Blake."

"Not *the* Larry Blake?" I said enthusiastically.

"Yes, *the* Larry Blake," Cliff said matter-of-factly.

"Well, then, would you mind telling me one thing, Cliff?" I asked.

"What's that?" he replied.

"Who's Larry Blake?"

Larry Blake had been a character actor in movies since 1937. He entered show business as an impressionist at 18, and he was then under contract to Universal. It made sense that Cliff would rather use him than pay an outsider like Lee to work with me. I explained the deal to Lee, and he understood. He never held the test against me. Instead he wished me good luck.

When I reported to Universal the following Monday, I couldn't believe my eyes. The size of the studio overwhelmed me. For someone who had grown up in the Midwest, a Hollywood movie studio was too much to comprehend. It was really a self-functioning community. Big-name stars hurried in and out of their dressing rooms, which, for the higher-priced talent, were designed like little cottages complete with the luxuries of a real home. Each unit had its own kitchen, living room, bedroom and bathroom. Some stars even had their own private dressing rooms.

Technicians kept moving lights from one stage to the next. The sound stages were the size of airplane hangers! There was even a barbershop in the backlot, as well as separate departments for the technicians, the soundmen, and the film editors. I never saw a complex bustling with as much activity. Best of all, the studio even had its own commissary . . . just in case I got hungry!

The test was set to be filmed on Stage 3. Larry was there waiting for me with the entire crew. I met everybody after they put me through makeup. Christy was directing the test, so I felt relaxed right away. He reminded me of a salty seaman who had seen everything during his career. He had been directing movies since they used tin cans for microphones! He also had directed silent pictures for D.W. Griffith starring Douglas Fairbanks. He immediately put me at ease for the test when he instructed, "Just do your act, Joe. Be yourself."

For fifteen minutes Larry played straight man to me, and we recreated my entire vaudeville act. The crew was unable to control their laughter, which was all right with me. Their laughter couldn't hurt the test. Maybe it would help influence the hierarchy at Universal into signing me.

The test wasn't as smooth as you might think, however. A real scare was thrown into me minutes before the cameras began rolling. After Larry and I finished rehearsing, I went to sit down on a bench to conserve my energy. Just then, a studio light came crashing down on the bench, just missing me by inches! That's all I needed, a cheap haircut! I was bald enough as it was!

The crew turned their backs on me in horror when they saw the light fall because they thought I was dead for sure. After the dust cleared they realized I wasn't when I screamed, "What happened?" Once they heard my voice they came rushing to my side to make sure I was okay. They all started laughing when I said, "Ooh, you cowards, you. Where were you a minute ago?"

I assured them that I was okay, and one stagehand in particular stopped me and said, "Joe, in show business, that's considered a good omen!"

I failed to see how almost getting killed was supposed to bring me good luck, but as it later turned out the man was speaking the truth.

When the test was completed, Christy told me he hoped to have an answer for me in a week. In the meantime—wary after this exhilirating experience—I returned to performing at the Orpheum Theater for two more weeks. By the end of the second week, I still hadn't received word from Universal. Frustrated, I couldn't wait to return home. Ernie was back in Astoria, and even though she was excited for me because of the test, she wished I could be with her. So did I.

My plans changed when actor Wally Ford paid me a visit at the theater on closing night. Wally and I were old friends. I first met him when he and Pat O'Brien were starring in a legitimate theater production called, *The Nut Farm*, at a theater in Cleveland. I was performing two doors down at the Palace Theater. Now Wally was a critically acclaimed British actor who had settled into Hollywood in the early thirties. After a few semileads in Tod Browning's *Freaks* (1932) and John Ford's *The Informer* (1935), he was doing primarily character roles.

Following a brief chat, Wally invited me to stay at his home in Encino for a couple of days until Universal handed down their decision. Wally was under contract there so he advised me, "The executives are probably too busy picking their noses. Give them time. They'll come through."

I certainly didn't have anything to lose, except time. I stayed with Wally and phoned Ernie to tell her I wouldn't be home for another week.

My staying at Wally's home presented one itsy-bitsy problem, however: When Cliff got word from the Universal executives to go ahead and sign me for *Hot Steel*, he couldn't find me! He called the Knickerbocker Hotel where I had been staying, and desk clerk informed him that I had checked out. He then called the manager at the Orpheum Theater who told him, "Joe Besser? Heck, he finished his act *weeks* ago!"

Desperate, Cliff finally sent out a search party to find me. He instructed them: "Find him. Look everywhere. But find him. I want Joe Besser, alive!"

Cliff never realized I was right under his nose!

The day all this confusion over my whereabouts had started, Wally reported to the studio to resume filming on his latest feature, *The Mummy's Hand*, which Christy Cabane was also directing. Dick Foran, Peggy Moran, Tom Tyler (the mummy) and Cecil Kellaway, who were also starring in the picture, were mingling with Wally between takes when he overheard Cliff talking to several members of the "search party."

"Did you guys locate Joe Besser yet?" Cliff asked, mopping the sweat from his brow.

They all shook their heads, "no."

Dressed in an expeditionary outfit, Wally sauntered over to Cliff and said, "You want Joe Besser? He's at my house!"

Cliff smacked his forehead in disbelief. "You wouldn't be joking with me now, Wally, would you?" he said.

"No, I wouldn't, Cliff. You want Joe," Wally said, "I'll go back home and bring him here."

Still in costume, Wally drove out of the studio. Meanwhile, production of the movie was held up until he brought me back with him. When I finally arrived, Cliff couldn't wait to put his arms around me.

"Joe, I've been looking all over for you," he said. "We want you in *Hot Steel*!"

After Wally picked me up off the floor, Cliff had the contracts drafted and sent them to my agent. I received $2,000 for working in the picture—and what a picture! The cast of characters who starred opposite me represented a Hollywood "Who's Who." They included such luminaries as Richard Arlen, Andy Devine, and Peggy Moran, (boy was she ever busy!). With a cast like that the movie couldn't miss. Filming started two weeks later, so I sent for Ernie to join me in the meantime.

Hot Steel was one of Universal's B-productions. But the script still packed quite a wallop for being low-budget fare. The story took place in a small steel town where Arlen discovers a new method of taking impurities out of steel. I was put in as comic relief, playing Siggie Landers, a steel worker. The script, which was written by Clarence Upson Young and Maurice Tombragel, also called for me to do some dramatic acting.

I remember one scene where Richard, Andy, and I were working at the steel mill, and a worker suddenly fell off a girder into a vat of boiling steel. My big moment arrived when, after seeing the man fall, the camera turned to me, and I grimaced before delivering the line that moviegoers waited for: "Oh, God!" You can bet I didn't win any Academy Award nominations that year!

Andy Devine was crazy about me. Andy always talked in a whiney, gravelly voice and had made his living starring in character roles. He had long been a favorite of mine, and even though we had never formally met, he knew who I was. I'll never forget why.

The year before when I was playing in a show in Los Angeles at Christmas time, Ernie went along with me. We heard that every year the Hollywood

Chamber of Commerce sponsored a Santa Claus Lane Parade on Hollywood Boulevard that many big stars participated in. So we attended it, and I shot home movies of the entire parade.

Riding in the lead car with Santa Claus was Andy Devine. Ernie and I weren't more than five feet from his car when he rode by. I remember taking movies of Andy and watching him through the lens when he waved and hollered, "Hi, Joe!" Here among three thousand spectators, with a camera in front of my face, Andy still managed to recognize me. I never forgot this incident, and Andy remembered it with a chuckle when we started working together on *Hot Steel*.

After we wrapped up filming *Hot Steel* in April of 1939, I returned to New York on a cloud with visions of sugar plums. I could see it now! A limo would drop me and Ernie off at the front porch to our twenty-two acre estate. A red carpet would roll out from the car to the front door, and I would walk out splendidly garbed in top hat and tux. The butler would take my hat and coat as dinner was steaming on a dining-room table the length of a football field! Pretty good dream, if I say so myself!

But that's all it was—a dream. When Ernie and I returned to our *real* home in Astoria there was no limo, no red carpet, no butler, no servants, and, darn it, no sugar plums! Just Anna waiting with a table of bite-sized sandwiches and a pot of coffee!

I guess Hollywood wasn't quite ready for me yet because after *Hot Steel* was nationally issued to theaters on May 24, 1940, no concrete offers resulted. Producer Boris Morros from RKO Radio Pictures called and offered me a job in his new picture, *Second Chorus*, with Fred Astaire and Paulette Goddard. But that deal fell through. Boris knew me from my days with the Parmount Publix circuit when he was a stage producer. He had also worked with Ernie before. His offer became the extent of Hollywood's knocking on my door.

I was far from discouraged, however. I've always been the type who doesn't get his hopes up. If something is going to happen, it's going to happen. If it doesn't, there's nothing you can do to change it. I still had my first love to keep me busy: working on stage. So I played the Roxy Theater and other big circuits, but without Lee Royce.

Lee had left my act to pursue other career roads after Universal signed me for *Hot Steel*. The man I found to replace Lee couldn't have been more qualified. Jimmy Little had been playing straight man to comedians all his life. In June of 1940, he became my new straight man, and we incorporated the drill routine into my act.

I broke Jimmy in at the Lyric Theater in Paterson, New Jersey, the hometown of another famous comedian, Lou Costello. At first, Jimmy seemed lost working with me. On our first night together after rehearsing before doing a live show he admitted, "Joe, when I rehearse with you and then actually do the act I wonder whether I want to stay with you or not. You're a different person when you go on stage."

Jimmy was right. During rehearsal,we would rehearse the lines to the act, but that was all. When we actually performed, Jimmy got flustered because I ad-libbed a lot. I would start throwing in gestures and mannerisms that he never saw during rehearsals. He finally realized I wasn't doing this on purpose. I explained to him that my movements had to be spontaneous. They couldn't be rehearsed because I based my actions on how the audience reacted to me. My energy always grew with the intensity of the audience. When Jimmy realized this, he told me in confidence, "I'll never think wrong of you again."

Jimmy was a good man. He was always faithful to me. He never double-crossed me or spoke ill of me. He never took any other jobs without first consulting with me. He respected and understood that everything I did was for the best of the act. He considered our relationship a partnership, even though we were never a team. I always gave him the same consideration.

Jimmy was a loud, boisterous, but nervous type. He wanted to succeed badly. I think while he was working with me the pressures to succeed finally got to him. I noticed on some nights his behavior radically changed. He'd walk into the dressing room in a fog. In other words, he was drunk.

Jimmy started turning to alcohol more and more during his first year with me. I discovered this problem several months after we had started working together. One night he came reeling into the theater minutes before we were supposed to go on. I could tell that Jimmy had been drinking by the smell of his breath. We went ahead and performed the act, and he was fortunately coherent enough to deliver his straight lines without the audience ever realizing that he was inebriated. After we finished, we went backstage, and I was faced with making a decision. Should I look for another straight man? Could I work with someone coming to the theater drunk every night?

I deciced to give Jimmy a second chance by putting a stop to his drinking before it put a stop to his life. Once we were back inside the dressing room, I told him off. "Jimmy, if you ever come to this theater, or any place we play with liquor on your breath again, you're through!"

Jimmy remained sullen the whole time, then nodded that he understood. I'm not sure what problems he had had in the past, but from then on he sobered up and never drank before a show again. This incident became the only entanglement in our entire working relationship.

Otherwise Jimmy was a credit to his craft, and he was the perfect partner for me. We worked like a well-oiled piece of machinery, without any cogs gumming up the works, and critics howled with laughter at our every move. In every city we played in, we received favorable reviews.

The following year, 1941, my drill routine took on even more significance when the United States declared war on Germany and Italy. With the everyday horrors of this global confrontation, theatergoers wanted to laugh more than before. Consequently, more wartime propaganda films and cartoons were produced and comedies showed the war in such a way that helped us to forget our own troubles.

Comedians were also called to duty to serve their country by entertaining troops at the various camps: Bob Hope, Abbott and Costello, Jack Benny, Fred Allen, Jerry Colonna, Andy Devine, Jack Oakie, George Burns and Gracie Allen, Olsen and Johnson, and myself. In fact, Olsen and Johnson were responsible for getting me involved in the first place.

Their real names were John Sigvard Olsen and Harold Odgen Johnson (whose nickname was "Chic"). John was born in Peru, Indiana and intended to be a professional violinist; Chic hailed from Chicago, Illinois and entertained the idea of becoming a pianist. John changed his name to "Ole" (borrowing it from his younger brother,Ole, who I had worked with before) when he entered show business.

In 1912, when Ole was playing the violin with a singing group called the "College Four," Chic became their new pianist when the original one quit. From then on Chic and Ole began to throw in comedy ad libs and went on to develop a vaudeville routine. Then they began entertaining at businessmen's luncheons in the Midwest before they became convinced that audiences wanted something funny to happen every minute. This became the basis for their humor—a kind of anything-goes format. Audiences flocked en masse to their shows like big kids at heart.

I first met Chic and Ole one night after my performance at the Paramount Theater. They caught my drill routine, and after they shook the tears of laughter from their eyes, they asked me to work a benefit at Fort Jay in their place. The camp was located on Governors Island, so you had to take the South Ferry from the Winter Garden over to the island. Jimmy was unable to go because he fell ill at the last minute, so Ole Olsen took Jimmy's place and played straight to me. The Radio Rogues and a pantomimist name Harry Reso also worked in the show with us.

Ole and I were such a big hit with the servicemen—numbering in the thousands—that afterwards Chic and Ole considered me for a new Broadway show they were casting called *Son's of Fun*, which they promised would be "bigger and funnier" than its predecessor. J.J. and Lee Shubert were producing the show, and apparently Chic and Ole convinced them to go after me. By the time they did, however, my value had risen considerably.

Actor, writer, song plugger and toastmater George Jessel, who also was a theatrical producer, had approached me first about working his new show, *High Kickers*. It was set to feature such name stars as Sophie Tucker and Jack Haley. How I got to star instead in *Son's of Fun* I can thank George Jessel for.

When Chic and Ole informed me that the Shuberts wanted me in *Son's of Fun*, my mind was in a quandary. Jessel's show was going to be a typical musical revue; Olsen and Johnson's was going to be a madcap comedy revue. I really wanted to work with Chic and Ole, but I didn't want to offend George. After telling Ernie about my dilemma I finally got up the nerve to discuss the matter with George in person.

When I arrived at his office George welcomed me with open arms and we quickly got down to business. I informed him that Chic and Ole wanted me for *Son's of Fun* and that the two coinciding offers had put me in a bind.

"I feel a sense of loyalty to you, George, because you showed interest in me first," I said.

George was always open-minded, and he could see how much working with Chic and Ole would mean to me. So he took matters into his own hands to change that.

"I'd hate to see you get left out, Joe," he said. "Let me call J.J. I'll fix it."

George dialed J.J.'s number and when J.J. got on the line, he said, "J.J., I hear you want Joe Besser!"

"Yes, you're darn right I want him," growled Shubert.

Jessel, who knew how to con Shubert, said, "Well, you can't have him. He's with us. He's working in my show."

There was silence on the phone. J.J. groveled a bit, then he said, "I can't believe you're going to pay him what we're going to pay him." (Jessel's offer to me was for $350 a week.)

"Yes, I am," said George firmly. "You'd be foolish to think I would let a top talent like this get out of my hands."

More silence on the phone. Jessel had J.J. where he wanted him. J.J. finally spoke up. "We'll pay him more than you can."

The smoothie that Jessel was, he said, "If you don't sign him, I'll grab him away from you, J.J. So think about it."

End of conversation.

Meanwhile, I sat there stunned. "George, that was beautiful what you did for me," I said.

"You deserve it," he said. "You're a funny guy and I want you to get the best. I think you'd do better working with Olsen and Johnson than you would if you worked in my show."

Now how do you like that? George was a class guy all right. He put *my* best interests before the best interests of his own show. Not many men would have given as much as George did that day. He wanted to help me—and he did.

The Shuberts immediately signed me to a contract for $500 a week, and Chic and Ole were the first to congratulate me. As Jessel had predicted, *Son's of Fun* was a great boost to my career. In the end it helped me realize more dreams than I ever thought were possible.

Chapter 10

Playing Around with the Son's of Fun

As the first week of rehearsals for *Son's of Fun* began in late September of 1941, Chic and Ole soon proved to me why they were being called "geniuses of hokum comedy."

By now vaudeville, as I remembered it, was losing ground. Local theaters were foregoing the usual stage-show productions before the screening of their main features. The biggest reason was because big-budget productions had taken their place. But they were only played on the larger circuits—like Pantages and Shuberts. As smaller circuits began eliminating the stage-and-screen formats, theater owners began filling in time with additional movie shorts. (In many ways, it was cheaper for them to book a major MGM musical than a star-studded stage revue.)

Olsen and Johnson were responsible for prolonging the life of the talent-laden musical comedy vaudeville revue a while longer. Their screwball doings in *Hellzapoppin* proved that there was still an audience for this type of show. *Son's of Fun* promised to be just as successful, if not more.

I found it was no problem blending my crazy style of comedy with Chic and Ole's. It was a pleasure to work with them in such a wacky production. They always treated me with the utmost respect and let me have free reign on stage. They never insisted that I adhere to the script, as they knew my main strength was my ability to ad lib. If something came to my mind on the spur of the moment that I liked better than the scripted word, they encouraged me to use it. In other words, they were not selfish people and never restricted my creativity. As Chic once explained to me, "After all, Joe, we're all here for the same purpose—to entertain."

I was excited about working in *Son's of Fun* for a number of other reasons, too. My years of hard work were finally paying off. For fifteen years I had toiled and sweated for this moment. I had never been in a *successful* Broadway show before, so I prayed that this show would be the turning point in my career.

Meanwhile, I was thankful for the stages my career had taken thus far. I had gone from being an underpaid magician's assistant to a top-paid vaudeville comedian. The time it had taken me to achieve this actually seemed less than fifteen years. I loved what I was doing so much that I never paid much attention to the years swiftly going by me. It was only now that I had the time to reflect on how far I had come. At 34 I firmly believed in my ability and that the right break would come. It was just a matter of when.

Rehearsals went along rapidly during the three weeks before *Son's of Fun* opened at the Shubert Theater in Boston. Ernie was able to bask in my glory as she came out to join me. To show how confident the Shuberts were in the show, which they also bankrolled, I remember Lee and J.J. spared no expense in producing *Son's of Fun. Hellzapoppin* had been produced on a much skimpier budget with a bare minimum of sets and fewer players. *Son's of Fun* used more players, and the costumes glittered as did the props and backgrounds.

The Shuberts also went whole hog on grabbing up name talent at top dollar. The main cast was set to feature Carmen Miranda (the fruit bowl queen, complete with alternating headgear), whose South American rhumbas always tantalized; song-and-dance extraordinaire Ella Logan; piano satirist Frank Libuse (assisted by Margot Brander); Spanish dance team Rosario and Antonio; puppeteers Walton and O'Rourke; comedian Milton Charleston; the Biltmorettes; and dancers Valentinoff and Ivan Kirov, among others.

Chic and Ole oversaw every facet of production before the show debuted. I remember they were perfectionists in every sense of the word. They worked tirelessly to make the show a success. They monitored the construction of the props and scenery. They reread and rewrote the script numerous times, even if that meant laboring over one line until it sounded absolutely right. One time Ole almost got hurt trying to convince Chic he was right, however.

It happened one day when we were still in rehearsal. Ole went to Chic with a new routine he wanted to add to the show. It involved Chic's disappearing on stage (Ole had a trap door planted in the middle of the stage). When Ole presented the idea, Chic was unenthusiastic. No amount of persuasion on Ole's part could convince Chic that the gag would be safe.

"Come on, Chic," Ole insisted. "There's nothing to it. You stand on top, the stagehands pull the trap door open, and you fall straight through, with your hands down at your side."

Ole never saw past his enthusiasm; Chic saw himself getting injured.

Ole finally realized he was getting nowhere with Chic, so he said, "I'll demonstrate it for you, fraidy. You'll see."

So Ole stood on the trap door, the stagehands did their thing and—whoosh!—Ole fell from sight! In the process of falling, however, he forgot to pull his hands in and almost broke both arms as he went down. I remember afterwards Ole was in pain, but luckily he wasn't seriously hurt.

Chic didn't offer much help—or sympathy. He just laughed, looked down at Ole and said, "Oh, that's the way you do it, eh? You break two arms, two legs, and live happily ever after!"

Although the gag was never used, Ole was still able to perform, with the bruises to remind him of his not-so-brilliant idea.

At least Chic and Ole's preproduction efforts didn't totally go to waste, for *Son's of Fun* became a gigantic hit on opening night: Friday, October 31, 1941. It also was a welcome relief to theatergoers and critics alike caught up in the war overseas. The show spewed out rapid-fire laughs, and box office cash registers never stopped ringing all week long. The Shuberts immediately began recouping their investment, and the show also made Olsen and Johnson millionaires! It ended up running for almost three years, and they earned $5,000 a week, plus a quarter of the gross profits from the box office receipts.

But the bottom line, in my opinion, is that *Son's of Fun* entertained. The show became a swift course in lunacy, and the sounds of laughter from theatergoers still echoed in the air even after they had exited the theater. The critics only complaint about the opening show was its length; it lasted five hours! So Chic and Ole took scissors to the script and cut the show to three hours the next night. Otherwise critics reacted unanimously: Olsen and Johnson had another hit on their hands!

I recall a critic for the *Boston American* wrote: "*Son's of Fun* is a melange of the maddest and most enchanting performers ever to hit the stage. (It's) a lusty, rowdy, dignity-deflating and occasionally lilting entertainment."

Son's of Fun might also be best described as an earlier version of Rowan and Martin's *Laugh-In*. Like the popular sixties TV show, it contained one comedy blackout after another and nothing was sacred! Something was likely to happen at any minute, in any direction. The successful formula also let the audience feel as though they were participants. All night long players popped up in theater boxes or ran down the aisles to annihilate the audience with their humor. It was an outrageously funny show.

I can still recall various scenes in the show which stood out. Before the curtain was ever raised, Frank Libuse appeared in the orchestra pit as a heavily wigged musician and demolished an entire set of symphonic music! His comical zaniness was a prelude to a silly musical number sung by the stagehands, a scrubwoman, the usherettes and the washroom attendents. It was called: "The Joke's On Us."

The show kept alternating from musical numbers to comedy skits, but not before enduring its share of interruptions. As I said, players would pop up in theater boxes all night, including my straight man, Jimmy Little. After Ole finished introducing my act, Jimmy suddenly started warning somebody next to him to stop smoking.

"I asked you not to smoke that pipe!" he'd say, enraged. "I can't stand the smell of a pipe! I asked you several times to stop it!"

When the man wouldn't respond, Jimmy would turn finally turn even more delirious. "You won't, huh?" he'd say. "Well, take that!"

Jimmy would then supposedly hurl the man (actually a dummy) into the audience. Then the ushers ran down the aisle in the dark and hauled the dummy away!

A similar gag was used later in the show when another performer started complaining to a woman in a box seat to take off her hat because he couldn't see the show.

"Lady, will you please remove your hat?" the man would insist angrily. "Will you please take off your hat?"

She, too, wouldn't listen. So finally the man would scream, "Take off your hat!" and he would knock the woman's head off! The woman would then get up from her seat, pick up her head and hat and exit from the box!

Chic and Ole acted aloof during this buffoonery and resumed the show as though nothing had happened at all. They'd either introduce another skit or exchange snappy dialog until another act was ready. I recall Ole and Milton Charleston kept the audience rolling in the aisles with laughter over their nonsensical patter. Ole would start talking to Milton about what his occupation was:

"Say, what do you do?" Ole would ask.

"I'm sort of a traveling salesman," Milt would proudly reply. "I work for a corset concern; I take measurements for tailormade corsets."

"Wait a minute!" Ole would say, blushing with his eyes bugging out. "Do you mean you go around the country taking measurements for . . ." He indicates busts, hips, and legs.

"I sure do," Milt would reply.

"Ever make any mistakes?" interrupted Chic.

"Oh, once in a while," says Milt, "I pull a *bloomer!*"

Son's of Fun also had running gags galore. One man kept intermittently rolling a bowling ball down the middle of the stage waiting for the sounds of falling pins. Another time a loud and boisterous woman (Mrs. Johnson) kept popping up throughout the show searching for her husband, Oscar. On her last go-round, there were Oscars with willing answers all over the theater! A man also kept reappearing on stage in a straightjacket trying to worm his way out by doing a Russian dance! What craziness!

Between such madness there were several other striking musical performances that kept the show light and lively. Carmen Miranda helped people forget their troubles as she sang and danced her sultry South Anerican rhythms. Wearing gorgeous Brazilian costumes, she electrified the audience with her meaningful gestures. Ella Logan was at her engaging best singing "Mighty Fine Country," "It's a New Kind of Thing," and "Happy in Love." On the humorous side, Ella took her comic jabs as Panama Hattie (a Broadway character immortalized by Betty Hutton) and with Chic Johnson as "Charlie's Aunt" in a number retitled, "Oh, Auntie!" These numbers, which were written by Jack Yellen and Sam E. Fain, added smartness to the show.

Chic and Ole also showcased me in five different skits. My three main bits were the paint bucket gag, the drill routine, and the water bit. The water bit was a progressive gag like the woman who was trying to locate "Oscar." As Chic and Ole introduced a different act, I would run on stage, each time a little faster, carrying a cup. I would prance over to a water cooler on the other side of the stage, fill the cup, then run back off stage. The audience's laughter kept building as they soon realized I was up to something. By the third time I successfully finished refilling the cup, Ole finally stopped me upon my return and asked, "Wait a minute! What's going on here? What's with all the water?"

Flustered I'd say, "Ooh, don't stop me! It's not for me. The men's room is on f-i-r-e!!"

The Army drill routine got even bigger laughs for me. Ole and Jimmy Little also participated in this skit. Ole played an army captain while Jimmy played an army sergeant. This was the same routine I had first popularized in *You're in the Army*—only this one was a revised version. The routine took place on the first day new recruits report to camp. I was the bad apple of the bunch—a lisping soldier with a temper! I fulfilled the secret ambition of every rookie by impersonating the sarge and disregarding any orders I didn't like!

I acted like a kid at heart, which was my natural character anyway. During a drill I'd run across the stage trailing my gun after me as if it were a scooter. When Sarge confronted me, I'd react to him as though he was the neighborhood bully. I'd slap his hand and say, "You old c-r-a-z-y! I've had enough of your meanness!"

As a result, confusion continually reigned! When Sarge asked me to carry my gun correctly, I'd complain, "But it's too h-e-a-v-y!!" I never got anything straight, even his order of "right shoulder arms!" I thought meant putting the rifle on the right shoulder of the recruit next to me! The audience really howled with laughter when the Sarge changed it to "left shoulder arms" because I finally screamed, "Make up your m-i-n-d!"

This bit always produced laughs and helped pave the road to my future success.

In December of 1941, when *Son's of Fun* moved to the Winter Garden Theater in New York, the show's success with the critics and the public remained unspoiled. Even on the night Pearl Harbor was bombed, according to *Variety*, we were "the only show to play to standing room" audiences.

The New York critics—everybody from Walter Winchell to Ed Sullivan—were especially kind toward me. They all gave me undeserved raves. But Sullivan's review gave my career a gigantic boost. In his column, "Little Old New York," for the *Daily News*, on December 3, 1941, he said:

> "Yet out of the maelstrom of sound and fury there emerged on opening night a genial comedian who ran away with the show. He is Joe Besser. In the character of a lisping soldier, Besser's voice found querulous fault with every command. And by the time the scene was over, the audience had elected him unanimously as the top hit of the evening. The Winter Garden stage has served as the incubator of many comedy stars; Besser was given his Academy sheepskin on opening night."

Sullivan couldn't have been kinder. Even Dorothy Kilgallen, writing for *Cosmopolitan*, predicted great things for me. I recall she wrote: "The next comedian to hit the laughter jackpot of the nation in the manner of Bob Hope and Abbott and Costello is Joe Besser. It probably won't be too long before he will be larger than life on everybody's neighborhood screen."

I was definitely touched that Dorothy rated me this highly, but I never thought much about my future, nor about becoming a great movie comedian. For the moment I was just gratified that Chic and Ole had given me the opportunity to work in their show and that George Jessel was kind enough to act on my behalf. Jessel's gut feeling about *Son's of Fun* couldn't have proved truer. That show helped lift my career out of the doldrums for good.

Ernie was certainly proud that her Joey had finally done good! She and other entertainers had been telling me from the beginning: "When you've made it, you'll know."

I finally understood what they meant.

Chapter 11

Teaming Up with Benny, Allen, and Cantor

For the next three years, the Winter Garden became my permanent home. At the beginning of 1943, my third year in *Son's of Fun*, my career skyrocketed into another medium: radio.

I enjoyed working steadily at the same theater. It enabled me to spend time at home with and Ernie and Anna. I still kept in touch with Momma and Poppa, although I didn't do it as often as I had in the past, since I worked six days a week with only Mondays off.

However, Momma and Poppa were thrilled with my success, and my lack of communication didn't make them any less thrilled. I was disappointed that they never saw me in a single performance of *Son's of Fun*. I understood. But it's a shame they missed out on all the fun!

Being home meant Ernie and I could develop new friends and socialize on a regular basis. We spent most of our time visiting Ole Olsen and his wife, who lived on a farm in Malverne, Long Island. Ole threw the greatest parties, and his sense of humor always shone through.

At Christmas time, *Son's of Fun* racked up record business as people came to the theater in droves. Even though heavy snowstorms devastated most of the city's transportation system, somehow audiences always found ways to get there.

Servicemen on leave became my biggest boosters. They loved the drill routine. Some soldiers even pasted my photo next to pin-up girls like Betty Grable or Dorothy Lamour. Although I didn't have the legs of Grable or Lamour, one soldier wrote,

> Dear Mr. Besser:
>
> You are really the camp riot here. How's about a photo, Joe? I'd sure get a kick out of hanging it up in the barracks with our "Pin-Up Girls"—Choo Choo Johnson, Betty Grable, and the works. How's about it, please?

Signed,
Ben McMorrough, Private
Army Air Corps

Name personalities like Spike Jones, Al Jolson, Sophie Tucker, and Irving Berlin flocked to see our show. One man liked my routines so much, he wanted to write me into his weekly NBC radio show. He was considered the stingiest man in America, and his long pause and emphatic "Well!" had become a national institution. If you haven't guessed who he was already, he also played a lousy violin! His name was Jack Benny.

On Monday night, January 11, Jack and his wife, Mary Livingston, saw a performance. After seeing the show, he saw great possibilities for me and couldn't wait to contact me. He phoned me the next day, but I wasn't home. It was a cold, miserable day, but I had reported to the Winter Garden as usual, where we were performing an afternoon matinee.

When the call came through, Ernie answered the phone, but when the caller identified himself as "Jack Benny," she thought it was a prank.

"Come on," she said. "This must be a gag. You're drunk. Go home and sober up!"

Then she hung up.

Jack, as I later found out, was pretty even tempered. However, you could only test his patience so far, then he'd lose his cool and get mad. He called again. Ernie still didn't believe who he was. Again she hung up.

By now Jack was furious! He had his agent call Ernie, and before she could hang up he said, "Ernie, don't hang up. It's really Jack Benny who's been calling. This is his agent!"

That's when Ernie fainted!

Jack was told he could reach me at the Winter Garden. So when I returned to my dressing room after the matinee, Jack was waiting there for me.

"Jack Benny!" I screamed.

"Yes, Jack Benny. Who did you expect, Oscar Levant?" he cracked. "And would you please tell your lovely wife it was really me who called!"

Jack told me what had happened with Ernie, and we laughed. Then he became serious.

"Joe, I want you on my show," he said. "You're a very funny man."

Well, you can imagine after hearing a show business giant like Jack Benny praise me, I got scared. I had never been on radio before and working with Jack frightened me. Every week his program attracted the largest listening audience in the country! I developed "mike fright" and looked for every possible excuse to change Jack's mind.

"Look, Mr. Benny," I said. "I've . . . I've . . . I've got a bad throat. See, I can't talk. Honest. I can't talk above a whisper. See?"

Faking an illness didn't work. Jack saw right through my cover.

"Come on, Joe, quit the clowning. I'm serious," Jack said. "I want to feature you in this Sunday's broadcast."

Still nervous, I said, "I don't know, Mr. Benny."

"Call me Jack."

"I don't know, Jack."

"Call me Mr. Benny."

Jack had hoped that by kidding around he'd make me more comfortable. It didn't.

"Seriously, Jack," I said. "I'd be awfully nervous working the entire show."

Jack realized he was going to have to pamper me if he was going to succeed. "That's no problem, Joe," he said, "I'll cut down your part. Then all you'll have to do is stick your head in the studio several times, so the audience gets a chance to see you, say your lines, then leave."

Jack hadn't quite convinced me. There was one other snag: I had worked with only one straight man for the last several years. "I'll go on if you let me use my straight man," I said.

"I don't want your straight man," Jack said patiently. "I'll be your straight man!"

It was settled: I would appear on his show Sunday night and Dennis Day would pick me up three hours before the show on Sunday afternoon to rehearse. Dennis was to meet me at the Winter Garden after we finished performing the matinee.

I probably should have told Jack the entire truth behind my being scared, so I wouldn't have offended him. In late 1933 Rudy Vallee had asked me to appear on his radio show, *The Fleischman Hour,* which he hosted and produced. Rudy was a pioneer of radio variety programs. His show first aired in 1929, and it paved the way for radio drama, situation comedy, and documentaries. His program had introduced such talents as Beatrice Lillie, Ezra Stone, Edgar Bergen, Phil Baker, Alice Faye, and many others.

Vallee had sought my services upon the recommendation of Joe Bigelow, a staff writer who later wrote for *The Edgar Bergen and Charlie McCarthy Show* and who became one of my closest friends. Rudy wanted me to perform my entire RKO vaudeville act and said he would serve as my straight man. This was my first offer to appear on radio and I cautiously accepted.

I rehearsed the day before the show with Rudy and everything seemed good until the following night—the night of the broadcast. I froze. I was so scared, I couldn't leave the house. "Honey," I said to Ernie, "I'll be a nervous wreck. I don't want to go." And I didn't. I never showed up.

Bigelow panicked. He had stuck his neck out for me, and when I didn't show he told Rudy, "We've got to get somebody." Rudy recommended another comedian, Joe Penner, who needed work but wasn't yet a household name. They found Joe and put him on the show. Penner performed my entire act, with the exception of his own catch phrase, "Wanna buy a duck?" and became famous overnight!

The next morning several critics pointed out that: "Joe Penner did Joe Besser on radio last night. Penner obviously stole Besser's material." That didn't stop Penner from becoming successful. Afterwards he was in several feature length movies, and Jack Warner signed him to a contract at Warner Brothers to work in movies as comic relief.

Because Rudy Vallee had used another comedian with my material, I wondered what would prevent Benny from doing the same thing if I didn't show up. Would he also get another comedian? And would that comedian also succeed before me?

I had another reason for being sensitive. Most of my humor is visual. I didn't see how it could possibly click on the air. On stage, theatergoers watched and listened to me. On radio I could only be heard.

Dennis picked me up at the appointed time on Sunday and drove me to the Park Central Hotel, where Benny lived when he was working in New York. I rehearsed my bits with the entire cast: Mary Livingston, Don Wilson, the show's announcer, Oscar Levant, and, of course, Dennis. I was still nervous as we rehearsed, but Jack immediately soothed my nerves.

"Don't be nervous, Joe," he said. "Everything's going to be all right. You'll see."

Jack had heard how it took additional convincing on Dennis' part to get me into the car. I said I wouldn't feel comfortable going on Jack's show unless he allowed me to wear my costume from *Son's of Fun*. It was a stripe-colored vest and pants and a tiny hat, and it was my security blanket. Every comedian has one. Dennis said, "Sure, bring it along. Jack won't mind."

During rehearsal I received more assurances from everybody. No matter what I said, they were hysterical. They laughed at things I didn't even find funny. For a while I remained leery and thought they were making fun of me. Finally, I protested. "I'm not going on," I said, "you're just laughing to make me feel good. And you're making fun of me."

They laughed again.

Jack then stepped up to me and said, "Joe, we're on the level. We love everything you're doing."

I'll admit it was stupid, but I was frightened.

On Sunday night, January 17, 1943, I made my radio debut when *The Jack Benny Program,* sponsored by Grape Nuts, was broadcast—live—from the NBC Studios in New York. The show was performed before servicemen on leave. Every branch of the service was in the audience: the Navy, the Army, and the Marines. It was my kind of crowd, and the studio was packed!

Jack warmly welcomed me when I arrived at the studio. He handed me a revised copy of the script and wished me good luck. Ernie had stayed home with Anna because she was afraid being there would make me more nervous. She was right! I was so nervous I could have eaten an entire case of Grape Nuts! I got even more nervous as I read the new script. Jack had reneged on his promise to use me only as a walk-on. Instead I was on throughout the whole show! I tried calming myself down because I had something to prove this time. I wanted to avoid another Rudy Vallee fiasco.

Jack opened the show with a funny monologue that was followed by several skits. Meanwhile, Dennis kept me company. We sat in offstage chairs. I went over my lines until Don Wilson gave me my cue. Dennis leaned over and said, "Knock 'em dead, Joe!"

Then Don waved me on, and I ran out. I had forgotten my hat! But it was too late. There was the sound of a knock at the door.

Benny: "Now, who's that? Come in! (door opens) Yes, sir!"

Joe: "Is this 'The Jack Benny Program'? I'm supposed to be in your play tonight."

Benny: "Oh, yes, you were going to play the villain. What's your name?"

Joe: (softly) "Joe Besser."

Benny: "Messer?"

Joe: "No, B-e-s-s-e-r!"

(Applause)

Benny: "Well, I'm sorry, Mr. Besser, but we're not doing a play this evening."

Joe: "Now, wait a minute . . . I want to accttt!!"

Benny: "All right. Calm down. I'll find something for you."

Joe: " You better, you ol' crazy yooouuu!!!"

Benny: (Laughing) "Now sit down, please."

From then on, everything I did clicked. Jack brought out the best in me that night. Once I heard the audience laugh, my spirit soared, and I was on my way. Without my hat!

After I finished I returned to my seat, and Dennis pointed to my hat. I realized that I didn't need a funny costume or a funny hat to be funny. People were laughing at what I *did*, not at what I wore. In future performances, I dressed normally in a sports jacket or coat.

In the next skit Jack kept the audience in helpless laughter. I was included in a panel of experts that was a satire of another popular radio program: *Information, Please!* Jack was the host, "Clifton Bennyman." Mary Livingston, Oscar Levant, Abe Leiman, Dennis Day, and I made up the panel.

Jack read questions that had been submitted by "listeners." For each question we answered incorrectly he gave the lucky listener a page from *The Encyclopedia Britannica* and one Grape Nut flake! Jack had tried several times to get an answer from us for one question. Finally he repeated the question one more time: "Give me the name of a president whose name begins with W."

I raised my hand and Jack said, "Ah, Mr. Besser, I see *you* have the answer!"

Squirming uncontrollably in my seat, I said with great distress, "Ooh, it's not for tha-a-a-t!!"

Following the program, the switchboards at NBC lit up like a Christmas tree. The board was flooded with calls, all wanting to know who "the guest comedian" was? The next morning critics filed their reviews and, to my surprise, they were all raves. I remember one critic wrote: " 'The Jack Benny Program' was Besser's initial radio appearance, but it obviously won't be his last. His childlike, high-pitched expressions have a disarming quality that registers solidly over the air. With suitable material, as for instance, his participation in Benny's 'Information Please!' takeoff, Besser's possibilities for radio are broad."

I heard Danny Kaye had been sitting backstage at the Imperial Theater in New York, listening to the broadcast. He reportedly told an acquaintance: "Listen to this guy, Besser. He's the funniest man on Broadway and folks are just discovering him!"

I was very flattered that critics and other entertainers felt that way about me. I thought anybody could have done the character I did. Then I thought it was because I always tried to radiate happiness through my character. With our country at war, people didn't have much to be happy about in those days.

I think that part of my success over the last five decades has been because of everybody's secret yearning to forget how old they are and all their responsibilities and their wish to just act like a kid again. I've done it for them. That's probably why I've always been so well liked by fans of all ages and by critics.

With the flood of critical kudos coming in, Jack asked me back on his program for several more weeks. He told me that the ratings for his show were continuing to beat out the competition. One of his arch rivals, Fred Allen, also noticed this alarming fact.

Fred had been "feuding" with Jack since the mid-thirties. Jack's show aired on NBC from 7 to 7:30 P.M. every Sunday night. Fred's program started at 8 P.M., one half hour after Jack's was finished. According to Jack, the feud had started as a joke one night when Fred introduced a talented ten-year-old violinist named Stuart Canin on his show, who played Franz Schubert's "The Bee." When Canin finished, Fred cracked, "Jack Benny should be ashamed of himself."

The following week Jack picked up on Fred's crack and insisted that he could play "The Bee" when he was ten. Well, Jack's comment added fuel to the fire. The following week Fred brought on a character actor who claimed he was a neighbor of Jack's from Waukegan, Illinois, Jack's hometown. The man swore that Jack hadn't played well enough at ten to play "The Bee" or "any other song."

After Fred had wrung every laugh out of that story, he started getting personal. He was a noted writer with a natural wit, and every week he came up with a series of attacks on Jack: "Before shoes were invented, Jack was a heel . . . His false teeth are so loose they are always clicking . . . Jack has more hair than an elbow . . . I don't want to say that Jack Benny is cheap, but he's got short arms and carries his money low in his pockets."

Jack got in his share of put downs about Allen. "Fred's so tight that when he finally spent a five-dollar bill, Lincoln's eyes were bloodshot!" Then he said, "Fred looks like a butcher peeking over two pounds of liver."

Jack and Fred also feuded about their guest: They each wanted the best talent on their shows. After Jack had had me on his show for four weeks in February of 1943, Fred had me on his show for eight weeks! Each time Fred used me as a guy who popped in by mistake. On the first show I came in looking for the studio they broadcasted the Lone Ranger show from. Fred gave me the directions so fast, and I got so confused, I finally said, "Ooh, I'm going to be late. Tonto will be so a-n-g-r-y!!"

Despite his media-created feud with Fred, Jack was the first to congratulate me. He sent me a telegram the next day:

You were great on Allen's program last night. Working easier than ever. Please wire me at the Ambassador East Hotel in Chicago where I can call you some morning before I leave for California.

Best wishes,
Jack Benny

Fred loved having me on his show, and we began to socialize with each other frequently. Once a week, Fred, Joe Bigelow, Irving Mansfield and his wife Jackie Susann (who became a best-selling novelist),Artie Hershkowitz, Ernie and I would go to a different restaurant for dinner. Our favorite hangout was Dave's Blue Room, which was frequented by all the performers in New York. Afterwards we'd drive over to Bigelow's apartment on 59th Street, one-half block from Irving Mansfield and Jackie Susann's place, to play cards. Fred never played, but he was often the life of the party.

Because of the exposure on Fred's and Jack's programs, I rapidly became "the most talked about comedian in America" according to *Time* magazine. *Time* wrote an in-depth article about my career, and the writer called my catch phrases "national exclamations." More radio offers poured in. I had so many offers, I had to turn many of them down. It was impossible to work on all these shows while continuing to work in *Son's of Fun* three times a day. I chose my best offers.

My next appearance was on the CBS radio mystery program, *Ellery Queen,* with Gypsy Rose Lee as a guest detective. The program was based on the character created by Frederic Dannay and Manfred Bennington Lee, and it had made its debut in 1939. Each week a different celebrity served as an armchair detective and tried to solve the mystery before Ellery Queen revealed the actual answer. The producers of the show were elated over my performance; I joked around with Gypsy until the conclusion, and it kept the show light and lively.

After those appearances I started feeling more comfortable with radio broadcasts. There was no more mike fright. I had no more worries about people stealing my material. And I didn't need funny costumes to stimulate laughs. I had finally overcome my worst fears. I was thankful I had come this far.

Success brought imitation. Within a very short period of time, other performers started using my famous catch phrases on their shows. (These phrases later showed up in several Warner Brothers cartoons!)

Eddie Cantor was the first. An established vaudeville and Broadway star, Cantor starred in his own radio show, *The Eddie Cantor Show* (which was later called *The Chase and Sanborn Hour*). Eddie had brought national attention to many up-and-coming performers including Deanna Durbin, Dinah Shore, and Bobby Breen.

Affectionately called "Banjo Eyes," because of his large, expressive eyes, Eddie didn't need my material to get laughs. But he used it and so did his guests. Bert Gordon impersonated me one week, followed by Lionel Stander the next. On another broadcast Eddie used my "Not so fast!" business in repartee with actress Janet Blair.

This use of my material didn't come to my attention until several friends, who had listened to Cantor's show, called me and after I had read several items in the newspaper. I never filed any legal action against Eddie because I felt his use of my catch phrases didn't hurt me. People knew they were mine. Every time Eddie got laughs using them, it reaffirmed in people's minds that "that's Joe Besser."

However, somebody felt differently about it because on Monday, March 14, 1943, I got a shock while reading the morning edition of the *The New York Post.* A banner headline read:

BESSER ASKS CANTOR TO STOP USING HIS GAGS

What? I had never made any such statement or taken any action. But the article said I did. It clearly said that I had wired Cantor to refrain from using my "trademarked expressions" on his radio show. Friends including Jack Benny and Fred Allen called me and sympathized with my situation. I played along; I had no idea how the story got started until my good friend Joe Schoenfield of *Variety* in New York phoned me. He told me *he* had sent the telegram and signed my name! He also planted the article in the *Post* because he was outraged by Cantor's use of my material.

I didn't get mad at Joe because I really didn't care what Cantor did. But if the incident got me work, well, that was another story!

Joe sent me a copy of the telegram he wrote to Cantor. It said:

> My dear Mr. Cantor:
>
> I know you would not willfully harm me, but your use of two trademarked expressions identified with me is certainly not helping me. When you did them yourself two weeks ago I deemed it a compliment. But in turning them over to Lionel Stander, it was plagiarism. I am just getting started in radio and my trademarks are very valuable to me. Please stop using them.
>
> Yours very sincerely,
> Joe Besser

Well, Schoenfield's telegram worked all right. It generated a visit to Cantor from my agent Bill Miller. It also got the following reply from Cantor, dated March 2, 1943:

Dear Joe:

As time goes on and you become even more successful in radio, you will find not only Eddie Cantor and Lionel Stander and Phil Baker, but all the comedians using your catch phrase. It happened with the late Joe Penner's "You Wanna Buy a Duck?" It happened with Jack Pearl's "Vos You Dere Sharlie?" It happened with my own Mad Russian and his expression, "Shall I Tell Em?" You should be heartened by the compliment, rather than taking it to heart. To stop the use of a popular catch phrase would be like stopping our American boys at Guadalcanal or any place where they start going. Don't be a silly little boy. If it was my desire to hurt you, I wouldn't have spent an hour with your agent last Friday trying to arrange a deal where I could have you exclusively for radio.

Kindest regards,
Eddie Cantor

That Guadalcanal comment killed me; as though I wasn't patriotic! I sold war bonds and did my share of benefits during the war. Eddie just blew the entire incident out of proportion. But he apologized to me the following week by signing me as a regular on his show for twelve weeks!

Eddie never regretted having me on his show either. Critics said my appearances bolstered the show. One critic reported, "Not since he first hit the airwaves as a guest on the Jack Benny program has Joe Besser clicked the way he did on the Eddie Cantor program last week. Besser again demonstrated he's got something distinct and unique for radio."

I continued to ride a roller coaster of success with Cantor and in *Son's of Fun* until tragedy struck. In late March of 1943, I quit taking on extra jobs when Ernie became seriously ill. We had gone to Chic Johnson's farm in Connecticut, which was surrounded by acres of tall grass and cows grazing in the fields. While I visited with Chic, Ernie and Chic's daughter June went to milk the cows. Afterwards June gave Ernie a fresh glass of milk, straight from the cow.

That night Ernie became violently ill. I called our family physician, Dr. Hertz, who rushed her to the Doctor's Hospital in downtown New York. She had a high fever, and Dr. Hertz discovered after he examined her that she had paratyphoid. Hertz believed Ernie got the disease from drinking milk that was unpasteurized and contained harmful amounts of bacteria that poisoned her system.

Dr. Hertz needed twenty-four hours to break Ernie's fever. Despite her contagious condition, he allowed me to visit her. A nurse dressed me in a surgical mask and gown before going into her room. I stayed with her until the visiting hours were over. Before I left, Dr. Hertz pulled me aside and said, "Joe, we're going to do everything in our power to break Ernie's fever. I promise."

I worried about Ernie all night. She was everything I had. Without her, life meant nothing to me. I slept a half hour at most that night.

The following morning I went back to the hospital before reporting to the Winter Garden. When I got there, Dr. Hertz had a big grin on his face; Ernie had broken her fever! He predicted a full recovery in about a week, but decided to keep her hospitalized for two weeks to avoid a relapse. Ernie gave me an okay sign when I visited her. Every day after that I came to see her when my work schedule permitted it.

Meanwhile, many performers from the show who heard about Ernie's illness sent her daily get-well cards. I have never forgotten their thoughtful outpouring of love. Baskets of flowers and potted plants crowded her room, and that brought joy to my little angel.

By the time Ernie returned home she was still weak, and it took another week of rest before she could stand on her feet. Anna, who possessed an incredibly strong will, helped out when I wasn't at home, and she gave Ernie lots of encouragement.

Just as Ernie started to progress, however, I almost set her back for good. Following her release from the hospital, she started having problems sleeping at night. I had had similar problems, so sometimes I took sleeping pills to sleep. A bandleader I had worked with during an engagement in Washington, D.C. had recommended them to me. So I gave Ernie two tablets to put her to sleep.

Dr. Hertz had always told me never to worry about how much sleep I got. He said, "Rest is the next best thing to sleep." I should have remembered those wise words when Ernie told me about her insomnia because after she took the pills she never woke up. I finally read the directions on the bottle, which said, "Take tablets according to your weight." Oh, my God, Ernie should have taken only half of one pill.

I frantically shook Ernie, but there was no response. I called Dr. Hertz, and he said, "Joe, walk her. Give her coffee." So Anna boiled a pot while I walked Ernie around. A half-hour later I almost gave up when Ernie still showed no signs of coming out of her slumber. Then suddenly, she started coughing. She woke up and wearily asked me, "Where was I?"

I hugged and kissed Ernie and told her how stupid it was of me to have given her a pill (I won't repeat what she said!). Afterwards I stopped using them. I threw the rest away and took Dr. Hertz's advice. I never worried about sleeping again.

Once Ernie was fully recovered, I began taking on more work. I would soon realize another dream: starring in motion pictures.

Chapter 12

My Hollywood Dream

In April of 1943 my elusive dream to become a full-time Hollywood movie star came one step closer to becoming a reality.

Charlie Kerner from RKO Radio Pictures had been scouting me at the Winter Garden for weeks. He was the studio chief in charge of production. When he finally approached me, it was worth the wait. He offered me a four-year contract, at $2,000 a week, to star in a series of comedy features opposite comedian Wally Brown (who later became the funny half of the comedy team Brown and Carney, also for RKO).

I was as thrilled as could be by RKO's offer. At last, after three years of waiting, my chance to work regularly in motion pictures had arrived! Every imaginable dream ran through my mind: a mansion in Bel Air, a heated swimming pool, and a harem of girls. A harem of girls? . . . Wow! Wow! Wow! Now *that's* Hollywood!

Before I signed my name on the dotted line, however, I told Olsen and Johnson about the offer. I respected their opinions and I figured they'd know whether RKO's offer was fair. They immediately encouraged me to take it.

"We won't stand in your way." Ole said.

"Yeah," quipped Chic, "now you'll be a Hollywood c-r-a-z-y!!"

Even the stoic J.J. Shubert seemed genuinely excited about RKO wanting me. When I asked for a release from my contract from *Son's of Fun*, he also suggested that I sign with RKO right away before they changed their minds.

That night I followed their advice and set up a meeting with Kerner at the Winter Garden for the next day. Charlie was happy that I had reached a favorable decision, and he immediately wired the studio's head of publicity to start grinding out a promotional package about my signing.

Everything looked promising until, minutes before my meeting with Kerner, the Shuberts called me into their office. Apparently J.J. had spoken to Lee about RKO's interest in me, and they had a sudden change of heart.

"Joe, we've reconsidered your offer from RKO," said J.J. "We can't let you go. I'm sorry, but we feel you're too valuable to the show."

Red-faced, I apologized to Kerner for the misunderstanding and for days I was heartbroken. The best deal any studio had offered to me had just gone up in flames . . . So had my dream for a mansion in Bel Air, a heated swimming pool, and a harem of girls!

I guess the Shuberts had their business interests to protect and I was one of them. I didn't stay mad at them for long, as I've never held a grudge toward anyone. I've always forgiven and forgotten.

Afterward, however, I used extreme caution when a movie producer expressed interest in me because I knew the Shuberts couldn't be trusted.

In the meantime, I had lots of employment. I still worked eight shows a week at the Winter Garden, and I appeared weekly on Eddie Cantor's radio show. When that contract expired, I again became a frequent guest on Jack Benny's and Fred Allen's programs. I received more offers than I could handle. And knowing people wanted me, my spirits were once again high.

Even though my career rode a boundless wave of popularity, two weeks after the RKO deal fell through, I was struck with devastating news. Momma was dead. She had died peacefully in her sleep of natural causes. She had passed away without any warning and without ever showing any signs of slowing down.

Momma's death crushed me. The morning Poppa called with the news, I was headed out the door to the Winter Garden.

"Momma's gone, Jessel. She's gone . . . " Poppa said. His voice trailed off as he fought back the tears.

I searched for the proper words to console my dear father, but nothing came out. Shock overcame me, and everything else that had been happening now seemed meaningless. Ernie took over the call.

I sat alone for several hours, sorrowful and unable to find the energy to report to work. My memories of Momma flashed before me as though they had happened yesterday. I saw her putting me to bed as a child. I could see her tending to my needs—especially my large appetite! I remembered her reveling in her fairy tales in front of the burning stove. I could see her painfully rubbing the rheumatism out of her hands. I saw her many acts of charity. I remembered all the times I had run away, and heard Momma say "Next time, at least let us know when you plan on running away!

I finally found the strength to go to the Winter Garden. Poppa had told

Ernie that Momma would be buried the next day. She was to be interred on Jewish soil, which was the custom of our faith. In order to attend her funeral, I needed to get permission from the Shuberts. I went in to see J.J. about getting some time off but, to show how heartless men in power can sometimes be, he wouldn't let me go.

"Joe, your duty is here, to this show," said J.J., as though Momma's death had no merit. "How could we replace you on such short notice?"

I didn't even put up a fight. I was too stunned! Besides, what was the use? I realized then that the Shuberts didn't care about my well-being. There was only one kind of language they understood. How to make money. They were not interested in any of my problems.

So I remembered Momma the way I had seen her: cheerful as always with a kind word and a happy greeting. Now when I look at the picture of her in my den it's as though she's not gone at all. She still lives in my heart everyday.

That night, at the Winter Garden, I paid homage to Momma the best way I could. I lived up to the old tradition of many show business people: "The show must go on!" I went on. Before the first show, I choked back my emotions and looked up toward heaven, "This one's for you, Momma!" I'm sure she was watching me.

After Momma's burial ,I invited Poppa to come and live with us. Although he hadn't been to New York since he and Momma had first arrived in America, he knew his way around. And I thought that if he got tired of sightseeing, he would have Anna to socialize with.

When Ernie and I picked Poppa up at the train station, however, we saw a changed man. The spirit and driving force had been drained from him. After Momma's death he seemed to have no desire to live.

A short time after Poppa arrived, he developed a terrible cough that worsened each day. He had always been a heavy cigar smoker, but now he coughed from the moment he woke up until the moment he went to bed. I worried about him a great deal. Finally I had Dr. Hertz give Poppa a complete physical.

Afterwards Hertz pulled me aside and gave me his prognosis: "Joe, your Poppa hasn't long to live. He has lung cancer."

The thought of losing Poppa, too, was very difficult for me to bear. "Is there anything you can do, Doctor?" I asked "If he stopped smoking would that help?"

"Why should he stop now?" he replied grimly.

Each day Poppa's health rapidly deteriorated. Each day he had less energy than the day before. I tried making his last days cheerful. I bought him two expensive new suits. I knew how much Poppa loved fancy clothes, so I hoped they would lift his spirits. Ernie and I took him to the finest New York restaurants. We took him to the most popular Broadway shows. I even had our dentist implant dentures in place of Poppa's old teeth, which had begun to rot away. But nothing seemed to help. I realized that Poppa was going to die.

Although I tried hiding my grief, my spirits were lower than ever. Working in *Son's of Fun* became my only means of escape. But even my work never lifted spirits completely.

Then in early May of 1943 two scouts from Columbia Pictures joined the audience to scout me: producer Irving Briskin and director Charles Barton (who preferred to be called "Charlie"). They had flown in from Hollywood to consider me for an army comedy they were casting titled *Hey, Rookie!* Ann Miller was already set to star as the female lead and Barton was going to direct it.

During the show Barton supposedly turned to Briskin and called my performance "Chaplinesque." Irving agreed. Afterwards he was sold on signing me. "We've got to get this guy," he told Charlie enthusiastically. "We've just got to."

Backstage in my dressing room, Irving immediately offered me a contract. At first the offer overwhelmed me; it was better than RKO's previous offer. My salary would start at $3,500 a week, guaranteed for six weeks, with an option to make another picture if my first one was successful.

As thrilled as I was, I was also scared. I was afraid the Shuberts were going to try and doublecross me again. I never let on to Irving and Charlie about my dilemma. Instead I tabled their offer.

"I have to check with the Shuberts," I said. "But I'm not promising you anything."

"Do what you can," said Barton. "We'll wait, but we're not going back to Hollywood unless we take you with us."

I checked with J.J. about leaving *Son's of Fun* and this time he assured me that there would be no hanky-panky on his and Lee's part. Well, like before, his word lasted one day.

The following afternoon, J.J. and Lee called me back into their offices with an ultimatum: They would let me go provided I signed a separate contract with them that would entitle them to half of my earnings from *Hey, Rookie* and half of all my future film assignments.

I was shocked. How greedy could they get!

This time, however, I called my attorney, Artie Hershkowitz, and asked him to review my new contract. He said it was sound and legal and he told me I had no choice but to agree to the Shuberts' terms if I wanted to star in *Hey, Rookie!* I didn't know what to say. Artie had been my legal counsel for years. So I signed.

Columbia Pictures made it official the last week in May. They announced in the trades that *Hey, Rookie!* would be "featuring comic sensation, Joe Besser, direct from Broadway's *Son's of Fun*." The movie was set to roll in June. Despite my dealings with the Shuberts, I was starting to get excited. Hollywood, here I come!

I had good reasons for being excited. Columbia Pictures had become a major force in the motion picture industry. After years of squandering itself as a member of Hollywood's Poverty Row, the studio had turned out many top-grade films, which included: *It Happened One Night* (1934) with Clark Gable and Claudette Colbert, which won five Academy Awards; *Mr. Deeds Goes to Town* (1936) with Gary Cooper and Jean Arthur; *You Can't Take It With You* (1938) and *Mr. Smith Goes to Washington* (1939), both starring James Stewart.

The man responsible for turning Columbia into a respected multimillion dollar giant was movie mogul Harry Cohn, the studio's president. Cohn was either loved or hated by those who worked for him. In spite of what people thought of him, nobody could argue with his success.

Poppa was still of major concern to Ernie and me. Since we were heading west by train, we made arrangements to drop Poppa off in Little Rock, Arkansas, where he would stay with my sister Esther, who happily took him in. But it was the last time I saw him. One month later, he died.

I was saddened by losing Poppa, but there was no looking back. It was time to get my career in order. Momma and Poppa would have wanted it that way.

Happier moments followed when *Hey, Rookie!* started production the second week in June of 1943. The screenplay, which was written by Henry Meyers, Edward Eliscu, and Jay Gorney, was based on a popular musical show of the same title. With World War II still going strong, it was a timely feature film.

I was cast in the rôle of an army rookie named "Pudge" Pfeiffer. Pudge helps another soldier (Larry Parks), who's a stage producer who's been drafted, produce a show for the servicemen that features a leading lady of Broadway, Winnie Clark (Ann Miller). The movie was a good blend of comedy and music. I managed to convince director Charlie Barton to use my straight man Jimmy Little. Jimmy played my drill sergeant, and together we brought a revised version of my army drill routine to the screen.

Most of the scenes were shot outdoors at Fort MacArthur, a real army camp located in San Pedro. As part of the arrangement for using the camp, Columbia paid to have an indoor swimming pool built for the soldiers. The remaining scenes were shot indoors on Stage 7 at Columbia.

There were pressures, of course, in being the star of the film. A lot of responsibility rested on my shoulders; Columbia's investment in the film was at stake and so was my career! I'll admit I was nervous until Ernie began coming to the studio with me every day to calm my nerves.

Filming *Hey, Rookie!* wasn't like work at all. It was a continual party five days a week! The atmosphere was loose and lively and the reception Harry Cohn, Charlie Barton, and the entire cast and crew gave me made me wonder why I hadn't been in Hollywood before.

Charlie Barton set the tone the first day. He came up to me, put his arm around me and discussed his ideas for the picture. Charlie was only 5 feet, three inches tall and he was in a big man's job. But his heart was always in the right place. He had gained his experience by working for Cecil B. DeMille as an assistant director and by working as a director at Paramount before he jumped to Columbia.

Charlie knew situations and how to handle people. They were his greatest assets. He never yelled at anybody. Never. He always consoled you with his comforting voice. If you had anything you wanted to try in a scene, he would let you. He definitely fit in at Columbia; Harry Cohn wanted artists with fresh ideas who were not afraid to loosen the reins.

Several days into the picture, I realized that Cohn had given me his best in Charlie. I recall telling Charlie, "You know, I have a feeling that I'm lucky I got you to direct my first starring picture. I feel as though you're going to watch over me, so I'll do the right things."

Charlie liked that. Afterwards we became the best of friends. He and his lovely wife Roma gave Ernie and me the grand tour of California. We spent a fun-filled weekend in the mountains at Big Bear. We soaked up more scenery when we took drives up the coast. They showed us around Hollywood and introduced us to the best restaurants and theaters.

On nights when filming ran late, Charlie always stopped at the Knickerbocker Hotel for dinner, which is where Ernie and I were staying. His favorite meal soon became Ernie's pork chops. He couldn't eat enough of them. After dinner we finished the evening with a game of hearts. We never played for money, just for matches!

Ann Miller also made me feel at home in Hollywood. The first week of production she threw a party at her spacious hilltop home overlooking the San Fernando Valley. The party was catered and the tables were stocked with food and spirits (not the *ghostly* kind either!)

The party was memorable for me in many ways. It was my first Hollywood party. And it almost became my last!

Charlie and Roma drove Ernie and me to Ann's house. Neither Ernie nor I drove a car yet, but after that day we considered taking lessons immediately! I never realized until then that Charlie could be quite a daredevil at times. The only way to get to Ann's home was up a series of winding roads. We missed one near-miss after another climbing those roads. But Charlie nearly got us killed when he turned the car around in an open curve. I got a very *close* glimpse of the Valley—as he almost backed the car off the cliff!

"Charlie, stop the car!" I screamed.

Charlie immediately slammed on the brakes. I could hear pebbles falling off the cliff—tumbling below.

"What's the matter?" asked Charlie casually. "Is there something wrong?"

More pebbles cascaded off the cliff.

"You almost got us killed, that's what!" I said.

Charlie was always as cool, collected, and brave as General Patton. He had a different perspective.

"We would have made it!" he said cheerfully.

The final day of filming *Hey, Rookie!* was filled with just as many surprises as Charlie's driving! My first starring feature became a sentimental journey at the last take. Before the lights were doused, Charlie asked me and the cast to gather around. A stagehand appeared wheeling out a big cake. Actors usually gave the crew a party once a picture was finished, but instead the crew had decided to give me a party!

The cake was layered with vanilla frosting and the inscription read, "To Our Joe, May You Always Roll in the Dough!" (And they didn't mean Pillsbury e-i-t-h-e-r!)

"Cut the cake!" Ann hollered.

I blew out the candles, then tried cutting the cake. But, to my surprise, I found the cake was nothing but a glump of unbaked dough covered with icing! The whole thing wobbled like a Jello mold! Everybody laughed and afterward the stagehands brought out another cake. This one was real.

As everybody gobbled down their cake, Harry Cohn joined the party with a surprise of his own. Harry had become a second father to me during my six weeks at Columbia. He always dropped by to check on me.

He'd walk on the set carrying a whip cane. Then he'd slam it down on a chair, and ask, "How are you doing, Joe? Is everything okay? Are you happy?"

Harry cracked the whip to intimidate people, but he never intimidated me. Although I may have been like the Cowardly Lion at times, Harry didn't scare me. I'll admit his method for saying "hello" was strange, but I knew Cohn truly cared about me.

Some people have said the opposite about Harry Cohn—that he was a heartless, ruthless individual. They're entitled to their opinions, but flattery will get them nowhere! Sure, Cohn had many bizarre traits. I remember when you walked into his office, his desk was raised on a platform so that wherever you were sitting, you always had to look up at him. I know several people were offended by this because they believed Cohn considered himself "godlike." I guess if you let those kind of things bother you, you probably are resentful. I didn't.

I met Harry behind the doors, in front of the doors, and between the doors and he was always friendly toward me. I treated him with respect and like he was a normal human being—never as someone in a position of authority. Maybe that's why he liked me.

Cohn's visit at the party fortified my feelings towards him. He had come back from viewing most of the rushes for *Hey, Rookie!* He was so satisfied with the final results, he said "Joe, we want to pick up your option. We want you to be with Columbia for a long time!"

Boy, that was a surprise!

A feeling of joy ran through me, but it was shortlived. Suddenly I became depressed, and Harry noticed this.

"Joe, something's wrong, isn't it?" he said. "I can tell something's worrying you. You didn't smile. You always smile. What is it?"

I didn't want to burden Cohn with my troubles, but his offer to pick up my contract revived a bad taste in my mouth that I had already swallowed once before.

"You're right, Mr. Cohn, something is wrong," I said. "I didn't want to tell you this, but I don't want you to pick up my option."

Harry was flabbergasted. "Why?" he asked.

I told him how the Shuberts had cornered me into signing an additional contract before coming out to film *Hey, Rookie!* and that it entitled them to half my earnings. Well, Harry couldn't believe it. He exploded!

"That's a lousy thing to do!" he said, in a huff and a puff. "I'll take care of the Shuberts. Don't you worry!"

I didn't. Cohn was like E.F. Hutton. When he spoke, people listened!
After an emotional goodbye, Ernie and I bid farewell to tinsel town and returned to our home in Astoria. The morning after we arrived an article was in the entertainment pages of *The New York Times*. The headline read:

JOE BESSER DROPPED BY COLUMBIA

The article said Columbia's president Harry Cohn had announced that the studio was not going to pick up my option and that they were cancelling my contract effective that day. Cohn had planted the story with *The Times* to deliberately deceive the Shuberts.
It worked.
Since the Shuberts believed Columbia had given me the boot, they thought they would no longer profit from any of my earnings from future films. My attorney Artie Hershkowitz joined in on this scam with Cohn and went to the Shuberts right after the story was published. Cohn believed they'd want to get rid of me fast. I was now damaged goods in their eyes.
Artie never saw two grown men say "yes" faster in his life when he suggested: "You know, it's silly to keep Joe Besser. Columbia dropped him, so you're not going to make anything now. So let's make a deal. You wanted half of Joe's salary. We'll give you $10,000 and the case will be closed."
Artie's Perry Mason delivery convinced the Shuberts, and I bought out their contract with me. I still had a separate arrangement, however, to work in *Son's of Fun*. So I returned to the show that week.
The Shuberts thought they had come away with a bargain after I paid them off. But Cohn wasn't through yet. He phoned me that night and asked how the Shuberts reacted to my buying them out.
"They would have signed a release in blood," I said, "if they had to."
Cohn laughed like hell. "Wait till tomorrow!" he said.
The next day *The New York Times* ran a follow-up story. It said:

COLUMBIA PICKS UP BESSER'S OPTION
"Hey, Rookie!" Star Signs New Contract

The Shuberts nearly choked themselves after reading this story. In August of 1943, *Son's of Fun* made its final bow after 742 consecutive performances. I signed a new three-year deal with Columbia, which called for me to star in one feature film a year at the same salary.
This time I had the last laugh!

Chapter 13

Uncle Miltie and the Shoe That Didn't Fit

Harry Cohn's efforts to keep me at Columbia paid off for the studio, immediately.

Hey, Rookie! was released on April 6, 1944. It became a critical hit and a top moneymaker for Columbia that year. The first weekend many theaters did a record business. I remember *Variety* called the film "one of the best shows of its type to be produced since the beginning of the war cycle."

Immediately after the success of *Hey, Rookie!*, Cohn readied two more properties for me to star in: *Eadie Was a Lady*, also with Ann Miller and Larry Parks, and *Talk About a Lady* with former model turned actress Jinx Falkenburg and Forrest Tucker. Both were musical comedies.

Eadie Was a Lady went before the cameras in late April of 1944 and again I brought Ernie with me to Los Angeles. The story and screenplay for this film were written by screenwriter Monty Brice, and my co-stars, besides Ann and Larry, included Jeff Donnell and my straight man Jimmy Little. I played a goofy professor called Professor Diogenes Dingle, who teaches classical drama at Glen Moor College in Boston, where a student named Eadie Alden (Ann Miller) is starring in the school's annual Greek Festival. Arthur Dreiffus directed and Michael Kraike was the producer.

It was fulfilling to know I had finally become a permanent part of the Hollywood system. I was grateful to Harry Cohn for believing in me, and I carried out making this film with pride and dignity. Of course, I also threw in a little fun and games for good measure!

Eadie Was a Lady was even more fun to make than *Hey, Rookie!* Ann Miller enjoyed working with me for a second time, and she was as warm towards me as she had been before. With Larry Parks back, we started feeling like an old vaudeville team—we were inseparable! We lunched together at the commissary, we sat in each other's dressing rooms and told funny stories, and we played practical jokes on each other from time to time.

We had more laughs than Barnum and Bailey! Except for our director.

Arthur Dreiffus was a competent director, but he was not as well educated in comedy as Charlie Barton had been. In fact, during the first week of filming it became painfully obvious to me that Arthur knew nothing about comedy. He had previously directed film dramas such as *Baby Face Morgan* (1942) and *The Pay Off* (1943). Arthur Dreiffus was a German immigrant, who had started in show business as a child conductor and had later become a choreographer. So while he was quite adept at directing Ann's dancing sequences, comedy wasn't his bag.

Arthur disappointed me one day when, at the suggestion of Michael Kraike, he decided to cut a gag from the script before it was filmed. I argued that the gag was important to the scene's overall continuity. Arthur said he didn't want to film the extra footage needed to build to the scene. In the intended sequence, after leaving a building on campus, I was supposed to jump over a hedge and fall into a puddle of water. That's right, one of the oldest comedy gags in the book! I loved the bit, but my pleas to keep it in fell on deaf ears.

Then the man with the whip cane walked in—Harry Cohn. He came to my rescue—again. When Harry made his usual rounds that day he arrived on the set shortly after Dreiffus had decided to strike the scene from the script. Cohn noticed I wasn't smiling.

"Joe, you're not your jovial self today," he said. "What's wrong?"

Again, even though we were the best of friends, I hated to trouble Cohn with such a petty thing.

"Nothing!" I said.

My eyes gave me away, however. They say if you look straight into someone's eyes you can tell whether they are telling the truth or not. Cohn realized I wasn't.

"Joe, you can level with me," he insisted.

So I told him.

This time Cohn never showed any anger in front of me. All he said was: "Don't worry, I'll see that it's back in."

The next morning it was.

Later, Cohn brimmed with satisfaction as *Eadie Was a Lady* became my second straight hit for the studio. Released on January 23, 1945, the film rolled up as many profits as *Hey, Rookie!* and film critics were unanimously sold on my performance. I remember one noted critic said the film was "well produced largely due to Ann Miller and Joe Besser . . . Besser is funny when given a break."

With two hits in a row, Cohn rushed my next film into production. *Talk About a Lady*, which took only five weeks to film, was wrapped up in March of 1945. I then returned to New York to be with Ernie, who had gone home after *Eadie Was a Lady* was finished.

Until Cohn decided on my next project, I was able to consider other offers for the first time in a year. *Talk About a Lady* would premiere in theaters in the spring of 1946—and would be my third consecutive hit. Afterwards Cohn was unsure about my future. In the meantime, he gave me his blessings to accept any work that came my way. The offer I accepted came from an unlikely source: Milton Berle.

Berle wanted me to appear as a guest on his weekly NBC radio program, *Let Yourself Go*, which was sponsored by Eversharp, the world's leading manufacturer of pens and pencils. Each week Berle did a thirty-minute Ziegfield-styled variety show. He was capably aided by regulars such as Connie Russell, Ray Bloch and his Orchestra, and Kenny Roberts, the show's announcer.

Milton's material was always geared to insult his guests or members of the audience, making him a "master of the put-down." I remember once when he turned to a gentleman in the audience and said, "Oh, I see it's novelty night. You're out with your wife!"

Miltie had caught my earlier performances on Benny's and Allen's programs. Since that time he'd followed my career with interest. Irving Mansfield, the show's producer, made Berle's offer to me and I immediately accepted it. I trusted Irving because he was such a good friend. I couldn't think of anyone I'd rather work for than Berle; he was a class comedian in every respect.

My first appearance on Berle's program was on April 18, 1945, and it created a hit with listeners, who deluged NBC with mail for weeks. After that Berle made me a regular. I remember Milton was having a terrible time with girls on one show, and he needed to talk to somebody who was an "expert on women." Kenny Roberts introduced me the same way he did every week. "Well, it just so happens, Milton, we have an expert waiting outside . . . Come in, come in! Will you please come in!"

"Don't rush m-e-e-e!!" I'd scream, prancing out like an elf. "Stop p-u-s-h-i-n-g!!"

"Besser," says Berle stunned, "don't tell me you're an expert on women?"

"Why certainly, you crazy yooouuu!!"

"Well, then, Besser," says Miltie, "tell me how do you make out with women?"

"Well, the other night, I went over to my girl's house," I'd explain, "and I bought her a box of chocolates . . . And pretty soon she turned the lights down *real* low . . ."

"She turned the lights down low?" repeated Berle.

"Yes."

"What happened then?" asked Miltie.

"I ate the ch-o-c-o-l-a-t-e-s!!!"

When Berle wasn't frustrated with women, he was in a quandary over how he was going to put on a banquet for his sponsors. I happened to be a banquet connoisseur:

"Besser, what did *you* ever have to do with any big parties?" Berle would ask.

"Well, last week," I explained, "I handled a big party of 300!"

"A party of 300?" says Berle. "What was it?"

"My girl S-o-p-h-i-e!!"

"Besser, I'm not talking about your girl Sophie," he'd say. "My sponsor likes fancy dishes. Do you know any fancy dishes?"

"Well, the last banquet I arranged," I'd explain, "I tried something new. I put Mexican jumping beans in the meat loaf!"

"Well, how did the guests like it?" asked Berle.

"What?"

"I said," he repeated, "how did the guests like it?"

"I don't know . . . They haven't come down yet!!!"

I remember the audience laugh-o-meter practically broke its decible readings another week when Milton portrayed a frustrated playwright and I played an established playwright waiting in the wings.

"Besser, if you're a playwright," said Berle, "tell me, how many plays have you written?"

"I wrote 3000 plays in two weeks!" I boasted.

"Come, come, Besser," says Berle in disbelief, "How could you possibly write 3000 plays in two weeks?"

"I used carbon p-a-p-e-r!!"

"Besser, I want you to write a play I could be in," said Miltie.

"I've got a play," I said. "It's called, 'One Meat Ball.'"

"'One Meat Ball'?" said Berle. "Is there a *role* in it for me?"

"Of course not," I'd say. "You get *no* rolls with just one meat b-a-l-l!!"

Miltie and I had a million laughs working together. He never held back my creativity. Besides anybody who could put up with my ad libbing couldn't be all that bad! I ad libbed a lot on Berle's show and each time I did, he busted up laughing in the middle of his straight line. Finally he would retort, in razor-sharp fashion: "There'll be no ad libbing on my show, son!"

At first Berle started me out as an infrequent guest on his program. I played the "Mr. Know-It-All" character on his show who happened to come out just at the moment when Milton needed advice. My bits usually lasted ten minutes. I was either the world's greatest traveler, a famous baseball player, an income tax authority, or a country western teacher. You name it, I played it!

Each week the zaniness continued.

Meanwhile, with me being a permanent fixture on Berle's radio program, Ernie and I decided to make a more permanent home in the New York area. We rented out our old house in Astoria and bought a new home in Jackson Heights, which is a suburb of Long Island. The house was quite a spread and more than we actually needed, but with the money I was making at Columbia and as a regular on Berle's show it was silly to put it into anything else.

Our home had three floors. In the basement we set up a mini-theater with seats and an enclosed projection booth, so that when company came over we could screen a popular movie after dinner. Harry Cohn had an arrangement with me that if there was ever any Columbia film I wanted to borrow, it was okay with him.

The main floor to the house included a spacious living room, a Colonial-styled dining room and kitchen. Upstairs we had four bedrooms and two baths. Anna occupied one room, while Ernie and I slept in the master bedroom. The other two rooms were guest rooms for when we entertained.

It took us less than a year to completely settle in. In January of 1946, we decided to bring in the new year right by throwing a housewarming party. The party was also meant to toast my new success as a regular on Berle's radio show. We invited more than fifty guests including Fred Allen, Jack Benny and Mary Livingston, Artie Hershkowitz, Al Hirschfield, Joe Bigelow, Irving Mansfield, Jackie Susann, Eddie Cantor, Kenny Roberts and, of course, "Mr. Comedy" himself: Milton Berle.

Ernie and I spent more than two hours preparing for the party. We decorated tables, set out party favors and worked with a professional caterer we had hired. (I sampled the food to make sure it was edible.) We spent close to one thousand dollars just on food and champagne.

The party was a big disaster, however. For wouldn't you know it, it snowed that night!

By 8 p.m. more than six feet of snow had fallen on New York. And more was coming by the bootloads! It crippled roadways and transportation systems, and we couldn't get out of either the front or back doors; they were snowed in, solid. The milkman let us out the next morning when he shoveled our driveway to make his delivery!

Our party was ruined. None of our guests showed. They all called to bow out at the last minute. I was so miserable afterwards I cried in my champagne!

On nights like those, when Ernie and I were shut ins, radio was the only form of entertainment to keep us from getting bored. But around that time, I remember spotting small boxes with five-inch screens in store windows. They began sprouting up all over New York and throughout the country and they were selling for $495 apiece at some stores. Blurry images danced across the screens. The programs that were broadcast were "experimental," and I remember when somebody said these things called televisions were eventually going to put movie theaters out of business I laughed. Then on May 9, 1946, I became "a guinea pig" on the first live, hour-long entertainment series of any kind produced for network television. It was a variety series called *Hour Glass*.

Standard Brands, which had been one of the first sponsors of one-hour radio variety shows, sponsored this historical first. It was broadcast on NBC, and aired locally on NBC's affiliate WNBT. The show followed the standard radio formula of songs, comedy acts, and skits, punctuated by a long commercial. I re-created my famous army drill with Jimmy Little. The rest of the program's roundup featured Doodles Weaver, doing a comedy rabbit act, actors James Monks and Paul Douglas in a smart melodrama called *Moonshine*, and the Spanish dance team of Enrica and Novello. The show was hosted by Evelyn Eaton and it was an instant hit with local audiences. More than 20,000 people (approximately 3,500 sets) tuned in for the first broadcast!

There were several minor drawbacks to this first commercial broadcast, however. Television was such a primitive medium that nobody had the proper knowledge of how to light sound stages to filter out shadows without burning the cast alive! On the night of the broadcast we performed on a small sound stage that became so hot from the multitude of lights,each performer had to swallow salt tablets and water before going on. It was worse than a sauna!

The images that appeared on television screens were fuzzy. Everyone looked like a demon straight out of a Universal horror movie! In time, of course, television resolved those technical problems and became a very competitive medium. Many of radio's greatest comedians pioneered the new medium. I was there, too.

In the summer of 1946, when Milton Berle's radio program went into hiatus, I had plenty to whoop about (but decided *no* parties this time) when the Eversharp people gave me my own radio program. It was a thirty-minute variety show called *Tonight on Broadway*. It also featured Jane Froman and Kenny Roberts and was broadcast on CBS every Sunday night. I recreated my Mr. Know-It-All character for listeners, using new material. I starred in the show all summer long. Kenny Roberts and I then returned to Berle's program in the fall as regulars, where we remained until the show was cancelled in 1948.

One night, while *Tonight on Broadway* was on the air a famous theatrical producer showed up in the audience. Leonard Sillman was his name. Sillman had a real affection for the theater, and he had helped promote the careers of such potential stage celebrities as Henry Fonda, Imogene Coca, John Lund, Libby Holman, and Eve Arden. He had lent a helping hand to the highly successful productions of *Low and Behold* and *Fools Rush In*. Now Sillman was producing a swing version of the Cinderella tale entitled, *If the Shoe Fits*. He was interested in having me star in the show.

I had met Leonard briefly before. The night Berle's program went on hiatus, Sillman expressed his interest in seeing me perform again. I suggested he could come and watch me do my show with Jane Froman.

"Should I sit in the audience," he said, "and watch you?"

"Yes," I told him, "and you'll see a nice reaction."

It was apparent Leonard knew very little about me until that night. When I walked out at the beginning of the show the audience roared with laughter and never stopped. When the show was over, Sillman visited me backstage. His eyes were bugged out and he was stunned by the audience's reaction.

"Gee, I didn't know you were that well known!" he said.

Never one to brag, I said: "You want to know something? Neither did I!"

Afterwards Leonard sat down with me and my agent and quickly worked out an agreement. I was to star in the role of Herman, an amorous barrel-chested mouse who turns into a coachman. My salary would start at $1,000 a week and I was to receive top billing with Leila Ernst, who played the part of Cinderella. Also in the cast were Florence Desmond as Lady Eve, a most unusual fairy godmother, and Eddie Lambert as rotund King Cole. Musical arrangements for the show were by David Raksin, and the choreographer was Charles Weidman. Edward Gilbert's settings, which included an operable storybook, brought life to this famous fairy tale.

After two weeks of rehearsal, *If the Shoe Fits* opened in the third week of November 1946 at a theater in Detroit. I was ready to quit the first week there. I have never been a quitter, but so many things went haywire with the show—which I warned Sillman about—that I contemplated leaving more than once. Not even a fairy godmother could have helped me!

In the first place, Leonard never gave me the billing we had agreed upon. In Detroit, the theater had me billed at the *bottom*, in small letters.

"I don't go on," I told Leonard, "unless that's changed to the same letters as Leila. Otherwise you can get somebody else."

Well, workers hurried like employees on an assembly line and pulled down the old letters and put up the new ones. This temporarily satisfied me, until other problems surfaced that made working in the show unbearable.

After one week in Detroit, where reviews were poor, the show moved to Cincinnati. On opening night my opening scene was completely ruined when the chariot I drove broke down—and it could have been prevented. Designed in the shape of a pumpkin, the chariot was actually battery driven. The chariot had a lever that was turned to steer it instead of a normal steering wheel. I had warned Leonard, on numerous occasions, the lever was incompatible with the size and weight of the chariot.

"One of these days," I warned, "this damn thing is going to cause you trouble if you don't fix it."

Leonard never listened.

Consequently, during the scene, I was unable to straighten out the chariot. The lever jammed and the chariot made a perfect bullseye into the storybook, which was resting on another platform on top of the stage. It shattered the platform.

I was able to climb down from the chariot unhurt and lend a hand to Florence Desmond (who I had been trying to pick up). I was displeased with what had happened, but I turned to the audience and said, "A very cheap pumpkin . . . Very cheap!"

I got laughs, although I was sick at heart.

The show closed in Cincinnati after one week, where critics were just as harsh as they had been in Detroit. Our next stop was Boston, which looked as though it would be the show's burial grounds. Instead, my attorney Artie Hershkowitz came to the rescue. He brought a writer named Nat Hiken with him to Boston. (Nat later developed TV's *Sgt. Bilko*, which starred Phil Silvers).

Artie had heard rumors that the show was in trouble. It was no rumor, and he hired Nat to write new material for me, which definitely helped. I worked the material in while we were in Boston, and reviews for the show improved. I found out, however, that one man cannot save a show.

Even though the audiences loved my performances, I wasn't satisfied with the show as a whole. It was overwritten and the music was overdone, which caused the story to suffer. For the most part, I remember the musical numbers were terrible. We sang songs with such catchy lyrics as: "Early in the morning the birds begin to sing/Early in the morning I don't know a thing!"

Songwriter David Raksin even had a special song written for me, which I also hated. It went like this: "I'm a little mouse/I never get soused." One night I finally asked the orchestra leader, "Who wrote this *thing*?"

As a result, *If the Shoe Fits* closed in Boston after one week. The final test followed in New York. We opened on December 5, 1946, at the Century Theater near Central Park, but the show flopped. Critics raked us over the coals. I recall one critic said "the Cinderella story has been steamed up, boiled down and steeped in so-called sophistication until its *originator* wouldn't know it."

Well, Cinderella's originator certainly wouldn't want to remember Leonard Sillman's version, especially after what happened at the Century Theater on opening night. It was one for the Guiness Book of Records!

In the scene that introduced me in the show, the storybook opened up and, revealed a woodpile box with a stool set in half a room with a doorway. I was the mouse, dressed in a gray mouse suit with an itsy bitsy tail, who came out of the woodpile. To do that I had to run beneath the stage and come through a secret door that led to the woodpile. The audiences were always in awe over my appearances, since I always appeared out of the woodpile just as the book finished opening. They often wondered, "How did he do that?"

On this particular night, they found out "how" when the trap door got stuck! The music crescendoed to my entrance as the storybook opened mechanically, as scheduled. But, whaddya know? No Joe! I was underneath, pounding on the trap door!

Nothing worked, so I finally ran up the stairway to the top of the stage and then skidded across the stage. The audience laughed and applauded when I said dramatically: "I made it! The trap door was stuck!"

I got more laughs joking about how *bad* the show was, which really was unfortunate because the show could have been good. As it turned out *If the Shoe Fits* closed, for good, one week later.

Meanwhile, through most of 1947, I made personal appearances at movie theaters where I reprised my old army drill routine. And what happened to Leonard Sillman? *If the Shoe Fits* put him into rags instead of riches.

Chapter 14

The Movies and Lou Costello

For the first time in three years, I was faced with several uncertainties about my future at Columbia. Uncertainties with a capital "U."

In December 1947, even though he didn't have any properties for me to star in at the beginning of the year, Harry Cohn renewed my contract for another year. Earlier he had starred me in a comedy two-reeler called *Waiting in the Lurch*, billed under Columbia's "All-Star Comedy" banner. But it wasn't released until two years later. At that time Cohn reassigned me to my own short subject series, entitled "Joe Besser Comedies," and for the next six years I filmed one short subject a year, under the direction of Jules White . . . Yes, the same man who once said I wasn't cut out for motion pictures!

Meanwhile, my present situation made me anxious for more work. I still performed every Sunday night on Milton Berle's radio program, but it wasn't enough. I realized Hollywood could be a *jungle* at times (at least that's what Johnny Weismuller once said!). So, in order to survive in this business, I had to get other deals cooking. If not, I would be cooked!

Since my contract at Columbia never prohibited me from working for other studios, in January of 1948, with my single ambition being to make more movies, I talked Ernie into letting me return to Hollywood to look for work. I set up house at the Knickerbocker Hotel and before I even had a chance to start looking for work, my phone rang. It was producer Leonard Goldstein from Universal Pictures calling. Boy, word traveled f-a-s-t!!

"Leonard Goldstein!" I exclaimed.

"Joe Besser!" Leonard exclaimed back.

"Ooh, you copy!" I quipped.

Leonard laughed, then he turned serious with me. He told me that my old friend George Sherman was directing a new picture for Universal called, *Feudin' Fussin' and a-Fightin'.*

"*'Feudin' Fussin' and a-Fightin'*?" I said. "That sounds like the life story of Rocky Graziano!"

"No, Joe," said Leonard, "it's a comedy."

"Oh."

George had directed me in *Talk About a Lady*, so he had recommended me to Leonard for the role of a small-town sheriff, Sharkey Dolan, from the town of Rimrock. The film was a comedy western and starred Donald O'Connor, Marjorie Main, and Percy Kilbride. I couldn't refuse with this kind of company.

Universal was also quickly becoming a comic's haven. The studio's most popular feature film series starred Abbott and Costello, who were the studio's biggest moneymakers. Later, Universal created two new comedy feature film series: Ma and Pa Kettle, with Marjorie Main and Percy Kilbride, and Francis the Talking Mule.

I hoped to become a part of Universal's stable of talent. Even though I considered Columbia my home, I realized Universal was clearly a land of opportunity (which was more than I could say for some swamp land I owned in Florida).

Fortunately, I had no trouble fitting in. Donald was a delight to work with. We became good friends. Everyday after filming he stopped by to visit with Ernie and me before going home. Our paths had crossed once before when he was part of a dancing act with his mother and brothers. They played on the same bill with me at the RKO Keith Theater in Union, New Jersey. Donald was the youngest entertainer there; he was five years old.

But age never stood between us. Donald was pretty outgoing when he introduced himself to me at the age of five. "Mr. Besser," he said, impishly. "I'm Donald O'Connor. Mother has told me quite a lot about you."

"Don't believe everything you hear!" I said.

Donald blushed, then he said, "No, honestly, I'm glad you're working with us."

Well, what could I do for an encore?

I took Donald on a trip to the drugstore. Every day, between shows, I used to take him to the corner drugstore and buy him a candy bar or we would play the pinball machines. Donald could never reach the handles, so I always lifted him up so he could shoot the pinballs.

From playing pinball Donald went on to become a big star. At age 12, he made his film debut in the 1938 musical, *Sing You Sinners*, with Bing Crosby, long before his great fifties musicals. The film was a tremendous hit, and after that Donald's career flourished. Later, in 1952, Donald's dancing talents were further exploited in the MGM classic. *Singing in the Rain*, that co-starred Debbie Reynolds and Gene Kelly. Oh, yes, I almost forgot. Donald also played second banana to Francis the Talking Mule in the same series of films for Universal in the 1950s.

When Donald and I were reunited for *Feudin' Fussin' and a-Fightin'*, seeing each other was like turning back the hour glass. We reminisced about our vaudeville days and talked shop in general. Donald frequently asked me for tips on how to play comical scenes. Now the only difference from the first time we had worked together was that when we played the pinball machines together Donald could reach the handles himself!

Marjorie Main also made filming *Feudin' Fussin' and a-Fightin'* a pure joy for me. She was every bit as funny in person as her horsey characterization on the screen, but in a quiet way. She was always gentle and kind and more subdued when she was not working.

Marjorie's voice was real, too. At first I thought she gargled with rusty razor blades to get her voice that way, but I later found that this rumor wasn't true.

Seriously, Marjorie had to be the most health-conscious person I have ever met. She would have put Jane Fonda to shame! She never wrote a diet and exercise book, but she did ride her bicycle around the studio to keep in shape. She also was one of the fussiest women I ever knew.

I remember Marjorie was deathly afraid of catching other people's germs. When George Sherman first introduced me to her, Marjorie reached out to shake hands with me, only her hands were covered with white cotton gloves! She never shook hands without them. She would have made the surgeon general wary!

With my new film career taking off, I became convinced I needed to make Hollywood my permanent home. New York was suitable for actors who worked on stage and on radio, but not for actors who were motion picture stars. The minute you left Hollywood and you later returned for work a producer would say: "What's your name again?"

I kept this in mind in early June of 1948 when Leonard Goldstein called. The studio was planning a promotional tour in conjunction with the July release of *Feudin' Fussin' and a-Fightin'*. The tour was going to make stops in midwestern towns such as: Omaha, Nebraska; Sioux City, Iowa; St. Cloud, Minnesota; Tulsa, Oklahoma; and many other towns east of the Rockies. Leonard said they would be sending Percy Killbride, Marjorie Main, and a new star the studio wanted to promote—Shelley Winters. He wanted me to participate in the tour, too. (Donald O'Conner was unable to go because he had begun production on a new picture for Universal.)

Rather than travel from coast to coast every time I was needed in Hollywood, Ernie and I decided to follow Horace Greeley's advice. We sold our homes in Jackson Heights and Astoria, packed our bags, and moved west to an English Route-styled home in North Hollywood, where we still live. We arrived by train the first week in July of 1948 and brought Anna to live with us.

I was thrilled to be in California. It meant no more harsh winters (and no more milkmen to dig Ernie and me out). No more cabs or subways to catch. No more muggy summers. Nope. We were in the Sunshine State: the land of the milk and honey, the home of the California orange, the capital of . . . cough, cough, cough . . . smog! (Well, you can't have everything, you know!)

Universal hired a band of movers to transfer all our belongings. The moving company was called the Seven Brothers. But, as it turned out, only *six* of them worked because our furniture never arrived the same day we did. Our house also wasn't carpeted. What dilemmas!

The tour left the next day. Rather than worry, I rented a couple of beds for Ernie and Anna to sleep in and cooking utensils for them to cook their meals in before I left. I also came up with another brainstorm (of course, everything in my brain *is* a storm!). I phoned Leonard Goldstein about buying carpet from Universal. Since the studio purchased their carpet wholesale and in bulk, it would be cheaper for me to buy mine from them. "Joe, don't worry about it," said Leonard. "It's as good as done."

In the meantime, I went on the Universal promotional tour, and the crowds who turned out at the theaters were overflowing. The lines stretched a block long and wrapped around the theaters! I did my old comedy act, including the water bit, with Jimmy Brown, who worked as my straight man and was also the master of ceremonies for each show.

Marjorie and I performed a vintage comedy skit together. The old hot water bottle gag where she stuck a funnel down in front of my pants and then poured water in it while I counted to ten before dropping a coin into the funnel from my head! (Ooh, was the water c-o-l-d!!)

Shelley Winters wowed audiences with her singing and, when the tour ended, we all celebrated in Shelley's hotel room. (She didn't write about *that* in her book!)

During the party, Leonard Goldstein called. He had good news for me. "Joe," he said, "you've been doing a great job for us so I have a surprise for you. Your house has been completely carpeted."

I couldn't believe it. I thought there had to be a catch somewhere. "How much do I owe you?" I asked.

"You owe us exactly nothing!" Leonard said.

"Nothing?" I repeated.

"Yes, Joe," Leonard said, "nothing! It's a gift from me and from Universal to you and your lovely wife for all the good work you've done during the tour."

When I returned home, I could have cried with happiness. Sure enough, Leonard had the entire house carpeted: the living room, dining room and hallway. The carpenters he had hired did such a good job that we still have the same carpet in our house today.

While I was gone, however, Anna's health had begun to fail. She was 87 years old and suffering from a severe case of glaucoma (which, during its critical stage, can make a person go blind) and homesickness. When we came out to California on the train, Anna had told Ernie and me shortly before we left the New York train station, "Children, this will be my last ride."

After we moved to California, I noticed Anna was starting to deteriorate physically. She wasn't used to the new surroundings she was in and she didn't know her way around like she did back in Jackson Heights. And this contributed to her slow demise. Taking her out of her familiar environment was probably a dumb move. I had thought the warmer California climate would help prolong her life. Anna refused to accept her new surroundings, however. In August of 1948, she died of natural causes.

Anna's death left a definite void in our lives, as Ernie and I had grown accustomed to her company. Anna had been a big part of our family and her death was, of course, very sad for both of us.

About this time, Leonard Goldstein phoned me again. Universal wanted to send the cast of *Feudin' Fussin and a-Fightin'* on another promotional tour through the western part of the United States. When I told Leonard Ernie's mother had just died, he immediately offered his condolences and suggested a remedy for Ernie's grief. "Joe, take Ernie with you," he said, compassionately. "It will be good for her to get out of the house and I'll pay for her way."

Well, bless Leonard's soul. Bringing Ernie along with me proved to be the best tonic for her. We locked up the house, and for two weeks Ernie enjoyed the company of Marjorie Main, Percy Kilbride, and Shelley Winters. The tour was just as successful as the first one and there wasn't one person in one theater who didn't yuck it up, including Ernie. The laughter helped mend her broken heart.

Meanwhile, working at Universal helped me in another department:

I broadened my contacts. I did more handshaking and "how do you dos" than the President of the United States! Thus, more people became aware of my talents, which I hoped would ensure more jobs for me along the way.

Likewise, Ernie and I created a new group of friends now that we were permanently entrenched in Hollywood. Marjorie Main and Ernie became good friends. And I ran into an old acquaintance at a nearby drugstore who lived less than one mile from me on Auckland Avenue: Shemp Howard. Shemp invited Ernie and me over for dinner to meet his wife Gertrude. In no time, we began seeing each other every week. We also visited again with my old film pal Charlie Barton and his wife.

Another man also came back into my life at this time. We went on to become very dear friends, and he later confessed to me that he had idolized my character for some time. He had visited me on the set of *Feudin' Fussin' and a-Fightin'* and he was known throughout the world as the "Heeey, Abbott!" kid: Lou Costello.

Lou's real name was Louis Francis Cristillo. He was born in Paterson, New Jersey, where he first embraced the idea of becoming a comedian. I remember he once told me his first opportunity to show off his comedic talents came when he won a prize at a Halloween party for his impression of his idol, Charlie Chaplin. In school, Lou was always getting into trouble. One day, his teacher made him write one hundred times on the blackboard: "I'm a bad boy!" (This later became one of Lou's trademark phrases.)

In 1927, Hollywood-bound, Lou left home with his childhood friend Gene Coogan and became a stuntman at MGM. After his partner became homesick, however, Lou returned to Paterson, which is where we first met in 1928. I was playing at the Lyric Theater, and for one week Lou attended every show to watch me perform. Lou was thinner then; he was not the roly-poly funnyman everybody remembers.

After every show Lou came back to my dressing room to talk about comedy. He never left my side. I soon became his favorite, and I later realized my style and mannerisms undoubtedly influenced him. When Lou became the comic half to Bud Abbott, he incorporated some of my childlike inflections in his own character. Not intentionally, though. I'm sure these things just rubbed off on Lou from hanging around with me. It's only natural, and I never begrudged him one bit for what he did. Instead, I was honored that he had such a high esteem for my work.

In 1928, Lou heard that the Lyceum, a local vaudeville theater, was searching for a Dutch comic. Evidently the comic straight man on the bill, Bud

Abbott, made the request after his partner became sick. It was this historic engagement that brought about Lou's teaming with Bud Abbott and from then on their joint careers knew no bounds. They signed with Universal Pictures in 1940 and by 1942 they were named "America's number one box office attractions." Their fast-talking routines, including the classic one "Who's on First?" left audiences hysterical. At Universal, their films reportedly grossed more than one hundred and forty million dollars, lifting the studio out of mediocrity. This tremendous success story prompted one studio executive to say: "Thank God for Abbott and Costello!"

Lou married a beautiful brunette chorus girl by the name of Anne Battler while they were appearing together in a show in New York, in 1934. Lou and Anne later became the proud parents of three lovely daughters—Patricia, Carole Lou, and Christine. Louis Francis, Jr. (nicknamed "Butch"), their only son, who tragically drowned several days before his first birthday.

Lou's name never came up in my life again until 1945. At the time I had left *Son's of Fun* and Bud and Lou were headlining at the Roxy Theater in New York, where they were doing a benefit. One night the manager of the Roxy called and asked me to replace them when Bud and Lou got into one of their bad rifts, so bad that they were not speaking to each other.

I went on in their place and performed my army drill. Even though the audience realized Abbott and Costello were supposed to headline the show, they laughed at my antics anyway. After the first show I realized how much the comedy team of Abbott and Costello meant to the American public when a reporter from *The New York Times* called me.

"There's a rumor," he said, "that you're going to take Lou's place and work with Bud Abbott. Is that true?"

I had replaced them at the Roxy and I was already being picked by the media to succeed Lou. This wouldn't be the last time, either. Later, after they split up, Bud called me about joining him for a new act. He wanted me to play Lou's part, but I graciously declined. Nobody could replace Lou. (Bud needed the money then, however, so he got Candy Candido to team up with him instead. They played a series of nightclub engagements but their act fizzled faster than seltzer water.)

Meanwhile, I flatly denied there was any truth to the rumor.

"If that's true," I said, "I've never heard about it. Besides, nobody can ever replace Lou."

The man continued to persist. I finally put his aggression to rest when I said, "They'll never split up and you can print that!"

And, they didn't break up—until twelve years later in 1957.

Meanwhile, Lou read *The Times* article and the next day I received the following note from him. It said:

Thanks, Joe, for sticking up for me. You are truly a friend.

Best wishes,
Lou

In 1946, I finally saw Lou for the first time since his heydays with Bud Abbott. He and Bud were filming their latest comedy for Universal, *Little Giant*. I was in Hollywood at the time and went by the studio on a whim to see him. Lou gave me a big bear hug and the Universal publicists had a field day. They sent for their best photographer and together Lou and I posed for a series of photographs in which I pretended to smash him with my fist!

Later, when Universal put me in *Feudin' Fussin' and a-Fightin'*, Lou looked me up again. He always stopped by to watch me run through my scene. He and Bud were filming a comedy feature for Eagle Lion at the time, *The Noose Hangs High*, Lou and I became good friends.

Following Anna's death, Lou asked me if I would be interested in working with him and Bud in their next picture. They were making a comedy spoof of every Hollywood jungle movie called, *Africa Screams*. It was being filmed at the old Nassour Studios in Hollywood (which is now the Los Angeles TV station, KTTV-Channel 11), where the boys were on loan from Universal.

Lou was the type of person who always surrounded himself with his friends. He never forgot them. Thus, the film's supporting cast came as no surprise. Lou cast boxing greats Max and Buddy Baer, both friends of his, in minor roles, as well as Hillary Brooke, a future member of the team's TV series, and Shemp Howard (then a member of the Three Stooges, taking Curly's place), as a near-sighted gunman, who also was a favorite of Lou's. (Shemp had previously appeared in a handful of Abbott and Costello features at Universal.) To add authenticity, big game hunter-actor Frank Buck and lion tamer Clyde Beatty made brief appearances in the film, too. And Lou's old friend—and mine—Charlie Barton was brought in to direct the picture. Charlie had directed the best of the Abbott and Costello films, including *Abbott and Costello Meet Frankenstein*. I played a comedy butler in *Africa Screams* and Charlie asked me to re-create the old water bit I had first used in *Son's of Fun*.

Many times the off-camera shenanigans were funnier than anything we did on film. I had heard many funny stories about what it was like to work in an Abbott and Costello film, and every one of them was true. Between scenes, Bud and Lou gambled in their dressing rooms—many times for high stakes. For fun they ran all over the sound stage with custard pies and seltzer bottles. Lou went around throwing pies at everyone. He did it to relieve tension between scenes. Each day on his way to the studio Lou would pick up custard and cream delicacies from a bakery in the San Fernando Valley. He spent close to $4,500 on pies alone for this one picture! In Lou's mind it was worth it. "They're too good to eat!" he said.

One day Max Baer was bragging to everyone about how he hadn't been hit by a pie yet. Little did he know that Lou was plotting to hit him next and I was in on Lou's plan. Somehow Max found out. When Lou ran in front of Max, taking dead aim with the pie, I was standing to Max's right on the sidelines and I burst out laughing. Max ducked and I was the one who wound up with the pie in my face!

Bobby Barber also contributed to the fun. He was Lou's "stooge." He was a nice little guy, bald like me, and everybody picked on him, including Lou. He'd either get stuck with the dirty work, or he'd take the brunt of Lou's own dirty work. I remember one day when we were eating at the studio's commissary, Lou took a bowl of soup and, for no reason, spilled it over Bobby's head. It was chicken noodle, so the noodles clung to Bobby's face like worms. Bobby took it all in stride, though; he picked up Lou's bowl of soup and splashed it over Lou's head!

This kind of fooling around annoyed Eddie Nassour, the studio president. He never liked Bud and Lou's childish pranks, especially Lou's, since the film went over budget. Originally, *Africa Screams* (nicknamed "Nassour Screams" because of Eddie's frequent outbursts over the film's rising costs) was scheduled to be filmed in seventeen days; instead it took twenty-seven, ten days over budget, to complete.

Some actors who were deathly serious about their craft also found it hard to deal with Bud and Lou's antics. You had to possess a certain temperament to work in such a circus. Hillary Brooke admitted to me that she considered quitting after the first day. This was her first picture with Abbott and Costello, and she had never experienced so many looney tunes in her life. Lou's constant ad libbing in their scenes together also killed her. Hillary had come from working in the theater, so she was accustomed to actors following their cue lines; Lou didn't. She finally phoned her agent and wanted out of the picture. Her agent convinced Hillary to give it another try. She did, and, afterwards, I'm sure, Hillary never regretted it.

Hillary rolled with the punches (and pies) and started coming up with silly things on her own. One day Hillary and I were on our lunch hour, still dressed in our expedition costumes, when she suggested we pull a stunt on Harry Cohn. We walked over to Cohn's office in the Columbia studios. When we walked in, Harry was busy working on some paperwork. He looked up and gave both of us the strangest look—especially me. I was carrying an elephant gun and I said, "Okay, Harry, when's my next job?" Harry bowled over with laughter and the story that I "held up the boss" circulated the studio for days.

One of the best incidents during the shooting of *Africa Screams*, however, involved Shemp Howard. Shemp was afraid of everything and anything, from French poodles to water. I remember in one scene the entire cast was supposed to take a ride on a raft in the studio tank, representing the Congo River. Shemp got extremely nervous (the raft was being pulled by another boat). The raft was stacked to the rim with trunks and supplies and Shemp and I sat on top, back to back, to guard the cargo. The water was only four feet deep, but it was deep enough to launch Shemp into a frenzy. He was afraid he was going to drown.

"Shemp, the water's only four feet deep," I reasoned.

"I know," Shemp panicked, "but you can drown in there."

"No, you won't," I said. "Put your hand in back and hold on to me."

So Shemp took a grip around my shirt, and he gripped it so hard that he almost tore it off! He was that scared!

Finally, they had to stop filming when Shemp got seasick. Everybody abandoned ship but they left poor Shemp up there by himself. He wanted to come down but nobody would help him. "Will someone get me down from here?" he screamed. "How much longer do I have to stay up here? Hurry up, fellas, I'm getting sick!!"

Everybody laughed uproariously and finally I said, "Fellas, he's really sick." So we helped Shemp down to safety and the first stop Shemp made was the bathroom.

That evening, when Shemp and I returned to our dressing rooms, I witnessed another dimension of Shemp's anxiety: his fear of death. The dressing rooms were below street level and the only way of getting above ground was by way of a stairway that led up to the street. Shemp and I shared the same dressing room and as he began washing off his makeup over the sink, a terrific earthquake shook the building. Shemp had his pants half way down so he kept tripping over his costume as he made a run for it.

"Every man for himself!" Shemp screamed. "Goodbye, Joe. This is it!"

"Oh, shut up!" I said. "We're not going anywhere."

I must admit, I laughed a lot watching Shemp trip over himself even though I was scared, too. Finally, we climbed up the stairs near the dressing room and the stairs shook so bad that I had to drag a frightened Shemp up to safety.

Later, after Shemp and I returned to redress ourselves, I offered to give Shemp a ride home. Another fear: he was afraid of automobiles; he didn't drive. What next? (I knew Shemp wasn't kidding. He used to take the bus to go fishing in his spare time. He would take the bus to Hollywood and then transfer to a street car that took him to the Santa Monica pier.)

"Shemp, that's hogwash," I said. "There's nothing to be afraid of."

"Oh yeah," he said shaking. "The brakes will probably go out and we'll be killed!"

"Trust me, Shemp," I said. "I'll drive real slow."

I had been driving less than a year at the time. Believe it or not, Shemp's premonition proved true: my brakes *did* go out! Shemp didn't know, however, because I just whistled and sang songs as though nothing was wrong. Then I remember an old trick a friend once told me: if your brakes ever go out, use the hand brake instead and put the car in third when it comes time to stop. Fortunately, it worked and I got Shemp home safely before he caught on.

During the months that followed the filming of *Africa Screams* and its eventual release in 1949, Ernie and I became quite close to Lou Costello and his family, spending hours visiting him, Anne, and the kids at their Longridge estate in Sherman Oaks (the place had twenty-two rooms and it was Lou's palatial playground). Lou was a good-hearted and giving man. I never detected the kinds of things several writers have written about him—that he was always having temper tantrums or that he was demanding.

On screen, Lou played a sweet little guy who made a lot of mistakes and was the perfect patsy for Bud—or anyone else. In real life, however, Lou was a good family man and he made most of the decisions for the team, including which routines they would use in their films. Lou had a human side, too; he had his good days and bad days like everybody else. But I can easily say he had more good days than bad ones with me.

As far as Bud Abbott was concerned, I never knew him as well as I did Lou, so I cannot delve into his personality. I do know that Bud was always quiet and even-tempered and that he never let his personal problems interfere with his work. If he was frustrated, he would take it out in the dressing room, whereas Lou would take out his frustrations in front of people.

They say comedians eventually grow into their characters; in Lou's case, he was childlike in his actions and I'm sure he never meant any harm. Charlie Barton once illustrated my point with a very funny story about Lou. At Universal Lou carried a tremendous amount of clout and he used it in a playful way. During almost every Abbott and Costello picture Charlie directed, props would inevitably disappear from the set. Once a grandfather clock was missing. Nobody knew where it went. It turned out Lou had had a truck come to the studio, pick up the clock, and deliver it to his house! Another time, a canoe disappeared. It had become a planter in front of Lou's house!

Aside from his childlike antics, Lou was a very generous man. Together, he and Bud raised fourteen thousand dollars to pay off the mortgage of St. Anthony Catholic Church, where Lou had attended mass as a boy in Paterson. Later, they contributed thousands more to help build a new church. Then, during World War II, he and Bud raised millions of dollars selling war bonds nationwide. The proceeds went to the Emergency Relief Fund for soldiers' dependents.

Lou's most active charity, however, became the Lou Costello Youth Foundation, which is still in operation. With Bud's help, Lou created this recreational center for underprivileged children in the memory of his son, Butch. The center included libraries, medical clinics, a gymnasium, a baseball diamond, and many other facilities for children. The costs to run the center ran close to eighty thousand dollars a year, and Bud and Lou shared the costs on a fifty-fifty basis until Lou later absorbed most of the costs himself.

Every year at Christmas, as part of the center's annual activities, Lou would hold a Christmas party for the children in the gymnasium. As a favor to Lou, I would come dressed as Santa Claus and help him hand out the presents to the children. I remember Lou worked many long months before the party soliciting merchants in the area for toys that could be donated. Sometimes I don't know where Lou found the time, but he did because he loved children. Lou always felt the work was worthwhile when he saw the smiles on their faces.

Ernie and I really got our first taste of Lou's generosity at Christmas time. He and Anne loved Christmas. Their home was always decorated with multicolored lights, stand-up Santa Clauses, and gold garlands strung along the bottom of the roof. Ernie and I were the only non-family members who were invited to spend Christmas with Lou and the children. (Even though I was Jewish, Ernie and I celebrated Christmas instead of Hannukah.)

Ernie would help Anne decorate the tree, while Lou and I would sneak away into the projection room downstairs in the basement. Lou had converted this area into a minitheater, complete with theater-styled seats, after he bought the house. He owned the largest collection of old movies, next to William Randolph Hearst. He had prints of Universal classics such as *Frankenstein* and *Dracula*, as well as prints of his own films and many popular television shows. Lou gave me carte blanche to borrow films from his collection. I was welcome at any time, even when he wasn't home.

At Christmas, Lou handed out the presents inside the theater. He always bought so many expensive gifts that they were stacked on a pool table as high as the ceiling. Ernie and I helped Lou bring in the gifts and then took our places in the front row.

In 1949, our second Christmas with the Costellos, Lou proved why he was known as "Mr. Christmas" on his block. Ernie and I hadn't decorated our house with lights, so the week before Christmas Lou asked me, "Joe, don't you have any lights?"

"No, Lou," I said, "I didn't put up any because I don't own any. Besides, nobody else decorates their house on our block, so why should I?"

These words horrified Lou. It was un-American not to decorate your house at Christmas. Wait until Santa Claus heard about this!

"What are you, Scrooge or something?" he asked, wistfully.

"No."

"Well, then, you're going to decorate this year," he said, in his typical childlike voice.

"But, Lou," I reasoned, "I have no lights."

"You're going to get 'em," he said. "You're going to put 'em up even if I have to help ya put 'em up!"

The next day Lou came to the house with fifty boxes of lights. (Lou definitely believed in the old adage, "The more, the merrier.") When I opened the door, I saw a stack of boxes, but no Lou. Then I heard his voice.

"Joe, it's me," he said, struggling. "Here's your lights!"

I removed the top ten boxes and, sure enough, Lou was behind them. That afternoon, he helped me string the entire house and by nightfall we witnessed the wonders of our work: the entire house lit up! Lou had me string lights over every window, completely around the house, on the weather drains, across the roof, around the door frames—everywhere. He even brought candy canes to put around the front yard that also lit up. Our home looked like a substation for the electric company!

Afterwards Lou looked at me proudly, like a little kid seeing his dream come true. "See," he said. "I told ya you was going to have lights!"

Indeed we did—thanks to Lou.

Chapter 15

Hey, Stinky! You're a TV Star!

In 1950, all my handshaking at Universal proved worthwhile. I would appear in three feature films for the big "U" scheduled for release that year, and my career would prosper even more during the fifties.

I was constantly amazed that my career had already spanned three generations of fans, a world war, and six U.S. presidents. I had more lives than Morris the cat! It seemed my style of comedy was ageless. In the fifties, society went through rapid changes: teenagers started rockin' and rollin'. Many subjects—which I won't mention so this book will not be X-rated—that had previously been considered taboo were now deemed appropriate for movies. In the meantime, I never changed. I could play any character, in any time in history. Even if I put on a leather jacket, boots and sunglasses, I was still Joe Besser, and audiences continued to accept me.

I was grateful that my career had seen so many peaks and few valleys. The work at Universal couldn't have been more plentiful for me—not to mention convenient. The studio was only one mile from my home, so I didn't have to drive far. I could have jogged there in twenty minutes . . . but I'm not that crazy!

My next feature for Universal was an Arabian adventure film called, *The Desert Hawk*, starring Richard Greene, Yvonne DeCarlo, George Macready, Jackie Gleason, and a young Rock Hudson. Leonard Goldstein, who produced the film, remembered me from *Feudin' Fussin' and a-Fightin'* and hand-picked me for the character of Sinbad, a seller of phony maps. My partner in crime was Alladin, played by Jackie Gleason, a master of the old shell game. We were cast as the film's comic relief. Our director was Frederick DeCordova (who preferred to be called "Freddie"), now the producer of NBC's *Tonight Show* with Johnny Carson.

I had more fun working with Jackie Gleason on that film—and not only in front of the cameras either! Jackie was a one-man arson squad on the set. He was always up to no good. I think after all these years he's felt guilty about what he did to me during this film because for years prior to his death he sent me a Christmas card every year without fail. It just goes to show you what guilt will do.

Jackie was always playing practical jokes on me (of course, I always got even, so I was no saint). I remember we had to dress up every day in tunics (a costume that was like being wrapped in a bedsheet). Every morning we spent one hour wrapping ourselves in these cloths before reporting to the sound stage where we were filming. Since these wraps never had any pockets, I always improvised by pinning my money in a pouch inside. Jackie noticed how I concealed my pouch and already was scheming.

One morning before Jackie finished helping me wrap my tunic, he asked me to do him a favor. "Joe, if I give you my pouch of money," he said, "would you put it with yours?"

I obliged. "Sure," I said. "What are pals for?" I should have never used the term "pals" so freely, especially with Gleason.

As we started towards the set Jackie suddenly stopped me. "Hey, Joe," he said, "I want to buy a pack of cigarettes. Would you please give me my pouch?"

I unwrapped my tunic, and I took off the pin that held his pouch inside. I pulled it out, and Jackie said, "Give me one dollar."

I gave Jackie one dollar. Then I put back his pouch, repinned my tunic, and we headed for the sound stage. But twenty minutes later, following a take, Jackie called upon me again. "Joe, I want to buy a sandwich," he said, "and ice cream at the commissary. Can I . . . "

I dug inside my tunic, unwrapped each cloth, took off the pin that held his pouch, pulled it out, gave Jackie one dollar, put back his pouch, repinned my tunic . . . and that was that!

Jackie really had my number that day because by the time we finished filming he had asked me for this pouch one dozen times! By the thirteenth time I finally caught on. "Take your pouch," I said, disgusted, throwing it at him.

Jackie started laughing. "I wondered when you were going to catch on!" he said in his raspy voice.

Jackie didn't stop there. He was always a festival of laughs. Another day he went around telling everybody that he had studied to become a hypnotist. He decided to demonstrate his hypnotic powers in my dressing room. We all had our own portable dressing rooms on the sound stage, but everybody always hung around in mine. This time everybody crowded into my dressing room to see Jackie at work.

When there were no takers for Jackie's experiment, I volunteered. "Great," said Jackie. "It won't be dangerous. I can snap you out of it in no time."

Jackie and I sat opposite each other. He immediately placed his right hand on mine and started rubbing it to relax me. Then he took a gold medallion and began twirling it in front of my eyes, slowly and hypnotically.

Meanwhile, Yvonne DeCarlo, Richard Greene, and several other cast members looked on intently as I started nodding off. I remember Jackie telling them, "See, it looks like Joe's starting to go already."

My eyes kept getting heavier and heavier, then Jackie said, "How are you doing, Joe?"

Acting drowsy, I said, "I'm doing fine, Jackie. I'm doing . . . I'm . . . " Plunk! I was out.

Elated, Jackie jumped from his chair. "There you are everybody," he boasted. "See, I did it!"

Everyone applauded Jackie until I opened my eyes and said, "Jackie, when are you going to put me to sleep?"

Jackie hit the ceiling and chased me out of the dressing room.

He always managed to get even. The next day I was resting in my dressing room with my sandals on, and he came sneaking in on me. When I wasn't looking, he planted a match at the bottom of each shoe and lit them. Boy, did he ever give me a hot foot! I hopped all over the room like I was doing a Russian dance until the sting finally went away.

But I got even. The following morning Jackie was on the set sitting in a director's chair. I came up behind him and lit *three* matches in each one of his shoes. He danced so wildly that Freddie DeCordova thought Jackie was auditioning for one of the Arabian dance numbers in the picture!

Another funny incident between Jackie and me was more scary than funny. One afternoon while filming on location, we were supposed to ride down a dune in the desert on horseback—even though neither one of us knew how to ride a horse . . . especially Jackie. In the scene, we made a fast entrance by charging down the dune, then stopped abruptly at the bottom. When the cameras got rolling, Jackie's horse stopped all right, but Jackie didn't. Jackie went flying forward. He looked like a Warner Brothers cartoon character: he stopped in mid-air then fell to the ground. Fortunately, he was all right; no serious wounds. Only his pride was bruised.

"No more of that!" Jackie told Freddie DeCordova while he brushed himself off. "From now on I'm *walking*!"

Aside from my madcap moments with Gleason, I spent most of my time with Rock Hudson. Rock's first movie role came in the 1948 film, *Fighting Squadron*. Shortly afterwards he was signed by Universal where they started him in Western films and melodramas. So Rock was still a little wet behind the ears when I met him.

Every day after Rock and I did our scenes, we would lunch together at the commissary. Rock was a shy fellow, quiet and reserved, but determined to succeed. I could tell because he always cared about how good his scenes were.

"Joe, am I doing all right?" he'd ask, "Are my scenes good?"

Rock may have been young and inexperienced at the time, but I didn't fool with him. After all, he was the Rock (he was built like one, too!). So I always answered him honestly and gave him a boost of confidence.

"Rock, let me be the first to tell you," I said, "that you're going to be a big star. You have the star material in you."

"Gee, Joe, do you really mean that?" Rock would say, surprised.

"I wouldn't have said it if I didn't mean it."

The days following our first meeting Rock was more enthusiastic than ever about doing his scenes. He acted beautifully in them. And he did become a star, didn't he?

Years later when I ran into Rock at the studio he always embraced me and introduced me to people as "the man who helped me believe in myself."

Following *The Desert Hawk*, I appeared in two more films for Universal: *Woman in Hiding* with Ida Lupino and Howard Duff, in which I played a salesman at a convention, and *Outside the Wall* with Richard Basehart in a bit role as a chef. I also made one more film that year, *Joe Palooka Meets Humphrey*, for Monogram Pictures. Each film proved to be a new challenge for me, and my workload increased threefold with the added exposure these pictures gave me. Thus, a word that had been missing from my comic vocabulary recently returned to the forefront: television.

Since my first TV appearance in 1946, television had made great strides. I owed these tiny boxes with rabbit ears a lot of gratitude. My career remained strong thanks to them, and, fortunately, my contract at Columbia never prohibited me from working in TV. In time, I received so much work in this medium that many producers thought I had had myself cloned!

By now television had become an extension of vaudeville. (The term "vaudeo" was coined—meaning vaudeville on television.) Many of the early television programs were variety shows molded like vaudeville shows, featuring one act after another. These included: Milton Berle's *Texaco Star*

Theater; *The Ed Wynn Show*; *Your Show of Shows* with Sid Caesar and Imogene Coca; *The Red Skelton Show*; and NBC's *Colgate Comedy Hour*, which featured a different guest comedian as its weekly host, from Fred Allen to Abbott and Costello to Jack Benny to Martin and Lewis. Many comedians, after years of basic training in vaudeville, burlesque, the theater, and on radio, switched to television. The only difference was, unlike vaudeville and burlesque, a comedy act never had time to properly construct and develop their material. Instead, during the early days of live television, they had to succeed immediately. Every performance was like opening at the Palace.

At first, television's progress frightened me. There was talk that TV would eventually cripple the film industry by causing people to stay home rather than go to the movies. While I feared TV would mean fewer job opportunities in the movies, I actually became one of the most productive character comedians on television. Work I later received in feature films directly resulted from my appearances on the boob tube.

In March of 1950, my fears about TV waned when I started to receive many excellent offers. One was a pilot for a weekly TV series. It was a comedy detective show entitled, *The Private Eyes*. Eddie Nassour was the producer of the show, and by now he had forgiven me for my active involvement in Lou Costello's pie escapades. Jimmy Brown, who had gone on tour with me for *Feudin' Fussin' and a-Fightin'* as my straight man, wrote and submitted the script for this pilot to Nassour (Jimmy was later a writer for Pinky Lee's TV show). Nassour showed the script to his money man who liked what he saw. After their meeting, Nassour called and asked me to come in and discuss the possibility of starring in the project.

Even though Nassour felt strongly about the idea, he was concerned about the strength of the script. "Joe, I don't want Jimmy as a writer for this show," he said. "The script is weak and poorly written, so it will need to be rewritten."

"I don't care who you get to rewrite it," I said. "As long as the material is good, I'll do it. If it isn't, I won't."

Nassour agreed. Then, remembering that there was a part for a second detective in the show, Nassour asked me who I'd prefer to work with. I immediately suggested Sheldon Leonard, who was my favorite comedian at the time. Nassour liked the idea, so he contacted Sheldon right away. Sheldon accepted the job after Nassour told him, "Joe didn't want anybody but you. He refused to do the show without you."

Sheldon never disappointed me. He was great in the show. We played two detectives trapped in a haunted house trying to solve a murder mystery. The pilot was filmed at Nassour Studios in one week. Nassour then started screening the program for executives from all the major networks and for potential sponsors. The sponsors loved the show, but the executives from the networks didn't. They thought the show was "too ahead of its time." So the show never sold.

Naturally, I was disappointed. Television was starving for new ideas, but I didn't remain disappointed for long. I received an offer which was just as tantalizing.

In the summer of 1950, Ken Murray, who was starring in his own one-hour variety show for CBS, contacted me about becoming a regular on his show. Ken and I had worked together in vaudeville, of course, and his show was the perfect format for me. It was an act-filled program in the fashion of vaudeville. Each week Ken had different acts sprinkled throughout his show and he kept the program together with his own witty chatter between acts.

I was definitely interested in working with Ken again, but there was one drawback: the show was broadcast live from New York, and I wasn't too keen about returning to the East Coast. I enjoyed being in California, but Ernie finally convinced me. She said she would come along and enroll at a college in New York and take classes while I worked. So I accepted Ken Murray's offer and was added to the cast of regulars that already included Darla Hood (formerly of "The Little Rascals"), Joe Wong, Tony Labriola, Jack Mulhall, Betty Lou Walters, and the Enchanters. The program aired every Saturday from 8 to 9 P.M.

Each week I performed a different bit with Ken—and Ken gave me more material than I gave *him* in vaudeville. The first night I appeared on the show, October 7, 1950, I recreated my army drill routine with Jimmy Little; in the following appearances Ken played straight to me. Ken also used me in sketches and skits that were similar to the ones I had done with Milton Berle on his radio program.

I remember one week I appeared as a famous poet. Ken was searching for help on how to become a published poet, and he called on me:

"Besser, if you're a poet," says Ken, "what have you ever written?"

"I once wrote a poem on Grant's Tomb," I boasted.

"You wrote a poem on Grant's Tomb?" repeats Ken. "What happened?"

"They erased it!!"

"Besser, I don't believe you ever wrote a poem in your life," says Ken.

"Oh, no?" I'd say. "I have one right here that I just wrote, smarty."

I'd hand Ken a piece of paper without any writing on it.

"What kind of poem is this?" asks Ken. "There's nothing on the paper."

"It's *blank* v-e-r-s-e!! . . . Ooh, you're such an ignorant!"

My favorite spot was the week I played an inventor. Ken was thrilled to have an inventor on his show until he realized my inventions were as phony as my claim:

"I've never heard so many silly inventions in all my life," says Ken.

"Silly, eh?" I'd say. "Wait until you hear about my new dollar bill invention. It has Lana Turner's picture instead of Lincoln's."

"What's so good," says Ken, "about having Lana Turner on a dollar bill?"

"That way," I'd say, "you don't mind *kissing* your money g-o-o-d-b-y-e!!"

"Look, Besser," says Ken, "how long have you been inventing things?"

"Ever since I was a child," I'd say.

"You had your own little work shop?" Ken would say.

"Of course. Why, when I was five years old, I worked eight hours a day," I'd explain. "Then, when I was six years old I worked ten hours a day. And at the end of the sixth year do you know what happened?"

"No," says Ken, "what happened?"

"I was seven years o-l-d!!"

"Have you invented anything else? asks Ken.

"Yes," I'd say, "I just invented a new chocolate monkey wrench."

"A chocolate monkey wrench?" repeats Ken. "What is that for?"

"To tighten the nuts in Hershey b-a-r-s!!"

I remained a regualr on *The Ken Murray Show* for half the season before my personal feelings began to interfere with my work. I became homesick. Even though the opportunity of starring in a weekly show was advantageous, I finally talked Ken into letting me go.

Afterwards, Ernie and I returned to Hollywood where I filmed several new Columbia two-reel comedies, which carried me halfway into the new year, 1951.

I didn't return to television until almost the end of that year, when I appeared on *The Alan Young Show*, on CBS. The Canadian-born Young was one of the hottest young comedians on television. I remember critics applauded his gentle, intelligent humor and versatility, calling him "the Charlie Chaplin of television." Alan also starred later as the character Wilbur Post in TV's *Mister Ed*.

Alan's 1951 show was a half-hour long, and each week he opened with a brief monologue, a song or two, and two complete skits. I had worked with Alan on Ken Murray's show, and when he got his own program, he invited me to appear with him. Alan and I dressed up as two little kids in Buster Brown outfits. It was on *The Alan Young Show*, dressed in the Buster Brown outfit that my most famous television character was born: a malevolent brat named "Stinky." The character wasn't called Stinky yet, however.

In the skit in which we dressed as children, Alan and I romped through the house playing together and destroying everything in sight. We would share things, but, in my customary way, I'd smack him for taking my toys. The sets for these skits were built eight times larger than us—including the furniture—to reinforce the illusion that we were children. So when we appeared on stage we were only four feet tall!

I thoroughly enjoyed doing the show with Alan, and after it aired one night my friend Lou Costello called me. Ernie and I were in the middle of screening a movie for several friends on the patio—which had become a regular social event with us—when the call came through. Lou had seen my appearance on Alan Young's show, and he liked my character very much—so much so that he wanted me to re-create it for a weekly syndicated TV series he and Bud were going to star in for CBS. It was called, *The Abbott and Costello Show.*

"The character needs a name, though," said Lou. "You got any ideas, Joe?"

"No, Lou," I said. "I'm fresh out of ideas. I used up my last one an hour ago."

"Well, gee, Joe, you're always such a stinker," says Lou. "Why not Stinky?"

I wouldn't have wanted that name on my driver's license, but for a TV character it sounded good to me. Besides, I relished the thought of working with Lou again. It was always like filming home movies with him; everybody seemed so natural and so did the laughs that resulted.

In the spring of 1952, we began filming *The Abbott and Costello Show* at the old Hal Roach Studios in Culver City, which had lately become an active television production company. Lou kept everybody in stitches, as usual, with his off-camera comedy exploits, and the atmosphere was always relaxed. If you made a mistake, Lou never cared. He saved it and later used it in a blooper reel he could show people at his home.

In the show, Abbott and Costello played a pair of unemployed actors who lived in a boarding house where most of the comedy situations took place. The show was hokum comedy at its finest. Lou was gullible as ever; Bud was the perfect con man who always put Lou to work, then stood-by idly watching. They re-created many of their classic routines, and Lou balanced the show's comedy with a cast of cutups that included: Sid Fields as their landlord, who was constantly trying to get the boys to pay their back rent; Hillary Brooke as Bud and Lou's neighbor (and Lou's part-time girlfriend); Gordon Jones as Mike the cop, Bud and Lou's perennial nemesis; Joe Kirk as Mr. Baciagalupe, who worked in a variety of jobs, from a barber to a grocer (he also was Lou's real-life brother-in-law); and, of course, yours truly, as Stinky.

Twenty-six episodes were filmed for the first season, and I appeared in thirteen of them. Alex Gottlieb produced the first six shows before he gave way to Lou's brother, Pat Costello, who succeeded him as the series' executive producer (Lou believed in keeping things in the family). Jean Yarbrough directed the series, (after turning down a similar offer to direct *I Love Lucy*), and each episode was filmed like a movie. We often filmed segments for three different shows in one day. So, for instance, all our scenes in the boarding house were at once, while our scenes on the mock street were filmed later . . . Believe me, filming that show became as confusing as the scripts themselves!

The budget was $15,000 per show—but this figure often ballooned because of Lou's penchant for ad libbing. I remember Jean Yarbrough salvaged as much footage of Lou as possible by keeping two cameras on him at all times, so he wouldn't miss any funny business. Once these shows were completed, they would screen each one before a live audience at the old Santa Monica Theater. The audience's laughter was then recorded and later added to the soundtrack of each show before they were broadcast. (No "canned laughter" in those days!)

On December 5, 1952, *The Abbott and Costello Show* sponsored by Chevrolet, premiered on CBS, airing every Friday night at 10:30 P.M. As usual, the critics were less enthusiastic about the show than the viewers. Critics were tired of seeing the boys use the same old material from their movies. But viewers didn't care. They were enthusiastic enough for the show to last two complete seasons. So much for critics!

Throughout the series, the rivalry between Lou and me was constantly played up. I was Lou's bratty playmate—and antagonist (that's a good word, too!). Lou would tangle with me, but he'd always back off when I'd threaten him with, "I'll harm you!!!" or when I'd smack him with a lollipop. I was as bad as any kid could be. I represented a child's scheming mind, always getting in trouble and never aware of the difference between right and wrong. Lou and I were supposed to be "friends," but you wouldn't have known it by the way I treated him.

To add to the effect, I donned a Little Lord Fauntleroy outfit, complete with napkin collar and short pants. I also wore a saucer-shaped hat with a ribbon. I'll admit that the idea of a forty-year-old man playing a little kid each week was bizarre . . . but it was a living!

In the show's first episode "The Wrestling Match," Lou and I got into a scuffle in front of the boarding house when Lou runs into me. I started belting him in the stomach, being my bratty self, and I kept screaming, "He started it! He started it!" until Mike the Cop arrives on the scene to break things up. Mike then suggests if we want to fight each other we should participate in a policeman's benefit wrestling match that night at the local auditorium. The winner will receive a $25 defense bond.

"For some reason," says Lou skeptically, "I don't think this is on the level . . . "

To show what kind of hokey comedy we did, Mike gets upset. "It ain't on the level?" repeats Mike. "Everything I do is on the level. I'm an officer of the law. There will be no favoritism shown . . . Absolutely not, or I ain't Stinky's uncle!"

"So long, Uncle Mike!" I'd say, sticking out my tongue at Lou before giving him one last belt in the stomach.

Of course, the night of the wrestling match, Lou fixes it, so I cannot participate; he gives me twenty-six malted milks which make me sick. Mike brings my kid brother to replace me, however: a real goliath named Ivan the Terrible. He tears phone books in half for a living, with Lou as his next victim.

I truly loved doing this series because I had room to grow with the Stinky character. Lou always gave me the best spots, and each time I got the best of Lou.

I remember that in another episode entitled, "Lou's Birthday Party," I menaced Lou while doing something as simple as riding a scooter. I made a hand signal to turn left, but Lou knocked me down because he never saw me.

"Why don't you look where you are g-o-i-n-g!!" I'd say, pouncing on Lou like a lion. "I gave you a warning signal!" Then I'd hit him again. "You're such a dangerous pedestrian, that's what you are!!"

I'd take off on my scooter before Lou even had a chance to defend himself.

The childish situations Stinky would get into were real, yet funny. For example, in an episode entitled, "The Drugstore," Lou played a soda jerk. My mother decides to punish me for biting Lou on the hand by asking Lou to mix a glass of castor oil and Coke for me:

"Mom, not th-a-a-a-t!!" I'd moan.

"Castor oil mixed with Coke?" repeats Lou. "Why don't you like castor oil mixed with a Coke?"

"I just don't like it!! . . . I'm always getting it!!" I'd complain. "She's always making me drink castor mixed in chocolate syrup . . . in pineapple juice . . . in grapefruit juice. It makes me sick, sick, sick!"

"What's wrong with that?" asks Lou innocently.

"I just like *plain* castor o-i-l!!"

Lou turns green at the thought—and so did I when we filmed that scene. Just like Stinky would do to him, Lou plotted against me by pulling another one of his many pranks on me. Before I drank down the stuff in that scene Lou actually put castor oil in the glass!

Like all good laughs, however, my role in *The Abbott and Costello Show* came to an end in 1953. I left the series after the first season when Lou decided to revamp the show's format—including the cast. I was replaced by, of all things, a chimpanzee named Bingo who dressed like Lou. I never lost out to a chimp before, but I never resented Lou for making this move. He had done plenty for me just by being my friend.

My appearances on *The Abbott and Costello Show* put my face in front of many prominent television producers on a weekly basis, so I never lacked for employment. From 1953 through 1955, I appeared on a record thirty television shows including: *Mr. District Attorney; The Spike Jones Show; My Little Margie; My Favorite Story;* (which marked my TV dramatic debut); *The Millionaire* (as a hobo named Harvey Blake in the series' premiere episode, which was directed by Stooge director Edward Bernds); *The Martha Raye Show; The Damon Runyan Show;* and *I Married Joan*. Between lunch hours I also worked on *The Jack Benny Show* (in seven episodes replacing Eddie "Rochester" Anderson who was seriously ill at the time); *The Ray Milland Show; Private Secretary; The Dennis O'Keefe Show; December Bride; Willy;* and even *The Gene Autry Show.*

I also found time to perform in such feature films as: the original *I, the Jury*, in 3-D, with Biff Elliott and Peggie Castle; *Sins of Jezebel* with Paulette Goddard, who I had worked with before on Milton Berle's radio show; *Abbott and Costello Meet the Keystone Kops*, starring who else?; *Mad at the World* with Frank Lovejoy; *Headline Hunters* and a 1956 release, *Two Gun Lady*. Phew, I thought I'd never finish!

Between these many appearances, Ernie and I took several vacations since we both loved to travel. Ernie also kept herself busy taking classes in painting. So when she wasn't with me, she was working on her latest Van Gogh.

By the end of 1955, however, my career suddenly took an unexpected nosedive when the well of jobs started to run dry. There was no explanation for this period of drought, other than that actors tend to go through them all the time. I guess I was long overdue. The situation remained the same until fate stepped in to save me: I became a Stooge.

Chapter 16

The Third Stooge

It was two days before Thanksgiving, 1955. Ernie and I were gearing up for Thanksgiving and Ernie was already planning her shopping list for Christmas.

The holiday season was our favorite time of the year. With Christmas right around the corner, I knew my old pal Lou Costello would be coming over again to help us decorate. It also meant the den would be converted into Ernie's little mystical workshop. Each year she bought different yuletide figures and assorted decorations to personally hand wrap gifts for our friends. We delivered gifts to more than forty friends annually, so Ernie's fingers kept busy right up until Christmas Eve.

In the meantime, I took time to reflect about my future. This December my contract with Columbia would be up for renewal, so I would be meeting shortly with Harry Cohn to reevaluate my future. I was scared about what my future would hold, especially now that my workload had drastically fallen off for the first time in years. We were fortunate to own our home outright, and we had all the material things we ever needed, but I would have felt more secure knowing what my next job would be. If worse came to worse, I could have always auditioned for a job as a Salvation Army bell ringer!

My holiday spirit became even more diffused that year when I received some shocking news about my dear friend, Shemp Howard. Shemp had become an established comedian in his own right since I first met him in *The Passing Show of 1932*. He had gone on to become a versatile comedian throughout the years by co-starring in films with W.C. Fields, The Andrew Sisters, John Wayne, Broderick Crawford, the Dead End Kids, and, of course, Abbott and Costello. He also had starred in his own short subject series for Vitaphone and Columbia Pictures. Then, in 1946, after his brother Curly Howard suffered a stroke, which immobilized him until his death in 1952, Shemp returned to the Three Stooges act to take over the third stooge role.

On the night Ernie and I began preparing for Thanksgiving, Shemp went out with two friends to the fights at the Hollywood Legion Field. Shemp had plenty to celebrate that night. The Stooges had signed a contract earlier with Columbia that marked their twenty-second year with the studio. The boys had about four films left to make on this new contract and things couldn't have looked better for them. They continued to make personal appearances, in addition to meeting their rigorous film commitments, so Shemp was making a decent living being a Stooge, taking all those the bops and whacks.

The Stooges had another week-long nightclub engagement booked for the following week in Miami, Florida. So this particular night was Shemp's only chance to relax. The fights were his outlet for relaxing. After the fights, Shemp took a cab home, and began chatting with one of his friends, Al Winston, about the outcome of the bout. During the conversation, Shemp lit up a cigar. When his friend Al began giving Shemp his account of the fight, Al looked down and saw cigar ashes burning through his suit; they were from Shemp's cigar.

Looking over at Shemp, Al nudged him and said, "Hey, Shemp, sit up straight. You're burning me with your cigar."

Shemp never answered.

"Oh, my God!" shouted Al. "Stop the cab!"

Shemp was dead. He had suffered a heart attack. He was 60 years old.

Shemp's death came as a great shock to everyone, and it was the second major setback in the Stooges careers; first Curly had died. Now Shemp. Even though I had worked only sporadically with Shemp, I mourned his death just as much as Moe and Larry did. We had remained in constant touch with each other ever since our *Africa Screams* days. Therefore, I felt a deep personal loss since I considered Shemp a close friend; he was like family to me. Already I missed his smart-alecky jokes, his warmth and kindness, and even that greased-down hair of his, parted over his loving-cup ears.

Somehow Shemp's wife, Gertrude, persevered. She undoubtedly had her hands full with her son Mort to raise. Ernie and I continued to visit Gertrude periodically, but it was never the same. Shemp's jovial personality, his sharp wit, and his ability to tell funny stories were sorely missed. Granted Shemp had his share of fears, but he was, without a doubt, the most entertaining man I had ever known.

Most people don't realize that it was Shemp not Curly who was the original third stooge. Unfortunately, this fact is often overlooked because new generations of fans are fooled by the reruns of the old shorts on television which show Curly, Moe, and Larry as the original trio.

I remember that for Shemp the hardest part of returning to the act after his brother Curly suffered a stroke was the studio's initial hesitation about Shemp's replacing his ailing brother. Several studio executives, including Harry Cohn, felt that Shemp too closely resembled Moe and that pairing them together would create an identity crisis with the audience as to who was the boss of the trio. Somehow Moe got his way and Shemp rejoined the act. How Moe manipulated the brass at Columbia to go along with his way of thinking we will never know.

Moe always maintained that Shemp's joining would be temporary until Curly was well enough to come back (actually, though Moe said this, the general feeling is that he hoped his words would serve to boost Curly's sagging health and morale by leaving the door open). Unfortunately, Curly never got a chance to rejoin the Stooges. Six years later, following a series of stokes, the most naturally gifted comedian the act had ever known died.

For days I couldn't get Shemp off my mind. My mind flashed a kaleidoscope of memories that I had almost forgotten, all putting into perspective what a great tragedy Shemp's death was. Whenever we used to get together, Shemp loved to swap stories. Naturally, his favorites were from his vaudeville days with Moe and Larry, as well as his film days as the third stooge. He had many stories to tell and I thoroughly enjoyed each recounting.

I'll never forget one story he told me from his days with Moe, Larry, and the great Ted Healy when they were headliners in vaudeville. They enjoyed some crazy adventures—actually misadventures—together. A classic story I enjoy recalling involved Larry and Shemp and a turkey dinner that came back to haunt them in 1927, a time when Moe was away from the act to be closer to his family. (His daughter Joan was born that year.)

Shemp and Larry were working in Chicago with Ted Healy at the Cohan Theater. During their engagement the boys rented an apartment at the Croyton Hotel, known then as an "apartment hotel." As Shemp told it, five girls lived next door to them at the hotel, and one night the girls went out to the McVickers Theater to attend a midnight show. At late shows, such as this one, the theater gave away door prizes in a drawing held to pick the lucky winner. The door prize that night was a live turkey, and, as luck would have it, the girls won the prize!

After the show, the girls returned to their hotel room, and accidentally awakened Shemp and Larry due to all the commotion in their room. Larry and Shemp went next door to investigate. The girls were trying to figure out how to kill the turkey so they could roast it for dinner the next day. One of the girls asked Larry if he would kill it for them, but he backed off, saying. "Not me, brother. Are you kidding?"

When the girls asked Shemp to perform the duty, the same man who couldn't hurt a fly, said, sheepishly, "Oh, no, not me. I couldn't harm the little fella."

In a flash, though, Larry saved the day with a brainstorm: "Look, I have an idea. There is an all-night drugstore downstairs. I'll go down and buy some chloroform. That'll do the trick!"

Larry raced downstairs, picked up the smallest bottle available of this potent stuff, ran back upstairs, soaked a handkerchief, and placed it over the turkey's face. In seconds the turkey was knocked out. The best part of the story is yet to come: Shemp and Larry thought the chloroform killed the turkey . . . little did they know.

The girls quickly plucked the turkey clean, then placed it in the refrigerator, figuring they would stuff it in the morning. The next morning when they opened up the refrigerator, did they ever get a surprise: the turkey, completely skinned, staggered and jumped out of the refrigerator. Still asleep, Shemp and Larry heard a blood-curdling scream next door and came running. When one of the girls opened the door to their room, the turkey, still on its feet, staggered right by Shemp and Larry, outside the hotel and down Michigan Avenue!

What a sight that must have been!

Another vintage Shemp story that flashed into my mind involved an act that was billed once with the Stooges as part of their vaudeville act. The act was called "Stevens Wrestling Bear." Imagine Shemp sharing center stage with a real, live ferocious bear. I wish I could have been there to have seen that.

The routine for the act was simple—wrestling with the bear was the act! The bear would come on stage, and there would be interplay between the bear and the Stooges. The act began with Moe going out to wrestle with the bear, the idea being that he would get it angry enough to chase him off stage. Once he succeeded and the bear followed him into the wings, Moe would then return on stage with a dummy bear that had a rope attached to it (Shemp was in charge of holding the rope). Teaching the bear a lesson, in Stooge-like fashion, the gag called for Moe to throw the fake bear into the audience; Shemp would then retrieve it by reeling in the rope. This part of the act always went over well, frightening and making the audience laugh at the same time.

The bear act was a huge success until during one performance Mother Nature took over. Everything was going fine. As usual, Moe took his place on stage to wrestle the bear. While wrestling, the bear apparently decided to ad lib. He left a little gift right in the middle of the stage. The audience roared, Moe buckled over and laughed his sides off. And the bear? What could he do except take a bow for his exploits.

Oh, and Shemp? He fainted dead away backstage.

Shemp took his lumps as a Stooge, too. I never laughed so hard as the time he told the story about a scene between him and Christine McIntyre from one the boys' pictures. I think the title was *Brideless Groom.* Shemp gave his all in each performance, and this story, if any, proved it. In the film, Shemp had a few hours in which to get married if he wanted to inherit his uncle's fortune. He calls on Christine McIntyre, who mistakes him for her cousin and greets him with countless hugs and kisses. Naturally, when the real cousin phones to say he'll be late, she accuses Shemp of kissing her under false pretenses and, at one point, she is supposed to slap Shemp around.

Lady that Christine was, she couldn't do the scene right; instead of crowning Shemp, she dabbed at him gingerly. Finally, after a couple of bad takes, Shemp pleaded with her. "Honey," he said, "if you want to do me a favor, cut loose and do it right. A lot of half-hearted slaps hurts more than one good one. Give it to me, Chris. Just let it rip."

Christine got the courage and in the next take she gave it to Shemp all right. The slaps rang out like pistol shots. She slapped Shemp all over the set, with the final blow sending him through the door.

A bit groggy, Shemp pulled himself off the floor, feeling like a doormat that's been stepped on one too many times. He looked at Christine, who hovered over him apologetically and said, "It's all right, honey! I said you should cut loose and you did. You sure as hell did! Wow!"

Besides the fun times Shemp always shared with me when we visited each other, the one part of his personality I remembered—and shall always remember—was his loving, gentle side. Shemp was always giving to assorted charities and helping those less fortunate than himself. For example, at the conclusion of a booking in Birmingham, Alabama in the late 1940s, Moe, Larry, and Shemp headed by train to their next engagement in Miami, Florida. The train ride was a long one—nineteen hours—due to several unexpected detours taken because of a serious accident on one of the tracks.

As a result, things got desperate when the train ran out of food. At one of the last stops before reaching their destination, one of the engineers located a farmer who brought a wagon full of food to the train to help feed the passengers.

Now Shemp, who loved children, when he saw the farmer alongside the train, said to Larry, "Larry, the kids on board must be starved. Let's go out and see if we can't buy some apples for them from the farmer."

Like a pied piper, Shemp bought several bushels of apples and other fruits and, with the help of Moe and Larry, distributed the fruit throughout the train to all the children. That's the kind of man Shemp was—always thinking of others before himself. Like a rare gem, his kind is hard to find.

After Shemp's death there was talk through the grapevine at Columbia that Moe Howard wanted to disband the group altogether. He couldn't see continuing with the team after Curly's and Shemp's deaths, and I can't say I blame him. In his mind Moe probably thought, what else could happen?

Moe changed his mind, however. Later he met with Harry Cohn to contemplate the team's future. Moe suggested that he and Larry could finish their present contract as "The Two Stooges," but Cohn balked at the idea. The American movie-going public could never accept just two Stooges; it had to be three or nothing at all.

Moe and Larry completed the four remaining films of their contract by altering the films' storylines, shooting new footage with a double named Joe Palma, who looked like Shemp (although you never actually saw his face), and combining the new footage with stock footage from four earlier comedies with Shemp. In the meantime, Cohn dropped the entire matter of finding a permanent Stooge replacement until after Christmas of 1955. That's when he authorized Jules White to call and offer me the job of the third Stooge.

Before saying "yes" I met with Jules to discuss specifics about my joining. But first, since I was between agents, I needed to find an agent to represent me. So I called on my old friend, producer Harry Rogers. Harry had moved to Hollywood and he was now working as a manager at the Pantages Theater. He really missed being involved in the talent end of the business, so I figured I'd help him out by giving him a commission if he'd handle contract negotiations for me with Jules. I trusted Harry because he had booked acts in nightclubs before, so he definitely knew the ropes. I wasn't so sure, however, after Harry asked me before our meeting with Jules: "How much should we ask for?" Momma always told me there would be days like this!

That afternoon, Harry and I met with Jules in his office. Jules immediately laid out his plans to me. Moe and Larry had two years remaining on their present contracts with Columbia, with the studio having an option to pick up their contracts after the second year. Harry Cohn suggested to Jules that, since my contract was up for renewal, it would be a good idea to have me take Shemp's place as the third Stooge. My joining was contingent upon Moe Howard's approval because he had the final say on any new partners to be hired for the group. Moe happily approved my becoming a Stooge.

Jules liked Cohn's suggestion that I become the third Stooge because he thought my character was child-like, like Curly's. So the basic situations Jules had used before with the boys could be reused if I joined the team. I almost backed off on the deal, though, when Jules asked me to shave my head completely (what little hair I had I intended on keeping). He wanted me to look like Curly.

"No, Jules, I'm going to be me," I said. "I don't want to be Curly. Besides, I'm not taking Curly's place anyway. I'll be Joe Besser."

Jules never argued. The matter was settled, so he said, "Well, Joe, what do you think? I'd love to have you take Shemp's place and work as a member of the Three Stooges. How about it?"

I waited for Harry to speak up on my behalf by suggesting to Jules what my salary would have to be per week. But Harry just sat there in his chair and looked at me for help . . . Some agent!

"I'd love to take the job, Jules," I said. I wasn't working much at the time and I definitely needed the money.

"Well then," said Jules, "how much do you want per week?"

"The same salary I received when I made features here," I said, "$3,500 a week!"

Jules suddenly became quiet. He lit up a cigar, leaned back in his chair, and playfully blew smoke rings in my face.

"You got it, Joe," he said. "I'm not going to argue. I'll see that you get it."

Jules and I shook hands and the deal was complete. I walked away with a better deal than the Stooges; they were only making $2,500 a week. I also walked out of Jules' office door as a new member of the Three Stooges.

Outside, Harry almost fainted in the hallway. "Joe, you don't know what I was going to ask Jules for," he said. "I thought $1,500 a week would be enough!"

So much for Harry as my agent!

On January 1, 1956, I officially became a member of the Three Stooges when I signed a two-year contract to that effect. I would make sixteen comedies over the next two years with Moe and Larry, all directed by Jules, who also produced them. The screenplays were written by Felix Adler and Jack White, Jules' brother, and the film editor on these films was also from the White clan—Jules' other brother Harold. This was definitely a family affair operation.

By now Columbia began turning out fewer short subjects than before, as the market for two-reelers had begun to dwindle. In fact, Columbia was the only active producer of comedy two-reelers left. The other major studios had shut down their respective departments when theaters began going less and less with the two-reel subjects. So the budgets for our films were comparatively less than those for the Stooges films that were produced during the height of the Stooges careers. Our films were also shorter in length; they ran roughly fifteen minutes.

On the average, we took anywhere from one to four days to film each comedy. Since my physique was similar to Curly's, the scriptwriters cleverly wrote stories matching old stock footage from comedies featuring Curly and shaped them around new footage of me. Those comedies usually took one day to film. They also developed new stories for me, which were more like television situation comedies; these films took between three to four days to shoot.

There also was a changing of the guard in the Stooges' stock company when I came aboard. New faces populated our films, as well as some old ones. The beauteous Greta Thyssen became the new heroine in our films, replacing Christine McIntyre, who had formerly held that position. And several other newcomers also joined forces with us, namely: Harriette Tarler, Milton Frome, Muriel Landers, and Dan Blocker (who earlier had starred in one of my two-reel comedies at Columbia and later became famous as Hoss Cartwright). Several veteran Stooge company players also appeared in our films, including Emil Sitka, Gene Roth, and Joe Palma.

At first my wife Ernie was not completely happy about my joining the Stooges, purely for the reason that she thought their comedy style was too physical for me. I, too, had some trepidations about whether it would work. I had had a very successful career on my own up to this point. I had starred in my own feature films and short subjects, I was popular on television and radio, and, more importantly, I was pretty well-known individually for my work. How would becoming a Stooge change that? Would the public accept me as Shemp's replacement. Would Moe and Larry ever regret bringing me aboard? As it turned out, my fears all washed away after my first day on the job.

I'll never forget my first film with the boys. It was called *Hoofs and Goofs*, and it told the story of our long-lost sister Birdie (actually Moe in drag), who is reincarnated as a horse. The horse in the film was Tony the Wonder Horse, who was easy to work with and with whom we all became instant friends. The film also co-starred Benny Rubin and Harriette Tarler, who worked for more than a bundle of carrots each day.

This film was the first time I had seen Moe and Larry since becoming the new third Stooge; we never had a formal meeting beforehand to discuss our future as a team. Sure, we ran into each other occasionally at the studio when I was making my own short subject series, but our run-ins were mostly comprised of quick "hellos." So on that first day of shooting we spent time getting reacquainted.

No sooner did I finish getting my makeup put on when this voice echoed in my ear, "Joe, there you are!" It was Larry; he was the first to welcome me aboard. "I've been looking all over for you. I figured you'd be on the set by now."

"It takes the makeup man longer because of my beautiful bald head," I cracked, rubbing the top of my head.

"You funny guy. I see you haven't lost your sense of humor." Larry said warmly. "Hurry up if you can. Moe is anxious to go over the script with you. You know Moe, he's already going over his lines."

We both chuckled. Everyone at Columbia knew how dedicated Moe was to his work. We used to kid that he carried a flashlight with him to work in the morning because not even the engineers were up that early to turn the studios light on for him.

Makeup complete, I grabbed my script and darted to Stage 7, where we were filming that day. The minute I set foot on the set Moe noticed me out of the corner of his eye. "Joe," he said, putting down a cigarette, "I'm happy to see you," extending his right hand to shake hands. "You're looking as fat as ever!"

"Then I'm perfect for the part," I remarked.

"Joe . . . " Moe started, before I interrupted. "What is it, Joe?"

"Moe, I have to tell you how sorry I was to hear about Shemp. I loved him, too; I considered him family. And I just want you to know that I feel bad about replacing Shemp under these circumstances. I know how special he was."

Touched by my remarks, Moe dabbed his eyes, fighting back the tears. "Joe," he managed, "let me be the first to say that I'm sure Shemp is looking down with approval."

Throughout the rest of the day it was like old home week for us. I felt like I had known Moe and Larry all my life, and it showed in our work together, I think. Their making me feel welcome was just like both of them. I couldn't help recalling the same warmth they showed me when we met for the first time during *The Passing Show of 1932*. Their greeting was as special then as it was on that day in 1956. I could sense from that first day as a "new Stooge" that we were going to make it as a team.

Chapter 17

Stooging Around with Moe and Larry

I'll admit that on that first day on the set with Moe and Larry I was nervous about succeeding Shemp. Shemp was a gifted comedian and a tough act to follow. Moviegoers had associated him longer in the third Stooge role than me, but if our roles had been reversed and the opportunity had come Shemp's way, I'm sure he would have done the same.

Moe and Larry never compared me to Shemp and Curly, however. I never heard them say after a take, "Curly would have done it that way," or "Shemp would have done it that way." I'm sure now and then when Moe went to slap me he saw visions of Curly and Shemp dancing in his head, but that was only natural. He never talked about his brothers.

On film, I'd have to say we were more like "The Two Stooges, Plus Joe Besser" at times, but that's because I wanted it that way. As part of my accepting the job, I had a special provision written into my contract that prevented Moe or Larry from causing me serious bodily harm in our scenes together. I let Moe give me an occasional poke in the eye or belt in the stomach, but otherwise serious stunts were out with me. I wasn't used to doing the Stooges' brand of slapstick; I felt more comfortable hitting others back because my character called for that. I was a feisty, little kid.

I'm especially glad the boys were agreeable to this provision because too often I had heard stories about serious injuries that occurred in their films. Shemp once told me about one film where Larry invented a fountain pen that wrote under whipped cream. The scene called for the pen to be demonstrated in a mixing bowl. It was to be positioned in front of the mixer, then fly off uncontrollably in the process, hitting Larry square in the forehead. Of course, the prop department rigged it up so the pen would spring right into the center of a metal plate planted in Larry's forehead, disguised with makeup. Jules White assured Moe, after much disagreement, that the gadget was foolproof. So much for the best-laid plans of mice and men. The pen flew into the plate all right. It also went straight through the plate and into Larry's head. Moe got so mad afterwards that he ran Jules White off the set.

When I felt it was necessary, I asked Jules to replace certain breakaway props that Moe planned to use on me so I wouldn't get injured. In *Hoofs and Goofs*, the script originally called for Birdie (Moe) to crown me on the head with a rolling pin. At my request, Jules changed it to a casserole dish from which Birdie/Moe dumped the contents on my head!

Moe and Larry never held these changes against me. They, too, realized my character was unlike Curly's and Shemp's, and they treated me like an individual. They were always willing to work out any differences with me.

"Don't worry, Joe," said Larry. "If you don't want Moe to hit you, I'll take all the belts."

Moe was just as understanding. "Joe, if there's any hitting going on," he said, "and you don't want it, let me know because I'll cut it out."

But even when Moe did hit me, it was a pleasure because he had such a feathery touch. He never really hit me; he always faked it. Sometimes he would miss his mark and I'd feel the force behind his blow, but most of the time he just made his hitting look real when it wasn't. And, combined with sound effects which were added later by Joe Henrie, the studio's sound effects expert, you'd think Moe was beating the bejeepers out of us everytime!

Actually, when I think about it now, I may have done the Stooges a big favor by having them tone down the violent mayhem in the act. Later, when Columbia released their shorts to television, they had to clean up their act anyway to appease angry, protesting parents whose children loved the Stooges!

So in *Hoofs and Goofs* this new Stooge-team formula was introduced, and I remember the critics were very receptive. As a result, each day I reported to the studio with new-found enthusiasm. Eventually I started making other suggestions for the good of the team.

In our second film together, *Muscle Up a Little Closer*, where we helped find my girlfriend "Tiny's" engagement ring which had been stolen, I introduced yet another dimension to the team: new haircuts. I suggested to Jules that Moe and Larry would look more like gentlemen if they combed back their hair every so often. Moe didn't mind retiring the old bangs now and then, and I know Larry started losing hair everytime he frizzed his out, so they were both agreeable to the idea. In this film we used it for the first time, but Jules used the new hairstyles sparingly thereafter when we wanted to match old stock footage of the boys from their old films.

I'll say this much about Moe and Larry; they were always professional in how they treated me, and we developed the greatest respect for one another. We also had a lot of fun together. And, in time, I would learn more and more about Moe's and Larry's contrasting personalities.

I found that Moe always focused his mind on what was best for the team. He was serious most of the time on the set, and he kept himself involved in every aspect of our films from scriptwriting to whipping up the pies. He was truly a perfectionist. I also noticed he was always on the set early and seemed to have a tremendous amount of nervous energy. He could never sit still; he always had to be busy.

There was no arguing one other point about Moe: he was truly "the boss" of the team. He understood the Stooges' style of comedy better than anybody, so he made sure that our routines and impressions on film lived up to certain standards. If they didn't, he'd always tell Larry and me, "Fellas, this routine isn't written right. Larry, you should be saying Joe's line here, and Joe, you should be saying Larry's line here." On more complicated matters, Moe would hold what he called "bull sessions" with Jules to discuss more elaborate reworkings that needed to be made to the script, or concepts that he didn't agree with.

But there was a human side to Moe, too. Although he pretty much kept his feelings to himself, occasionally he would share a story or two about the Stooge's early days, which showed that he was a sentimentalist at heart. Moe certainly had a vivid memory and, when he was on, he was a great storyteller.

I'll never forget one hilarious story Moe told me about the time he, Larry, and Curly played a benefit show at a local mental institution, where, as Moe said, "We belonged in the first place!"

While stagehands took care of setting up the stage, Moe walked around the grounds. He tried to be very jovial, since a mental institution is a very depressing place. When he met a patient, he said, "Pardon me, I'm one of the Three Stooges. We're going to entertain here tonight."

"Don't worry about it," the patient said, "I was Napoleon when I got here!"

Moe thanked the patient for his time, then walked around the grounds some more until he found himself in front of a nice little cottage where a fellow was walking around completely nude except for a derby on his head. Spotting the gentleman, Moe walked up to him and said, "Hey, fella, you ought to be more careful walking around like that in the open where the public can see you."

"Oh, nobody ever comes to see me," the man said.

"Well, that's fine, but you shouldn't be walking around like that," Moe reasoned.

But the man insisted, "Well, nobody ever comes to see me."

Finally Moe said, "Well, then why are you wearing the hat?

"Well," the man said, "that's in case somebody comes."

Then Moe told how the next man he ran into was painting a brick wall, which was one hundred and forty feet long and eight feet high, with a little artist's brush.

Moe stood there and watched this fellow until he turned around and noticed Moe. "You know," the man told Moe, "you must think I'm silly or something."

"No, no," Moe said politely.

"Actually," the man babbled, "I'm killing time here. I have $200,000 in gold hidden on top of Lookout Mountain, under a rock. Now if you go up there and get it, we'll split it and then we'll go out and have a good time."

Moe figured he had nothing to lose; anything to help the poor man. So the man instructed Moe, "You go up Laurel Canyon Boulevard to Lookout Mountain Road, go up the hill twenty paces to the right and you'll find a big pine tree. Twenty paces behind that there's a big boulder. And under the boulder, there's the tin box with the money."

So, the next day, Moe went there, followed the man's instructions step for step, and returned to the institution the next day with a full report. He informed the man, "Hey, buddy, something's wrong someplace. There's no gold up there."

"Did you go up Laurel Canyon Boulevard and then down on Lookout Mountain Road?" the man asked. "And did you find the pine tree?"

"Yes, I did," Moe replied.

"Did you see the boulder?" the man asked next.

"Yes, I did," Moe answered again.

"Did you move the boulder and look for the tin can?" the man said.

"Yes, I did," Moe said.

"Go get yourself a brush!" the man said, laughing.

Like any human, Moe had his share of idiosyncracies. One of them was getting things in his eyes. I remember he was real cautious about that because of some earlier injuries he had sustained as a Stooge. I learned about Moe's fear when we made *Oil's Well That Ends Well.* We were going to film a scene where Moe would unstop a pipe with a screwdriver to draw oil and the oil would squirt him in the face. When Moe read the scene, he told

Jules, "We have to talk about this scene, Jules."

Moe reminded Jules of how he almost had gone blind many years before while making *Three Troubledoers* with Curly. "In that film," he said, "I stood directly behind Curly who was holding a bazooka, which backfired and shot soot in my eyes. My eyes became so inflamed that doctors feared I'd never see again."

Although Moe proved the doctors wrong (even though he later suffered from glaucoma) Jules agreed to help Moe on the scene. Moe told Jules, "Jules, I'll count to three, and when I do, I want the oil to come out on three. No sooner." It did and Moe closed his eyes on cue, with not one drop of oil getting into his eyes.

Earlier in this film, in a scene where we blasted for uranium, Moe and Larry escaped injury by having Jules use rubbermade rocks to fall on them after the explosion. In that same scene, I surprised Moe and Larry with one of my on-camera ad libs after Moe pushed me aside for being no help. I walked to the camera and lipped the words, "I hate h-i-m." I had originally used the gag in *Hey, Rookie!*, and Jules loved the bit so much that he kept it in.

Later when we filmed *Outer Space Jitters*, Moe was faced with yet another dilemma. He hated shell fish and in one scene we were supposed to eat clam shells and drink battery acid for dinner! Since Moe wouldn't eat shell fish—let alone taste it!—he asked Jules to substitute the real clam shells with artificial ones. Jules did; we ate fortune cookies which were shaped like clam shells.

Larry's personality was altogether different than Moe's. He was carefree and rarely punctual. He just wanted to have fun. I can remember Larry would strike up a conversation with anybody, while Moe was more selective about who he talked to. Larry was the warmest, kindest man, too. Did I mention funny? He was also that. Like Shemp, he enjoyed telling stories and he always started them off by saying, "Did I ever tell you about the time . . . "

During the first month I worked with the Stooges, Larry was the first to invite me and Ernie to his house. He was definitely a social butterfly. Moe never made any attempts to socialize with us because he and his wife, Helen, had their own circle of friends, mostly doctors, lawyers, and politicians. But Ernie and I visited Larry and his wife Mabel at their beautiful Griffith Park home several times. During those precious visits I really got to know Larry. He talked a lot about his glorious past with the Stooges. He kept me in stitches with stories about him, Moe, and Curly. You could tell by the sparkle in his eyes that had been the happiest period of his life.

Larry was a doll!

Through Larry's stories, I sensed there was a deep caring between him and Moe, like brothers. By the time I joined the team, they had known each other over 30 years. That's a long haul to be with someone, working together and socializing together. The Howards and the Fines held family get-togethers periodically, so they actually had very few moments apart.

Like brothers often do, they played practical jokes on each other when the moment seemed right. Larry once told me about such an incident when the boys—Moe, Larry, and Curly—were booked at a theater in Kansas City, Missouri as part of a personal appearance tour. Appearing on the same bill with them was European lightweight boxing champion George Carpentier (he had fought Jack Dempsey, the world's heavyweight champion, a few months earlier and lost).

For a boxer, George was a quiet, unassuming type. He was very handsome and could easily have been mistaken for a movie star. In between shows, Larry, who loved all kinds of sports, naturally cornered George to wring out of him some ringside tales. While discussing some of George's more memorable fights, a falling object exploded on Larry's head from above—a blueberry pie, hitting him squarely on the head and splattering his face. Wiping the dripping goo from his eyes, Larry excused himself and told George, "I'm going after whoever dropped that pie."

Finding the pie-throwing culprit wasn't easy. First Larry checked all the dressing rooms, thinking that whoever plotted the scheme would have a second pie in waiting. Of all places, Larry found a pie in the dressing room belonging to the Mangean Sisters, a duo sister act. The pie was sitting in plain view, and the sisters seemed like the culprits all right, since their dressing room was located directly upstairs overlooking the spot where Larry and Carpentier were chatting.

Determined to get even, Larry picked up the pie, found the Mangean Sisters downstairs and smeared it all over their faces, hair and costumes. Totally aghast, one of the girls screamed, "What are you doing . . . are you mad?"

"Don't kid me," Larry insisted, still wearing the evidence, "you dropped that pie down on my head and you know it."

At that very moment, Larry heard someone laughing uncontrollably, doubled up on the floor with a piece of blueberry pie in his hand. It was Moe, of course. Between laughs, all Moe could muster was, "Larry, Larry, when are you ever going to learn."

"You win this one, Moe," Larry remarked, fuming, the pie boiling on his face. "But every dog has his day."

With that remark, Larry chased Moe out of the theater. But I'm sure it wasn't the last time Moe succeeded in getting the best of Larry.

Another thing I remember about Larry and how he was different from Moe was how he enjoyed his stardom. Whenever he could use it to his advantage, he would. When people heard he was one of the Three Stooges, they always gave him the red-carpet treatment. And Larry lapped it up everytime. One time, however, Larry's celebrity status backfired on him and Curly. While playing an engagement at the Strand Theater in New York, Rocky Graziano and Harold Green were squaring off in a middle weight bout at Madison Square Garden. The hottest ticket in town, Larry tried everything possible to rustle up three tickets for him, Moe, and Curly.

The boys got nowhere at the box office. Disgusted, Moe said "Now how are we going to get in, it's sold out."

His wheels turning, Larry remarked, "Don't worry, Moe, I'll work something out."

At the entrance, Larry approached the doorman and, without batting an eye, said, "Do you have three tickets for the Three Stooges?"

Recognizing them instantly, the doorman answered, "No, I have no tickets for you, but I think I can arrange to let you boys in to see the fight."

Calling over an usher, the doorman consulted with him and then told the Stooges, "Look, fellows, follow the usher."

So far so good. The plan worked brilliantly. Moe patted Larry on the head for "using an ounce of brains for once," they took their seats, and were delighted at being let in to see the fight.

In public Moe and Larry never looked like they did onscreen; Moe usually combed back his hair, as did Larry. Of course, Curly never had that luxury; his head was always shaven. The only way he disguised his personality was by wearing hats all the time.

Things continued to fare well until Curly made the mistake of removing his hat. Instantly a man from the balcony spotted him and shouted, "Curly, what newspaper do you work for?"

All heads turned in the Stooges direction, including the head usher, who recognized them. They were never so embarrassed in their lives, and shortly afterwards the usher escorted them out of the arena never to darken the door again.

Even though Larry never concerned himself with every aspect of our films, as Moe did, there was one time he did and became the hero of the day. In *Merry Mix-Up*, in which we played a set of identical triplets, the film became a test of Jules White's talents with special effects. A real merry mix-up almost developed when we were filming the master shot of all three sets of triplets. Three separate shots were taken of each trio, costumed differently, of course. These shots were then carefully blended to give audiences the illusion that all of us were standing next to each other in the same room.

Jules thought that Larry was standing behind a different marker than in the previous shot, but Larry insisted that he was standing in the right spot.

"I think you had me stand behind the wrong marker," he told Jules after the shot was taken. "I was supposed to stand in the center of Moe and Joe, and you placed me to the right of them."

"What are you talking about, Larry?" argued Jules. "I had you in the center."

I was ready to get out the boxing gloves when Moe finally interjected. "I don't think you know what you're talking about, Jules," he said emphatically. "I believe Larry is right."

Nobody ever asked me—but I couldn't help them anyway. My stomach started growling during that scene; I was too hungry for lunch to remember.

Finally Jules decided to view the rushes of that scene and it's a good thing he did. Larry was right and Jules was wrong. If Jules hadn't listened to Larry, the studio would have ended up spending thousands of dollars more for a retake . . . Good ol' Larry.

I also found Larry to be more natural on screen than Moe. Moe would ham it up more, while Larry appeared to be playing himself on screen and rarely mugged.

In *Merry Mix-Up*, I remember we did a routine that showcased Larry's natural talent for stealing laughs. It also typified the kind of silly patter that became our trademark in the films we did together. In this particular scene we were mourning the fact that our brothers, also veterans of war, were probably lost in action. I began by saying tearfully, "All these years we've never been able to trace our dear brothers."

"Poor guys must have been lost in action," interjected Moe.

"What a break. Gosh, what a break," sobbed Larry. "Worst break I've ever had . . . they all owed me money!"

"Quiet, Porcupine," said Moe, poking Larry. "And, speaking of money, how about the twenty dollars you owe me?"

"Oh, yeah," said Larry, "I only got ten, so I owe you ten," handing a ten dollar bill to Moe.

"Thanks," said Moe.

"Hey, Moe," I said. "You owe me twenty."

Moe and Larry graciously welcoming me as a member of the Three Stooges in our first comedy together, *Hoofs and Goofs*.

What looked like a normal cigar wasn't! From *Quiz Whizz,* a 1958 Stooge comedy.

Actor Dan Blocker (the monster) probably wanted to forget ever working with us before becoming Hoss Cartwright on TV's *Bonanza*. From *Outer Space Jitters*.

Thanks to Larry a real mixup was avoided in staging this scene of Stooge triplets. From *A Merry Mix-Up*.

Moe and Larry were receptive to a few changes in our films, like occasionally combing back their hair. From *Muscle Up a Little Closer*.

Our swan song became a bullfight picture with Greta Thyssen called *Sappy Bullfighters* (1959). The bull stayed employed, we didn't.

Comedian Joey Bishop put me back on my financial feet by making me a regular on his weekly TV series from 1962 to 1965.

My animated counterpart, Babu, from Hanna-Barbera's *Jeannie*, 1973.

Sharing my favorite holiday, Christmas, with my wife Ernie.

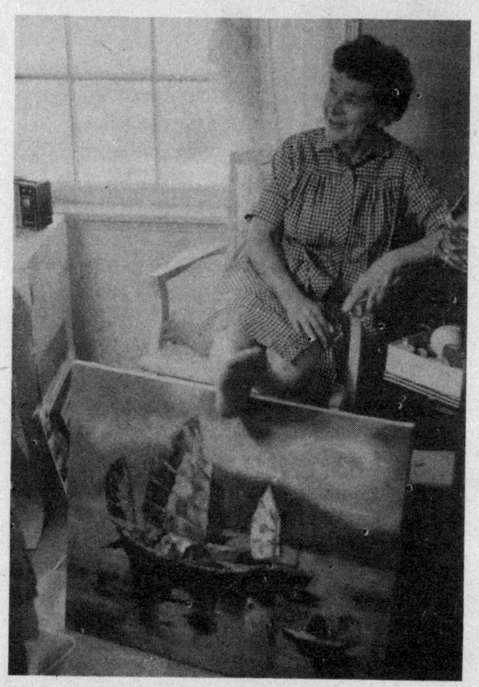
Ernie with one of her many paintings.

The big moment . . . unveiling the Three Stooges star—fifty years of Stoogery finally recognized!

With my "boys" Jeff and Greg Lenburg.

"Here's ten," said Moe, handing me the same bill Larry gave him. "I'll owe you ten."

"Ah-ah-ah," Larry remembered, looking at me. "You owe me twenty."

I handed him the same bill. "Here's ten," I said. "I'll owe you ten."

Then, quickly thinking, Larry hands the bill to Moe. "Here's the ten I owe you."

"Here's the ten I owe you," Moe says gleefully now passing the bill to me.

"Here's the ten I owe you," I remark, giving it back to Larry.

"Good," says Larry, "now we're all even."

In most of our films where stunts became too risky, Jules always substituted stunt doubles in our places. I'll admit these doubles looked about as much like us as the ceiling, but at least we saved in the bandage and gauze department. However, some minor injuries were inescapable.

In *Horsing Around*, the sequel to *Hoofs and Goofs* where we save our sister Birdie's mate, Schnapps, from the glue factory, I obtained my first injury as a Stooge. It happened in the scene where Jules had us ride down a bumpy road in a wagon.

Since most studio wagons and stagecoaches were stored outside the prop warehouse, the damp midnight air often caused these props to decay. So, when the script called for me to step down from the wagon, I stabbed my left hand on a one-inch splinter on a portion of rotted wood. I realized the splinter had gone into my hand because my hand started bleeding profusely and the pain was just unbearable. I looked like a Mexican jumping bean! Jules noticed the accident and he immediately sent me to see the studio's doctor, which turned out to be a fate worse than death.

Columbia's studio doctor must have flunked medical school, because I don't think he ever learned what a splinter was. When I showed him the wound (which was obvious because the area around it was red and sore), the doctor just glanced at it. "Gee, Joe," he said, "I see nothing wrong with your hand."

It's not as though the doc had a flood of patients pounding at his door, but the way he made his remark, in a fleeting sort of way, gave me the impression that he was bored with his work. Maybe for a little excitement I should have had Moe break a vase over my head to prove to the doctor that I was injured.

"Are you crazy?" I said, fuming, "I feel something in my hand. I'm sure it's a splinter."

The doctor just yawned and stood firm. "No, it isn't, Joe," he said. "You can go back to work now. It will be all right."

That weekend, I remember my hand began festering badly. Ernie looked over the wound and agreed that something was wrong. I decided to wait and see the studio doctor again on Monday; this time maybe he'd realize I actually injured my hand.

Meanwhile, on Sunday morning, I had chores to do around the house. I remember I went outside to change the light on the front porch which had burnt out. I climbed up the ladder to fix it and began removing the old lightbulb from the socket. During the continuous turning motion of removing the bulb, the splinter popped out of my hand and fell to the pavement below. My hand instantly felt better, but my temper didn't.

On Monday, I saw the studio doctor and brought the splinter in with me as evidence. The doc had malpractice suit written all over his face when I walked in. "I just want to show you," I said, "that I had a splinter in my hand but that you were too busy to see that!"

The doctor didn't know what to say; actually, there was nothing he could say. Several other actors had complained about his practice, too, so by the end of the week Harry Cohn finally gave him the ol heave-ho.

By December of 1956, Moe, Larry, and I finished the balance of our film quota for that year (I had also appeared in a film without the Stooges, *The Helen Morgan Story*, 1957), but not without a scare. In late August of 1956, we had a short break before our next picture. We had just finished filming a sci-fi comedy entitled, *Space Ship Sappy.* I should have taken time to rest but a neighbor asked me if I'd help him put the finishing touches on a new pool he had just built. Why not? I figured the outdoor recreation would do me good. The only exercise I had been getting lately was walking from my dressing room to the sound stage!

The hot summer sun beat down on us as we painted the bottom of the pool, and the air was filled with smog, but not enough to prohibit us from doing our work. After we finished putting on the last strokes of paint, I returned home to rest in the den. I sat down and suddenly felt a sharp twinge of pain near my heart. I was having a heart attack.

I called for Ernie and she had me lay down in bed and rest while she phoned our family doctor, Dr. Garson. The doc arrived a few minutes later and gave me a thorough check-up. He diagnosed the pain as a minor heart attack and recommended that I rest completely for two weeks before going back to work. Fortunately, I didn't have to be hospitalized; I recovered at home. My illness delayed the filming of our next Stooge comedy for a while, but it could have been worse; the Smiley Brothers could have been sizing me up for a pine box!

Moe and Larry were shocked by the news, of course. The last thing they wanted was another disaster to strike them down. Larry came by to visit, but Moe never did. Instead Moe called to see if I was going to be okay, which showed me that he cared about my well-being. I never doubted that he did, anyway. It's just that Moe had problems showing his true emotions, although he always showed them when it counted.

Following our first year together as a team, Harry Cohn expressed his satisfaction to us over the money our films were making. He was especially pleased with these results considering that the market for short subjects was declining daily. Theaters were beginning to book more double features instead of "curtain-raisers," another term for short subjects, and, according to Cohn, our films were the only two-reelers that were continuing to make money.

Therefore, before we started filming our first comedy of 1957, *Fifi Blows Her Top*, Cohn entertained the notion of putting us in a weekly television comedy show in addition to our short subject series. Harry saw that more studios were producing programs for television, so he thought that the obvious direction for us would be that same medium. However, for reasons that are still unclear to me, Cohn scrapped the project at the last minute. Instead, he kept us in short subjects for the rest of the year.

Thanks to Harry allowing us to continue with our series, I received my first pie in the face as a Stooge in a film called *Pies and Guys*. Pies had long been the Stooges' specialty and it's true that Moe threw all the pies in that film, as well as the other Stooge pie comedies. Moe always had a muscle-bound property man offstage stirring up the pie goop in a vat while Moe piled the stuff on pie plates; the ingredients were Moe's own special recipe.

I had never been hit by a pie before—on camera, that is!—so when we did the party scene where pies went a-flying I wasn't sure how to react when I got mine until Jules instructed me. He made me count to three and on three I was to be prepared for Moe to smack me with a pie. I remember Moe tossed the pie on schedule but when it struck me I just stood there wondering what I should do next. Finally I started eating the pie off my face. Then, looking straight into the camera, I said, "Oooh, that's delicious!" Jules, Moe, Larry, and the entire crew just burst out laughing.

Of course, every comedy team had its share of stinkers. We certainly did. The film I hate the most is *Sweet and Hot*, featuring Muriel Landers with Larry, Moe, and me playing separate roles. (Moe played a psychiatrist in that one). A fan had sent me a print of this film, so one night Ernie and

I invited a Burbank city councilman and his family over for dinner. Afterwards I decided to screen the film for them. Well, I realized what a dog it was when the councilman and his family started falling asleep—and so did I.

The filthiest film we ever made—and I don't mean language—would have to be *Oil's Well That Ends Well*. It was a remake of *Oily to Bed, Oily to Rise* with Curly, where we strike—what else?—oil! I remember one scene that called for me to sit on top of an oil gusher to plug it up so we wouldn't lose any oil. I became "an unsuccessful cork" when the gushing oil suddenly shot me up in the air, with me riding on top of the gushing oil. I was never too crazy about floating near outer space in that scene. They hoisted me upward on a crane for close-ups. The shot was so tight you never could see the wires which were holding me up.

Of course, Moe and Larry had the worst view; they were standing down below so the oil drenched them more than it did me. After we finished the scene, we scrubbed forever to get clean. We were so filthy, not even Mr. Clean could have helped us!

Moe and Larry were not always saints on the set. Now and again they would doublecross me in a scene. When we did *Quiz Whizz*, in which we played wards to M.M. Montgomery ("That means we'll be Montgomery Wards!"), we had one scene where we dressed up like children. A gangster (Gene Roth), posing as Montgomery, becomes wise to the fact we are adults in children's clothing, especially after I spot a pack of cigars close by and start smoking one.

"Oh, does Joey like cigars?" Roth cracks.

In an attempt to keep our identity intact, Moe says, "Oh, no. He don't like to smoke them."

"He likes to eat them," Moe adds.

Moe then forces me to eat the cigar, which makes me sick. But the cigar I really smoked was not the one you saw in that scene. At the last moment Moe and Larry planted an explosive cigar in its place; after I lit it up I looked like little black Sambo (unfortunately, that scene was cut from the film).

If this was what it was like to be a Stooge, I wish I could have been one forever.

Chapter 18

A Stooge Solos

December 20, 1957: We finished our latest comedy, and on this fateful day our futures at Columbia Pictures were decided. We had fulfilled the balance of the two years on our contracts, with an option for a third now to be discussed. That option, of course, was out of our hands, but we remained hopeful that we would continue with our relationship at Columbia and as a comedy team for years to come.

Those final minutes that Moe, Larry, and I spent together making the last film of our contract seem even more precious now, considering the decision that was to be handed down and how my life would be turned upside down.

With the final scene in the can, the boys and I were on our way to our dressing rooms. Moe said, "Well, fellas, let's keep our fingers crossed that Harry Cohn thinks we're worth another year." Larry and I just nodded; there was nothing else anyone of us could say.

In our dressing rooms, we slowly undressed, removed our makeup and awaited word from the studio hierarchy. I don't think we uttered one word during the whole time we were in there. Cohn and several studio executives were in closed-door meetings that very hour, so we hoped word would reach us soon about their decision.

It did.

Jules White walked in and we could tell the news wasn't good by the pained looked on his face. "Boys, I have bad news," he shrugged. "Columbia Pictures is letting you go."

Just like that we were finished. Three unemployed comics. Cohn had made the decision we all feared. He wasn't going to pick up our option. He was letting us go and possibly we could strike a deal with another studio. But since we were short-subject comedians, we knew no offers would be forthcoming. The writing was on the wall. We had outlived our usefulness, at least that's what we thought at the time.

When we received the news, Moe, Larry, and I were naturally downcast. We affectionately patted each other on the shoulder, turned around to finish dressing, and sat quietly with our own thoughts. I'm sure we were all thinking the same thing, mostly how Columbia had made millions on the Stooge films (and on mine as well) and how unfair it now seemed that they were letting us go. For Moe and Larry this decision meant an end to twenty-four consecutive years with the same studio. And I had been with Columbia for fourteen years. It didn't seem fair, but I guess it had to be expected. Like they say, all good things come to end.

While Moe and Larry left after hearing the news, only saying they would be in touch soon, I somehow found the nerve to see Harry Cohn one last time. Harry seemed surprised that I would come up to his office after he had made what was probably one of his toughest decisions. Never one to be remorseful, I looked him straight in the eye, smiled and said, "Harry, people can say many bad things about you, but you've been awfully good to me and I want to thank you."

Looking up from his desk, his eyes gleaming with emotion, Harry said, "Joe, I'll miss you and the boys. You've always come through for me. But what can I say? Television is the rage. Even though your films have made money, short subjects are dead. I wish I could say it was the reverse."

I thanked Harry Cohn again for sticking with me with all those years. Afterwards, I was actually relieved that he had let us go, because I had my own problems at home.

Ernie had suffered a heart attack one month before our dismissal from Columbia, so I was naturally concerned about her health. When I had last talked to Moe and Larry about our future as a team, they hadn't given me any indication of what might lay ahead. In the meantime, I cared for Ernie, cooked all her meals, and tended to all her needs.

By early January of 1958, Ernie had fully recovered, and she urged me to go back to work. We needed the money, as the medical bills almost devastated us. Any further financial plight was avoided when director Frank Tashlin called me from Twentieth Century-Fox and offered me a co-starring role in Bing Crosby's upcoming feature, *Say One For Me*. I immediately accepted this offer.

It was just before that picture that Moe contacted me about going on tour with Moe and Larry. During our meeting, Moe said, "Joe, Larry and I want you to stay with us. We feel you've fit in well with us as a third stooge."

"Yeah," said Larry, "there's nobody who could take your place."

"Well, thanks, fellas," I said. "But I hate to be the bearer of bad news.

I can't go with you on the tour. I've signed a contract to work with Bing Crosby, and I really need to be close to home in case Ernie needs me."

I was never told until later that one reason Moe suggested we go on tour was that Larry needed the money. Moe was a smart businessman; Larry wasn't. Larry had never properly invested his money so at that stage Larry was almost broke. If he didn't work, he would have to claim bankruptcy.

But neither Moe nor Larry let on to me that Larry was in this predicament. All Moe said was, "Joe, I'm sorry to hear that. But let me be the first to say that we'll miss you."

"I'll second that," Larry added.

We shook hands, patted each other on the backs, and went our separate ways for good.

Wasting little time, Moe found another replacement. He signed a burlesque comedian named Joe DeRita as my successor, who shaved his head and adopted the nickname of "Curly-Joe." Curly-Joe became a capable replacement, especially when the boys later experienced a tremendous resurgence in popularity in 1959.

In the meantime, my career took a different direction; I was on my own.

Landing the job in *Say One For Me* saved me from the throes of unemployment, but as time wore on I battled the greatest Hollywood curse of all: typecasting. I inevitably returned to doing what I did before I joined the Stooges—features and television shows—even though the jobs were few and far between.

I'm afraid the old adage of "once a Stooge, always a Stooge" prevailed on producers' minds. Consequently, in the months ahead, I would go to one audition after another only to go home disappointed. The casting directors would be looking for "a fat comedian type." I would show up, but so would *three hundred* other wideload candidates! Each of us were given a number and I felt as though I was at a cattle auction on the O.K. Corral! Finally, the auditions became a lost cause for me, until my performance in *Say One For Me* resulted in more work for me.

By now Ernie was feeling normal again, which made me happy. She was getting around more and doing more with her friends. She was getting into painting again, which was good therapy for her; it kept her mind off her troubles. Once I saw this sudden change in Ernie's behavior, I stopped worrying about her (well, not completely) while I went to work.

In February of 1958, *Say One For Me* started production, and I couldn't have found three greater individuals to work with than Bing Crosby, Debbie Reynolds, and Robert Wagner, the stars of the film. They certainly helped me forget my troubles, as did Frank Tashlin, a masterful comedy director. I played Robert Wagner's agent in the film, and I earned $2,500 a week (one thousand dollars less a week than I made with the Stooges). Bing donned a priest's cassock for the third time in his career (the first time was in *Going My Way*).

I think Bing was undoubtedly one of the most popular American entertainers of the twentieth century. He had had an equally impressive career in radio, music, and the movies, and his recordings had sold close to 400 million by the time I met him. Bing's real name was Harry Lillis Crosby and his laid-back singing style brought pleasure to the ear.

On screen, Bing was easy and relaxed, but off screen I saw just the opposite. He was all work and no play. We had one thing in common from the start: my brother Manny. They had worked together in vaudeville when Bing was relatively unknown. Bing was not real talkative. I found him to be a cold person; one you couldn't get close to because he put a protective shield around himself. I figured he must have been hurt badly at one time in his life, so he was slow to trust people.

Bing trusted me, however. I guess he sensed my sincerity and he liked working with me. After we completed the picture, I remember he surprised me with a special gift. As a token of his appreciation for my work, he gave me a St. Christopher's medal, which was blessed by the priest at Bing's parish, with an inscription on the back that read: "To Joe. From Bing. We'll 'Say One For, You!' "

I remember Debbie Reynolds was her bouncy, bright-eyed self most of the time when we made this picture. She had, of course, hit her mark in many musicals in the 1950s and she remained a big box office attraction well into the 1960s. I found her mood sometimes fluctuated as we got deeper into the picture, however. She seemed the happiest when her two-year-old daughter, Carrie Fisher (of *Star Wars* fame), came to visit her on the set. But I saw that Debbie appeared downcast over her messy divorce from Eddie Fisher; the memory still lingered on.

One day after we broke for lunch, I found Debbie sitting on the floor of the sound stage all alone, depressed. Carrie had just visited her and left. I was returning from the commissary where I had bought a pocketful of chocolate candy bars. I felt sorry for Debbie, so I walked up to her to see if I could put a smile back on her face. One thing about being a comedian is, I've always known when people are down.

"Debbie doll!" I said. She smiled. "How about having a piece of candy with me?"

Debbie perked up and the girlish look returned to her face immediately. "I'd love to have a piece, Joe," she remarked softly.

Like a little girl, Debbie removed the wrapper to the candy bar, daintily. A smile creased her face the minute she bit into the rich, milky chocolate. "Mmmmmm," she purred. "This is heavenly!"

Finally, I saw the Debbie Reynolds of old. She started kidding around with me and from that day forth I think she felt she found a new friend. She always came to me when she needed a little cheering up. Later, Debbie showed her gratitude to me for being her friend by treating me to one last candy bar!

Working with Robert Wagner was also a real treat. He was always full of the dickens, and we enjoyed one laugh after another when we rehearsed our lines together in his dressing room. A beautiful brunette often graced us with her presence, too: Natalie Wood, Wagner's wife. She was as beautiful in person, if not more, than she was on screen. We laid the jokes on so thick sometimes when she came in that I remember Natalie couldn't control her laughter. "Stop, you two!" she'd scream between heehaws. We never did, and Natalie never stopped laughing either.

After I finished *Say One For Me*, Frank Tashlin broached the subject of starring in another picture with me. It was called *The Laughing Man* with Maurice Chevalier and Mary Costa, Tashlin's wife. The film would have been my dramatic debut and was to be filmed in France, with production starting in the fall of 1959. I was set to portray an elderly widower who gets into pathetic situations. Unfortunately, the deal fell through, but several producers heard from Tashlin about my good work in *Say One For, Me*. I received jobs in several more features at Twentieth Century Fox—*The Rookie* with Tommy Noonan and Peter Marshall, in which I played an army medic, and *The Story on Page One*, with Rita Hayworth and Gig Young—and another feature, *The Plunderers of Painted Flats*, for Republic Pictures.

Following those appearances, however, I didn't do much else except worry about what my next job would be. In the spring of 1959, I made several television appearances on *The Kraft Music Hall*, both times with Milton Berle. With Berle, I knew I would be well represented throughout the show—and I was. We hadn't seen each other in years, but you wouldn't have known it by our performances. We had no difficulty picking up where we had left off. We showered the audiences with our usual brand of zaniness. On one show we did a takeoff on the Oscars called, "The Annual Milties Awards." Edgar Bergen and Charlie McCarthy were guests on another broadcast.

Edgar Bergen thought the world of me. Charlie McCarthy was a fan of mine, too. Bergen enjoyed talking about comedy with me between takes. I'll never forget how we were introduced. The day of the show I was walking by his dressing room and he was sitting there with Charlie on his lap. The minute I walked in the door Bergen put Charlie to work.

"Hello, Joey!" Charlie said, in a wise Brooklynese accent. "Come on in!"

I did a double-take at first, but Charlie wasn't through.

"What's the matter?" he cracked. "The cat got your tongue?"

"Oh, shut uuuup!" I said, swiping my hand at him.

Charlie rolled his eyes skyward, then he said, "I knew you were going to say that!"

But after that period, jobs were scarce. For the first time since 1955, I was out of work frequently and sometimes I wished I was a dummy like Charlie McCarthy: he had no responsibilities and no worries. I never gave up, though. I had certainly been blessed up until now with great success.

Things didn't get any better for me though when I turned the calendar pages to the year of 1960. Shortly after Ernie and I rang in the new year, Ernie had her gall bladder removed. Medical bills piled up, and by this time I had been out of work for almost six months. I felt like a character from *The Towering Inferno*—everything was going wrong at once. And Charlton Heston wasn't around to save me!

I was so desperate for work that I filmed a pilot for an instructional television series entitled, *Better Bowling*. The show was produced by AMF and it presented instructions for beginning bowlers. I played a bowler learning to bowl for the first time. The show was so bad, viewers weren't sure which of us was the bowling ball—me or the ball!

One day, Frank Tashlin heard about my predicament and asked me to come by and visit him at Paramount. He was directing Jerry Lewis in his latest comedy, *Cinderfella*. I drove to the studio with renewed hope, and when I arrived Tashlin and I caught up on old times before he introduced me to Jerry.

As it turned out, Jerry had been a fan of mine for years. Following a warm embrace, Jerry remarked how glad he was to see me. "You've always been my favorite comedian," he said. "I remember you from when I was a kid growing up in Jersey."

Apparently Jerry and his father, Danny Lewis, who also worked in show business, used to come and watch me perform my vaudeville act when I played at a theater near his hometown, Newark. New Jersey. They used to sit up in the balcony and, as Jerry said, "We screamed our heads off laughing at you."

Jerry asked me what I had been doing lately.

"Nothing," I said. "It's been pretty rough for me lately, Jerry."

"You mean you haven't had any work," Jerry asked, surprised.

"I haven't worked in about six months!" I admitted.

Jerry sank low in disbelief.

"Well, we'll have to do something about that," he said. "I'll sign you to a contract and you'll have something to do. Don't you worry."

Jerry proved to be a man of his word. He put me under contract as a "gag man" and he kept me around the set in case something happened to Ed Wynn, who was co-starring in the film. Jerry and Tashlin were worried about Wynn's health, and they weren't sure whether he'd be able to finish the picture.

"Hang around, Joe," Jerry said, "until we see how Ed is. You'll receive a full salary in the meantime."

Well, I couldn't complain. Jerry paid me $1,000 a week for five consecutive weeks and I did nothing more than contribute a few gags now and then. Meanwhile, I developed a friendly relationship with Ed Wynn. I often visited him in his dressing room and we talked about comedy for hours. I had worked with Ed in vaudeville, and I had always admired his work. After all he was the granddaddy of comedy!

During our visits together I never saw any reason to believe that Ed was going to suddenly drop dead. He certainly had all of his faculties together. Finally, I went to give Jerry and Tashlin a full report, and I was completely honest with them. "Fellas," I said, "that man is as bright as the day he was born!"

Well, maybe I was *too* honest! A week later they let me go because they decided my services were no longer needed. But I didn't care. Ed finished the picture and I was $5,000 richer!

Later that year, Jerry called me back again to work with him in *The Errand Boy*, a 1961 feature he was starring in for Paramount. I was certainly touched that Jerry would think about me a second time. But, I guess that's how much he cared about me.

Originally, Jerry only wanted me for one day. I was playing an exasperated movie director. In the scene that was shot outside in a western setting, I was supposed to "direct" two cowboys. Jerry told me, "Do whatever comes to mind, Joe."

Jerry positioned himself next to the camerman who was seated atop a camera crane. Once Jerry yelled, "Action!" I responded by ad libbing the entire scene. The cowboys failed to take my direction, so I created utter chaos on the set. "Quiet on the set!" I said. When they ignored me, I stomped my feet like a little kid and screamed, "I said q-u-i-e-t!!" I did all sorts of other bits that are too difficult to describe because the whole scene was completely spontaneous.

Even though I never thought my scene was funny, I remember Jerry and the cameraman laughed so hard that the crane and camera started shaking! We ended up filming part of the scene over. After I was through, Jerry asked me to stay.

"Don't go away yet," Jerry said.

"You want me to stay?" I said.

"Yes, you just stay here."

Then the head casting director on the picture approached me as Jerry resumed filming. "Jerry wants you for the next four weeks on this picture," he said. "He has an idea on how he wants to use you."

I was kept on for four more weeks, at the same salary as before, but Jerry didn't use me again until the final week of filming. He decided to cut my scene as a movie director. Instead he used me in a scene where I was part of a panel of studio executives who were viewing the rushes to Jerry's new feature that had an errand boy as the star.

I'll admit it was silly of Jerry to keep me around just to film this one scene, but that's the way he is. He wanted to help me out by letting me have the salary. Heck, I didn't care. I needed the money so badly that Jerry could have asked me to mop the studio floors and I would have. Anything to work!

After working in the two Lewis features, things started to pick up for me again. I appeared in one more feature for Twentieth Century Fox, *Let's Make Love*, with Marilyn Monroe (whom I never met because I only worked in the picture for one day). I also made two television appearances. The first was on *The TV Guide Awards Show* with Fred MacMurray and Nanette Fabray in two sketches as a "mailman" and "milkman" and the second was on the *Shirley Temple Theatre* in an episode entitled *Babes in Toyland*, with Jonathan Winters, Carl Ballantine, Jerry Colonna, and me as pirates.

Early in 1961, it seemed as though I was going to be in for another drought. Although I kept landing one bit role after another, there was nothing substantial. I appeared in one feature, besides *The Errand Boy*, called *The Silent Call* with Roger Mobley and Gail Russell. On the television side of things, I did the voice of a fire-breathing dragon for *The Alvin Show*, featuring those lovable chipmucks: Alvin, Simon, and Theodore. I enjoyed the work but the money I earned went through my hands the minute I earned it.

Ernie's health was poor at the beginning of the year, so her medical bills continued to wipe out most of my earnings. Aside from the Lewis features and my scant television appearances, I continued to flounder. I was too proud to call people for work. After all, hadn't I done enough in this business for people to remember me?

Fortunately, my agent Phil Weldman of the William Morris Agency never gave up on me. He kept trying to scrounge up work for me, daily. When he made his normal rounds to the studios to meet with various producers, he often brought me along so I could impress these producers into hiring me.

One time we dropped in on the set of *Sergeants 3* at United Artists. I didn't realize it, but Frank Sinatra, Dean Martin, Sammy Davis, Jr. and Peter Lawford were working on this picture together. As soon as I laid a foot on the set, Sammy Davis saw me and went screaming after me like a wild man from Borneo.

"Joey Besser!" he said. "What have you been doin' man?"

I told Sammy that my agent had brought me by while he talked business with somebody.

"Come on," Sammy said, in his usual manner, "have you met Sinatra?"

"Yeah," I said, "when I was with the Stooges, Frank used to sneak over to the set and watch us make movies, and we would sneak over to the set and watch him make his."

Sinatra beamed and hugged me. Then a man,who had been a fan of mine for years, stepped up from behind Sinatra to meet me. His name was Joey Bishop (he was also in the film). I knew Joey from watching him do *The Jack Parr Show* several times.

"Joey," Sammy told Bishop, "I want you to meet another Joey." Sammy clapped his hands and laughed like he always does when he says something he thinks is clever. Joey spoke after Sammy contained himself.

"I feel I've known Joey Besser for years." he said. "When I was in the Army I was the head of the entertainment division and we owned a print of *Hey, Rookie!* We ran that thing for the servicemen until the sprockets fell off! Finally I had to order a new print."

For a few minutes, our conversation sounded like a meeting of the Mutual Admiration Society and afterwards Joey didn't forget me. I received a call from Phil Weldman in June of 1961. Joey had been starring in a new series for NBC called *The Joey Bishop Show.* He wanted me to appear on his show. Marlo Thomas, Bill Bixby, Joe Flynn, and Warren Berlinger were among the regulars, and Joey played a press agent named Joey Barnes.

I agreed to do the show and played a postman in an episode called "A Very Warm Christmas" that was broadcast on February 21, 1962. After I did the show, Joey called me back to do another show, then another, then another. I ended up appearing on the last six shows of the season and soon other job offers came in. Sammy Davis put in a good word for me, and I joined him and Charles Bronson in an episode of CBS's *General Electric Theater*. This was just the start.

After my appearances on the Bishop shows aired, NBC received thousands of letters from fans who wrote in and said, "Thank you for finding Joe Besser. We've missed him!" Joey heard about the deluge of mail my appearances on his show had elicited. So after we filmed the last show of the season, James V. Kern, the show's director, came to me. He said, "Joe, we're going to do a new series for next season. It's already been set and I've got news for you. You're going to be a regular, right from go."

The nightmare was finally over. Steady work at last! In 1962 I became a regular on *The Joey Bishop Show*. Getting the job helped save me from plunging further into debt. Ernie always told me to have faith. "Whenever we need help the most," she would always say, "God will be there." He sure was, and Joey was my guardian angel. They both came through in the nick of time. Working on Joey's show also helped me finally break the curse of being typecast as a Stooge. I had a tremendous revival of fans. The residue carried me through the sixties.

Before the season started, Joey hosted *The Tonight Show* in place of Johnny Carson. That night, Joey invited Ernie and me to the show. He told the millions of viewers tuning in that "my pal, Joe Besser, will be appearing in my new series for NBC this fall." Joey asked me to stand up in the audience and take a bow. The audience gave me a rousing round of applause. It was heartwarming, indeed, to hear the sounds of applause again, and I fought back tears as I realized how I had survived the toughest ordeal in my life. But now that was behind me.

In September of 1962, *The Joey Bishop Show* returned for a second season on NBC. It was completely revamped and had a new format and a new cast of characters. Joey kept the same character name of Joey Barnes, but now he was a *Tonight Show*-type television host. Each episode revolved around Joey's personal and professional life as a TV celebrity, with many guest stars appearing as themselves. Joey Barnes was married to a Texas girl named Ellie, played by Abby Dalton, and lived in the Carlton Arms Apartments. Joey's manager, Freddie, was portrayed by a gifted comedian named Guy Marks (who was replaced in 1963 by Corbett Monica as Larry Corbett). Mary Treen served as the Barnes' housekeeper, Hilda, and I was Jillson, the apartment building superintendent (in other words, I was the janitor!), who bungled more than he repaired things. The show ran until 1965, and went through some other changes. In 1962 the show was filmed in color, and the following season we switched to CBS. That was the year Joey's wife Ellie had a baby boy on the show. The baby was played by Abby Dalton's infant son Matthew Smith. In 1964, Dr. Sam Nolan, a pediatrician neighbor played by Joey Forman, was added to the cast.

The 1962 season opened with a bang! Critics loved the new format, even though the show's ratings slipped from the previous season (*The Defenders* was our main competition). I remember one critic said, "Bishop's new show is a lot like the old 'I Love Lucy' and Jackie Gleason 'Honeymooners' programs. It is sheer nonsense designed for nothing more than to make people laugh." The show reminded critics of the highly rated Danny Thomas show because of our similar format. Joey played an entertainer in family situations. This was no coincidence. Danny was the executive producer of our show!

Many hours of preparation went into filming each show. We rehearsed all week long, and on the day of the show we would go through a dress rehearsal hours before filming. Every Monday morning we reported to a special conference room where we sat around an executive-style table. Joey distributed the scripts to each of us, and then we spent the next two days memorizing our lines. By Wednesday, Joey handed us a new script, complete with revisions and changes, and we went over that. Initially I found it difficult to memorize a script for two days, then learn new pages of dialogue. Later I got smart! I was like a little kid who had found the easy way out. During the first days I acted as though I was memorizing my lines. Instead I waited until Wednesday! Nobody ever knew, except me!

Joey was a perfectionist. If one line of dialogue was off, he worked on it until he got it right—many times right up until minutes before we filmed. I vividly recall one time that Joey tried to change a line of dialogue on me just before I made my entrance. But it backfired on him. Joey frequently did this to others on the show, and his changes were always for the good of the show. But this time he didn't give me enough warning.

Joey and I were supposed to make our entrance together through the apartment door. We were standing behind the door when Joey stopped me. His exact words to me were: "Joey, when you come in, don't say this line, say that." When our director James V. Kern rolled the cameras I walked in and repeated exactly what Joey told me to say. I said, "Joey, when you come in don't say this line say t-h-a-t" Well, Joey busted up laughing and, in the future, he never changed a line on me at the spur of the moment like that again.

We often had name guests on the show. They included Danny Thomas, Buddy Hackett, Jackie Coogan, Zsa Zsa Gabor, Jack E. Leonard, Ed McMahon, Andy Williams, Jack Benny, Robert Goulet, Edgar Bergen and Charlie McCarthy (this time *I* did the talking to Charlie!) and several members of the Los Angeles Dodgers: Don Drysdale, Tommy Davis, Frank Howard, Willie Davis, Bill Skowron, and Ron Perranoski.

Milton Berle and his wife Ruth were guests in an episode called "Joey and Milton and Baby Makes Three," which aired during the third season. This was after Abby had given birth to Matthew and in the show Joey was learning the ins and outs of caring for his newborn son—from feeding him to changing his diapers. The kid cried so much that Joey finally asked me to install a doorbell chime that rang to the tune of "Rock-a-Bye Baby." I installed the chime, and I remember Berle was in that scene with me.

Everytime I tested the bell it rang off key and Berle was supposed to say, "It's too shrill! It's too shrill!" The line the writers gave me was not a funny line at all. I was supposed to say, "Okay, I'll take care of it!" Since I didn't think the line would muster any laughs, I surprised Milton with one of my ad libs.

When we actually filmed the scene, I tested the door chime, after which Milton said his line. Then I said, "All right, I'll *unshrill* it! I'll *unshrill* it!" Miltie doubled over with laughter because my line was funnier than the scripted one. James V. Kern, left the line in, even though Milton broke his composure.

Now and then I would run into other celebrities who were on the Desilu lot where we filmed. Marty Ingels had his own series for ABC which he also filmed there entitled, *I'm Dickens, He's Fenster!* Even though we had never officially met, I understood Marty was a great fan of mine. Our paths finally crossed one day, but I'm not sure it was in a way Marty Ingels would like to remember!

Marty was cleaning up his dressing room before a 6:30 P.M. interview with a newspaper reporter. Meanwhile, I was preparing to leave the studio. About three minutes before the reporter was due, Marty noticed a pile of animal droppings right in the middle of his dressing room floor. You could smell it for miles! Marty wasn't sure how it got there. Maybe a trained animal from another show got loose.

In a race to the finish, Marty scraped up the mess and dumped it in a copy of *Variety*. At approximately 6:28 P.M., Marty dashed out the door looking for a place to throw it. He no sooner tore around a stage corner when there I was—staring at him. Marty put on the brakes to stop from crashing into me (and, believe me, I had plenty for someone to crash into!). With only thirty seconds left before the interview, Marty tried hiding *Variety* from me, folding and carrying it under his arm like a time bomb ready to explode.

"Hello," Marty said abruptly, the sweat dripping down his face. "You must be Joe Besser. I've been wanting to meet you for years!" (Under a different set of circumstances, I'm sure.)

I struck up a friendly conversation with Marty as the seconds ticked away, but I could see that he was embarrassed and panicky. The sweat began dripping more profusely from his face. I had no idea why until I said, "Hey, Marty, could I check something in the *Variety*?"

Marty excused himself and said he would bring it back to me later. I'm still waiting!

As *The Joey Bishop Show* progressed, I was featured more prominently every week and I appeared in 89 shows in all. Soon the writers created more stories around my character, and I couldn't have been happier. My character became so popular, that I received telegrams from several network officials congratulating me. I was also made an honorary member of the local chapter of the janitor's union!

There are several favorite episodes from the show that I remember. One was called "Jillson and the Cinnamon Buns." In this show Joey and Abby tried putting me on a diet. My weakness: cinnamon buns! The story was like the movie *Lost Weekend* with Ray Milland, where Milland used to hide liquor bottles in the chandeliers and other secret locations. In my case I hid cinnamon buns in the lamps, under the couch, and in the closets of Joey's apartment! Joey finally discovered I had gone off my diet when he opened the hallway closet and an avalanche of cinnamon buns fell on top of him!

Another favorite of mine was "Jillson's Toupee." Joey and Abby thought I would look good in a toupee, so they bought me one as a birthday present. The children who lived in the apartment building didn't like it, however. They liked me bald. I, however, began to like it. I started feeling like a young swinger, and eventually I got a swelled head. Later, I gave in to the pleas of the children and tossed the toupee away when I found that they no longer liked me.

I think one of the funniest episodes had to be "Joey and Buddy Hackett

Make a Luau" from the 1964 season. At the beginning of the show Buddy promised Joey that he would never play another practical joke on him. But Buddy can't keep his promise when he learns that Joey plans to throw a luau for the sponsors of his talk show—so Buddy invites himself!

Buddy was permanently rearranging Joey's kitchen when I walked in to paint the kitchen.

"Buddy Hackett, you remember me," I said, "your ol' pal, Jillson?"

"How could I forget you?" Buddy said, pointing at my stomach. "You have my old body there!"

Buddy then saw a perfect opportunity to get into further mischief by telling me that Joey's wife didn't want the kitchen painted yellow.

"You ignored Ellie's orders," he said.

"Then what color did Mrs. Barnes want?" I asked.

"Polka dot!" Buddy said. "It goes with everything!"

He told me that I couldn't buy polka dot paint but that I would have to make it!

Buddy returned to the apartment later and cleared out all of Joey's furniture, turning it into a Hawaiian setting. On the night of the luau, Joey impressed the sponsors and Buddy was the hero of the hour!

In 1965, the laughs ended when *The Joey Bishop Show* was cancelled by CBS. Its final broadcast was on February 12, 1965, and I was sorry to see the show go. I had had four memorable years working with Joey and, like all performers, I didn't want them to end.

After the show was over I didn't go back to work right away. I spent more time with Ernie. Now that I was free from long working hours, we started going to the theater and doing more traveling. Ernie started taking more night classes at a local high school to further her education; she has always been a bug for knowledge. Then, one day in 1965, I thought I had lost my Ernie for good.

Ernie had a second heart attack. It was greater than the first one, and she was rushed to the Sherman Oaks Hospital. Ernie is a battler like her mother, so she never gave up. The odds are usually against you when you've already suffered one heart attack. Fortunately, Ernie beat the odds by fully recovering.

When Ernie returned home, I helped nurse her back to health, which became a full-time job. I only took on one job while she was sick, a cameo, in *With Six You Get Egg Roll* starring Doris Day. I played a chicken delivery man. My scene was shot only six blocks away from my house, or else I wouldn't have taken it because Ernie came first. I cooked all her meals, did all the grocery shopping, and maintained the entire house. I took on all the responsibilities that were normally hers.

This time I was more financially set than the previous times Ernie became seriously ill. So I could afford to stay home and take care of her. Unfortunately, by staying out of work for almost a year, I was temporarily forgotten by producers until I started making the rounds again. In 1966, I made a television appearance in an episode of *Batman* called "Hizzoner the Penguin" with Adam West and Burt Ward. Yep, I mixed villainy with comedy, but it was a job!

In 1967 I managed to avoid a further career tailspin by getting back into the thick of things. I received enough work to keep Ernie and me afloat financially. I appeared on several episodes of ABC's *Hollywood Palace* and on a Danny Thomas special, *It's Greek to Me*, as Hermes (spelled "Hermies" in the script) a Greek god.

Then my old pal Joey Bishop looked my up again. He was starring in a new show for ABC, a weekly variety talk program that was called *The Joey Bishop Show.* The program was similar to *The Tonight Show* with Johnny Carson. Joey had different guests on the show every night and he was the host.

The first year Joey created a special comedy act for the show called, "The Son-of-a-Gun Players" (*son-of-a-gun* was Joey's famous catch phrase). Joey made me one of the players, along with Joanne Worley and Ann Elder. We appeared in eight shows scattered throughout the season, and we always emerged from one of four doors on stage to perform routines with Joey. Later, a similar idea was used in TV's *Laugh-In* where cast members kept popping in and out of doors. Ours was better. We got more laughs every week on Joey's show, and our comedy ensemble had quite a following. Dean Martin and Frank Sinatra thought our act was their favorite spot on the show.

Unfortunately, Joey changed the show's format in 1968, so I was out of work again, even though the exposure on his show was responsible for keeping me employed. I appeared in two episodes of *The Mothers-in-Law* with Eve Arden and Kaye Ballard (in one show I was the bandleader of a Salvation Army-type band called, "The Friends in Need" and in another I was a hobo). I also worked on *That's Life* with Robert Morris as a delicatessen delivery man, on *That Girl* with Marlo Thomas as a juror, on *Hollywood Palace* as a necking stage manager, and on *The Don Rickles Show* as a Russian spy and as Aristotle Onassis.

My schedule became even more crowded in 1969, with more television appearances on many top shows, such as *The Good Guys* with Bob Denver and Herb Edelman; on *Hollywood Palace* as a hijacker; on *The Mothers-in-Law*, in my third appearance, this time as an innocent theatergoer; on *Burlesque Is Alive and Living in Burbank*, an NBC comedy special with Goldie Hawn that never aired; on *The Monk*, a TV-movie with George Maharis; and on *The Jerry Lewis Show* (plus another feature with Jerry, *Which Way to the Front?* as a comedy dockman). Heck, I did everything but blow bubbles on the Lawrence Welk Show!

I remained just as active the following year of 1970 by doing a wide range of parts. I kept my face before the television public by appearing on *My World and Welcome to It* with William Windom as "a chief of police," which was followed by *The Bing Crosby Christmas Special* for NBC as the character Lumpy, plus an episode of *Love American Style* ("Love and the Proposal," as a customer in a diner).

Suddenly, the parts dried up. In 1971 my only roles were in episodes of *Love American Style* ("Love and Murphy's Bed" and "Love and the Lady Barber" with Frank Sutton). Soon I found myself disillusioned with Hollywood and my career. Producers' tastes in filmmaking had changed drastically. Television programs and feature films were rapidly becoming more suggestive in their content, and there just didn't seem to be a place left for a comedian from "the old school" like me.

For the first time since I had entered show business, I decided maybe it was time to remove the greasepaint for good. Maybe it was time to retire.

Chapter 19

No Business Like Cartoon Business

In March of 1972 I saw the proverbial writing on the wall: there were fewer and fewer jobs for comedians like me. Producers were hiring a crop of young, up-and-coming comedians for their television shows instead of the more experienced veterans. I wanted to work badly, possibly in another weekly television series. But little by little the people I knew in the business were retiring or finding a place in the big film factory in the sky.

I still felt like a little kid inside, and my desire to work in show business had never been stronger. Now, after more than fifty years from the day I had run away with Thurston I still wanted to make people laugh. It was my daily goal.

Maybe if producers could have seen the bags of fan mail I received monthly, they would have hired me. I averaged almost two to three hundred letters a month! They were from fans of all ages who were either nostalgic and wanted to relive their childhoods through me, or were first-time fans. I've always appreciated the kind words many fans have expressed to me in their letters, and those letters that had deep sentimental value, I have kept over the years. My garage is bulging with boxes of fan letters dating back to my days in vaudeville! It would take a Bekins moving van to haul everything out!

But I started running out of room because of Ernie's paintings. By now she had built up a regular gallery of her oils to display. She still took night classes in painting at a local high school. But since she painted so much, I decided to convert the dining room into a studio for her. Now it looks like "Ernie's Paint Factory," with her easels and paints scattered all over. To me, the expense is no object as long as it keeps her happy. Besides, you know the old saying: "Easel come, easel go!"

In 1972, I was calling my agent at the William Morris Agency once a week about work. He always told me that he was circulating my name around to producers, but that nothing had come up as yet. Well, I went back to work, but by no miracle on my agent's part. One day I received a call from Friz Freleng. (Though I knew of Friz and his work, I had never talked to him before. He just called me out of the blue.) He had been an award-winning cartoon director at Warner Brothers where he co-created Bugs Bunny. He also created that pesky character Speedy Gonzales. Friz was now in charge of his own cartoon production company, DePatie-Freleng Enterprises, which produced cartoons for Saturday mornings.

"Joe, this is Friz Freleng," he said. "How would you like to come to work for us?"

"Work?" I repeated. "You mean a real job with a weekly paycheck and everything?"

"Why, sure, Joe," said Friz, "that's exactly what I mean."

"When do I start!"

Friz laughed. "Joe, you can start by coming down and taping an audition tape for us," he said. "We're doing a new cartoon series and we are interested in having you do the voice of one of the characters."

I wasn't going to say no.—I wasn't stupid, you know! Besides, Mr. Opportunity hadn't been knocking at my door lately.

The next day I taped the audition and the character I voiced was named Puttypuss, the cat of a thousand faces. He was one of the main characters in a *Mission Impossible*-type spoof Friz was producing entitled, *The Houndcats*, in which a group of animals that belong to a governmental intelligence agency undertake one impossible mission after another.

In April, Friz phoned me with the good news: the job was mine. Thanks to Friz, I never contemplated retiring again, as new opportunities opened up for me thereafter.

Meanwhile, the rest of the cast was selected, with Daws Butler as Stutz, the Houndcats leader; Aldo Ray as Musclemutt; Arte Johnson as Rhubarb; and Stu Gilliam as Ding-Dong. The first show we did was called "The Misbehavin' Raven Mission" and we recorded thirteen episodes in all.

In the months ahead, I found cartoons were more fun and easier to do than either television or feature films—so much so that I wondered where I had been all these years? I reported to the studio once a week, collecting $750 a week, to read my lines into a microphone with the rest of the gang. No fuss. No bother. No script changes. I never stuck to the script anyway, so that didn't matter. Friz always encouraged me to ad lib. He figured I had ad libbed all my life in show business, so why should I change now?

On September 9, 1972, *The Houndcats* premiered on NBC and it became one of the highest-rated shows in its time slot. This became a period when I started receiving feelers again from various people regarding work. Even though I wasn't seen in these cartoons, there was no mistaking my voice. "Joe Besser," they'd say "where have you been hiding?"

I always gave them a stock answer. "Well, I've been trying to beat Rip Van Winkle's record for sleeping," I'd say. "I figured one of these days you people would call to wake me up!"

One person who called was the producer of *Love American Style*. I had already appeared in three previous episodes (and the show was one of my favorites). They wanted me to do a fourth.

I filmed the show in November of 1972 with David White (formerly of TV's *Bewitched*). The episode was called "Love and the Lady Legend" and I played a duck hunter. The day before we filmed I remember the producer sent the script to me by special messenger. I tirelessly rehearsed my lines with Ernie. Then, two hours later, I received a revised script. This didn't bother me because every show I had worked on, I always received a revised script. So I memorized the changes, but apparently the producer wasn't through. Later that evening I received another script by messenger, with more changes. Then, at 10 P.M., a fourth and final script arrived. Well, that was it!

The next morning I reported to Paramount at 8 A.M. to film the show and told the producer off. I was so mad I wanted to "smash h-i-m!"

"You can't expect to change scripts on people like you have," I said. "This is a horrible thing to do. You can't expect an actor to learn and then relearn their lines on such short notice. I'm doing the scene *my* way and if you don't like it you can get somebody else!"

Well, the producer calmed me down and he finally apologized. "Joe, you're absolutely right. And I'm sorry," he said. "Just do what you feel comfortable with in the scene."

I did, but afterwards I stuck to doing cartoons. They didn't present half the hassles that a television show did.

If 1972 presented me with TV production hassles, it also marked the beginning of an unusual and wonderful new friendship. One day in November I met two people who, like most of my fans for their age at the time, had discovered me through reruns of old shows and first-time broadcasts of my performances on network shows. From the first day we met, they became an integral part of my life. Later they helped put me back in the spotlight once again. They were sixteen-year-old twins, and students at Loara High School in Anaheim, California ("near Disneyland," they said). As a class project, they wanted to interview me about my career in show business. I agreed, and they brought along their instructor and another friend.

When they arrived, I remember opening the front door and being faced with the pattern from two colored shirts. Rolling my head back, I made eye contact with "them." They towered over me like two redwoods and, yes, they were identical! One said, "Hello, Joe, I'm Jeff Lenburg. I spoke to you on the phone." Then, the other one, who sounded and looked the same, said, "Hi, Joe, I'm Greg Lenburg. It's really a thrill to meet you!" Already I was confused!

Ernie greeted the boys. "My God," she said, "your're tall. Where did you come from? Texas?"

The boys and I sat down in the den, and what a challenge it became for me to remember all the things I had done in show business. I rarely conducted interviews, but Jeff and Greg were an exception. I began recalling incidents and stories about people whose names and faces had been out of my thoughts for years. I began to realize I really had worked with a lot of people. The twins started to remind me of other films and TV shows I had appeared in.

Africa Screams with Abbott and Costello is one of our favorites . . . still is," spouted one of them.

"That's right, I did the water bit in that one." I interjected. "Now, how did you know that?"

"Looked it up."

Now they really had me. I asked them if they remembered any others shows I had worked in.

"*Son's of Fun* with Olsen and Johnson?"

"Yep."

"Let Yourself Go with Milton Berle."

"Yep."

"Stinky on *The Abbott and Costello Show*?"

"Yep."

"*The Errand Boy* with Jerry Lewis?"

"Yep."

"*The Jack Benny Show*? *The Fred Allen Show*? *The Eddie Cantor Show*?"

"Yep, yep, yep."

The kids fascinated me. They were real fans! Not only did they know all the films I had appeared in (some forty they said), but they had even done research on how many television shows I had been in (they were close to the 200 mark).

In the months and years ahead, my friendship with the Lenburgs blossomed. Ernie and I took in Jeff and Greg like they were our own sons. Since then, they've always been here when we've needed them and they still are. We've spent Christmases, birthdays, and summers together. We've also become close to their parents John and Catherine Lenburg and their older brother, John. Since I've known Greg and Jeff they've researched more about my career than even I can recall. Most of it is apparent in this book. Sometimes I don't know what I would do without them.

I was signed to do my second cartoon series entitled, *Jeannie*, for Hanna Barbera in 1973. It was a spin-off of the popular TV series, *I Dream of Jeannie*, starring Barbara Eden. But the story had a different twist. It involved a high school student named Corey (voiced by Mark Hamill later of *Star Wars* fame) who, one day, discovers a magic lamp on the beach containing Jeannie.

The studio artists developed a bumbling apprentice for Jeannie: Babu, the character I voiced. (There was more in that magic lamp than first met the eye!) The likeness between the character and me was unbelievable. It was as though they had me in mind from the start, since my voice fit Babu perfectly and the writers even developed a new catch phrase for me to say when Babu would disappear: "Yapple d-a-p-p-l-e!"

I really felt like I had arrived in the cartoon business with this role. The *Jeannie* series kept me busy until 1975. I later started providing voices for other characters in other cartoon shows, like *The Oddball Couple* (in an episode called, "A Day at the Beach"). I played a genie, of course!

Even though I had found a new role as a voice for cartoon characters, I wasn't able to elude the shadow of my former "Stooge" self. In late 1974, the Three Stooges went through a minor cult revival, and Stooge fans came out of the woodwork. I heard several colleges were actually studying our films and that fans of all ages were going around imitating me and the other Stooges. Of course, what helped matters was that most of us were still around.

Moe Howard was still active. He was lecturing at colleges and universities across the country and making appearances on such national talk shows as *The Mike Douglas Show*, reprising many old Stooge routines. Larry Fine was not as active. In 1970, he had suffered a stroke that left him partially paralyzed on his left side. He was living at the Motion Picture Country House, a retirement home and hospital for actors in Woodland Hills, California. But he was active in his own way. Larry and Babe London (who starred in *Scrambled Brains* with the Stooges and in Laurel and

Hardy comedies) visited schools in the San Fernando Valley area of Los Angeles, where they showed Stooge movies and conducted question-and-answer sessions with young fans.

I hadn't heard from Moe and Larry since the day we broke up as a team, in 1958. All of us had been busy with our own lives, so there was never any time to correspond. They led their lives. I led mine. Fans never understood this, however. A good portion of my fan mail came from Stooge fans who wanted to know more about my relationship with the boys. I would try and explain to them that the Stooges were only part of my career, but they always wrote back in disbelief, or, if I met them in person, they would give me a puzzled look.

It was at times such as these that I sympathized with someone like Leonard Nimoy of *Star Trek*. How would you like to be remembered the rest of your life for wearing pointed ears? In any case, this was a period of self-assessment for me. I was grateful to the fans who had remembered me, but I was surprised they only remembered me for being a Stooge. Ernie and I couldn't go anywhere without some fan coming up to me and saying, "Weren't you one of the Stooges?" I didn't even know those movies were being rerun on television!

Later I realized there was a purpose behind all this recognition, and I began to accept my role as an ex-Stooge. In January of 1975 Larry died of a stroke. Several months later Moe was ill with cancer, and he started to write me. Moe recalled working with Ernie in *A Night in Spain* in 1929, plus our first meeting on stage of *The Passing Show of 1932*. His letters interested me because during our years together I had always found him unable to express his feelings. Now, with his days numbered, I think he wanted to express some of those feelings to me.

In late April of 1975, Moe found the strength to call me.

"Joe, this is Moe," he said, his sounding tired and weak. "How have you been?"

"Moe, I couldn't be better," I said, touched by his call. "It's been a long time—eighteen years!"

Moe chuckled a bit. "Yes, it has, Joe. Those years were great times," he said. "I've been real sick lately so I'm sorry that I haven't answered yours and Ernie's letters, but I think about you daily."

"Well, I think about you, too, Moe," I said.

Moe started sounding weaker by the minute, so, finally, I decided to cut the conversation short. "I'll keep you in my prayers, Moe," I said. "God bless you and good bye."

Five days later, on May 4, 1975, less than four months after Larry's death in January, Moe died of lung cancer. He was 78.

I didn't attend Moe's or Larry's funeral because I would have felt out of place. I preferred to remember them the way I had seen them last. I had felt the same way about Momma and Poppa when they died and some of my closest friends. I found it more comforting to remember the happy moments we had shared together.

I have had plenty of time now to reflect on my final correspondence with Moe. It was as though Moe were passing on the Stooge baton to me and to Curly Joe DeRita, my replacement in the act. Moe realized he didn't have long to live, so he knew we would have to take over, in the years ahead, as spokesmen for the team. In 1976, when Curly Joe's health started to wane, I would become the sole spokesman.

Moe's and Larry's deaths were a turning point for me in terms of my feelings about the Stooges. Before that, I had only remembered the awful time I had had finding work after I left them. I had had mixed feelings about being known as a Stooge. Now, however, when I think back to my days with the boys I don't have any regrets. Their memories live with me, and I'm glad that I was part of them.

In 1976, for the first time in nineteen years, my identity as a Stooge finally started working in my favor. Jeff and Greg Lenburg began acting as my press agents. They began sending press releases to Hollywood trade papers about all my activities and they sent promotional fliers to producers, announcing that I was available for work. Well, I started seeing results in no time. I received a dozen job offers within two months after those first notices were mailed. Even though I said I would never work on television again, I knew I would reconsider if I could work with someone I had worked with before.

Among those who contacted me in 1976 were two old faces from the past: Hal Kanter and Sam Denoff. Hal Kanter was then executive producer of *Chico and the Man* with Freddie Prinz and Jack Albertson, and Sam Denoff was producing a new summer variety show for CBS starring Bert Convy.

Sam's office was at CBS where the Convy show was also taped. We hadn't seen each other since he produced *That Girl* with Marlo Thomas. Bert Convy sat in on the meeting. They were looking for a comic to play off Convy.

Bert stood up to greet me when I walked in. "Joe Besser," he said, "I haven't seen you in years! You're looking good. Are you going to work with us?"

"I hope so," I said with a laugh. "I was entertaining audiences at CBS before you were even born!"

Sam and Bert discussed the show over lunch with me, but nothing concrete was said. They never made an offer or explained whether or not they wanted me. After saying goodbye to Bert, Sam escorted me outside. Finally, I said, "Sam, why did you bring me out here?" The lunch was great, but why?"

"Joe, I'm sorry you had to come out all this way for nothing," he said apologetically. "But before you arrived the network executives decided they wanted to go with *young* comedians, instead of old ones . . . I'm real sorry."

"So am I, Sam," I said. "So am I."

Sam and I shook hands and I started walking toward my car. I was instantly mobbed by fans who wanted my autograph . . . Too bad the CBS executives never saw that!

Naturally, I remained disappointed for a while over this incident, for I felt a comedian never grows old. A comedian can always fit into a different situation or become a different character because he's ageless; his work is never finished. I've always considered a comedian to be like one of Santa's elves; everytime he prances on stage to entertain people he brings joy into their hearts—not just at Christmas but year round. Therefore, I remained an elf, wanting to entertain and waiting for the right chance to come along.

It looked as though I was finally going to be given that chance after I met with Hal Kanter during the week of our country's bicentennial celebration. Apparently Hal had created a role that was, if I got the job, for me to be an irregular on *Chico and the Man*. James Komack, the show's producer, liked the idea, and he sat in on the meeting with Kanter and me.

"I don't know who else could do this role except you," Hal told me. "It features all your mannerisms and expressions."

I read the script and Hal was right. He had written a part for me as a car owner who took his car in to be serviced at Ed's Garage. Freddie Prinz would greet me and we would get into a bit of business over what needed to be done to my car. Finally, after Freddie confused me, I would tap him on the shoulder and yell, "Leave me alone, you c-r-a-z-y y-o-u!!"

When I finished reading the part, Kanter and Komack were hysterical. Hal told me, "We'll try it, and if the executives at NBC like you, we'll put you in every so often."

I didn't hear from Hal again until December of that year. He had finally received the okay from the network to use me and I agreed to take the job. Our first rehearsal was scheduled for February 14, 1977, Valentine's Day. I couldn't wait to step before the cameras. It had been five years! Finally I would be given the opportunity to show people that "the elf" was still alive in me and prove to the executives at CBS who had wanted "new comedians" that I could still make people laugh.

I was never given the chance, however. Two weeks before the show's filming, Freddie Prinz committed suicide. His death put the show's future in limbo. Later, after Kanter and the company regrouped, Hal asked me if I would be interested in becoming a regular, but I declined. I was too disturbed over Prinz's death and had no desire left to perform on the show. Instead, Hal convinced George Gobel to take my place.

When all the other offers I received for television roles also fell through, I returned to my old standby: voicing cartoons. For the next two years, I became more established in this field by working in a number of popular cartoon shows.

In 1976, I provided the voice of a "giant" character for *Misterjaw-Supershark* (the episode was called, "Shark and the Beanstalk"), which was produced by DePatie-Freleng to cash in on the *Jaws* craze. In 1977, I became a regular on another Hanna-Barbera series called *Scooby's All-Star Laff-a-Lympics*, reprising my characterization of Babu. I also played the character of Simple Simon in an episode of *Baggy Pants and Nitwits* with Arte Johnson and Ruth Buzzie for DePatie-Freleng. I joined the science fiction craze when I became a regular on *Yogi's Space Race* for Hanna-Barbera, and did the voice of Scarebear (a bear who splits into every direction the minute he gets scared!).

By the spring of 1979 I couldn't wait to start working the new season. I believed my future in the cartoon business would only get brighter. I was content doing cartoons and enjoyed working with people such as William Hanna, Joseph Barbera, Friz Freleng, and David DePatie. They all treated me like a king.

One day Joe Barbera called me to see if I would be available again in the months ahead in case he needed me. I told Joe I didn't see any problem. "I'm *always* available!" I said. After the excitement of talking to Joe, I suddenly started feeling rundown. Ernie had had her usual ups and downs lately, so I worried about her and took care of her around the clock. At times I was doing the work of two people without fully realizing it, so I began to wear out faster than usual.

After lunch I decided to sit down in the den and rest when all of a sudden my left arm began shaking wildly. I tried calling for Ernie, but I only managed to utter some high-pitched sounds—no words. I tried putting something into my pocket, but I couldn't. My arm felt like a piece of lead. Finally, I managed to push my hand into my pocket, but everything fell out. "What's happening to me?" I thought. Again I tried yelling for Ernie, but nothing came out. A few minutes later I stopped shaking and the entire episode was over. I didn't realize it then, but I had suffered a minor stroke.

Ernie told me to lie down and rest while she phoned our family physician, Dr. Richman. Richman told Ernie to get me to the hospital right away. Because she didn't drive, I drove us to the Tarzana Hospital after resting for a while. Richman put me through a series of tests, and I was hospitalized for one week. He also gave me my first complete physical. I had never had one because I was always afraid that doctors would tell me something was wrong with me. Under these circumstances, however, I had no choice. So, scared or not, I gave in.

Once the test results were in, Richman gave me the bad news. "Joe, we're going to put you on a salt-and sugar-free diet," he said. "We found that something blocked an artery in the back of your neck, which caused you to have the stroke. We've also discovered that you're suffering from diabetes."

"Can you explain that in English for me, Doc?" I cracked.

"Yes, I can," Richman said with a chuckle. "It means you'll have to lose weight and watch what you eat."

I didn't argue, because Richman knew best. Besides, he told me I was a very lucky man. I emerged from the stroke without any serious side effects or paralysis. I was able to walk out of the hospital, which was more than most stroke victims could say for themselves.

My battle of the bulge began immediately. Richman had the nurses feed me nothing but salt-and sugar-free foods. I remember the foods tasted pretty bland at first and I would dream about having glazed donuts and chocolate cakes. At the same time I kept thinking about the theory of mind over matter. And, boy, did I have a lot of matter! I weighed in at the hospital at 220 pounds. Two months following my discharge from the hospital and extensive dieting, I had lost sixty pounds!) I was a new streamlined version of Joe Besser. I could even bend over and tie my shoes for the first time in years (as well as see them)!

I have to credit the lovely nurses who saw to my needs for helping pull me through this ordeal. With all the tubes they put in me, you'd think I was training to be a space shuttle astronaut! I was definitely the life of the party at the hospital. The young nurses always checked up on me. Once word got out that I had been a Stooge, the number of nurses who made rounds to my room increased considerably. In order to appease them, Ernie brought me a batch of Stooge photographs to autograph. I must have signed one hundred photographs while I was there!

The day Richman released me from the hospital, Jeff and Greg drove me home. I was relieved to be at home. But at the same time I got misty eyed when I thought of working again. I told the boys I had decided it was time to take it easy. Having the stroke made me realize that life was too short, and I had too much left to enjoy. I didn't need to push anymore. Of course, if somebody offered me a job and it seemed right, I would take it. As it happened, I received an occasional call to voice another character, but for the next three years I was less active.

I didn't need the fame and fortune anymore. What was more important to me at this stage in my life was having Ernie. She was everything I had in the world and I decided it was time I devoted more time to her needs everyday. Unfortunately, once I got well again Ernie went through some more physical problems—she had a cataract removed and a pacemaker implanted—so I didn't have time to do anything more than take care of her. Through it all, our love for each other carried us through and our love for each other continues to be as strong, if not stronger, than the day we met. In November of 1982, we celebrated our fiftieth wedding anniversary, a tremendous feat considering how very few Hollywood marriages last today.

When I wasn't caring for Ernie, I did find time to sit back and reminisce about the good days gone by, my many achievements in show business, and the millions of fans who supported me throughout the years. I realized more than ever that it was time to be thankful for all that I had done and to ask God to give me time to continue my work, savor more ovations and applause, and be remembered.

As long as people remembered me, I would be happy.

Chapter 20

Once a Stooge, Always a Stooge

The producers in Hollywood may have forgotten me, but my fans never have. Thousands of fans still write to me year after year, recalling my days with the Three Stooges and as Stinky on *The Abbott and Costello Show.* In 1982—taking me quite by surprise—my popularity skyrocketed to new heights when the Stooges and I received what every artist yearns for: international recognition.

During that year I experienced tremendous fan revival because of my association with the Three Stooges. The Stooge fan phenomenon had broken out like a runaway train! Every newspaper, radio, and television station carried stories about the Stooges and how millions of fans—college age and older—were flocking weekly to revival shows of Moe, Larry, Curly, Shemp, and me. The amazing part was that kids were paying $4 and $5 a ticket to watch these films, even though many television stations in their areas were also showing them daily!

My fan mail increased twofold. Fans were asking me dozens of questions about the Stooges, and I was more than happy to answer their questions. I only looked back on the good times I had shared with the boys during my stint with them. I didn't mind as much anymore that, even though my career had encompassed so many other roles, I was primarily being remembered for being a Stooge. I guess I had mellowed with age.

As a result, I would have to say that the greatest thrills lay ahead for Ernie and me. In 1982, Hollywood proved that it was still a glamorous and loving town. Especially when it came to honoring those who had contributed to the business in the days gone by.

In October of 1982, I was honored at the National Film Society's Movie/Video Expo '82 at the Universal Sheraton Hotel in Hollywood where my pals Jeff and Greg Lenburg conducted a salute to the Three Stooges. I headed a guest list that included Phyllis Fine Lamond, Larry's daughter; Stooge producer Norman Maurer and his wife, Joan Maurer, Moe's daughter; director Ed Bernds; screenwriter Elwood Ullman; and actress Julie Gibson, who had worked in several Stooge comedies with Curly.

The people from the National Film Society really gave me the red carpet treatment. Ernie was unable to come because her arthritis was acting up, but she convinced me to attend the salute anyway. I'm certainly glad I did. When I walked in, the audience gave me a standing ovation and for two hours straight, the outpouring of love never stopped. Fans asked me questions about Moe, Larry, Curly, and Shemp and I couldn't say enough to please them. After the program was finished, I was mobbed from every corner by fans wanting my autograph. It was during this exchange that I realized how crazy the young people of today were about me. Many fans brought old theater posters and lobby cards from my Columbia features, as well as photographs of me with the Stooges, to autograph. Several girls leaned over to kiss me and photographers crowded around to snap pictures. Their flashbulbs were a kaleidoscope of light explosions that almost blinded me.

I was on a cloud for days after the ceremony. The honors and tributes to me and the Stooges were just beginning. In February of 1983, radio personality Gary Owens, then of Los Angeles station KPRZ, mounted a nationwide write-in campaign to induct the Stooges in the Hollywood Walk of Fame. Almost every big name in show business had received a bronze star on Hollywood Boulevard—Bob Hope, Abbott and Costello, Jerry Lewis, Frank Sinatra, and John Wayne—but for years we Stooges had been slighted. What an injustice! Apparently, the members of the Hollywood Chamber of Commerce, who annually nominate thirteen candidates for stars felt that the Stooges were low-brow comedians undeserving of such an honor.

Well, Gary saw to it that this great injustice was amended. He and my pals Jeff and Greg Lenburg formed a committee known as "A Star for the 3 Stooges Committee," which received the support of Joan Maurer, Barry Koltnow, a local newspaper columnist, and many nationally syndicated columnists. They received endorsements from noted celebrities such as Steve Allen, Tim Conway, Mel Brooks, Arte Johnson, Carl Reiner, and Frank Sinatra, Jr.

But that's not all!

Their committee amassed more than 25,000 letters from fans around the world, all supporting their Stooge star drive. The news media also got full swing behind the campaign. A local TV show, *Eye on L.A.*, did an investigative report on the Stooges which showed that attempts had been made in the past to get us a star but that the Hollywood Chamber of Commerce had ignored these pleas. Soon more television station news shows aired reports, and a ground swell of national and international support in Canada and Australia followed.

By April 24, 1983, the pressure on the Hollywood Chamber of Commerce became so intense that Bill Hertz, the chairman of the Walk of Fame Committee of the Hollywood Chamber of Commerce, and Bill Welsh, the president of the Hollywood Chamber of Commerce, announced on Gary Owens' radio program that the Stooges would receive a star on August 30, 1983 in "the largest ceremony in Hollywood ever."

It's funny but, as I told Jeff and Greg, I had had a dream several months before the campaign that we were going to receive a star and that I would be asked to say a few words on behalf of the boys. I would look up to the sky and say, "See, I told you they were going to do it!" So who says that dreams don't come true!

The day of the ceremony, I was a nervous wreck. I wasn't one to make speeches, but I knew people would be disappointed if I didn't. This event would also mark the first public meeting of me and my successor, Curly Joe DeRita. However, due to poor health, Curly Joe was unable to attend. So, I would be the sole spokesman for the team.

Ernie and I rode to the ceremonies in style in a chauffeured black limousine with our friends Frank and Helen Berry and Hank Pollard. As the Hollywood Chamber of Commerce had promised, the event was as glamorous and exciting as an Academy Awards presentation.

Los Angeles Mayor Tom Bradley proclaimed the day "Three Stooges Day," and fans started lining up in front of the star in the wee hours of the morning. At 11:30 Ernie and I arrived at the Brown Derby restaurant for a pre-ceremony luncheon. The restaurant was only one block away from the site of the star, and during the luncheon I conducted last-minute interviews with scores of reporters. *Entertainment Tonight* filmed the event for the opening story on their program and referred to the Stooges getting a star as "one of the top stories of 1983." Local Los Angeles TV station KTTV also aired the ceremonies live as part of their noonday news. I could not remember the people of Hollywood ever going to the lengths they did that day for us Stooges.

During the luncheon I saw Milton Berle, who was invited to say a few words about the Stooges since he had had us on his television show when Shemp was the third stooge. Milton gave me a big hug and said, "This is your moment, Joe." Immediately, Milton and I started recalling many of the old routines we did on his radio show, and we re-created them to the delight of the audience.

I was also touched by others who showed up that day to remember me and the boys: Jamie Farr, of TV's M*A*S*H, Adam West of TV's *Batman*, Norman and Joan Maurer, Phyllis Fine Lamond, and Paul Howard, Moe's son, whom I had never met. But the best was yet to come.

The ceremonies began at noon and nearly three thousand fans crowded around the star. The area was so packed, some fans had to stand on top of billboards and automobiles to watch the presentation. It was like a gigantic political rally, and I felt like I was being nominated for the President of the United States!

Several policemen escorted Ernie, me, and the entire group of guests through the crowd. The cheers swelled as I neared the platform to represent "the boys." Fans started imitating me and the "Hey, Joes!" became as deafening as their applause.

Bill Welsh opened the ceremonies by giving a speech about the contributions we had made as a team. Gary Owens appropriately served as the master of ceremonies. Then, one by one, the guest speakers took turns giving their testimonials. The best came from Jamie Farr and Milton Berle.

Jamie summed it up most succinctly when he said: "I don't think there's anyone in the world who doesn't know who the Three Stooges are."

Then Milton, who has never been at a loss for words, expressed his feelings and at the same time kept the crowd entertained with one one-line after another. What Milton said seemed most appropriate considering that Moe, Larry, Curly, and Shemp were not around to enjoy the ceremony with me. "What these men gave to the world is timeless," he said. "These great gentlemen, who brought laughter to millions and millions of people, will never be forgotten."

At one point I couldn't resist interrupting Milton, however, just like old times. A fan had interrupted him so it only seemed fitting for me to do the same when Milton told the fan: "There will be no ad libbing here, son . . . One fool at a time!"

I then ran up to Milton, tapped him on the shoulder, and screamed, "Did you call m-e-e-e!!"

Berle looked at me and laughed, and the audience gave me a loud ovation. One of four that day! But the biggest ovation was to come later. After many more speeches, including one by my pals Jeff and Greg Lenburg, bedlam cut loose! Gary introduced me for the unveiling of the star! First he asked me to say a few words.

Fans screamed and cheered, waving banners and hollering "You crazy y-o-u!!" I only hoped that I would know what to say when I stepped up to the podium. In the meantime, I cherished the moment and blew kisses back to the crowd in gratitude, which brought me more cheers until I finally quieted them down.

I said what came most naturally to me, in my familiar whiney voice. "I'm not gonna say m-u-c-h!!" I said.

The crowd went crazy and after they quieted down again, just like in my dream, I looked up toward heaven and said: "I noticed there are four clouds up there, and you know who's looking down on all you wonderful people? The boys. They loved every minute they had together, and my two years with them was one of the highlights of my career in show business. I loved the boys and we had a lot of fun, and I know you had a lot of fun watching us . . . because we love you as much as you loved us!"

The crowd became delirious. Afterwards Gary squeezed my hand and brought me down to the location of the star. An army of news photographers and cameramen crowded around as Bill Welsh announced: "Ladies and gentlemen, the 1,767th star of the Hollywood Walk of Fame . . . The Three Stooges!" Bill Hertz, Bill Welsh, Joan, Phyllis and I knelt down as we pulled the tassled, gold velvet cover away and there it was: a star bearing the team's name! Hundreds of cameras clicked in unison and the thousands of onlookers cheered and clapped wildly.

For a moment, I wondered what Moe, Larry, Curly, Shemp, and Curly-Joe were thinking. I was only sorry that they couldn't have been there to stand beside me. What a celebration that would have been! We all had played an equal part in the success of the Three Stooges, and now, as the star shined, tourists and fans who had laughed at us from the around the world would have a constant reminder of our years of fun and antics.

At the end of the day, the limousine driver took Ernie and me home, and I was still euphoric. Hollywood had finally recognized the Three Stooges, and they had also indirectly paid me back for all that I had contributed to the world of show business.

This world called comedy is a funny thing. In my darkest moments when I thought I would never reach stardom, something good always came my way. Regrets? None. I wouldn't sell my life in show business for a million dollars. Either singly or as a Stooge, I've worked with the most beautiful people and some of the biggest names in show business. I've also had the most loyal fans an entertainer could ever hope for. The deluge of love in the form of fan letters has only made me want to entertain more. It's hard to believe that, as of this writing, I'm now entertaining my seventh generation of fans. Pretty good for someone who started in the business at the age of thirteen!

I am proud to be a part of the world of comedy. I do wish, though, that today's comedy world would clean itself up. It's a shame that there are so many comedians who are so talented—who resort to below-the-belt humor. I'm annoyed when I read an answer to who influenced these comedians the most, that they invariably say, Abbott and Costello, Laurel and Hardy, the Marx Brothers and, of course, the Three Stooges. Let's not forget them.

If this is how we influenced them, I'm surprised. I'm proud to say that in all of my performances—even those with the Stooges—I never, ever used a *hell* or a *damn* for the sake of getting a laugh. It wasn't necessary then, and it isn't necessary today. For the most part, the only comedians today who I think are throwbacks to us comedians of old are guys like Chevy Chase, Bill Murray, Steve Martin, and John Candy. As long as they continue in this vein, I think the future of comedy is in good hands.

In a way I feel sorry for comedians today. They don't have the training grounds we had years ago to develop their character and material. It's tougher to break into the business. For those young, aspiring comedians out there wanting to fulfill their dreams, I say, stick to those dreams, but remember it takes hard work, perservence, and originality if you're ever going to make it.

I've been asked numerous times by fans of all ages, "What's your proudest moment, your proudest accomplishment?" That's a tough question to answer. I'm proud of every moment, actually—67 years of uninterrupted laugh-making. I'm especially grateful to the people who gave me opportunities when I needed them the most—Olsen and Johnson, Jack Benny, Lou costello, Jerry Lewis, Joey Bishop—all of them allowed me to blossom, unselfishly and uninhibitedly.

I am deeply thankful for my association with the Three Stooges. In every sense, my years with them turned out to be a blessing. I'll be the first to admit that, for years, it bothered me that my Stooge role overshadowed some other great work in my career. But as time has passed and I've mellowed with age, I realize that thanks to the Stooges and my association with them, fans are able to appreciate my work with the boys and rediscover my other work.

It seems fitting then to end this book by saying: To Moe and Larry, thank you, from my heart. I was not just a Stooge, but because of you and our years together, I can now rest assured that I will be remembered forever. And for that, my life in show business, and with you, was worth every moment.

Filmography of Joe Besser

Feature Films Starring Besser, 1944-46

All films are black and white and were released to theaters by Columbia Pictures.

1. *Hey, Rookie!* (1944). Directed by Charles Barton. An army rookie, Pendleton "Pudge" Pfeiffer" (Joe Besser), helps another soldier (Larry Parks) produce a show for the servicemen that features Winnie Clark (Ann Miller), a Broadway leading lady.
2. *Eadie Was a Lady* (1945). Directed by Arthur Dreifuss. Professor Diogenes Dingle (Joe Besser) teaches classical drama at Glen Moor College in Boston where a student named Eadie Alden (Ann Miller) is starring in the school's annual Greek Festival.
3. *Talk About a Lady* (1946). Directed by George Sherman. Janie Clark (Jinx Falkenburg) travels to New York with her guardian, Roly Q. Entwhistle (Joe Besser), to find out why she was named heiress to an estate.

Feature Films With Besser in Supporting Roles, 1940-76

All films are black and white unless otherwise noted. Role played by Besser follows director on each film listed below.

1. *Hot Steel* (1940). Universal, directed by Christy Cabane, "Siggie Landers."
2. *Feudin', Fussin', and a-Fightin'* (1948). Universal, directed by George Sherman, "Sharkey Dolan, Sheriff of Rimrock."
3. *Africa Screams* (1949). United Artists, directed by Charles Barton, "Harry the Butler." Also features Shemp Howard of the Three Stooges.
4. *Woman in Hiding* (1950). Universal, directed by Michael Gordon, "Fat Salesman."
5. *Joe Palooka Meets Humphrey* (1950). Monogram, directed by Jean Yarbrough, "Carlton the Hotel Clerk."
6. *Outside the Wall* (1950). Universal, directed by Crane Wilbur, "Chef."
7. *The Desert Hawk* (1950). Universal, technicolor, directed by Frederick de Cordova, "Sinbad."
8. *I, the Jury* (1953). United Artists, 3-D, directed by Harry Essex, "Elevator Operator."
9. *Sins of Jezebel* (1953). Lippert, Anscocolor, directed by Reginald LeBorg, "Yonkel the Chariot Man."
10. *Abbott and Costello Meet the Keystone Kops* (1955). Universal, directed by Charles Lamont. "Hunter."
11. *Headline Hunters* (1955). Republic, directed by William Whitney, "The Coroner."
12. *Mad at the World* (1955). United Artists, directed by Harry Essex, "Gas Station Attendant."

13. *Two Gun Lady* (1956). Associated Film Releasing, directed by Richard H. Bartlett, "Town Drunk."
14. *The Helen Morgan Story* (1957). Warner Brothers, directed by Michael Curtiz, "Bartender."
15. *The Plunderers of Painted Flats* (1959). Republic, Naturama, directed by Albert C. Gannaway. "Andy Heather."
16. *Say One for Me* (1959). Twentieth Century-Fox, DeLuxe Color and CinemaScope, directed by Frank Tashlin, "Joe Greb."
17. *The Rookie* (1959). Twentieth Century-Fox, directed by George O'Hanlon, "Medic."
18. *The Story on Page One* (1959). Twentieth Century-Fox, directed by Clifford Odets, "Gallagher."
19. *Let's Make Love* (1960). Twentieth Century-Fox, DeLuxe Color and CinemaScope, directed by George Cukor, "Lamont the Joke Writer."
20. *The Silent Call* (1961). Twentieth Century-Fox, CinemaScope, directed by John Bushelman, "Art."
21. *The Errand Boy* (1961). Paramount, directed by Jerry Lewis, "Studio Projectionist."
22. *The Hand of Death* (1962). Twentieth Century-Fox, directed by Gene Nelson, "Gas Station Attendant."
23. *With Six You Get Eggroll* (1968). National General, Color, directed by Howard Morris, "Chicken Delivery Man."
24. *The Comeback* (1969). Congdon Films, directed by Donald Wolfe, "Sightseeing Bus Driver." Never-released.
25. *Which Way to the Front* (1970). Warner Brothers, Color, directed by Jerry Lewis, "C.W.O. Blanchard."
26. *Hey Abbott!* (1978). ZIV International, Color and Black-and-White, Directed by Jim Gates, Compilation of *The Abbott and Costello Show*, "Stinky" (old footage) and Joe Besser (new footage).

Joe Besser also served as an uncredited gag writer on *Cinderfella* (1960/Paramount) starring Jerry Lewis.

Columbia Shorts Starring Besser, 1938-56

All films are black and white and were released to theaters by Columbia Pictures. Running times are 16-17 minutes. For more details, see *The Three Stooges Scrapbook* (Citadel Press, 1982).

1. *Cuckoorancho* (1938). Directed by Ben K. Blake. Joe is mistaken for an American millionaire by a poor hacienda owner.
2. *Waiting in the Lurch* (1949). Directed by Edward Bernds. An addiction to chasing fire engines almost makes Joe miss his own wedding.
3. *Dizzy Yardbird* (1950). Directed by Jules White. Joe becomes the hero of the

day when he rescues his Army sergeant from a mess hall fire.
4. *Fraidy Cat* (1951). Directed by Jules White. Joe and comic straight man Jim Hawthorne are detectives hired to catch a jewel-stealing gorilla. A remake of *Dizzy Detectives* (1943) with the Three Stooges.
5. *Aim, Fire, Scoot* (1952). Directed by Jules White. Besser and Hawthorne are drafted into the Army of Starvania where the sergeant takes a liking to Joe's wife. Joe reprises his "Army Drill" routine.
6. *Caught on the Bounce* (1952). Directed by Jules White. Joe must remit $2,500 or the mortgage on his trailer home will be foreclosed.
7. *Spies and Guys* (1953). Directed by Jules White. Joe joins the Republic of Yugonutzland Army and goes on a spying mission with a female soldier.
8. *The Fire Chaser* (1954). Directed by Jules White. Joe wins back his fiancee, whom he lost when she found out about his addiction to chasing fire engines. Stock footage from *Waiting in the Lurch* (1949).
9. *G.I. Dood It* (1955). Directed by Jules White. Joe is promoted to sergeant when he recovers some stolen documents. Stock footage from *Dizzy Yardbirds* (1950).
10. *Hook a Crook* (1955). Directed by Jules White. A reworking of *Fraidy Cat* (1951) with some stock footage.
11. *Army Daze* (1956). Directed by Jules White. A reworking of *Aim, Fire, Scoot* (1952) with some stock footage.

Miscellaneous Shorts Starring Besser, 1953-59
1. *A Day in the Country* (1953). Lippert. 3-D Anscocolor. 15 minutes. Produced by Jack Rieger. Joe narrates the daily activities of two young country boys.
2. *The Woodcutter's House* (1959). Walt Disney Productions. Color. 10 minutes. Joe is "The Green Man," a live-action elf surrounded by animated characters, in this one-reel screen test. Never-released.

Three Stooges Shorts Starring Besser, 1957-59

In 1956 Besser joined the Three Stooges replacing Shemp Howard who died in 1955. He made the following 16 two-reel comedies with the two original Stooges, Moe Howard and Larry Fine. All of these films are black and white and were released to theaters by Columbia Pictures. Running times are 15½-17 minutes. All are directed by Jules White. See *The Three Stooges Scrapbook* (Citadel Press, 1982) for a comprehensive Stooge filmography.
1. *Hoofs and Goofs* (1957). Joe dreams that their sister Birdie has been reincarnated into a horse.
2. *Muscle Up a Little Closer* (1957). Moe and Larry help Joe find his girlfriend's stolen ring.
3. *A Merry Mix-Up* (1957). The Stooges portray three sets of identical triplets separated during the war, who are reunited years later.
4. *Space Ship Sappy* (1957) The Stooges encounter three cannibalistic Amazon

women on the planet Sunev (that's Venus spelled backwards).

5. *Guns-a-Poppin'* (1957). Larry and Joe take Moe on a hunting trip to calm his nerves.
6. *Horsing Around* (1957). The Stooges save Schnapps, Birdie's mate, from the glue factory.
7. *Rusty Romeos* (1957). The boys mistakenly propose marriage to the same girl.
8. *Outer Space Jitters* (1957). The Stooges help a professor study the lifestyle on a planet, and almost become zombies.
9. *Quiz Whizz* (1958). Moe, Larry, and Joe pose as children in order to recover Joe's TV winnings.
10. *Fifi Blows Her Top* (1958). Joe is humorously reunited with his sweetheart from the war.
11. *Pies and Guys* (1958). A professor bets another that he can turn three plumbers into gentlemen.
12. *Sweet and Hot* (1958). Joe and Larry take their sister, Tiny, to a German psychiatrist (Moe) who cures her fear of singing in front of people.
13. *Flying Saucer Daffy* (1958). Joe becomes a hero when he takes a picture of a real flying saucer.
14. *Oil's Well That Ends Well* (1958). The Stooges find an oil gusher while searching for uranium on their father's property.
15. *Triple Crossed* (1959). Larry is two-timing Moe's wife and Joe's fiancee.
16. *Sappy Bullfighters* (1959). A jealous husband tries to foil the Stooges from performing their comedy bullfight in Mexico.

Three Stooges Features Starring Besser, 1959-

1. *Three Stooges Fun-O-Rama* (1959). Columbia. Directed by Jules White. Compilation of the Stooge shorts with Joe Besser.

Television Appearances

Weekly Television Series Co-Starring Besser, 1952-68

The following is a listing of television programs on which Besser was a series regular. Role played by Besser follows names of cast members on each series listed below.

1. *The Abbott and Costello Show* (Syndicated CBS, December 5, 1952 to May 29, 1953). 30 minutes. With Bud Abbott, Lou Costello, Sid Fields, Hillary Brooke and Gordon Jones. "Stinky." 13 Episodes: "The Wrestling Match," "The Drugstore," "The Birthday Party," "Alaska," "The Vacuum Cleaner Salesman," "The Army Story," "The Charity Bazaar," "The Haunted House," "Peace and Quiet," "The Music Lovers," "Getting a Job," "Bingo," and "The Actor's Home."
2. *The Joey Bishop Show* (NBC, February 21, 1962 to September 1964; CBS, September 29, 1964 to September 1965). 30 minutes. B/W and Color. With Joey Bishop, Abby Dalton, Corbett Monica and Mary Treen. "Jillson." 88 Episodes: "A Very Warm Christmas," "Surprise, Surprise," "Must the Show Go On?" "Route 78," "A Show of his Own," "The Image," "The Honeymoon," "Penguins Three," "Three's a Crowd," "Door-to-Door Salesman," "Joey's Replacement," "The Fashion Show," "Baby It's Cold Inside," "Joey Takes a Physical," "Deep in the Heart of Texas," "The Honeymoon is Over," "Chance of a Lifetime," "Joey's Lucky Cuff Links." "Kiss and Make Up," "Double Time," "Jillson and the Cinnamon Buns," "Freddy Goes High Brow," "Joey Leaves Ellie," "Ellie and the Talent Scout," "A Crush on Joey," "Joey's House Guest," "We're Going to Have a Baby," "The Baby Formula," "Joey's Dramatic Debut," "Joey and the Laundry Bags," "The Masquerade Party," "Joey, the Good Samaritan," "My Son the Doctor," "The Expectant Fathers' School," "The Baby Nurse," "My Buddy, My Buddy," "The Baby Cometh," "Joey and Milton and Baby Makes Three," "The Baby's First Day," "Joey Plugs the Laundry," "Joey's Mustache," "Danny Gives Joey Advice," "The Baby Sitter," "Joey's Lost Whatchamacallit," "Joey's Surprise for Ellie," "Joey Jr.'s TV Debut," "Bobby Rydell Plugs Ellie's Song," "The Baby's First Christmas," Ellie Gives Joey First Aid," "Two Little Maids Are We," "Joey's Hideway Cabin," "Zsa Zsa Redecorates the Nursery," "Double Play from Foster to Durocher," "Joey Insults Jack E. Leonard," "Joey the Comedian vs. Larry the Writer," "Joey and Roberta Sherwood Play a Benefit," "Joey and Buddy Hackett Have a Luau," "Hilda Quits," "Joey and the Los Angeles Dodgers," "Every Dog Should Have a Boy," "Weekend in the Mountains," "Joey, Jack Jones and the Genie," "Joey Introduces Shecky Greene," "Andy Williams Visits Joey," "Joey is Invited to Washington" (never aired because subject matter was about President Kennedy who was assassinated prior to scheduled

broadcast date), "Joey Goes to CBS," "The Nielson Box," "Joey the Patient," "Joey and Larry Split," "Joey vs. Oscar Levant," "Joey Discovers Jackie Clark," "In This Corner, Jan Murray," "You What? Again," "Jillson's Toupee," "The Perfect Girl," "Joey's Courtship," "Ellie Goes to Court," "Rusty Arrives," "Rusty's Education," "Joey Entertains Rusty's Fraternity," "The Sultan's Gift," "What'll You Have," "Do-it-Yourself Nursery," "Testimonial for Sergeant Murdock," "Joey Changes Larry's Luck," "Never Put it in Writing," "Larry's Habit," and "Joey the Starmaker."

3. *The Joey Bishop Show* (ABC, April 17, 1967 to September 1968). Color. 60 Minutes. One of the "Son-of-a-Gun Players" (with Joanne Worley and Ann Elder) in 8 appearances on Bishop's late-night talk show.

Miscellaneous Television Appearances, 1946-84

Joe Besser has made more than 185 television appearances. Aside from the listing below, Besser also was featured on countless shows for which the authors regretfully are missing air dates, episode titles, and character names.

These shows include *Mister District Attorney, I Married Joan, The Jack Benny Show, The Ray Milland Show, The Dennis O'Keefe Show, Willy, December Bride, Private Secretary, The Gene Autry Show, The Eddie Cantor Comedy Theatre, Better Bowling* (pilot), *The Big World of Christopher Wells* (pilot), and *Arnie*.

Stooge film historian Richard Finegan reports the following episode titles for other television shows on which Besser appeared. They are:

December Bride: "Skid Row"; *The Ann Sothern Show:* "Give it Back to the Indians (1958); *The Jack Benny Show:* "Rochester Falls Asleep" (1955), "Jack Goes to the Races" (1955), and "The Tennessee Ernie Ford Show" (1956); *Make Room for Daddy:* "Kathy Delivers the Mail" (1960); *My Sister Eileen:* "The Leasebreakers (1960). According to Besser, at least four other appearances were made by him on Benny's program.

In 1950 Besser was the star of a television pilot for his own series called *The Private Eyes*. The pilot was produced at the Nassour Studios and co-starred Sheldon Leonard. As the title suggests, Besser and Leonard were private eyes.

Besser also was cast in three television commercials. His first was for Caesar's Palace Hotel in Las Vegas (filmed July 12, 1966).

Joe's second and best-remembered commercial was for *Off!* mosquito repellent and was titled "Don't Forget." He played a man pestered by mosquitos while using an outdoor barbecue. This commercial was filmed at the Columbia Studio Ranch on February 3, 1971, and ran on television until the summer of 1977.

Besser's third commercial was for Scope mouthwash, filmed on May 6, 1971. His role in this commercial and whether it aired are unknown.

1. *Hour Glass* (NBC, May 9, 1946). 60 minutes. With Evelyn Eaton, Evelyn Knight, Paul Douglas and Doodles Weaver. Joe performs his "Army Drill" routine on this first hour-long variety-entertainment series ever produced for network televison.
2. *Hollywood House* (NBC, December 2, 1949) 30 minutes. With Dick Wesson, Jim Backus, Florence Bates, Connie Haines and the Paul Cavanaugh Trio. "Irate Hotel Guest."
3. *The Ken Murray Show* (CBS, October 7, 1950) 60 minutes. With Herbert Marshall, Alan Young, Darla Hood and the Enchanters and Oswald. Joe recreates his "Army Drill" routine.
4. *The Ken Murray Show* (CBS, October 14, 1950). 60 minutes. With Van Heflin and Mel Torme. Various.
5. *The Ken Murray Show* (CBS, October 21, 1950). 60 minutes. With Bob Burns and Tito Guizar. Various.
6. *The Ken Murray Show* (CBS, November 4, 1950). 60 minutes. With Margaret O'Brien and her mother Mrs. Gladys O'Brien. Various.
7. *Colgate Comedy Hour* (NBC, January 7, 1951). 60 minutes. With Abbott and Costello, Evelyn Knight, Hal LeRoy and Sid Fields. Various.
8. *The Alan Young Show* (CBS, November 22, 1951). 60 minutes. With Connie Boswell. Joins Young in a sketch as two children playing in a room full of oversized prop furniture.
9. *Colgate Comedy Hour* (NBC, November 29, 1953). 60 minutes. With Eddie Cantor, Eddie Fisher, Frank Sinatra, Brian Donlevy and Connie Russell. Various.
10. *The Spike Jones Show* (NBC, February 20, 1954). 30 minutes. With Spike Jones, Helen Grayco, Eddie Arnold, Ruth Foster, Betty Grayco and the Borden Twins. "Jailhouse Warden."
11. *Saturday Night Revue* (NBC, September 11, 1954). 90 minutes. Hosted by Eddie Albert. With Alan Young, Paul Lynde, Wally Boag, Pat Carroll, Carol Richard, Kay Nelson, Richard Eyer and Tiny Thompson. Recreates children's sketch from *The Alan Young Show.*
12. *My Little Margie* (NBC, Airdate unavailable, 1954). 30 minutes. Episode: "Vern's Butterflies." With Gale Storm and Charles Farrell. "Butterfly Catcher."
13. *My Favorite Story* (Syndicated, January 13, 1955). 30 minutes. Episode: "No Tears." Hosted by Adolphe Menjou. With Patsy Moran, Ben Walden, Jack Lomas, Ken Christy, George Chandler and Jack Henderson. "Smalltown Mayor."
14. *The Millionaire* (CBS, March 2, 1955). 30 minutes. Episode: "Harvey Blake." Directed by Edward Bernds. With Marvin Miller. "Hobo."
15. *The Damon Runyan Theatre* (CBS, July 9, 1955). 30 minutes. Episode: "The Mink Doll." Hosted by Donald Woods. With Sally Bracken, Dorothy Lamour, Harry Bracken, Wayne Morris and Frankie Farrell. Character name unavailable.

16. *The Martha Raye Show* (NBC, December 13, 1955). 60 minutes. With Martha Raye, Jack Carson, Cesar Romero, Paul Lynde and Julius LaRosa. "Maintenance Man" who loves Raye.
17. *Club Oasis* (NBC, March 29, 1958). 30 minutes. With Spike Jones and His City Slickers (George Rock, Freddie Morgan, Gil Bernal and Billy Barty), and Helen Grayco. Joe becomes a member of Spike's band for one night.
18. *The Kraft Music Hall* (NBC, April 1, 1959). 60 minutes. With Milton Berle, Edgar Bergen and Charlie McCarthy, Peggy King, Billy May and announcer Ken Carpenter. Various.
19. *The Kraft Music Hall* (NBC, April 8, 1959). 60 minutes. With Milton Berle, Janis Paige and Ken Carpenter. In a take off of the Oscars entitled "The Annual Milties Awards."
20. *The Chrysler Corporation TV Guide Awards Special* (NBC, March 25, 1960). 60 minutes. Hosted by Robert Young. With Fred MacMurray and Nanette Fabray. Appears in two sketches, the first as a "Mailman" with Fred MacMurray and the second as a "Milkman" with Nanette Fabray.
21. *Shirley Temple Theatre* (NBC, December 25, 1960), 60 minutes. Episode: "Babes in Toyland." With Shirley Temple, Jonathan Winters, Carl Ballantine and Jerry Colonna. "One of Three Pirates."
22. *General Electric Theater* (CBS, January 8, 1961). 60 minutes. Episode: "Memory in White." Hosted by Ronald Reagan. With Sammy Davis, Jr. and Charles Bronson. "Fight Manager."
23. *Batman* (ABC, November 22, 1966). 30 minutes. Color. Episode: "Hizzoner the Penguin." With Adam West, Burt Ward and Burgess Meredith. Filmed September 6, 1966.
24. *The Hollywood Palace* (ABC, October 10, 1968). 60 minutes. Color. Hosted by Milton Berle. With Kaye Ballard, Irving Benson, Professor Irwin Corey and the Bottoms Up Troupe. "Stage Manager."
25. *The Danny Thomas Special: It's Greek to Me* (NBC, December 2, 1967). 60 minutes. Color. With Danny Thomas, Juliet Prowse, Vic Damone and Buddy Hackett. "Hermes the Greek God."
26. *The Mothers-in-Law* (NBC, April 28, 1968). 30 minutes. Color. Episode: "How Not to Manage a Rock Group." With Eve Arden, Kaye Ballard, Roger Carmel and Herbert Rudley. "Bandleader of the Friends in Need."
27. *That's Life* (ABC, October 1, 1968). 30 minutes. Color. Episode: "Bachelor Days." With Robert Morse, E.J. Peaker, Tim Conway, Nancy Wilson and Jackie Vernon. "Delicatessen Delivery Man." Filmed August 16 to 18, 1968.
28. *That Girl* (ABC, October 10, 1968). 30 minutes. Color. Episode: "Eleven Angry Men and That Girl." With Marlo Thomas and Ted Bessell. "Juror." Filmed June 20 to 21, 1968.
29. *The Mothers-in-Law* (NBC, November 24, 1968). 30 minutes. Color. Episode: "The First Anniversary is the Hardest." With Eve Arden, Kaye Ballard, Richard Deacon and Herbert Rudley. "Hobo." Filmed May 27 to 31, 1968.

30. *The Hollywood Palace* (ABC, November 30, 1968). 60 minutes. Color. Hosted by Milton Berle. With Martha Raye, Joey Forman, Barrie Chase, Rosey Grier and the Third Wave. "Necking Stage Manager." Filmed September 23 to 27, 1968.
31. *The Don Rickles Show* (ABC, December 27, 1968). 60 minutes. Color. With Don Rickles, Gene Baylos, Dick Clark and Gary Owens. "Russian Spy." Filmed December 15, 1968.
32. *The Good Guys* (CBS, February 12, 1969). 30 minutes. Color. Episode: "Win, Place and Kill." With Bob Denver, Herb Edelman and Joyce Van Patten. "Mr. Gerard." Filmed January 7 to 10, 1969.
33. *The Jerry Lewis Show* (NBC, March 4, 1969). 60 minutes. Color. With Jerry Lewis, Joanne Worley and John Byner. "Tailor." Filmed February 25 to 28, 1969.
34. *The Mothers-in-Law* (NBC, March 16, 1969). 30 minutes. Color. Episode: "Two on the Aisle." With Eve Arden, Kaye Ballard, Richard Deacon and Herbert Rudley. "Innocent Theatergoer." Filmed December 15, 1968.
35. *The Hollywood Palace* (ABC, March 22, 1969). 60 minutes. Color. Hosted by Don Rickles. With Phyllis Diller. "Hijacker." Filmed March 12 to 14, 1969.
36. *The Jerry Lewis Show* (NBC, March 25, 1969). 60 minutes. Color. With Jerry Lewis, Buddy Greco and Michele Lee. Various.
37. *The Jerry Lewis Show* (NBC, April 8, 1969). 60 minutes. Color. With Jerry Lewis, Michele Lee and the Osmond Brothers. Various.
38. *My World and Welcome to It* (NBC, October 13, 1969). 30 minutes. Color. Episode: "The Night the House Caught Fire." With William Windom. "Fire Chief." Filmed August 6, 1969.
39. *The Good Guys* (CBS, Air date unavailable, 1969). 30 minutes. Color. Episode: "No Orchids for the Diner." With Bob Denver, Herb Edelman and guest star Phyllis Diller. "Guard." Filmed August 14, 1969.
40. *ABC Movie of the Week:* "The Monk" (ABC, October 21, 1969). 90 minutes. Color. Episode: "You Can't Judge a Book." With George Maharis, Janet Leigh, Rick Jason, Carl Betz and Jack Albertson. "Fish Peddler." Filmed in San Francisco on April 23 to 24, 1969.
41. *Burlesque is Alive and Living in Burbank* (NBC, Scheduled for November 24, 1969, but never aired). 60 minutes. Color. With Carl Reiner, Sid Gould, Bobby Darin, Goldie Hawn and Jack Burns. "Stage Manager" in a sketch with Hawn and Darin. Filmed July 29 to 30, 1969.
42. *Love American Style* (ABC, January 5, 1970). 30 minutes. Color. Episode: "Love and the Proposal." With Warren Berlinger and Joan Hackett. "Restaurant Customer." Filmed June 25, 1969.
43. *My World and Welcome to It* (NBC, Airdate unavailable, 1970). 30 minutes. Color. Episode title unavailable. With William Windom. "Police Chief." Filmed November 13, 1969.
44. *The Bell System Family Theatre Presents Bing Crosby's Christmas Show* (NBC,

December 16, 1970). 60 minutes. Color. With Bing Crosby and Family, Jack Wild, Melba Moore and the Doodletown Pipers. "Lumpy." Filmed September 17 to 19, 1970.

45. *Love American Style* (ABC, January 22, 1971). 30 minutes. Color. Episode: "Love and the Murphy's Bed." With Jim Hutton and Jo Ann Pflug. "Next-Door Neighbor." Filmed December 8, 1970.
46. *Love American Style* (ABC, November 19, 1971). 30 minutes. Color. Episode: "Love and the Lady Barber." With Frank Sutton. "Toupee Salesman." Filmed September 10, 1971.
47. *Love American Style* (ABC, January 5, 1973). 30 minutes. Color. Episode: "Love and the Legend." With David White, Barbara Rhoades and Joanna Barnes. "Harley the Duck Pond Caretaker." Filmed November 6, 1972.
48. *NBC Nightly News* (NBC, April 23, 1976). 30 minutes. Color. Special Report: "The Three Stooges." Anchored by John Chancellor. Reporter Jack Perkins interviews Besser about how youngsters impersonate him and the other Stooges.
49. *The Funniest Guys in the World: Fifty-Years with the Stooges* (Syndicated April 10, 1984). 48 minutes. B/W and Color. Narrated by Steve Allen. Written, produced and directed by Mark Gilman, Jr. A profile of the Stooges career featuring interviews with friends and coworkers. Includes footage of Besser from *Africa Screams* (1949) with Abbott and Costello.

Weekly Animated Television Series Voiced by Besser, 1972-79

1. *The Houndcats* (NBC, September 9, 1972 to September 1, 1973). 30 minutes. Color. 13 episodes. Voice of "Puttypuss."
2. *Jeannie* (CBS, September 8, 1973 to August 30, 1975). 30 minutes. Color. 16 episodes. Voice of "Babu," a bumbling apprentice genie. Syndicated under the banner of *Fred Flintstone and Friends*.
3. *Scooby's All-Star Laff-a-Lympics* (ABC, September 10, 1977 to September 2, 1979). 120 minutes. Color. 12 episodes. Reprises his voice of "Babu" as a member of the Scooby Doobies.
4. *Yogi's Space Race* (NBC, September 9, 1978 to March 3, 1979). 90 minutes. Color. 26 episodes. Voice of "Scarebear" in the adventures of *Yogi's Space Race* and *The Galaxy Goof-Ups*.

Miscellaneous Animated Television Cartoons Voiced by Besser, 1975-82

In addition to the cartoons listed below, Besser also supplied his voice for one episode of *The Alvin Show* (1961), *The Marx Brothers* (1965, unsold pilot for Filmation), *Where's Huddles?* (1970), *Scooby Doo Meets Jeannie* (1973), *The Thing* (1979) and *The Shirt Tales* (1982).

1. *The Oddball Couple* (NBC, September 6, 1975). 30 minutes. Color. Episode: "A Day at the Beach." Voice of a "Genie."
2. *The Pink Panther Laff-and-a Half-Hour Show* (NBC, November 13, 1976). 60 minutes. Color. Episode: "Shark and the Beanstalk" starring Misterjaw Supershark. Voice of "The Giant."

3. *Baggy Pants and Nitwits* (NBC, November 1977). 30 minutes. Color. Episode: "Simple Simon and the Mad Pieman." Voice of "Simple Simon." Frank Nelson voices "The Mad Pieman."

Miscellaneous Animated Television Specials Voiced by Besser, 1983-

1. *My Smurfy Valentine* (NBC, February 13, 1983). 30 minutes. Color. Starring the Smurfs. Voice of "Cupid."

Afterword

For more than a half a century, Joe Besser brought laughter to millions, and created many precious moments on screen which will endear forever.

In recent years, he continued to entertain by providing his voice for new animated cartoons for television. He still found his greatest joy in bringing laughter to his fans.

Sadly, on March 1, 1988, Joe Besser died of heart failure, bringing down the curtain on one of Hollywood's most legendary acts. He completed writing this autobiography shortly before his death. Joe's wife Ernie passed away in the summer of 1989.

In his memory, the Joe Besser Memorial Fund has been formed to help others benefit from his death by aiding heart research. To make a donation, or to get more information, please write to:

The American Heart Association
Greater Los Angeles Affiliate
Attn: Joe Besser Memorial Fund
3550 Wilshire Blvd., 5th Floor
Los Angeles, California 90010

Index

"A Day at the Beach," 215
A Night in Spain, 82, 216
A Night in Venice, 82
"A Star for the 3 Stooges Committee," 224
"A Very Warm Christmas," 204
Abbott and Costello, 2, 97, 106, 142, 147, 149, 152, 159, 162, 167, 214, 224, 228
Abbott and Costello Meet Frankenstein, 148
Abbott and Costello Meet the Keystone Kops, 165
Abbott and Costello Show, The, 2, 162–163, 165, 214, 223
Abbott, Bud, 146–149, 151, 162
Adler, Felix, 174
Africa Screams, 148–151, 168, 214
"Ain't She Sweet," 47
Alamack Hotel, 19
Alan Young Show, The, 161–162
Albertson, Jack, 217
Alexandria and Olsen, 41, 43–44, 47, 51, 72
Alexandria, Eddie, 42, 45–46, 48
Allan K. Foster Girls, 55–56, 67
Allen, Fred, 2, 97, 115–117, 122, 133, 135
Allen, Gracie, 97
Allen, Lester, 78, 83–84
Allen, Steve, 224
Alvin Show, The, 202
Ambassador Theater, 29
American Theater, 19, 31
Anderson, Eddie "Rochester," 165
Andrew Sisters, The, 167
Annual Milties Awards, The, 199
Arbuckle, Fatty, 18, 85
Arden, Eve, 137, 209
Arlen, Richard, 94
Arthur, Jean, 125
Ash, Paul, 2, 51, 53–54
Astaire, Fred, 95
Babes in Toyland, 202
Babu, 215, 219
Baby Face Morgan, 132
Baer, Buddy, 148
Baer, Max, 148–149
Baggy Pants and Nitwits, 219
Baker, Phil, 111, 118
Ballantine, Carl, 202
Ballard, Kaye, 209
Barber, Bobby, 149
Barbera, Joseph, 219
Barnes Carnival, 30
Barnett and Clark, 53
Bartlett, Miss, 13–14, 18–20
Barton, Charles, 124–126, 127, 132, 146, 148, 151
Basehart, Richard, 158
Batman, 209, 226
Beatty, Clyde, 148
Benny, Jack, 2, 97, 110–113, 115–117, 122, 133, 135, 159, 206, 228
Bergen, Edgar, 111, 199–200, 206
Berle, Milton, 1, 133–135, 137, 141, 158, 165, 199, 206, 214, 225–226
Berle, Ruth, 206
Berlin, Irving, 110
Berlinger, Warren, 203
Bernds, Edward, 165, 224
Berry, Frank, 225
Berry, Helen, 225
Besser, Ernie, 57–58, 67–69, 71–72, 77, 85–86, 88, 90, 93, 107, 109–110, 116, 118–120, 123, 135, 141, 144–146, 152, 161–162, 165, 168, 174, 181, 192, 196–197, 200, 203, 207, 209–210, 215–216, 219–221, 225
Besser, Esther, 5, 20, 22–25, 27
Besser, Fanny, 5
Besser, Florence, 6, 21, 27
Besser, Gertrude, 5, 10, 27
Besser, Henrietta, 6, 27
Besser, Isadore, 6–7
Besser, Leopold, 6–7
Besser, Lily, 6, 27
Besser, Manny, 5, 14–15, 19, 27, 41–42
Besser, Molly, 5, 21, 27
Besser, Morris, 5
Besser, Rose, 6, 27
Better Bowling, 200
Bewitched, 213
Bigelow, Joe, 111–112, 116, 135
Biltmorettes, 102
Bing Crosby Christmas Special, The, 210
Bishop, Joey, 203, 205–206, 209, 228
Bixby, Bill, 203
Blake, Ben K., 88
Blake, Larry, 91–92
Blocker, Dan, 174
Bow, Clara, 51
Bradley, Mayor Tom, 225
Brander, Margot, 102
Breen, Bobby, 117
Brice, Monty, 131
Brideless Groom, 171
Briskin, Irving, 124
Bronson, Charles, 204
Brooke, Hillary, 148–149, 163
Brooks, Mel, 224
Brown and Carney, 121
Brown, Jimmy, 144, 159
Brown, Wally, 121
Browning, Tod, 93
Buck, Frank, 148
Buffalo Bill Traveling Show, 6, 14, 19
Bunny, Bugs, 212
Burday and Norway, 53
Burlesque Is Alive and Living in Burbank, 210
Burns, George, 97
Butler, Daws, 212
Buzzie, Ruth, 219
Cabane, Christy, 91–93
Caesar, Sid, 159
Calloway, Cab, 38

Calm and Gale, 53
Cambria, Frank, 53
Campbell, Arthur, 53
Candido, Candy, 147
Candy, John, 228
Canin, Stuart, 115
Cantor, Eddie, 2, 79, 116–118, 122, 135
Capps, Kendall, 78
Carnival Cocktail, 55, 58
Carpentier, George, 182
Carson, Johnny, 155, 204, 209
Carter-Waddell, Joan, 78
Caruso, Enrico, 10–11
Castle, Peggie, 165
Cavin, Alice, 72
Century Theater, 139
Chaplin, Charlie, 18, 146, 161
Charleston, Milton, 102, 104
Chase and Sanborn Hour, The, 116
Chase, Charlie, 57
Chase, Chevy, 228
Chevalier, Maurice, 199
Chicago Theater, 54
Chico and the Man, 217–218
Cinderfella, 200
Coca, Imogene, 137, 159
Cohan Theater, 169
Cohn, Harry, 125–126, 127–129, 131–133, 141, 150, 167, 169, 173, 192–193, 195–196
Cohn, Jack, 87
Colbert, Claudette, 125
Colgate Comedy Hour, 159
Coliseum Theater, 39
"College Four," 97
Colonna, Jerry, 97, 202
Columbia Pictures, 1–2, 83, 87
Columbia Theater, 27
Convy, Bert, 217–218
Conway, Tim, 224
Coogan, Gene, 146
Coogan, Jackie, 206
Cooper, Gary, 125
Costa, Mary, 199
Costello, Lou, 2, 96, 146, 148–149, 151, 153, 159, 162, 164, 167, 228
Costello, Pat, 163
Courtnidge, Cicily, 89
Craig, Jr., Richy, 48–50, 67
Crawford, Broderick, 167
Cristillo, Louis Francis (*see Costello, Lou*)
Critcherson, Sam, 69, 72, 77, 85, 88
Crosby, Bing, 2, 142, 196–197
Cuckoorancho, 88, 91
Daily Mirror, The, 40, 58
Dallon, Ethel, 55
Dalton, Abby, 204
Damon Runyan Show, The, 165
Dana, Dick, 69
Dannay, Frederic, 116
Davis, Jr., Sammy, 2, 47, 203–204
Davis, Tommy, 206
Davis, Willie, 206
Dawn, Julia, 55
Day, Dennis, 111–114
Day, Doris, 208
Dead End Kids, The, 167
DeCarlo, Yvonne, 155, 157
December Bride, 165
DeCordova, Frederick, 155, 157
Defenders, The, 205
DeMille, Cecil B., 126
Dempsey, Jack, 182
Dennis O'Keefe Show, The, 165
Denoff, Sam, 217–218
Denver, Bob, 210
Depatie, David, 219
Depatie-Freleng, 219
Depatie-Freleng Enterprises, 212
DeRita, Curly Joe, 1, 197, 217, 225
DeRita, Jean, 1
Desert Hawk, The, 155
Desmond, Florence, 137
Devine, Andy, 94–95, 97
Devoe, Frank, 69
Dixie Four, 39
Don Rickles Show, The, 209
Donnell, Jeff, 131
Douglas, Paul, 136
Dracula, 153
Dreiffus, Arthur, 131–132
Drysdale, Don, 206
Duff, Howard, 158
Dunedin, Queenie, 39–40
Durbin, Deanna, 117
DuVall Elementary School, 12
Eadie Was a Lady, 131–132
Eaton, Evelyn, 136
Ed Wynne Show, The, 159
Eddie Cantor Show, The, 116, 214
Eddy, Wesley, 53
Edelman, Herb, 210
Eden, Barbara, 215
Edgar Bergen and Charlie McCarthy Show, The, 111
Elder, Ann, 209
Eliscu, Edward, 125
Ellery Queen, 116
Ellington, Duke, 38
Elliott, Biff, 165
Ellsworth, Ann, 72
Ellsworth, Dorothy, 69
Enchanters, The, 160
Enrica and Novello, 136
Entertainment Tonight, 225
Ernst, Leila, 137–138
Errand Boy, The, 201–202, 214
Etting, Ruth, 51
Eye on L.A., 224
Fabray, Nanette, 202
Fain, Sam E., 105
Fairbanks, Douglas, 92
Falkenburg, Jinx, 131
Farr, Jamie, 1, 2, 226
Faye, Alice, 111
Feinberg, Louis, 81
Felix, Seymour, 57
Feudin' Fussin' and a-Fightin', 141, 143, 145–146, 148, 159
Fields, Sid, 163
Fields, W. C., 167
Fifi Blows Her Top, 193
Fighting Squadron, 158
Fine, Larry, 1, 78–81, 83, 168–179, 181–184, 191–197, 215–217, 223–224, 226–228
Fine, Mabel, 181
Fisher, Carrie, 198

Fleischman Hour, The, 111
Flynn, Joe, 203
Fonda, Henry, 137
Fools Rush In, 137
Foran, Dick, 93
Ford, Wally, 93
Forman, Joey, 205
Foster, Allan K., 58
Fox Theater, 73
Frances the Talking Mule, 142
Frankenstein, 153
Freaks, 93
Fred Allen Show, The, 214
Freleng, Friz, 212, 219
Froman, Jane, 137
Frome, Milton, 174
Gable, Clark, 125
Gabor, Zsa Zsa, 206
Gene Autry Show, The, 165
General Electric Theater, 204
Gerald, Ara, 78
Gershner, Nathan, 27
Gibson, Julie, 224
Gilbert, Edward, 137
Gilliam, Stu, 212
Glascoe Elementary School, 13
Gleason, Jackie, 2, 155–158
Gobel, George, 219
Goddard, Paulette, 2, 95, 165
Going My Way, 198
Goldstein, Leonard, 141, 143–145, 155
Gonzales, Speedy, 212
Good Guys, The, 210
Gorney, Jay, 125
Gottlieb, Alex, 163
Goulet, Robert, 206
Grable, Betty, 109
Grand Opera House, 19
Graziano, Rocky, 183
Green, Harold, 183
Green, Hazel, 38
Greene, Richard, 155, 157
Greenwich Village Follies, The, 86
Griffith, D. W., 92
Gus Edward's School Days, 20
Hackett, Buddy, 206
Hal Roach Studios, 162
Haley, Jack, 98
Hamilton Skydome, 17
Hamill, Mark, 215
Haney, Loretta, 82
Haney, Mabel, 82
Hanna, William, 219
Hanna-Barbera, 215, 219
Harmonica Rascals, The, 71
Hawn, Goldie, 210
Hayworth, Rita, 199
Hazard, Hap, 69
Headline Hunters, 165
Healy, Ted, 78–83, 169
Hearst, William Randolph, 153
Helen Morgan Story, The, 192
Hellzapoppin, 101–102
Henrie, Joe, 178
Herrmann the Great, 38
Herrmann, Alexander, 31
Herrmann, Madame, 38–39
Hershkowitz, Artie, 116, 125, 129, 135, 138
Hertz, Bill, 225, 227
Heston, Charlton, 200
Hey, Rookie!, 2, 124–126, 127–128, 131–132, 181, 203
High Kickers, 98
Hiken, Nat, 138
Hippodrome, 77
Hirschfield, Al, 135
"Hizzoner the Penguin," 209
Hollywood Chamber of Commerce, 1, 225
Hollywood Palace, 209–210
Hollywood Walk of Fame, 1, 224, 227
Holman, Libby, 137
Hood, Darla, 160
Hoofs and Goofs, 175, 178, 191
Hoover, Peggy, 78
Hope, Bob, 48, 97, 106, 224
Horsing Around, 191
Horwitz, Moses, 80
Hot Steel, 91, 93–95
Houndcats, The, 212
Hour Glass, 136
Howard, Curly, 1, 80, 83, 167–169, 172–174, 178–180, 182–183, 194, 223–224, 226–227
Howard, Frank, 206
Howard, Gertrude, 168
Howard, Helen, 181
Howard, Moe, 1, 78–83, 168–184, 191–197, 215–217, 223–224, 226–228
Howard, Mort, 168
Howard, Paul, 226
Howard, Shemp, 1, 78–83, 146, 148, 150–151, 167–169, 171–175, 177–178, 181, 223–224, 226–227
Hudson, Rock, 155, 158
Hutton, Betty, 105
I Dream of Jeannie, 215
I Love Lucy, 161
I Married Joan, 165
I'm Dickens, He's Fenster!, 206
I, the Jury, 165
If the Shoe Fits, 137, 139
Information, Please!, 114
Ingels, Marty, 206–207
It Happened One Night, 125
It's Greek to Me, 209
Jack Benny Show, The, 113–114, 165, 214
Jack Paar Show, The, 203
Jaws, 219
Jeannie, 215
Jefferson Theater, 73–74
Jerry Lewis Show, The, 210
Jessel, George, 98–99, 106
"Jillson and the Cinnamon Buns," 207
"Jillson's Toupee," 207
"Joe Besser and Company," 69
Joe Palooka Meets Humphrey, 158
"Joey and Buddy Hackett Make a Luau," 208
"Joey and Milton and Baby Makes Three" 206
Joey Bishop Show, The, 2, 204, 207–209
Johnson, Arte, 212, 219, 224
Johnson, Choo Choo, 109

Johnson, Harold Ogden ("Chic"), 97–98, 105, 118
Jolson, Al, 2, 47, 77, 79, 110
Jones, Gordon, 163
Jones, Spike, 110
Joyce, Teddy, 53
Kanter, Hal, 217–219
Kaye, Danny, 114
Kellaway, Cecil, 93
Kelly, Gene, 143
Ken Murray Show, The, 161
Kern, James V., 204–206
Kerner, Charlie, 121
Kilbride, Percy, 142–143, 145
Kilgallen, Dorothy, 106
King, Charlie, 71
Koltnow, Barry, 224
Komack, James, 218
Kraft Music Hall, The, 199
Kraike, Michael, 131–132
Kretschmer, Anna, 57–58, 109, 119, 144–145
Kretschmer, Erna Kay *(see Besser, Ernie)*
Kretschmer, Herman, 57
Labriola, Tony, 160
Lambert, Eddie, 137
Lamond, Phyliss Fine, 1, 3, 223, 226–227
Lamour, Dorothy, 109
Landers, Muriel, 174, 193
Landers, Siggie, 94
Lang, Harry, 69, 72
Langdon, Harry, 18
Laughing Man, The, 199
Laurel and Hardy, 215, 228
Laurie, Joe, 73
Lawford, Peter, 195
Lee, Gypsy Rose, 116
Lee, Lester, 68, 72
Lee, Manfred Bennington, 116
Leiman, Abe, 114
Lenburg, Catherine, 215
Lenburg, Greg, 1, 214–215, 217, 221, 223–226
Lenburg, Jeff, 1, 214–215, 217, 221, 223–226
Lenburg, John, 215
Leonard, Jack E., 206
Leonard, Sheldon, 159
Let Yourself Go, 2, 133, 214
Let's Make Love, 202
Levant, Oscar, 110, 112, 114
Lewis, Danny, 200
Lewis, Jerry, 2, 200–202, 214, 224, 228
Libuse, Frank, 102, 104
Lillie, Beatrice, 111
Little Giant, 148
Little, Jimmy, 95–96, 104–105, 126, 136, 160
Livingston, Mary, 110, 112, 114, 135
Lloyd, Harold, 18
Loew's Palace, 51, 53
Loew's State Theater, 85
Loew's Theater, 48
Logan, Ella, 102, 105
London Palladium, 67, 88
London, Babe, 215
Loper, Don, 73
Lorenz, Harry, 27–28
Lost Weekend, 207
Lou Costello Youth Foundation, 152
"Lou's Birthday Party," 164
Love American Style, 210, 212
"Love and Murphy's Bed," 210
"Love and the Lady Barber," 210
"Love and the Lady Legend," 213
"Love and the Proposal," 210
Lovejoy, Frank, 165
Low and Behold, 137
Lund, John, 137
Lupino, Ida, 2, 158
*M*A*S*H,* 226
Ma and Pa Kettle, 142
MacDonald, Dorothy, 78
MacMurray, Fred, 202
MacPhail, Addie, 85
Macready, George, 155
Mad at the World, 165
Maharis, George, 210
Main Street to Broadway, 53–55
Main, Marjorie, 142–143, 145–146
Man With The Claw, The, 18
Mangean Sisters, The, 182
Mansfield, Irving, 116, 133, 135
Marks, Guy, 204
Marsh, Charles, 55
Marshall, George, 78
Marshall, Peter, 199
Martha Raye Show, The, 165
Martin and Lewis, 159
Martin, Dean, 203, 209
Martin, Steve, 228
Marx Brothers, The, 78, 228
"Mary Astor's Dancing Dolls," 57
Maurer, Joan Howard, 1, 3, 224, 226–227
Maurer, Norman, 224, 226
McCarthy, Charlie, 199–200, 206
McCauley, Jack, 78
McIntyre, Christine, 171, 174
McMahon, Ed, 206
Merman, Ethel, 2, 48, 51
Merry Mix-Up, 183–184
Meyers, Henry, 125
Mikado, The, 20
Mike Douglas Show, The, 215
Milland, Ray, 207
Miller, Ann, 2, 125, 127, 131
Miller, Bill, 78, 88
Millionaire, The, 165
Mimic World, 57
"Minnie the Moocher," 38
Miranda, Carmen, 2, 102, 105
Mission Impossible, 212
Missouri Theater, 28
Mister Ed, 161
Misterjaw-Supershark, 219
Mobley, Roger, 202
Monica, Corbett, 204
Monk, The, 210
Monks, James, 136
Monroe, Marilyn, 2, 202
Moore and Pal, 55
Moore, Florence, 78
Moran, Peggy, 93–94
Morris, Robert, 209
Morros, Boris, 95
Mothers-in-Law, The, 209–210

Mount Hermon School, 31
Mr. Deeds Goes to Town, 125
Mr. District Attorney, 165
"Mr. Know-It-All," 135
Mr. Smith Goes to Washington, 125
Mulhall, Jack, 160
Mummy's Hand, The, 93
Municipal Opera, 20
Murray, Bill, 228
Murray, Ken, 46, 160–161
Muscle Up a Little Closer, 178
My Favorite Story, 165
My Little Margie, 165
My World and Welcome to It, 210
Nash, Charles Earnest Lee, 79
Nassour Studios, 148, 160
Nassour, Eddie, 149, 159
Neisen, Gertrude, 78
Niggemeyer, Charlie, 55, 57
Nimoy, Leonard, 216
Noonan, Tommy, 199
Norris, Jerry, 78
Nut Farm, The, 93
Nutter, Dolly, 57
O'Brien, Pat, 93
O'Connor, Donald, 2, 142–143
O'Connor, Frank, 40–41
O'Connor, Helen, 40–41
Oakie, Jack, 97
Oddball Couple, The, 215
Oil's Well That Ends Well, 180, 194
Oily to Bed, Oily to Rise, 194
Olsen and Johnson, 2, 97, 99, 101–106, 121, 214, 228
Olsen, John Sigvard, 41, 97–98
Olsen, Ole, 41, 45–46, 48, 97, 109
Oriental Theater, 53–54
Orpheum Theater, 19, 43, 87, 91, 93
Osterman, Jac, 78, 84
Outer Space Jitters, 181
Outside the Wall, 158
Owens, Gary, 1–2, 224–227
Palace Theater, 40, 43
Palma, Joe, 172–173
Paramount Publix, 49–50, 53, 68
Parks, Larry, 125, 131
Passing Show of 1932, The, 78, 82–84, 86, 167, 176, 216
Pay Off, The, 132
Penner, Joe, 112
Perranoski, Ron, 206
Pies and Guys, 193
Plunderers of Painted Flats, The, 199
Pollard, Hank, 225
Prinz, Freddie, 217, 219
Private Eyes, The, 159
Private Secretary, 165
Proctor Newark Theater, 85
Prospect Theater, 81
Puss, 45–46
Puttypuss, 212
Quiz Whizz, 194
Radio Rogues, The, 85, 97
Rainbow Gardens, 82
Raksin, David, 137, 139
Rancho Bango, 88
Randall, Lou, 86
Rappe, Virginia, 85
Ray Milland Show, The, 165
Ray, Aldo, 212
Red Circle, The, 18
Red Skelton Show, The, 159
Reiner, Carl, 224
Reso, Harry, 97
Reynolds, Debbie, 2, 143, 197–199
Richman, Harry, 2, 77, 89–90
RKO Golden Gate Theater, 69, 91
RKO Keith Theaters, 72
RKO Palace Theater, 70
RKO Polei Palace, 74
Roberts, Kenny, 133, 135, 137
Rogers, Ginger, 51
Rogers, Harry, 86, 172–173
Rookie, The, 199
Rooney and Bent, 73
Rosario and Antonio, 102
Ross, Benny, 29
Rotay, Dot, 78
Roth, Gene, 174, 194
Rowan and Martin's *Laugh-In,* 103, 209
Roxy Theater, 95, 147
Royce, Lee, 88–89, 91, 95
Rubin, Benny, 175
Russell, Mr., 32–33
Russell, Gail, 202
Santa Claus Lane Parade, 95
Say One For Me, 196–197, 199
Scarebear, 219
Scooby's All-Star Laff-a-Lympics, 219
Scrambled Brains, 215
Second Chorus, 95
Sergeant's 3, 203
Sessions, Almira, 53
"Shark and the Beanstalk," 219
Sharpe, Ernest, 78
Sherman, George, 141, 143
Shirley Temple Theatre, 202
Shore, Dinah, 117
Shubert Theater, 112
Shubert Theater Corporation, 77
Shubert, Eddie, 78
Shubert, J. J., 77, 83, 98, 121, 124
Shubert, Lee, 77, 124
Silent Call, The, 202
Sillman, Leonard, 137–139
Sinatra, Frank, 1, 203, 209, 224
Sinatra, Jr., Frank, 224
Sing You Sinners, 142
Singing in the Rain, 142
Sins of Jezebel, 165
Sitka, Emil, 174
Skouras, Charles, 28
Skouras, George, 28
Skouras, Spyros, 28–30
Skowron, Bill, 206
Snyder, Harry, 22–25
Son's of Fun, 98–99, 101–103, 106–107, 109, 112, 116, 121, 124, 129, 147–148, 214
Space Ship Sappy, 192
Spanish Omelet, 72
Spices of 1934, 86
Spices of 1935, 86

Spices of 1936, 86
Spike Jones Show, The, 165
St. Regis Restaurant, 40–41
Stander, Lionel, 117–118
Star Trek, 216
"Steven's Wrestling Bear," 170
Stewart, James, 125
"Stinky," 2, 162, 164–165, 214, 223
Stone, Ezra, 111
Stone, Maxine, 29
Story on Page One, The, 199
Strand Theater, 73, 87
Streisand, Barbra, 1
Sullivan, Ed, 106
Susann, Jackie, 116, 135
Sutton, Frank, 210
Sweet and Hot, 193
Talk About a Lady, 131–132, 142
Tarler, Harriette, 174–175
Tashlin, Frank, 196, 198–201
Ted Healy and His Racketeers, 78
Texaco Star Theater, 158
That Girl, 209, 217
That's Life, 209
"The Drugstore," 164
"The Joe Besser Ice Cream Cocktail," 57
"The Misbehavin' Raven Mission," 212
The Noose Hangs High, 148
"The Paint Bucket Routine," 72
"The Son-of-a-Gun Players," 209
"The Two Stooges," 172
"The Wrestling Match," 164
Thomas, Danny, 206, 209
Thomas, Marlo, 203, 209, 217
Three Stooges, The, 1, 83, 167–169, 215, 223, 227–228
Three Troubledoers, 181
Thurston, Harry, 31
Thurston, Howard, 31–37, 39
Thurston, Margaret, 31
Thurston, William H., 31
Thyssen, Greta, 174
Tombragel, Maurice, 94
Tonight on Broadway, 137
Tonight Show, The, 155, 204, 209
Tony the Wonder Horse, 175
Towering Inferno, The, 200
Treen, Mary, 205
Tucker, Forrest, 131
Tucker, Sophie, 2, 46–47, 98, 110
Turner, Lana, 161
TV Guide Awards Show, The, 202
Twentieth Century Fox, 2
Two Gun Lady, 165
Tyler, Tom, 93
Ullman, Elwood, 224
United Artists, 2
Universal Pictures, 2
Valentinoff and Ivan Kirov, 102
Vallee, Rudy, 111–113
Vici, Count Berni, 86
Wabash Railroad Company, 27
Wagner, Robert, 2, 197–199
Waiting in the Lurch, 141
Wallace, Dorothy, 69
Walters, Betty Lou, 160
Walton and O'Rourke, 102
Ward, Burt, 209
Waterson, Berlin, and Snyder, 27–28
Wayne, John, 1, 167, 224
Weaver, Doodles, 136
Webb and Hayes, 73
Weidman, Charles, 137
Weismuller, Johnny, 141
Weldman, Phil, 203
Welsh, Bill, 225–227
West, Adam, 1, 209, 226
"What's It All About?," 44
Which Way to the Front?, 210
White, David, 213
White, George, 32
White, Harold, 174
White, Jack, 174
White, Jules, 87, 172–174, 181, 184, 191, 195
White, Pearl, 18
Wild Cat Dugan, 68–69, 71–72, 78
William Morris Agency, 211
Williams, Andy, 206
Williams, Esther, 46
Willis, Frances, 55
Willy, 165
Wilson, Don, 112–113
Winchell, Walter, 106
Windom, William, 210
Winston, Al, 168
Winter Garden Theater, 67, 77, 97, 106, 109–111, 122–123
Winters, Jonathan, 202
Winters, Shelley, 143, 145
With Six You Get Egg Roll, 208
Withers, Jane, 71
Witmer, Ruth, 53
Wolf, Adele, 72
Woman in Hiding, 158
Wong, Joe, 160
Wood, Joe, 57
Wood, Natalie, 199
Work, Cliff, 91, 93
Worley, Joanne, 209
Wynn, Ed, 47, 79, 201
Wyse and Company, 69
Wyse, Jr., Ross, 69
Wyse, Sr., Ross, 69
Yarbrough, Jean, 163
Yellen, Jack, 105
Yogi's Space Race, 219
You Can't Take It With You, 125
You're in the Army, 86–88, 105
Youmans, Vincent, 11
Young, Alan, 162
Young, Clarence Upson, 94
Young, Gig, 199
Your Show of Shows, 159
Zimmerman, Ethel, 48